By the Author

Highland Fling

Love's Portrait

Highland Whirl

Visit us at www.boldstrokesbooks.com

Praise for Anna Larner

Highland Fling

"[This book] just kept surprising me at every turn! I had a few moments of 'Really did I just read that?' and 'Did she just say that?' I love when a book does this because you feel the writer is writing outside the box…All in all, I loved *Highland Fling* and think Anna Larner will definitely be an author I'll be watching out for."—*Les Rêveur*

"Take a day off, curl up and lose yourself in this lovely lesbian romance by debut novelist Anna Larner."—*DIVA*

"[T]his is one of those books that breathes 'good reading.' The author Larner has the perfect ear for a certain type of LGBT space, and weaves a convincing queer & lesbian psychogeography into the narrative, and her own experiences and previous work with archiving and creating space for LGBT history to be shared gives this book an authentic feel, not just in tone, geography and accent but also the emotional honesty that marks this book out as such a charming read."
—*Gscene Magazine*

Love's Portrait

"Author Anna Larner combines a satisfying mix of humor, bittersweet revelations, family and workplace dynamics, drama, opposites attract romance, and history."—*Omnivore Bibliosaur*

"This story was absolutely wonderful. The characters were dynamic and engaging, the flashbacks moved the story forward instead of dragging it down, the romance was sweet and awesome and perfectly paced. Just all around a great book, I enjoyed every second of it."—*Elisa Reviews and Ramblings*

"This book pulled me in so amazingly fast I'm pretty sure I got reading whiplash. It was awesome…What was most impressive about this novel was the emotion throughout the book, the whole novel seemed to vibrate with all sorts of different emotions. Especially the stuff that was set in the 1800s, which I loved. It was an amazing book, complex and compelling."—*From Bella to YLVA*

"I mean it as the utmost compliment that at times I felt I was reading a compelling C19th novel that just happened to be set in C21st Leicester with lesbians. It's not too much of a leap to say that, if Jane Austen was writing lesbian romance fiction today, she might have come up with something akin to *Love's Portrait*!"—*Sam O'Nions, Kenric Newsletter*

"Beautifully Romantic! I just got so lost in the romance inside the romance that I was genuinely in love with the story and blown away by the end. This is only the second story I have read by Anna Larner but I am in awe of her ability to capture such passion, longing, and love as she has with *Love's Portrait*. It was truly beautiful, even the more tragic elements, and I longed to learn that there was happiness and there was. I adored every second and became fully immersed in the story to the point I just couldn't put it down."—*LESBIreviewed*

"*Love's Portrait* is a perfect mixture of love, romance and belonging. Anna Larner's writing has a gentle beauty to it, an engaging tone throughout. Her characters feel real to me and she makes me want to know more about them. This is the second book I have read by this author and I must admit she has become a favourite of mine. A lovely story."—*Kitty Kat's Book Review Blog*

HIGHLAND WHIRL

by

Anna Larner

2021

HIGHLAND WHIRL

ISBN 13: 978-1-63555-892-0

This Trade Paperback Original Is Published By
Bold Strokes Books, Inc.
P.O. Box 249
Valley Falls, NY 12185

First Edition: December 2021

Credits
Editor: Ruth Sternglantz
Production Design: Stacia Seaman
Cover Design by Sheri (hindsightgraphics@gmail.com)

Acknowledgments

A heartfelt thank you to the BSB team, in particular, Len Barot, Sandy Lowe, and Ruth Sternglantz.

To my awesome beta readers, Bridget, Jen, Kay, Lis, Mary, Rita, Sue G, Sue L—thank you from the bottom of my heart for your amazing support.

To my wonderful partner, family, and friends—thank you, as ever, for your love.

To readers—a huge thank you! Writing for you simply means the world to me.

For Ang

Chapter One

"Hey, Rox."

"Evie Eds! Hi. Hold on a mo. I'm just at The Brewer's." With her mobile phone pressed against her ear, Roxanne Barns pushed against the brass fingerplate of the heavy door that opened from the street to the small porch of The Brewer's Arms. "So, how's tricks—wait, what the...?" No sooner had she stepped inside, than a pungent odour caught and stung at the back of her throat. She coughed out, "No way."

Eve chuckled. "That busy, huh? Well, it is a Friday night."

"It's pink. Like, totally pink." Roxanne stared in horror at her beloved pub. Nearly every wall and surface had been subject to a violent assault of eye-bruising, nausea-inducing pink paint. Even the floorboards, tacky under her feet, had not escaped the savage lick and slap. "Why? I mean...*why?*" Her disbelieving gaze eventually settled at the far corner of the room where the green felt of the snooker table seemed to float like an island in an ocean of strawberry milk. And was she imagining it, or could the circles on the dartboard really be expanding and contracting against the hallucinogenic wall? Was this what it was like to take acid? The space was trippy for sure but not in a good way.

"What's pink?" Eve asked, her voice piqued with concern. "You've not got a rash, have you?"

"No, I haven't got a rash. It's The Brewer's. It's been...violated."

"Oh no. What, like burgled?"

"Burgled? It's far worse. They've attempted to redecorate."

"Oh."

"Yep. Oh."

"You never know—it might grow on you."

"Yeah, judging by the smell, it's a distinct possibility."

Accompanied by Eve's pained laughter, Roxanne made her way to the bar. En route, she spotted a group of regulars standing huddled together by the open back door. They clearly figured a view of the bins was preferable to their usual seat and a lungful of toxic fumes.

"What the hell, Bel?" Roxanne said to her ex Belinda, who had bravely broken free from the group to risk a lifetime of certain asthma.

"It's supposed to be Crème de la Rose," Belinda said, casting her gaze from chair to wall to ceiling. "But dodgy Dave got a job lot from a mate, so it's more like Flaming Flamingo."

"You don't say?" Roxanne lifted her jacket collar across her nose. "Personally, I'm getting the vibes of Pepto Bismol."

Belinda laughed, which triggered a cough. She pressed her scarf against her face and gestured to the phone in Roxanne's hand. "Is that Eve?"

"Yep." Roxanne poked the speaker button and rested her mobile on the counter next to her pint of lager. Following an unspoken arrangement that had developed over the years, the barman had already drawn her pint. Roxanne's order never changed, after all, and neither did her need for a pint of Carling straight after her nursing shift in A&E. It wasn't a matter of habit. It was simply survival. Without another word, Roxanne drank down half her lager in one continuous thirsty gulp.

Belinda leaned in towards the phone. It was impossible not to notice her ample chest pillowing against the surface of the bar, not to mention the breath from her moist lipsticked lips misting the screen. "Hi, Eve."

Roxanne held her glass momentarily motionless to her mouth at the heady sight. A moustache of foam gathered and tickled at her top lip.

"Hi!" Eve shouted, startling Roxanne from the enchantment of Belinda's cleavage.

"I know you're in Inverness and everything, mate." Roxanne wiped at her mouth with the back of her hand. "But you don't have to shout. Modern technology, you know."

"Bugger off," Eve said. "I'm not shouting because I'm far away. I'm shouting because I thought it was a busy, noisy bar."

"I'll leave you guys to it," Belinda said with an amused smile. She paused to briefly lift Roxanne's chin so that their eyes met. "Obviously, we're not stopping. Come with us for a curry? And then maybe a nightcap at mine?"

There was nothing Roxanne wanted more than to forget her day with a nightcap. It always helped. Thank God for the urgent press of another's body against hers, dissolving her stress and worries into nothing but hot sensation. Until the morning that was, when her lover would hope for more, whereas Roxanne's only hope was simply to leave without attachment or regret. "I don't know, Bel...I don't want to, you know, mixed signals and everything."

Belinda raised her palms in the air in compliant surrender. "I know, you don't do relationships, you've made that clear *many* times. Nothing heavy tonight. I promise." She brushed her lips against Roxanne's ear and whispered, "Just casual. Just how you like it."

Tricky. Fair play, Belinda knew exactly how she liked it.

Roxanne hesitated. "Okay. Meet you outside." Roxanne watched Belinda curve and sway her return to her group. How she loved to watch her leave.

Eve loudly cleared her throat. "Er, hello, I'm still here. You do know that shagging her *is* giving her mixed signals, right?"

"That was a private conversation. And we both know Bel doesn't exactly do serious herself."

"That was on speaker. And we both know she's saying what she thinks you want to hear."

"Just a sec. I just need to..." Roxanne finished her pint and made for the street and the relief of fresh air. She leaned against the outside of the pub and took several deep breaths. All she could taste was the acrid tang of paint, not to mention the bitter after note of Eve's uninvited observation. A change of subject was called for. "So, what's up, bud?"

"What's up? Please don't tell me you've forgotten already?"

"No." Shit. What was it?

Eve gave a heavy sigh. "My birthday."

"Yes. Exactly. I knew that. Happy birthday."

"It's not for a fortnight yet."

"That's right, it is. That's how ahead of it all I am."

"Uh-huh. You're still planning on coming up, then? For my party?"

"Coming up? Erm...absolutely."

With a tone unmistakably rippled with hurt, Eve said, "You don't have to come, you know. If you don't want to."

"Evie, come on, don't be like that. I'm really looking forward to it."

"It doesn't exactly sound like it."

"It slipped my mind just for a second."

"What, just like all the other times when I've asked you to visit?"

Fair enough, Eve was right. How many times in the last three and a half years or so had she wriggled out of visiting Eve in Scotland? It was touching, in fact, that Eve continued to ask, given how often she'd given her the brush-off. Add to that, Eve was the one who'd faithfully done the travelling back and forth since her move. But the thought of visiting her best mate in her new home, and with her new love, and living her new life, well, it left Roxanne feeling like crap. And not just the crap that comes from being left behind and lonely, even, but the crap that comes from the scrutiny of comparison. She could sense people thinking—where was *her* new love and her new life?

The only thing that had changed or moved on for Roxanne it seemed was the paint job at The Brewer's. And to be frank, that's how she liked it. Did that make her a loser? No way. Had she ever cared about what other people thought of her, in any case? Nope. She had a life plan. Her life plan was to have no life plan. It was simple and perfect and resulted in her having no expectations, and therefore no disappointments. It was hard to disagree—it was perfect. Wasn't it?

Okay, so maybe, just recently, she might have wondered whether she was getting a bit tired of being footloose and fancy-free. Turned out keeping a life simple wasn't exactly simple. And, maybe, just *maybe*, finding someone special to share stuff with could be all right. But if she wanted a tweak to things or even a change, that was nobody's business but hers. Not even her best mate's.

"Evie, I'm sorry. I didn't mean to sound like I didn't care. I do. Seriously. You're turning the big three-oh. It's immense. And you're having a party. What's not to love about that? I wouldn't miss it for the world. And I can't wait to see you and to see your new pad in your new city."

"New pad? This is our second flat, and we've been in it for two years."

"New pad old pad, tomato tomahto."

Eve gave a sceptical, "I suppose. Please say you've booked your train?"

"Of course. Ages ago."

"You have?"

"Yes, sirree." She hadn't and now realized she should have done. She'd booked the time off work for the trip ages ago, yet for some reason she hadn't bought the train ticket. Maybe it had seemed a bit too much of a commitment at the time? There was always somehow something she should have done or something people were waiting for her to do. She always felt guilty and always pissed off at the thing that made her feel guilty. Why on earth did people expect so much of her?

Belinda stepped out onto the street. "Hey. You ready?" She wrapped her arm into Roxanne's and pressed Roxanne's arm tightly against the side swell of her chest. They began a leisurely stroll behind the group headed to the curry house.

"I've got to go, Evie. Sorry, mate."

"Right, sure. Well, I guess text me with your train times."

"Will do. Looking forward to it, really I am."

"Me too. Bye."

"Yep, bye for now." Roxanne shoved her phone deep into her jacket pocket.

"Ooh...what are you looking forward to?" Belinda asked with a tone infused with *Can I come?*

"Nowhere, nothing. I'm just visiting Eve for her birthday."

"Really? Scotland. Well, the Highlands are meant to be beautiful. I've never been."

"Nope, me neither."

"When do you go?"

Roxanne ignored the deflated note to Belinda's voice and shrugged. "Fortnight or so."

"You don't sound particularly excited."

"Honestly, I'm dreading it."

Belinda screwed her face into a frown. "Why? You get to hang out with Eve, who—and don't deny it—you miss loads, in, *hello*, one of the most stunning places in the world."

Roxanne shrugged again. "I suppose."

Belinda slowed their pace to a stop. "What's the problem, then? Is it Eve's girlfriend? I thought you were getting on okay with Moira."

"I am. She's fine. Despite my initial slight misgivings—"

Belinda laughed. "Slight misgivings? Didn't you tell Eve you thought she was too good for her, and that Moira was a heartbreaker?"

"Okay, let's agree Moira didn't exactly make a great first impression. I mean, come on, she has this fucked up past, and it was frankly inevitable that Eve was going to get hurt. And she did, and I had to watch." It might have been four years ago, but Roxanne could still feel the stress of it tighten in her veins. "But it turns out she's making

Eve really happy, and at the end of the day that's what matters most to me."

"Fair enough." They returned to their ambling walking pace. "I have to say on the few occasions I've met Moira, I thought she was hot. In a outdoorsy, older woman kind of way."

"Oh my God. What is it with older women? I just don't get it."

"Self-sufficient, financially stable, grown-up. Need I say more?"

"Are we back to the fact I still owe you a tenner?"

"It's twenty. And I'm even more confused now. You like Moira. You can't wait to see Eve. It can't be the midges, can it?"

"Crap, I hadn't thought about the midges." Roxanne shook her head. "Nope."

"What is it then?"

"Oh for goodness' sake, you're like a dog with a bone. If you must know, you've met Alice, right? Moira's stepdaughter."

Belinda momentarily stopped again to frown once more and shake her head. "Alice?"

"Yes, Alice Campbell. She came with me to The Brewer's that crazy night not long after Eve's family holiday and her Highland fling with Moira. You remember, when Moira turned up here at some talk at the library she'd contrived, without actually telling Eve she was coming, and just to confess that she wasn't exactly single."

Belinda pulled down her bottom lip and shaped a pained trying-to-remember face.

"Come on, you do know. She was trendy and tall with blond hair scraped back into a ponytail. She was arse-clenchingly uptight."

Belinda laughed. "Sorry, Rox. I can't quite place her."

"Yes, you can. She was having a meltdown over nothing really, just the revelation of her stepmum cheating on her dad by shagging Eve—"

Belinda put her hand over her mouth. "Oh yes. I remember her now. She told you to go to hell when you tried to help her see the truth."

"Bingo. That's who I have to face again."

"Okay, got it. But you can't deny she *was* hot. In a horrified what-the-chuff-am-I-doing-here kind of way. Poor thing, it looked for all the world that she'd honestly thought she'd stepped into a den of debauchery."

"Yeah, she kind of had." They both laughed. "Honestly, Bel, being in Alice's company that night was like being constantly stung by an angry wasp."

Belinda re-tightened her arm around Roxanne's as they started the final few yards to the restaurant. "I'm sure she's mellowed, Rox."

Roxanne gave a grumpy, "Maybe. Eve's been singing her praises."

"Well, there you go."

"She's been helping to teach Eve to drive, apparently. Eve even described her as cool."

Belinda nudged Roxanne's shoulder. "Cool? It sounds to me like you're worrying about nothing. Just go and have fun and come back. And you never know, by then we might even be able to breathe properly in The Brewer's."

"You never struck me as an optimist."

"And you never struck me as a big girl's blouse. And just to be clear, my dinner's on you." Belinda led the way into the restaurant.

Roxanne stared after her. Her gaze fell on the dining room beyond and on the glint of metal domed dishes catching the light. She let her thoughts drift with the melody of the sitar muddling itself with the hum of dinner conversations.

Was Belinda right? Was she over-worrying? Or was *she* right, and she had every reason to dread her first visit to the Highlands and everything and everyone that went with it?

Spring was, without question, Alice Campbell's favourite season, and April, in turn, was by far her favourite month. For winter with its consuming whiteness had at last relinquished its icy grip on the woods, heath, and moorland of Newland. Only the mountaintops, glinting white on the distant horizon, hinted at winter's recent brooding retreat.

Alice shielded her eyes from the searching soft rays of the morning sun that fell upon the grassy track that divided the burgeoning green of broadleaf woodland from a crofter's field and the heath beyond. She sat for a moment at the edge of the track with her back resting against a proud old oak and her legs stretched out. Her eyes closed at the feel of the warmth of the sun on her cheeks as she listened to the melodic sound of Newland bursting into life. For there was a percussion in the rhythm of the wind blowing through the long grasses and in the round tone of the xylophone-like notes of the water flowing over pebbles in the nearby stream. And then, as if a conductor had brought them in with a wave of his baton, a family of willow warblers called and answered in soulful harmony. There was simply no orchestra and no musician that could compete with the symphony of home.

She reopened her eyes at the gentle nudge at her boot.

"Hello, wee girl." She resisted the temptation to reach out to stroke the soft pink nose of the lamb now snuffling at her thigh. "I can't fuss you," she said, "and have you smell of me. Go to your mum. Go now." She stood to usher the inquisitive newborn back towards the throaty bleat of its mother and lingered for a moment to watch the lamb nestle beneath its mother's stomach with its tail frantically wagging with delight.

Alice gave a heavy sigh at the sight of a section of fallen fence that lined the boundary of the wood and the local crofter's field. First thing that morning on her weekly round of checks of the Newland Forest Trust's land, she had found two fence posts toppled onto the path. Their timber rails had fallen in piles like a discarded game of Jenga. She'd propped up the damaged posts against the side of her Land Rover while she phoned through to her colleagues at the Trust's education centre to get a helping hand to mend the fallen fence.

She couldn't have felt prouder to work for the Trust and alongside such a dedicated team of local volunteers. Together they cared for and shared their enthusiasm and knowledge of the community-owned forest and its surrounding heath and moors. As their education officer, every working day was different. She relished the variety of hands-on tasks that often went beyond what might be traditionally expected of her teacher training. For to work for the Trust was to be multiskilled. And as someone who had lived in Newland from the age of seven, she had learned to care for the land in the same breath as she had mastered tying her shoelaces or riding a bike or reeling off her times tables. Mending a fallen fence was simply a matter of daily life.

She checked her watch—quarter past ten. She glanced along the track to where it bent away towards the centre and beyond to the road that curled through Newland village. Help would be here any moment.

There was no question as to the fence-felling culprits. A telltale browse line of nibbled side shoots running along the lower edges of the oak's trunk marked the vandals' calling card, not to mention a clear trampled path leading into the denser woodland. Overnight rain had slightly obscured their prints, but a collection of their pellets sealed the deal. There was no doubt it was red deer. The young males would often gather and tussle and rub their stubby antlers against fence posts.

A trail of broken fencing and confused escapee lambs would be left in their wake.

With the persistence of youth, the lamb made its way once more towards Alice. "No, no," she said, through a smile. "Come now, haven't we had this chat about no cuddling?"

"It looks like you'll be having it again. That one seems pretty determined." Forestry officer Moira Burns, Alice's colleague, stepmum, and in every way mentor, arrived at Alice's side.

"Honestly, I've done nothing to encourage it." Alice gently clapped her hands towards the lamb. "Go on now, quick." The lamb gave a woeful bleat, as if Alice had broken its heart with her rejection. Alice looked back at Moira and said, "I didn't hear you arrive."

"I walked from the centre." Moira's cheeks flushed red with exercise. "I left a couple of volunteers to cover reception and to puzzle over next month's rota. I feel a bit guilty, but I couldn't have been more pleased when you rang and I could excuse myself to be up here." Moira's gaze settled beyond the field to the heathland falling away into the distance. The heath, punctured with spiky bursts of the vibrant yellow flowers of the common gorse, lit up the landscape in the morning sun. "Some days just seem to need taking in on foot. Spring has certainly arrived."

"I know exactly what you mean," Alice said. "Everywhere is just exploding with life, isn't it?"

"Aye. It's certainly a busy time for our natural world." Moira gestured with her chin to a crow raiding the lunch box that Alice had left unattended on her passenger seat. "I'm hoping you didn't want that apple."

"Oh, no way." Alice rushed towards the black-winged thief. The crow sat perched, unrepentant, on her half-open window with the ill-gotten trophy speared in its beak. She clapped her hands furiously to shoo it away, and the villain deftly escaped with the dull sweep of its wings in place of apology. "I swear, every animal in this wood is conspiring to wreck the joint and make my job as hard as possible."

Moira lowered her eyes from Alice's in a failed attempt to hide her amusement. "I don't think it's personal."

Alice gave a disgruntled, "Maybe. And speaking of making my job as hard as possible—tools?"

In that instant, Moira's tone lost a little of its lightness, as she replied, "Angus is bringing them. Before you say anything, I know, but he insisted. He'd called in at the centre just when you phoned, bright as sunlight, asking what was needed of him that day. He was totally oblivious to all the conversations agreeing for him to slow down and retire from volunteering altogether. Instead, he pounced at the half suggestion of mending the fence. I didn't have the heart to say no."

Alice nodded. "I get that."

"It feels so wrong. He was here at the beginning and such a key figure in securing the Trust." Moira looked about her. "This place, for us, for the community. It's just all so wrong."

"Yes. And cruel all round." Alice's heart ached for Moira. For Angus wasn't just her colleague. He was, along with his wife Elizabeth, to all intents and purposes Moira's family. From the moment Moira's parents had passed away, they had loved Moira like a daughter, unconditionally. And Alice, in turn, couldn't have loved them more herself. Life without them would be unimaginable. She hesitated to ask, "Did he seem worse this morning?"

Worry drifted over Moira's expression, shading her face momentarily in sadness. "Not really. Same, I guess. It's so hard to assess him." She leaned against the bonnet of the Land Rover. "I could do with spending some proper time with him. Quiet time. I'd even wondered about staying with them for a night or two…" She stared in silence for a moment at the ground before looking directly at Alice. "But then he never seems keen. Elizabeth understandably doesn't like to overrule him or make him uncomfortable. I think he can sense the scrutiny. I honestly don't know what to do for the best."

Very little seemed to fluster Moira. But when it came to those she loved, when it involved feelings, it was like she became lost, disorientated. Nature might be unruly, but it was predictable, and there was nothing, it seemed, that Moira could not work out. But love, on the other hand, seemed to fox Moira every time. And this left Alice in those moments without her mentor, and in every way utterly lost when it came to matters of the heart.

"You could," Alice carefully suggested, "look out for an occasion that would naturally lend itself to you staying over. Something that wouldn't raise suspicion because it makes sense. That sort of thing."

Moira straightened herself and stood free of the bonnet. "Actually, on that note, I have a favour to ask."

"Sure. What is it?"

"You can say no, of course…"

Why would Moira think she might want to say no? "That sounds a bit ominous."

"Can Roxanne stay with you at the croft the night of Eve's birthday party? I know it's a couple of weeks off yet, but I didn't want to spring this request on you last minute."

Roxanne? Alice folded her arms and squeezed them tight against her chest. She steadied her voice to say, "What?"

"Eve's best friend from Leicester."

Roxanne. A confusing rush of irritation, curiosity, and mistrust pressed at Alice's heart. How could she feel so much at just the mention of Roxanne's name? She'd only ever spent one evening in her company, just one, and four years ago at that, but without question, Roxanne had left her mark.

"I know who she is." Alice winced inside at the sight of Moira's cheeks flush in response to her curt reply. "I'm sorry, I didn't mean to snap like that."

She needed to calm down. Yes, she would breathe deeply and count slowly to ten. It was a simple technique her therapist had taught her, and it worked every time.

Moira gently rested her hand on Alice's shoulder. "I know that Roxanne coming here will bring up memories of when you saw her last and all the upset of the past. And I'm sorry for that."

A twist of embarrassment knotted Alice's stomach. She'd made such a fool of herself at The Brewer's pub in front of Roxanne. Panic had gripped her that night so tightly, that she could hardly breathe as everyone seemed to stare at her and laugh. She hadn't meant to be so angry and so defensive. She hadn't meant to be the person she'd worked so hard in these intervening years not to be. But then how could she not react that night? Her life was unravelling before her. Every truth seemed to be revealing itself to be a lie. And being taken to The Brewer's seemed to mock her and to rub her nose in her innocence and ridicule her naivety.

Why hadn't she realized Moira was gay? Why hadn't she pieced together the fragments of the past? Her own mum had loved Moira, and Moira had loved her. And yet no one, not even her father, thought to say. So how then could she have possibly known Moira was having an affair with Eve? She'd been kept in the dark her whole life and unwittingly caught up in a conspiracy of silence. Who wouldn't feel confused and hurt when the truth began to come out?

And she hadn't sought Roxanne's help. She hadn't asked to be escorted or to be rescued or to have her eyes opened by her to the obvious. And the last thing she'd hoped for was to feel so exposed in front of a complete stranger and, if first impressions were anything to go by, a cocky and insensitive stranger at that. And who could drink that much booze and stay upright or, for that matter, inhale food rather than eat it? So what if she was personable and clearly popular and good-looking, if bleached spiky hair and a freer-than-carefree appearance was your thing. And who was she attempting to win over with that annoyingly lazy grin…

"Alice?"

Alice cleared her throat. *Breathe.* "Really, don't be sorry." Alice briefly covered Moira's hand with hers. "Plus, it was ages ago, wasn't it. And all sorted now. We've all moved on, and for the better. Shall we rearrange those rails from their pile into a bit more order?" Alice let her hand slip from Moira's and turned away. She then made for the collapsed fence and began to lift the first rail free of the tumbled mess. She dropped the rail, which landed with a dull thud in its temporary place on the side of the track. She glanced over at Moira as she approached to lend a hand. Alice lifted another rail into her arms. "And what's more, I hardly remember meeting Roxanne."

Moira gave an amused shake of the head. "I think you might be in the minority. She certainly leaves an impression, that girl."

Alice dropped the rail with another thud onto the path. "Well, not on me. Zero impression." Alice brushed her palms together, brushing away wood dust and the pressing image of Roxanne. "Zero."

Moira lifted the last rail and rested it with the orderly stack they had now created. With a less than convinced tone, Moira added, "Aye, if you say so."

"I do."

"So I can tell Eve that Roxanne can stay with you?"

Wait. No. "Uh-huh. Sure."

"Thanks, Alice. It means a lot. The party will give Eve and me a good excuse to stay at Angus and Elizabeth's. And hopefully it might show Angus that having us stay there from time to time is a good thing and not some sort of threat to him."

A sense of shame for her selfish reaction crimped the edges of Alice's heart. "Yes. Sounds like a plan. Anything you need me to do to help, I will. Oh, talk of the devil."

They both looked towards the approaching red Fiesta bouncing over the dips and troughs of the track. The long grass that lined the centre of the track brushed against its undercarriage, and a fence post was poking out of each back window like tusks. Alice and Moira waved in unison to greet a smiling Angus.

Angus climbed out of the vehicle with gusto. He was dressed smartly, as always, in a green tweed country suit. His trousers were tucked into his boots, and he wore his flat cap tipped back so that his eyes were set in readiness by default to look to the sun and the heavens beyond. Alice's affection for him would always trigger a smile in her, for he had been her dear friend and protector for so many years. He was kindness and gentleness and wry wisdom personified. He was so easy to love and, therefore, so easy to worry about.

He scratched under his hat as he approached. "Now then, what have we here?" His attention soon drifted from the rails to the woodland. It was as if he expected to see the twitching ears and the flexed necks of the culprits just disappearing into the undergrowth.

"It looks worse than it is," Moira said. She looked at Alice who nodded in reply.

"Yes, just two new posts to dig in," Alice said. "And then the rails to fix in place again."

"So what are we waiting for?" Angus looked from Alice to Moira as if puzzled at their inaction.

"Nothing," Moira said. "I'll get the new posts from the car."

"And I'll prepare the ground for digging." Alice looked at Angus who was staring into the woods again. "You couldn't grab me the spade, could you, Angus?" she asked gently so as not to startle him. He turned and looked back at her. His expression was so blank it was like someone had taken a rubber to it, and only a faint outline of something that was once there remained. It was heartbreaking. She cleared her throat to add, "From your car."

"Well it's hardly in my pocket, young Alice."

Angus sometimes sensed when he drifted. He would promptly bat back a defensive comment as if to say, *I went nowhere. I'm here. Totally here.*

"No, of course. I didn't mean…of course." Alice turned her attention to removing any fragments of post left in the ground. She stole a glance and gave a sigh of relief when he'd returned to his car and fetched the spade. How could someone be with you and not with you at all?

Between the three of them it took less than an hour to mend the fence. Moira accompanied Angus on his return journey to the centre, and Alice was left alone once more, or as alone as Newland's woodland residents would allow. Alice's lamb eyed up the new fence from a hesitant distance.

"It's for your own good, wee one," Alice called out. "It will keep you safe."

She gathered the last of her belongings and made her way to the Land Rover and climbed in. She sat for a moment and looked back to where she had been. Her conversation with Moira bubbled to the surface. If only you could fence your heart to keep trespassers away. Not that Roxanne had ever sought to trespass. She probably didn't remember her, and if she did, well, it wouldn't be a good memory. She wound down the window fully to feel the cool spring breeze on her cheeks.

Would Roxanne have changed? These last four years had felt like a lifetime and no time at all. A prickle of offence itched at her skin. Why hadn't Roxanne visited Eve before? Were they just too boring and too rural for a city girl? Was that it?

She started the engine. Or maybe, was it more personal? It couldn't be, could it, that Roxanne wanted her best friend back at her side, even after all this time? Was Eve's birthday just a convenient excuse to come and stir things up?

Alice released her handbrake and swung the Land Rover round in the direction of the road. Well, she, for one, wouldn't be charmed or fooled. She might be obliged to put Roxanne up for the night, but that certainly didn't mean she was obliged to make her welcome.

CHAPTER TWO

Roxanne bellowed into her mobile phone, "Och aye the noo!"
"Hi, Rox! You've arrived, then?"
"Affirmative. Just stepping off the train. Fuck me, this rucksack's heavy." Roxanne stepped down onto the platform and hauled her rucksack from the carriage and over the gap between the train and the platform.

Eve gave a giddy squeal. "I. Am. So. Excited. You're actually here. Plus, I've pretty much got the whole week booked off work. Sorry I won't be there to greet you, but my meeting finishes in about an hour or so. I should be home around eight, give or take. I cleared Morrisons out of pizzas. Not to mention their house white."

"Awesome."

"Okay, have you reached the concourse?"

"Yep, squeezing my way through the ticket barrier. I think ScotRail are trying to propel out my haggis and tattie pastie." Eve laughed. "So, I can see a Costa…Oh, wait, there's a pub, The Ness and Thistle. Have you been in it? It looks nice."

"Is there a pub in the station? I'm normally rushing through there."

"Only you, Evie, could miss something so bloody obvious."

"Only *you*, Rox, could be in Inverness for less than thirty seconds and have sniffed out a pint."

"Fair comment."

Roxanne stared in through the pub's windows. Did she have time for an impromptu beer? No one need know. She couldn't think of a better start to her hols, that was for sure. With her phone held to her ear she made her way in. She dragged her rucksack past passengers who sat staring up at arrival and departure times on mounted televisions. As she arrived at the bar, she said in a half-whisper, "Pint of Carling, please," to the barman. Then back to Eve, "So, what's the planaroonies for this evening?" She gave the barman a thumbs-up as he placed her pint in front of her before presenting her with the payment machine. Roxanne rummaged for her bank card in the top pocket of her denim jacket and touched the card to the device. Would Eve hear the beep? Everything about this stop off felt illicit.

"Well, I thought tour of our flat followed by pizza and wine and catch-up natter."

"Perfect. And then where's our first port of call after that?"

"I wasn't really thinking of going out tonight, to be honest. Oh, I'm sorry, Rox, I've got to go—the meeting's starting. I'm guessing you've now come outside into Station Square."

Tricky. "Sort of."

"Great. Can you see Moira? She's waiting for you by the memorial statue of the Cameron Highlander, and just so you know, super brave soldiers wear kilts. It's a proud tradition—"

"Moira's here?" Roxanne gave a panicked look behind her, then stared at her full pint. *Shit.*

"Yes. I know you said you didn't need anyone to meet you, but we thought, it's your first time in town, and we didn't want you to get lost or feel alone."

"That's very sweet. But there's really no need."

"Yes, there is. I want you to feel welcome and wanted. We both do. I've got to go. Don't miss Moira. See you in a bit. Love ya. So pleased you're here."

"Love ya too. Bye bye bye." Roxanne lifted her beer to her lips. *You can do this. Down in one, it is.*

A large burp was not the way Roxanne had imagined greeting Moira. She had meant to say, *Hello and thanks for meeting me,* but well, plans and all that. To be fair, Moira seemed to take it in her stride and didn't blink at the beery cloud that momentarily enveloped them both.

"Hello, Roxanne," Moira said with a warm smile. "How was your journey? Uneventful, I hope."

"Hi." Roxanne dropped her rucksack onto the floor and rested it against the iron railings that surrounded the statue. A hug seemed somehow inappropriate and a handshake too formal. Moira had folded her arms in a casual way, and so Roxanne guessed she felt the same. "Yep, sped here in no time." In truth if there had been an event, Roxanne wouldn't have noticed. She had missed most of the last leg of the journey between Perth and Inverness by being distracted by the drinks trolley and the flirtatious blonde who wheeled it. She'd also slept quite a lot, and by the glare she received on waking from the couple opposite, she'd also probably snored.

To ease the awkwardness of the moment, Roxanne nodded to the statue. "He must feel a draft. And that headdress doesn't really say camouflage, does it?"

Moira laughed out loud. "Aye. Luckily, it's a ceremonial outfit."

Moira looked different. Gone was the plaid shirt and cords she had worn on those early visits with Eve to Leicester, and in their place, Moira now wore a funky T-shirt and jeans underneath a dark blue fitted mac. And more than that, her smile seemed to have found her eyes, and her cheeks had lost their pallor. Even Moira's shoulder-length curls appeared curlier. She seemed so much younger. No, she seemed… happier. Yes, that was it. It suited her. Life with Eve obviously suited her.

Whenever Roxanne had pictured Moira in the past, it was somehow always at that table in Carluccio's the night Moira had come to tell Eve that she was married. The same night she found out first and warned Moira that she would tell Eve if Moira didn't. Roxanne wasn't sure she'd seen anyone quite so uncomfortable and heartbroken either before or since.

Moira glanced across at the large station clock showing six forty. Its round face shone out in proud position overlooking Station Square. "Well, you've made good time," Moira said. Her gaze fell on Roxanne's rucksack and the crumpled free newspaper stuffed into the webbed front pocket. "Eve tends to read too when she takes the train back to Leicester. She says it helps pass the miles. She'll often finish a book, pretty much."

There had once been a time when Roxanne would have had to suppress the urge to say, *Yes, I know, Eve's a nerdy bookworm, so you don't have to tell me like it's news to me. Who's known Eve for longest? Who? That's right. Yours truly, johnny-come-lately.* But these last few years had proven beyond doubt that when it came to Eve's attention, and moreover her affections, no one could compete with Moira. Eve had found her one. And Roxanne understood that this was just as it should be. And judging by the soft expression that lit Moira's face at the mention of Eve's name, Moira's heart in turn belonged to Eve.

"Even though you had a good journey," Moira observed, "you must, nonetheless, be tired."

Roxanne shrugged. "A bit, maybe." In truth, she was exhausted. The beer on arrival and the several on-board mini bottles of wine were catching up with her. Thank God for the fresh Highland air to perk her up.

"There'll be opportunity before Eve comes home for you to rest a little and unpack. Shall I take that for you?" Moira gestured to the rucksack, which had fallen over and was causing people to awkwardly navigate around it.

"No, it's fine." Roxanne began to heave the sack to lean against the railings again. "I mean, it's very heavy," she said with effort. "I think I may have brought my whole wardrobe and that of my neighbours. Eve said to pack for all seasons, and so I literally did."

"That's good advice. It's not far—we're just round the corner. Let's go via the main shopping streets so you can get your bearings a little."

"Great." Roxanne tried and failed to lift the rucksack onto her shoulders. She had only managed to lift it at home by sitting on the bed and rolling into the rucksack and then standing to her feet in one push-up lift like a weightlifter.

"Are you sure I can't help you? Eve would never forgive me if I let you struggle."

"Obviously, you know, I wouldn't want you to get into trouble with Eve, so, please go ahead, be my guest."

Moira lifted the sack effortlessly over her shoulder. "Okay, let's go."

Roxanne glanced behind them as they moved off. Surely half the sack contents had fallen out, or Moira couldn't have lifted it so easily, could she? Wow.

They weaved their way through the eclectic streets. Grey stone Victorian Gothic buildings rubbed shoulders with simple mid-twentieth-century low-rise brick structures. Into the mix modern-day curved glass restaurants and cultural spaces glinted. High Street names and chains traded alongside independent stores, including traditional kilt makers and weavers, and whisky and craft shops. Inverness was definitely cool and definitely uniquely itself. Eve had commented to Roxanne many times that she had fallen for this city. And, even through a fine rain that had begun to fall, she could see why.

Roxanne brushed away the raindrops lightly catching on her eyelashes and dusting her cheeks. It didn't look like Moira noticed it was raining. But then, how much wild weather would Moira have seen in her time. What was fine rain, after all, when winter snow could, in some years, cover everything for months. Eve described it as a never-ending Christmas. Even for someone who enjoyed the festive season, less for family and more for its excesses, Roxanne thought that sounded like too much of a good thing.

Five minutes into their short journey, and an earthy river smell began to blend with the enticing passing aromas of food from takeaways and restaurants. High Street merged to become Bridge Street, and soon the glistening lights cast onto the water by Ness Bridge came into sight.

Just before they reached the bridge, Moira stopped outside a complex of shops and flats.

"Okay, we're here." Moira rested Roxanne's rucksack against a shiny metal exterior door which was inset from the building's facade. She rummaged in her mac pocket and pulled out a fancy digital fob. She then pressed the fob against a detector, and the light turned red to green.

Roxanne stared up at the place Eve called home. Even though Eve had described it to her when she first moved in, Roxanne wasn't quite prepared to be as impressed as she felt. It was clearly a high-tech development if the entrance door was anything to go by. It sat directly on the corner intersection of the route over the bridge that headed south out of the city, and the route that ran up and down the city side of the River Ness. In keeping with other buildings in the vicinity, it had a flat roof and only three floors. With a strain of her neck as she looked up, Roxanne could see that each long set of individual apartment windows appeared to have a balcony. Her gaze eventually settled on the busy hub of bars and restaurants that wrapped around the base of the building.

Moira took hold of the rucksack and pushed the entrance door open. "After you. We're on the third floor. There's a lift, but I find it's just as quick to take the stairs." Moira gestured through the entrance door to a polished metal staircase.

Roxanne's face must have betrayed her horrified reaction because Moira quickly added, "Or we could use the lift."

Er, yes. "No." Roxanne swatted away the suggestion like it was as unhelpful as a persistent fly. "It's all good. Get these legs of mine going after all that sitting." Roxanne performed a mini squat, which she immediately regretted. She hated exercise. She'd simply spent too many hours on her feet at work, and she grabbed any opportunity to sit and, if at all possible, to lie down. Even so, she would not lose face and nonchalantly changed the subject. "Eve said you could see the river from your flat."

"Yes, the view is what sold it to us."

"I bet." The on-site Zizzi restaurant, not to mention the all-you-can-eat Chinese buffet, would have sealed the deal quicker for Roxanne. "You're certainly right in the heart of everything."

"Yes, it's great. Inverness has got a nice energy. It's not too wild but still with the buzz of a city."

The last thing Roxanne would have expected Moira to comment on was the buzz of a city. Wasn't she all about Newland and rural self-sufficiency? And what about the rugged countryside and the wildlife and the wildness that was so much Moira? She couldn't help but say, "I never really thought of you as a city dweller."

Moira paused at the bottom of the stairs, and her gaze drifted off momentarily into thought before she replied, "I won't lie, for it's true I'm more at home amongst the hills. But I guess you could say Inverness is unique in that it's a community as much as it is a city. And the surrounding regions, including Newland, are just part of that, really."

"Gotcha," Roxanne said with a nod. "So, I'm to think of Inverness as a Highland hub?"

Moira's eyebrows rose, and she nodded with a smile. "Exactly."

Roxanne could tell Moira was impressed. A small wave of pride lapped at Roxanne's heart. She hadn't realized how much Moira's opinion of her mattered. She just hoped she didn't look as pleased with herself as she felt. And there was no need for Moira to know that she had read the slogan on the wall of The Ness and Thistle. No need at all.

As they began to climb the stairs, Moira added, "And from a practical point of view, it suits us here. As you know Eve's job with the university library and her volunteering often mean she works late or has evening meetings like tonight. And she insists on being independent in terms of lifts and such like. Therefore, as things stand, renting in the city makes total sense."

"Yep, I get that."

"And in any case, Eve loves it here, and ultimately that's what matters most to me. More than anything I want her to be happy."

Roxanne glanced back to Moira, and it looked like Moira was blushing. Roxanne had no idea why her cheeks tingled in response.

But then just like a yawn, there was nothing more infectious than embarrassment.

She quickly turned away, and they continued climbing the stairs until they reached their floor. It had the feel of a private and exclusive lobby. A discreet quick squeeze of a yucca by the lift revealed it to be real. And there were no unidentifiable stains on the carpet. In fact, there were no stains at all. It was hard not to be impressed and even harder not to mouth *wow* when Moira opened the door to flat 301, revealing the open-plan expanse within.

Roxanne made her way into the main space. Her attention flitted between the kitchen area and the living space and the dining room in turn. She then stood and stared in silent wonder at the wall of windows that looked straight out to the city and to the river and the hills beyond. The flat was so modern and cool, and yet it retained a cosy, comfortable feel. It was definitely the kind of home you would want to return to at the end of a busy day.

Roxanne recognized some of Eve's things from Leicester. She couldn't help but smile at the sight of the ever-wonky standard lamp leaning at an angle in the far corner. Nestled beside the lamp sat the familiar purple velvet armchair. The armchair was filled with a couple of the embroidered cushions that had endured many a pillow fight. How many times had Eve lost? She was always so trusting and so surprised when the pillow hit her. Roxanne hadn't prepared herself for the tug at her heart of the memory of her and Eve. How silly and young they were. It seemed so long ago.

A postcard stuck to the fridge with a magnet shaped like a thistle caught her eye. She wandered over to the kitchen area and pressed her fingers lightly on the picture of Berlin. She'd sent it to Eve last month, following an impromptu visit. She had no idea Eve still pinned the cards from her travels on her fridge, just as she had done in Leicester.

"Eve loves to receive your postcards," Moira said with a smile. "And to speculate where you might go next."

"She probably has a better guess than me. I'm not really a planning ahead kind of girl, unlike a certain birthday girl. I don't suppose she's forgotten to plan an itinerary for this week?"

"Ah. Let's just say it's unlikely you'll be bored. She wants you to have a good time. And so do I."

"Thanks. And for meeting me and having me stay. I appreciate it."

"It's really no bother. I know how much it means to Eve to have you here. So, you're in the spare room." Moira headed towards a door that led to a small corridor. Roxanne dutifully followed. "The bathroom's at the end there. You have it to yourself. Here you go." Moira pushed open a door and lifted Roxanne's rucksack onto a chair by the bed. "Help yourself to towels and toiletries in the bathroom." Moira looked at her watch. "Eve will be back, I'm guessing, in about three-quarters of an hour or so. Take all the time you need to settle in, and of course let me know if you want something to eat or drink. I'll get the pizzas all set up to go in the oven, so we can eat shortly after Eve gets in. I'll leave you to it."

"Cheers."

Roxanne sat on the bed and bounced. "Oh, comfy." The well-appointed room was beautifully decorated in soft tones of grey, cream, and dusky pink. It smelled of clean washing and fresh air. The comings and goings of the city played out through the floor-to-ceiling window. She watched, entranced, as winks of headlights danced early evening shadows onto the bedroom wall.

She kicked off her Converse and lay on the bed with her arms lifted and tucked under her head. She had the sensation of continuous movement that all long journeys leave the weary traveller with and that only sleep will stop. She closed her eyes, and the last thing she remembered before sleep overwhelmed her was Eve's face when she told Roxanne she was moving to Scotland. Her expression was full of determined resolve and fear. How brave Eve had been and how proud Roxanne felt of her. And how proud, even when she had misgivings, she always felt of her, in fact. She couldn't help but think that Eve was probably the gutsiest of them both, for hadn't she risked everything for love? How many people could say that? How many people would do that? Not her, for sure. No way.

"Knock, knock, it's just me." Alice wiped her shoes against the doormat and closed the McAlisters' door softly behind her.

Elizabeth McAlister stood at her Aga stirring milk in a pan. She called from over her shoulder, "Hello. Come in. Perfect timing—I'm just making our hot chocolate."

Alice couldn't quite remember when her Friday evening meetups with Angus and Elizabeth began. Like many routines it had all but formed itself, yet nonetheless, it had become a precious hour, which she treasured. It was the perfect end to her busy working week and the perfect beginning to her weekend. She would even make biscuits the evening before to bring with her. However, yesterday evening had been spent baking and preparing the buffet for Eve's birthday celebrations on Saturday night. It was clear Elizabeth had been busy too, as her kitchen table groaned with her own contribution to the celebrations.

"Goodness, you've been busy. But then I guess we do need a proper feast for everyone." Alice gazed in wonder at the abundance of mouth-watering delights. "My quiches and savoury pastries now seem rather inadequate in comparison."

"Nonsense. I've had far more time than you. And we both know how much Eve loves your baking."

"*Our* baking." Alice took a sneak peek under a tea towel covering a large round plate. A delicious selection of homemade rolls nestled underneath. Some of the rolls were wholemeal, some seeded, and some plain white. They were all waiting to be freshly filled in the morning. A waft of the scent of freshly baked bread settled in the air as she replaced the towel. If that wasn't temptation enough, two large cut-glass bowls, brimming with trifle, glistened under the kitchen lights. It took all of Alice's self-control not to dip a finger in the pillowy folds of berry-topped cream that had been generously smothered over rippled layers of strawberry jelly, boozy sponge fingers, and custard. Placed next to the trifles, two sets of large sandwich sponge rounds sat cooling, soft and golden, on wire racks. "Oh, Eve's cake," Alice said, smiling. "That's a fab birthday pressie you've given her."

"She was insistent that was what she wanted, and we weren't to get her anything else. I've prepared two, so that everyone can have a generous slice on the night."

"Good plan. And I love that she settled on traditional Victoria sandwich in the end. It was certainly a close call between that and chocolate. Good choice, if you ask me." Alice giggled, as she added, "Come to think of it, she did ask me several times. I got the impression she wanted her guests to enjoy the cake even more than her."

"Aye," Elizabeth replied with a distracted tone. Her concentration was clearly divided between Alice and the careful pouring of the milk from the pan into three earthenware mugs. She then tucked her palm under Alice's drink and carried it to the table. "I always fill it too full."

Alice pulled a chair from the table and took her usual place. "And I'm always pleased you do." The warmth of the exchange of a shared smile in response glowed bright in her heart.

"Eve's certainly a very thoughtful girl." Elizabeth smoothed a rainbow-coloured birthday napkin that had uncurled itself from its fold back in place. "And I couldn't wish her a happier birthday. She must be so excited. It's such a pity Eve's family couldn't make it." Eve's sister was recovering from an emergency appendectomy. "I know that Eve has been at pains to reassure them that she understands, but nonetheless, such a shame. Thankfully, the latest is Esther's doing well, so that's something. And, on the bright side, Eve's got her good friend from home, Roxanne, coming, so that will be nice."

"Uh-huh." Alice gripped her mug a little tighter.

"Eve was only saying on the phone to me yesterday how much she was looking forward to showing Roxanne round and having her meet us all. But then of course, you've met Roxanne before."

Alice said, "Yes. Very briefly." She then lifted her mug of chocolate so that it partially protected her face from scrutiny and took several slow sips.

Elizabeth in turn paused. Was she waiting perhaps to hear Alice's view of Roxanne? In all fairness, Elizabeth never pushed or pried, and after just a moment of Alice's silence, she continued with her news. "Well, I believe the plan is for all of us to have lunch together on Sunday. I think this will be a wonderful balance to Saturday night. Angus and I are certainly looking forward to the weekend."

"Did I hear my name?" A beaming Angus entered the kitchen from the dining room, and in one sweeping movement he captured Elizabeth in his arms and danced her round the kitchen several times. Her protests seemed to be more of an expression of delight than complaint. And for a moment it seemed like they were teenagers as they laughed and spun in time with the carefree world. They were love embodied, and this gave Alice hope that uncomplicated love existed in this complicated world. Alice felt a stab of pain at the thought of Angus's failing health, and that one day illness would separate them. The cruelty of it stung at her eyes, and she looked away to finish her drink.

"Please, Angus, you are embarrassing poor Alice. And my table is too full to suffer knocks. Now either sit quietly with us, or take your drink into the sitting room and out of harm's way."

Angus held his palms in the air in a gesture of surrender and sat next to Alice, his eyes twinkling with mischief and joy.

Elizabeth placed a gentle hand on his arm. "I was just saying to Alice how much we were looking forward to tomorrow night." Without missing a beat, she clarified, "Eve's birthday party."

"Ah, yes," he said. "Very much." He gave an emphatic nod into his drink.

"Me too. Although…" Alice shook her head.

"Although what?" Elizabeth rested her drink on the table and tilted her head.

"The thing is, as you know, Moira has asked me if I could host Roxanne for the night in the croft."

Elizabeth turned to Angus. "Roxanne is Eve's best friend."

"*Yes*, I know who Roxanne is." Angus's face shadowed for a moment in evident offence but lightened quickly again as he asked, "You don't want her to stay with you?"

"It's not that. Well, it is that. But it's not that I don't like her. I don't know her."

"Ah, but here's the thing—all our friends were once strangers, young Alice." Angus patted at the pocket of his jacket. There was a time he would pull out a pipe and then root around in other pockets for his tobacco pouch and matches. But now he patted, and almost at the same time, he seemed to forget what he was searching for. It was very much the remnants of a process lost in the fog of forgetting. He left his hand resting against his pocket for a moment and then returned to his drink.

"It is difficult to host a stranger," Elizabeth said. "But she's Eve's very best friend, and that says a lot for her."

Alice blurted out, "I'm not sure I trust her."

Elizabeth's expression spread wide in surprise. "No?"

Alice shook her head. "I know that sounds awful. And, like you say, she's Eve's best friend. It's just…I can't help wondering why she hasn't come to see her before now. What if, and I'm not saying for a moment that this is the case, but what if she's come for a different reason than to celebrate Eve's birthday?"

Elizabeth's brow furrowed in thought. "Well, what other reason could there be?"

"To tempt Eve back to Leicester?" Alice looked from Elizabeth to Angus before returning her focus once more to Elizabeth.

"But there is no sign of Eve being unsettled," Elizabeth said. "On the contrary, she seems to have built a lovely and, indeed, committed life with Moira. It doesn't make sense that Eve would want to return to Leicester. It's obvious she's very happy here. I would have thought Roxanne would know that too. Unless, has Eve said anything to you?"

"No. Not at all."

"Well, then—"

"I just, I don't know, I found Roxanne arrogant, as if nothing troubled her."

Angus tapped the edge of the table with his index finger. "Confidence is a valuable trait to have."

"She just didn't strike me as caring about others' feelings. I suppose that's it." Alice finished the last of her hot chocolate.

"But isn't she a nurse," Elizabeth said, rising from the table and collecting the mugs one by one. "Medical people have to learn to be dispassionate, so maybe that's what you've picked up on. And at the end of the day, you just have to remember that you are hosting Roxanne for Eve and Moira. And she'll be gone again in a few days, in any case." Elizabeth placed the mugs in the sink and then turned and leaned against it. "Now, moving on to our plans. What time shall we meet tomorrow? We've the rolls to prepare, and I want to finish Eve's cake. I'm thinking around ten thirty. Would that suit?"

"Perfect." Alice stood and gathered herself to leave. "I'll make the salad first thing and bring it over with me. Then when we're done, I'll head into town to collect the drinks order."

"Great. Eve mentioned that she would also be arriving with Moira and Roxanne about ten thirty to set the hall up. And they're bringing lunch for us all. Eve wanted everyone to have a chance to have a rest in the afternoon before the party begins. That reminds me—Angus, could you fetch down the blue wool blanket from the airing cupboard to go onto the bed in the spare room?"

"Of course. Has the bed complained it is cold?" Angus chuckled to himself.

Alice looked at Elizabeth.

"No, sweetheart," Elizabeth said with a delicate tone. "Moira and Eve are staying tomorrow night. Do you remember, they asked us if they could stay with us to save travelling back into town?"

Angus's cheeks flushed. "But I thought you just said they were staying with you, Alice?"

"Sadly, no. I have the pleasure of Roxanne."

"Alice…" Elizabeth shook her head. "She may surprise you yet, you know."

Alice gave a grumble in reply.

Alarm sounded in Angus's voice as he said, "Didn't you just say you don't want Roxanne to stay with you, Alice? I tell you what—why don't we have Roxanne, and then Alice can host Eve and Moira?"

"Really, Angus," Elizabeth said. "You can't ask Moira and Eve to sleep on a sofa bed that only just fits one person comfortably. Let's agree—it's decided. Please leave it there." Elizabeth turned away to begin to wash up the mugs.

Alice glanced at her watch. It was just past eight o'clock. With a final check to make sure she hadn't left anything, Alice said, "Okay, goodnight both."

Elizabeth moved to her and gave her a squeeze.

Speaking over her shoulder, Alice said, "Thank you for listening to my worries, as usual."

Elizabeth released Alice and held her lightly by the shoulders. "You worry too much."

Alice gave a small shrug. "Maybe."

Angus sat at the table, his expression bleached with evident confusion, and no doubt all the things he wanted to say.

Alice leaned forward and placed a soft kiss on his cheek. "See you in the morning."

"Aye. Goodnight, young Alice. Sleep well."

Alice's heart couldn't have felt heavier as she left the McAlisters' cottage and drove the short distance back to her croft. She knew that Elizabeth would have the same conversation with Angus throughout the day tomorrow. As always, she resolved to do her best to help them by reassuring, distracting, and cajoling where she could. But there was a limit to the help she could offer, and this limitation just felt cruel. And then there was Roxanne. She would have arrived in Inverness by now. She'd probably already dragged Eve into town, attempting to remind her of their wild social life and all that Eve might secretly be missing. And what about Moira? Had they left her behind? Would Eve leave her behind?

Alice pulled up outside her home and turned off the engine. She sat for a brief moment in the stillness of darkness. The prospect of sleeping well had never felt more remote.

❖

Was that knocking? Roxanne opened one eye and eased herself up onto her elbows.

"Rox!"

Eve? She shouted croakily, "Come in!"

"Yay!" Eve wrapped her arms around Roxanne's neck and

collapsed them both flat onto the bed. "I can't believe you're actually here."

Roxanne held Eve tight in a bear hug. "Me neither."

With her voice muffled and squeezed with their tight embrace, Eve said, "There's so much I want to show you. And so many people I can't wait for you to meet. You'll love it here. Honestly, I know you will."

"Don't doubt it for a minute, mate." She did doubt it. And not just for a minute, but for the last three and a half years since Eve's move. For wasn't this the place Eve abandoned her for? And, oh my God, imagine if everyone was like Alice Campbell. Roxanne released her hold of Eve a little. "Can't wait. Although, I won't lie, I'm a bit nervous."

Eve adjusted herself so that she sat up straight with her back against the headboard. An inquisitive expression played on her face. "Why? Everyone's so excited to meet you. I just know they'll love you, Rox."

"Everyone?" Roxanne was dubious.

"Uh-huh. Absolutely."

Eve was an awful liar.

Roxanne sat up next to Eve and gave a disbelieving half laugh. "What, even Alice?"

"Alice? Of course." Eve shook her head, and her overexaggerated confused expression left Roxanne in no doubt that Alice was looking forward to seeing her about as much as she was looking forward to seeing Alice. "Seriously, though, you've got nothing to be nervous about." Eve bumped Roxanne's shoulder with hers. "In fact, if anyone should be nervous, it's me." She rested her hand on her stomach. "My tummy's all churned up with excitement and nerves. I've got the pre-party jitters, and if that wasn't enough, the thought of my driving test on Monday just makes me want to puke."

"Yeah, try to hold that in. At least while you're on my bed."

Eve laughed. "I'll try."

Roxanne ruffled Eve's tidy hair so that her flicked-over fringe went into her eyes. "Look, I know you. And I know how much you'll have practiced for Monday, so your driving test will be a doddle. And as for tomorrow night, it will be *totally* awesome. You and me and the dance floor—what can I say? Match made in heaven."

Eve brushed back her fringe. "You know I can't dance."

"No, neither can I. Like I said, perfect match. And let's be honest, we'll be too pissed to recall the evening, so absolutely no probs in any case."

Eve shook her head. "I can't get too drunk."

"Dude, it's your birthday."

"It's just, I don't want to embarrass myself in front of everyone."

Roxanne shrugged. "Fair enough. I get that."

Eve wriggled forward to sit on the edge of the bed. "And in any case, you don't have to get pissed to have a good time, right?"

You don't? Roxanne couldn't immediately think of a good time she'd had entirely sober. "Err..."

Eve chuckled. "You're terrible. I miss you."

"Miss you too." Tears stung and surprised in Roxanne's eyes. She firmly bit down on her bottom lip to stop them falling. Okay, that was not good. *Keep it in.*

Eve placed her hand on Roxanne's shin. "You okay?"

"Me? Always. That's a fab view, by the way." Roxanne gestured out of the window to the view of the city and the river and the hills beyond. She then scrambled from the bed to stand at the window.

Eve joined her at her side. "Is everything okay back in Leicester?"

"Yep. Why wouldn't it be?" Eve wore a concerned frown in reply, and her eyes darted about Roxanne's face. "I'm fine, Evie. Really. So, is that Loch Ness?"

The tension in Eve's face eased a little to form a smile as she replied, "It's the River Ness. And that's Ness Bridge going over it."

"I'm sensing a theme."

They giggled together.

"You can tell me anything." Eve slipped her arm around Roxanne. "You know that, don't you? Just like the old days."

Roxanne nodded. "I know. Thanks." The old days? Was that how Eve thought of them? In the past? But then she was the one who had sidestepped invitations to visit. What was Eve supposed to think?

Roxanne's thoughts drifted with the River Ness as it sparkled in the reflection of the lamplights that lit the riverbank for as far as the eye could see. The beautiful scene evoked images of the Seine running through Paris or the Thames curling along the South Bank. It was easy to see why Eve choose this as home.

They stood quietly for a moment staring out at the water and at the traffic, how the cars and people moved with the water in a peculiar kind of harmony.

Roxanne glanced at Eve. "You and Moira have an amazing place."

"I'm really pleased you like it. We love it." Eve's demeanour seemed to brighten at the mention of *we*. "It's a fab building to live in. When I moved here, my first flat was in this block but looked out onto the street, not the river." Eve's hand dropped from Roxanne's waist as she tapped at the glass in the direction of the street to the side. "You couldn't swing a cat in it, to be honest."

"Yes, I remember you saying that I wouldn't believe that it was smaller than our place. I mean, *my* place. Obviously."

"It will always be our place. And, blimey, you remembered me telling you that? I'm impressed."

"*I'm* impressed I remembered." It was true. During how many conversations on the phone with Eve in these last few years had she been distracted by something—or, for that matter, someone? And yet, despite this, Eve never stopped ringing and never seemed to stop caring. Eve deserved better from her, that was for sure.

"Go on, mate. You were saying?"

"Oh yes," Eve said, "but I could afford the rent, and it helped me to begin my life with Moira and start my new job. And then I got my promotion—"

"Very cool. Congrats, again."

"Thank you. And Moira was like *How about I move in, and we get a flat with a view of the river and hills?* Although we'd spoken about her moving to the city if things were working out with us, somehow I thought it would be asking too much of her. I was so touched by it, Rox."

"Funnily enough, she was only saying earlier that what mattered to her was that you were happy."

"She said that?" Eve's eyes shone. "What else did she say?"

The last thing Roxanne was going to add was that Moira had said that she was more at home in the hills. "Oh, not much. You know Moira."

"Yes. She tends to keep things in. But far less now."

"That's good, Evie."

"And then this place came up for rent. I thought there was no way we could afford it. But Moira rented out her place, Foxglove, as a holiday let, and with a view of Loch Ness it rents out really well."

Roxanne nodded. "I bet."

Eve stared out towards the hills in the distance. "I do sometimes wonder what she's thinking when I see her looking out. If she's thinking of Newland. If she's missing living there."

"She'd miss you far more, mate. What's that look for?"

Eve had narrowed her eyes and curiosity teased at the edges of her smile.

"Nothing," Eve said. "I was just wondering. So, when did you become sentimental?"

Roxanne gave a shrug. "Oh, you know, people change." Hold on, where did that come from?

Eve's eyebrows rose in response. "I didn't think you were keen on change. Oh, pizza, Rox." The enticing aroma of pepperoni and cheese wafted through from the living space. "Smells like supper's nearly ready. You still like pizza, right?"

"Yes, yes, and yes. And, in any case, when I said change, I didn't mean *change* change, and certainly not the important stuff, like food."

Eve smiled and shook her head. "Okay. I'm starving." She made for the door. "Coming?"

"Defo. I'll see you out there."

"See you in a moment then." Eve closed the door softy behind her as she slipped away to rejoin Moira.

Roxanne sat back on the bed. Why was Eve so surprised at the thought that she might have changed? Did she doubt that she was capable of it? But then, had she changed? And was it less what she had said to Eve over the years and more what Eve had seen that made her form that conclusion? But then Eve hadn't been around these last years to notice, had she? Would anyone actually notice if she had changed or wanted to?

The thought prompted her heart to ache. Fatigue pressed once more, refusing to lessen its grip. She slapped at her cheeks. *Come on, Barns. It's your best mate's birthday.* This was no time for her to dwell on such maudlin thoughts stirred up by tiredness. *Get with the programme.* She could hear Eve laughing with Moira and the pop of a cork. *You can do this.* She took a deep breath, shook off her upsetting thoughts, and headed for the living space.

Moira handed her a glass of champagne and turned towards Eve. "Cheers! And happy birthday for tomorrow!" Moira held her glass briefly in the air, and Eve and Roxanne raised theirs in turn.

"Yes, happy birthday, Eddison. Up yer bum!" Roxanne all but drained her glass dry.

"Thank you! Cheers!" Eve said, giggling. "And thanks for coming, Rox."

"No problemo."

Eve turned to Moira. "And thanks to you for…" Eve swallowed back rising emotion. "For being my love."

The living room lights glistened in Moira's eyes. "Happy birthday, my sweet. Actually, now might be a good time to give you my gift. I'm guessing it'll be pretty hectic tomorrow." Moira rummaged in the pocket of her jeans.

Roxanne's chest tightened. What was she looking for? Oh my God, was Moira about to propose? Roxanne couldn't decide whether she was happy or horrified. Happy, because she loved Eve, and she wanted her to be okay and to have found her *one*. And yet she was horrified because that would be it, wouldn't it. They wouldn't be *them* any more. The old days really would be the old days.

The oven bleeped.

"I'll get the pizzas." Roxanne made for the kitchen area. She was grateful for the chance to give Moira and Eve some space. "You guys carry on." Plus she wasn't sure she could look. She heard Eve say, "Oh wow, that's beautiful."

"Here, let me," Moira said so tenderly that it made even Roxanne's heart twinge. "I had it made for you."

"It's so sparkly. Thank you."

It was an engagement ring, for sure. It went quiet. They were bound to be kissing. Now was not the time to turn round. "Ouch!" Roxanne was so busy earwigging that she caught her arm on the hot oven door.

"You okay?" Eve arrived at her side and rested a concerned hand on Roxanne's forearm.

"I'll fetch some cream from the bathroom," Moira said. "I won't be a moment."

"I'll just run it under the tap, and it'll be fine." Roxanne winced at the cold water. "So, anyway, congratulations!"

"What for?" Eve chuckled. "Wait a minute, did you think it was an engagement ring? You did, didn't you. It's a necklace. A really, really cool necklace." Eve lifted Moira's gift to show Roxanne.

A perfect ruby heart-shaped gemstone caught the light and sparkled as it hung, glistening, from a silver chain. Or was it white gold? Either way, it was classy and gorgeous.

"Here you go." Moira offered Roxanne a tube of cream. "It should help protect the skin from the air and lessen the burn. Sorry, you know that, I'm sure."

Roxanne nodded. "Great, thanks, Moira."

"Let's eat," Moira said, refocusing her attention to cutting the pizzas and sharing out the slices.

A contented silence settled over them as they ate.

Less than five minutes later, Roxanne leaned back in her chair and held her hand over her stomach. "Pepperoni pizza is the stuff of dreams. It's got to be my total favourite. Thanks for remembering, mate."

"It's not a fact anyone who has ever eaten it with you would ever forget," Eve said, smiling. She then licked her fingertips clean of tomato topping. "Now, I need to fill you in with the plans for your hols."

"Okey-dokey, I'm up for anything. Although, to be honest, tossing the caber's not really my thing." They all laughed, with Roxanne laughing the hardest. She wiped her eyes. "Sorry, Eve. Go on, you were saying."

"I confirm there'll be no Highland Games. Tomorrow's party day." Eve looked at Moira. "I'm so excited to celebrate with everyone." Moira moved her hand to rest on Eve's leg. "Then on Sunday, we've been invited for lunch with Elizabeth and Angus. You'll love them, Rox. Honestly, they are simply lovely. Elizabeth is so gentle and kind, and Angus is…" Eve's cheeks coloured a little as she stumbled over her words. "Well, he's been a little…not quite himself recently." Moira removed her hand and took a large mouthful of wine. The tension in that moment was palpable. Eve added, delicately, "But he's still such a character with a real twinkle in his eye."

What was the deal here? Maybe it wasn't her place to ask? "A twinkle, eh? He sounds just my kind of guy. Does anyone want those last two pieces of pizza?"

"I think we're done." Eve looked at Moira who nodded. "You go ahead."

Moira nudged the serving plate further towards Roxanne. "You should probably know we think Angus might have the beginnings of some sort of dementia or something. For love nor money we can't get him to see someone."

"Right, I see." Roxanne looked at Eve who'd taken Moira's hand and was staring at their hands held together. "I'm really sorry to hear that."

Moira nodded. "Thanks."

Roxanne gave a sigh. As a nurse she had held the hands of so many patients and their loved ones in just the same heartbreaking position as Moira. She took a deep breath and then added, "I doubt it's any consolation to hear, but sadly it's not unusual for the patient to resist the suggestion that they need help."

"Yes, I've heard that said before. Elizabeth's own GP told us the same." Moira cleared her throat. "Anyway, there's nothing any of us can do about it. Sorry, Eve, I interrupted you."

Eve squeezed Moira's hand. "That's okay. So, Monday morning I've got my driving test." Eve bit at her bottom lip. "Honestly, I'm so nervous. Thank God I've got a full weekend to distract me."

"You're ready," Moira said. "Don't worry."

Eve nodded. "I'm going to try not to. Then Tuesday, Rox, I've booked us in for a morning boat trip on Loch Ness. You can't go home without having done that, at least."

"Absolutely. Just one question—what are the chances of me seeing Nessie?"

"Almost certain," Moira said, deadpan. The edge of her lips twitched, betraying her amusement.

"Thought so."

Eve laughed, but her smile soon faded when she said, "Then Wednesday you're heading home." She looked down. "I just know it's going to go so quickly."

Roxanne swallowed away the rising lump in her throat. "Well then, we need to make sure we make the most of it. So where to next, after this? It's Friday night, and I can't believe for a moment that this cool city doesn't have a gay groove going on somewhere."

Eve screwed her face a little. "I don't know…"

"What's there to know? Haven't you mentioned in the past a pub run by a gay fella? The Gun something?"

"The Gunsmith."

"Yes. Perfect. Let's go."

"I'm not sure…"

"I don't mind if you pair want to catch last orders," Moira said, standing and collecting their plates.

Roxanne gestured towards Moira. "There you go."

Eve shook her head. "No, I'm okay. I'd rather be here tonight." Moira and Eve exchanged a tender smile. "But some other time, for definite. Maybe Monday after my test? I'll either need to be drowning my sorrows or celebrating."

"Monday? Okay. Sure thing. No worries." Roxanne couldn't

decide how rude it would seem if she went anyway. Maybe not on the first night.

As she cleared the dishes away, Moira said, "We mustn't forget the soup and the flasks for tomorrow's lunch. I'll write a note to remind us."

"Oh God, yes. Good thinking." Eve joined Moira at the kitchen counter. "And speaking of tomorrow, we've checked with Alice, Rox, and she's okay for you to stay in the croft with her tomorrow night. Moira and I will stay at the McAlisters'."

Roxanne choked on the last mouthful of her wine. "I'm sorry, what?"

"Tomorrow night. We're not going to want to trek back here from Newland after the party. And it seemed best to spend some time with Angus and Elizabeth. So we made plans for us to stay over."

Roxanne's chest tightened with alarm at the prospect of a night with the spiky Alice. "Really, you know, I don't mind getting a cab back here—"

"No, there's no need. Alice doesn't mind." Eve glanced at Moira.

"Not at all. She's, erm…" Curiously, Moira seemed to struggle to find the right thing to say. "It's fine."

"Great." Roxanne hoped that she didn't sound as horrified as she felt. "Can't wait." She could wait. She could wait a very long time before she had to see Alice Campbell again. A *very* long time.

CHAPTER THREE

This might have been Roxanne's first visit to the Highland hamlet of Newland, but that didn't mean she knew nothing of what to expect. Over the last few years Eve had described it to her in such detail and with such feeling that a three-dimensional picture of the place and its people had formed itself in Roxanne's imagination. *You have to see it, Rox, it's beautiful,* Eve would always say of Newland. How Roxanne's breath would be taken by the vistas that went on forever. And she couldn't miss the majestic green slopes of forested hills that swept down to the lochside. And then there was Loch Ness itself, of course. It was like the place had seeped into Eve's soul. She'd comment on its constancy but also its changing moods as if it was a knowing friend she revered.

It made no sense, then, that Roxanne should feel so unprepared for the impact of the striking scenery that developed before them on their ten-mile journey from Inverness to Newland. An overwhelming sensation of wonder left her staring, gobsmacked, at the dark, deep, and stretching expanse of water that formed Loch Ness. Never mind its moods or its constancy, you'd think Eve would have mentioned that Loch Ness was chuffing *huge*.

"All this is Loch Ness, right?" Roxanne wound down her window and gasped her words into the breeze.

"Sure is," Eve shouted from the front passenger seat.

"So, how big is it?"

"Well, it's got a surface area of about twenty-two square miles," Moira said, with her eyes focused on the road ahead. "Or to put it another way, if you took the scenic route to walk all round it, that would be about eighty miles."

"Wow. That's one big puddle."

Moira laughed. "I'm not sure anyone's referred to it as a puddle before."

Eve adjusted herself to briefly turn to face Roxanne. "It contains more water than all of the lakes in England and Wales combined."

"Well then, that officially makes it a very *wet* puddle."

Moira laughed again, but in contrast an oddly concerned expression washed over Eve's face.

"What?"

Eve looked decidedly uncomfortable. "It's just…you know I love you, right?"

"Yep. Ditto."

"Okay, please don't take this the wrong way, but if possible, try not to take the piss out of everything this week. I know it's a defensive thing you do. And I totally get that, and of course you mean nothing by it at all. But, well, I worry it could be misunderstood as maybe disrespectful. I know that wouldn't be your intention, absolutely not. But the thing is, others might not understand that."

A defensive thing? Roxanne didn't know what to say. She just thought she was being funny. Wait, had Eve always thought this?

Eve's eyes searched Roxanne's face. "I've upset you, haven't I. I'm probably over-worrying. I shouldn't have said anything. Sorry."

"No, I'm not upset at all. Message received. I shall be the very essence of diplomacy."

"I'm not saying don't be you, Rox—"

"Yeah, yeah, I know." She didn't know. And now she wasn't entirely sure how to behave. But she was certain of one thing—there was no way she was going to let Eve down.

"Okay, brace yourself as the hill up is a bit steep." Eve pressed a hand against the dashboard as Moira steered their Land Rover off the main road and began the ascent up a narrow side route to Newland.

Saying that the single lane road that led to the village was a bit steep was like saying an exploding volcano was a bit hot. As the Land Rover climbed up the hillside road, it felt in every way like the moment a plane takes off and you're forced back into your seat.

Roxanne closed her eyes. "Let me know when we're at the top."

"I don't remember you being scared of heights. You fly all the time," Eve said. "You're missing the view."

"Yep, I fly in a *plane*. You can tell me about the view later." Roxanne kept her eyes shut, and only opened one eye when she felt the Land Rover slowing and turning into what could be a driveway.

"Okay, we're just swinging by the croft on our way to the hall." Eve unclipped her seat belt. "Right, we're here. I wanted to catch Alice before she went over to Elizabeth and Angus. And it means we can drop your things off now, Rox, rather than later."

Alice. Roxanne struggled to resist the temptation to close her eyes again. She could do this. It was just one night. In fact, it would be twelve hours, max. And in reality most of that she would sleep through, so she wouldn't have to spend much time with Alice at all. It was fine. It would be totally fine.

Eve scrambled from the Land Rover and headed towards a barn-like building. Attached to this was a larger house, all but covered in flowers and ivy.

"You okay?" Moira was looking at Roxanne in the rear-view mirror.

"I'm fine. I have a slight headache. It's probably just altitude sickness."

Moira laughed. "Alice will have paracetamol if you need it. Just ask. I'll grab your rucksack."

Ask Alice? Yeah, not likely. "Thanks."

Moira jumped down from the Land Rover, lifted the rucksack from the boot, and rested it over her shoulder.

Roxanne climbed out of the Land Rover and followed Moira a few paces. She hesitated. It suddenly struck her that she was actually standing in the place where it all happened, where her best mate lost her heart to Moira, and nothing from that moment was ever the same again.

Eve was standing at the doorway, knocking.

"So, this is your place, then?" Roxanne gestured towards the barn.

"Yes, that's right. Foxglove Croft. Although it's Alice's place now."

"It's nice."

Rural simplicity and charm oozed out of the simple stone structure. Yellow pansies blew softly in the breeze from a pot by the door, and wildflowers bordered and brushed against the white render. It was certainly postcard-pretty. Roxanne squinted at the glint of the morning sun reflecting off the skylights tucked into the pitched grey slate roof. The deep-set windows, not to mention the red Land Rover parked at an angle just to the side, all pointed to the ruggedness of life here. How different it all was and how far it all felt from the city life she knew.

"I finished converting it a couple of years before I met Eve." Moira gave a small shake of her head. "It seems like a lifetime ago now. And the main house next door is Foxglove, my family's home. My great-grandfather built it, in fact."

Roxanne had formed the impression of Moira as a private, closed person, someone who was very much all action with few words. However, here she was, chatting casually with her and sharing the details of her life. Was this Eve's doing? Had Moira, by engaging her heart, engaged herself with her emotional life as well? Roxanne couldn't help but be impressed. Was this what love could do?

"It's great that you converted the croft yourself. And it must be nice to have a home that's been in your family for generations." Roxanne tried to recall her family home but failed. Her parents' divorce when she was small meant that *home* for her was more the contents of a holdall than bricks and mortar. Security had been the Eddisons. It was easier by far to recall their home. And hadn't she always thought of Eve as home. But then Eve left.

"Aye, the place means a lot to me. And it certainly felt good to work on the croft." Moira gestured to the house next door. "And then the cream rendered building to the left of the croft is Loch View. It's where Eve and her family stayed."

Roxanne shook her head. "It all seems a bit surreal to actually be here."

"I can imagine." Moira turned briefly around and pointed up the road. "To orientate you a little, the party tonight will be in the village hall, which is about half a mile or so just up the road. Elizabeth and Angus's cottage is then about three-quarters of a mile on from the hall. And if you carry on a bit further again from there, you'll come across a sign for the education centre. And that's where, as you know, Alice and I work."

Roxanne gave an affirmative nod. "Okey-dokey. Roger that. Thanks again for having me."

"You're very welcome here, any time."

Roxanne was surprised how much it meant to hear Moira say that she was welcome. Eve had always said how welcome she was, but somehow hearing it and believing it were two different things. Moira had no reason to say it, which gave Roxanne every reason to believe it.

An excited cry of "Happy birthday!" called their attention to the doorway and to the sight of a tall, slim, figure, holding Eve in a tight hug. Laughing, they released each other from their embrace and turned towards Roxanne and Moira.

Roxanne's chest immediately tightened. *Alice Campbell.*

Dressed in skinny blue jeans and a figure-hugging navy gilet, Alice was the embodiment of trendy. Her long blond hair was tied back into a ponytail just as Roxanne had remembered it. However, this time her pale skin caught in the softness of the morning light and revealed a delicate beauty that Roxanne wasn't expecting. In that moment, she might have been the most beautiful woman Roxanne had ever seen, but she was still certainly the most terrifying.

Alice's expressionless gaze flitted for the briefest of seconds upon Roxanne. For no rational reason, all Roxanne could seem to do in response was quickly look at the ground as she followed Moira towards the excitement.

"Morning, Alice," Moira said. "How are you?"

"Morning. I'm good, thanks."

"Great, can I just leave this inside for Roxanne?" Moira leaned into the croft and placed the rucksack in the hallway.

"And you've met Rox before, Alice," Eve said with a decidedly hesitant tone. "She'll be with us until Wednesday, which is just fab."

"Yes. Hi. Oh, one sec."

Roxanne lifted her gaze to say hello only to find it fall on an empty doorway. Alice had disappeared back into the croft. She looked at Eve, who gave an awkward smile.

"It's a busy morning," Eve said with an apologetic shrug.

"Right."

A small part of Roxanne had wondered whether she was doing Alice a disservice, and that maybe her memory of her had been skewed by the drama of that night. Nope. Alice's *hi* was so hollow and empty of welcome it practically echoed.

Alice reemerged clutching a piece of paper. "I nearly forgot the booze list for town." She tucked the list into her pocket and lifted a hessian shopping bag onto her shoulder. She glanced briefly at Roxanne, and at the same time gave the croft door a firm pull closed.

Roxanne looked away again. Had she imagined it, or was that door slam another way of saying *keep out*.

"Right." Alice patted the bag she was carrying. "I promised I'd take these food bits over to Elizabeth and help her with any last buffet prep before I head off into town."

"Thanks for running around so much," Eve said. "Come over to the hall for lunch."

"Yes, I will, thanks. I'll bring the booze with me then. And no worries at all, for I'm pleased to help. Teamwork."

"I'm a bit embarrassed to ask," Eve then added, with an apologetic tone, "but I have one more favour to beg."

"Oh, okay. Like I said, no worries. Anything. Just ask."

"Can you cover Moira at the centre on Monday morning, so that I can borrow her for a last lesson first thing before my test?"

"Oh my God, Evie," Alice said with feeling. "Your test."

Evie? Wait. Roxanne looked up and glanced from Eve to Alice and back to Eve. That was *their* nickname. It was Eve and Roxanne's special name together. What the...? A fizz of jealousy bubbled in Roxanne's veins.

Eve went ashen. "I know."

Alice hugged her bag against her. "I'd forgotten it's Monday. I'll have everything crossed for you."

Wind her up, why don't you?

"I've got to go. I don't want Elizabeth to worry." Alice then made her way to the red Land Rover and climbed in. She wound down her window and shouted, "And yes to covering. No probs."

"You're a star, Alice." Eve waved Alice off. Alice waved back before leaving in a swirl of dust.

Roxanne's heart pinched with betrayal. How could Eve be all over someone who was so rude to her best friend? Or had that changed? Was Alice now her new best friend?

Moira's hand on her shoulder broke her internal chuntering. "Let's head to the hall and make a start, shall we?"

"Yep. Let's go." She'd seen enough, that was for sure. *You're a star, Alice.* Yeah, whatever.

❖

Alice spent the entire journey into town and back thinking about Roxanne. It was beyond annoying. Thoughts of Roxanne had, in fact, consumed her so much that it felt like no time at all when she arrived back to the croft with a boot full of booze.

And before she knew it, she was rummaging in the linen cupboard for Roxanne's bedding and trying to answer the one question that particularly bugged her. Why had Roxanne appeared so subdued?

Alice shook a pillowcase flat with a sharp whipping motion. She stuffed the pillow into the case, resisting the petty temptation to leave it lumpy. She then reached again into the cupboard and dug under a couple of sheets for the guest duvet cover. She wrestled the duvet into submission by squashing and pulling it into place. If only wrestling her own thoughts was as easy.

Roxanne just wasn't behaving in the manner Alice had remembered or expected. She definitely *looked* like the Roxanne she recalled. For starters, her distinctive spiky blond hair remained unchanged, giving off that laid-back self-assured vibe that some might find attractive. And wasn't that the same denim jacket worn over a T-shirt and beat-up jeans that she recognized from when they first met?

No, it wasn't a change to Roxanne's physical appearance that struck Alice, but rather it was that Roxanne seemed off-kilter somehow. She was constantly looking at the floor and only now and then lifting her gaze to something that was said. It was weird. She might have still been tired from her journey, or more likely hungover from her reunion with Eve. Or was Roxanne simply reacting to her? Should *she* have been friendlier? No, she wouldn't be fooled. More likely Roxanne had found the floor more interesting. She was probably bored already and wanting to return to the city and its beer and bars and other…attractions. Anyway, what did she care? Not. One. Jot.

Alice carried the bundle of bedding downstairs and dumped it onto the sofa, only to rearrange it a few seconds later so it looked just perfect. She glanced around the sitting room. Yes, everything was in place. Her guest for the night might not have been particularly welcome, but it was a matter of dignity that her home was in good order and that Roxanne would be comfortable. Would she need an extra blanket? And perhaps a water glass? Wait, why was she still thinking of her when there were the hall preparations to finish? There were so many more important things than Roxanne.

How typical that Roxanne was the first person Alice should bump into when she arrived at the hall. But then she would have to accept the simple fact that, whether she liked it or not, there was no avoiding her.

Roxanne was balanced precariously on a chair trying in vain to hang bunting over the entrance to the hall. Alice's arrival seemed to make things worse as Roxanne wobbled at the sight of her and only just regained her balance before it was too late. She heard Roxanne growl, "Bloody bunting."

Yep, that was more like the Roxanne she'd been expecting.

As she made her way into the hall, Alice paused at the doorway. Annoyingly she somehow couldn't help but stare up at Roxanne.

"So, how's my bunting?" Roxanne gave Alice a wink and a grin.

If Alice didn't know better, it felt like her whole body blushed.

How did Roxanne always make her feel so flustered and exposed? She'd known this was what Roxanne would do to her. She'd known it.

"Wonky." And with that she made for inside and the safety of the company of Moira and Eve.

Eve was concentrating on the task of fixing a birthday banner to the wooden cladding at the back of the small stage. And Moira was moving tables and chairs into place, taking care to leave space in the middle for dancing.

"Hi, Alice," Moira said, looking up and smiling. "How did you get on?"

"Hi, great. All sorted. I've got the drinks in the boot. I'll bring them out when we've had lunch, maybe."

"Good idea. Angus and Elizabeth should be here any minute." Moira gestured to the nearest of the five large round tables that had been arranged together in a large circle. Each table had room for six people. "I'll lay out lunch for us here. How does homemade tomato soup sound?"

"Delicious, thank you."

"Hey, Alice," Eve said, jumping down from the stage. "Was Rox okay? She's a bunting first-timer."

"Define *okay*."

"Not collapsed on the ground with the chair and bunting on top of her."

"I'm fine." Roxanne sauntered into the hall shaking her head. "Bunting erectus, ye of little faith." She rubbed her hands together. "I am *so* hungry. I could literally eat this table."

"We're waiting for Elizabeth and Angus." Alice's comment came out sharper than she'd intended.

"There's crisps, which you could start with if it saves the furniture. Here you go." Moira carefully threw a packet of cheese and onion crisps, which Roxanne caught. Roxanne and Moira said at the same time, "Eve's favourite." An awkward silent second later, they all laughed.

"We should totally do an Eve quiz." Roxanne nodded enthusiastically.

Eve shook her head and held her palms in the air. "Really, I couldn't think of anything worse. Please don't."

"Dude, it'd be great."

"No."

Alice had never heard Eve mean anything so much before, except for the time when she'd told Alice in no uncertain terms that she loved Moira. She'd certainly never thought she'd see the day Roxanne blushed.

"Okay," Roxanne said, before adding under her breath, "I'd so win, anyway."

What? "Do you honestly think you know Eve better than Moira?" Alice placed her hands on her hips.

"It's fine, Alice," Moira said. "Roxanne and Eve have known each other all their lives."

"They may have known each other a long time. It doesn't mean they *know* each other." Alice wasn't sure why she wanted to beat Roxanne, but nothing in her wanted her to win.

"We know each other." Roxanne searched Eve's face. "Right, Eve?"

"Yep," Eve said, mock-punching Roxanne on the arm. "I can confirm where you're concerned, Roxanne Barns, I frankly know too much."

Unmistakable hurt broke over Roxanne's face. "You say that like it's a bad thing."

"Oh no, I didn't mean it like that." Eve gave Roxanne's hand a squeeze. "You know that."

Before Roxanne had a chance to reply, a bustle at the door announced the arrival of Elizabeth and Angus. Eve and Moira made their way to the entrance to greet them, leaving Alice with Roxanne. Roxanne began to munch forlornly on her crisps. Alice felt a twist of regret at having created the hurtful situation. She'd wanted to win, but now the victory felt hollow and pointless and mean.

"On second thoughts," she said, "you likely know her as well as Moira. Just differently."

Roxanne made a grumbling noise in reply and shoved the empty crisp packet in her pocket.

Alice turned away and began to fill mugs with steaming soup from large plastic flasks. She then turned her attention to unwrapping a foil bundle of buttered bread rolls. If there were two things Alice hated, they were inefficiency and waste. She proceeded to curl up the edge of the foil around the rolls to form a rudimentary plate and slid it into the centre of the table.

Roxanne gave a small nod. "Clever."

"Thanks."

"So, this is Rox." Eve guided Elizabeth and Angus towards Roxanne. "Rox, this is Elizabeth and Angus."

"Roxanne." Elizabeth held out both hands towards Roxanne, who in turn gently held them in hers. "How lovely to finally meet you. We've heard so much about you from Eve. In fact, we feel we know you already."

"Aye," Angus said. "Welcome to Newland, young lady."

"Thank you," Roxanne replied, with a warm and sincere tone. "I'm really pleased to meet you both."

"We will have time for a good blether at lunch tomorrow, but we mustn't miss today's." Elizabeth's positivity, as always, filled the room with generosity and lightness. "What a feast."

"Please, everyone, help yourself to crisps and rolls," Moira said, pulling out a chair for Elizabeth. "And there's some cans of fizzy pop and bottles of water if you need them."

Everyone gathered around the table, and moments later they were dipping their bread into their soup and chatting excitedly about the evening of celebration ahead.

Alice tried in vain not to watch Roxanne devour her roll in less than two bites. It was impressive in a can't-quite-believe-what-I'm-seeing way. Had she started on a table leg, it wouldn't have surprised her. Every now and then Roxanne would catch her eye, and Alice would have to quickly fake disinterest. She knew she was coming across as rude, particularly when Roxanne's eyes sparkled with amusement and not hate in response. But when it came to Roxanne, Alice had no idea how to be friendly. Wouldn't being friendly mean she was dropping her guard? That she was letting Roxanne in? Could she do that? Should she do that?

Roxanne let out a small belch. "Pardon. Fizzy pop. At least it's not the other end."

Angus laughed heartily and wiped at his eyes with his handkerchief. "Aye, every cloud." He then slipped his cap on his head and stood to his feet. He seemed a little bewildered as he began to look around him.

"You okay, fella?" Roxanne rested her hand on Angus's arm.

He blinked back at her as if attempting to clear away a fog. "Indeed I am," he said, at the same time touching the tip of his cap with his forefinger. "I wish you a fine rest of your stay."

"You'll see Roxanne this evening, sweetheart. At Eve's party." Elizabeth couldn't mask her concern at Angus's blank expression.

Roxanne quickly said, "You can't get rid of me that easily. And I'm relying on you to teach me a few moves this evening."

Angus laughed again. He laughed a lot less these days, so it was wonderful to hear. "It will be my pleasure." Angus lifted his arms in the air in a fling stance. Roxanne matched him.

She was such a fool. But she was also clearly a *kind* fool. And if Alice valued one thing, it was kindness.

Eve turned to Moira and smiled. "Maybe we shouldn't have introduced them."

Moira tucked her arm around Eve and gave her a squeeze. "I think we're all set for a memorable evening."

"I'll clear and take these to the car." Alice began to organize the lunch debris. "When I'm done, I'll grab the drinks."

"I'll help you." Roxanne scooped everything up, mixing clean items with dirty ones. She then dropped them in no order at all into a carrier bag. "Shall we?"

"But you haven't separated..." Alice followed numbly after Roxanne. After all, what could she say? And there was certainly nothing to say that would help with the fallen bunting flapping in the breeze.

Roxanne flung her arms in the air. "You're kidding me. Have you seen this?"

"See you this evening, both." Elizabeth gave Roxanne's forearm a consoling tap before tucking her arm into Angus's as they walked the few yards to their car. Angus gave a mischievous toot of the horn as they drove off.

Alice waved goodbye, then returned her attention to Roxanne and her bunting crisis. She could feel a smile teasing at her lips. "Oh. Tricky. Did you not mean for it to look like that?" Alice held Roxanne's gaze and watched it melt from crossness into playfulness into an idea.

"Do you think I could get away with saying it was my artistic vision?"

"No." Alice bent into the boot, which was full of boxes of wine, soft drinks, and kegs of beer and cider.

"Well, you're no help."

"And neither are you. Are you going to grab a box of booze or not?"

Roxanne repeated, "Are you going to grab a box of booze or not?"

"Honestly, my class of four-year-olds are far more mature than you." Alice dropped a box into Roxanne's arms. Roxanne turned puce. "Not to mention stronger. You seriously can't carry that, can you?"

Roxanne wheezed, "Maybe just take a couple of bottles out for me."

Alice lifted the box out of Roxanne's arms and handed her two bottles to carry, one in each hand. "Don't drop them."

Alice returned to the hall with the box of booze and the smug sensation of having had the last word. Roxanne followed quietly behind.

"Oh hey, you guys," Eve said, her face bright with excitement. "If you could just put the drinks over on that long table by the stage, that would be smashing. And then, I reckon, thanks to everybody's help, we're there."

"Sure thing." Alice made her way to the drinks table followed by Roxanne. She lifted the bottles from the box and organized them into reds and whites.

Roxanne placed her red wines amongst the whites.

Alice ignored it. After all, there was the slimmest chance it might not have been deliberate. Several more trips from car boot to hall later, and the drinks table was generously laden for the night of celebration ahead.

After their final fussing with the finishing touches for the hall, Eve and Moira joined them at the drinks table.

"How about we all rendezvous here at six thirty," Eve said. "Moira and I will bring the food and Angus and Elizabeth with us. The party officially starts at seven, but we don't want to feel rushed. Is that good with you pair?"

Alice glanced briefly at Roxanne. It was unclear whether she was listening, as her attention seemed to be everywhere except upon the conversation. "Perfect, six thirty it is."

It was frankly a surprise when Roxanne stuck up her thumb and said, "Absolutely."

"Great," Eve said with an amused smile. "Shall I take you over to the croft then, Rox, to settle you in, or Alice, would you like to—"

"No. No, that's fine. You take her. I'll be over shortly. I want to give you your birthday pressie, so wait for me."

"You didn't have to get me a gift. You've done so much already."

"Nonsense. I can't wait to give it to you."

"Okay, exciting. See you in a mo." Eve turned to Moira and gave her a kiss. "And I'll see you at the cottage in a bit. I won't be long, I promise."

Moira brushed Eve's cheek lightly with the back of her fingers. "There's no rush. I'll help Alice finish up."

"Okay, Eddison, I'm all yours." Roxanne wrapped her arm over Eve's shoulders, and they began to head off.

An uncontrollable urge to laugh pressed at Alice's throat as she heard Eve say, "Oh, the bunting. Has it possibly fallen down?" and Roxanne reply, "No. Unless…are you saying this isn't how you want it?"

Alice risked a look at Moira, who seemed to be working equally hard to control the urge to laugh.

Alice dug deep to compose herself and called over to Eve, "Don't worry. I'll sort it."

"You're a total lifesaver, Alice. Thanks."

Alice quickly returned her attention to the drinks table, not wanting to see Roxanne's reaction. Annoyingly, she felt sorry for Roxanne. Maybe she should have let her sort it herself rather than interfere and risk humiliating her. But this wasn't about Roxanne and her ego. It was about Eve and her party preparations. Not everything was about Roxanne.

"Alice?"

"Huh?"

Moira stood smiling at her. "Let's do the bunting together." She then shook her head. "She's certainly a character, that's for sure."

"Who?"

Moira replied, her tone signalling confusion, "Roxanne."

"Oh, her." Alice shrugged. "I hadn't really noticed."

"Right. Okay." It was clear Moira's reply continued with the unspoken *If you say so.*

Well, she had said so. Roxanne *who?*

Chapter Four

So, this is the place where the magic happened?" Roxanne glanced around the sitting room of the croft.

Eve shook her head. "I wondered how long it would take you to mention that. Please don't picture anything. Although, on the other hand…" A mischievous expression crept over Eve's face. "Yes, that's right, every room including outside."

Roxanne burst into laughter, only to stop abruptly. Wait. She studied the wooden-framed sofa and the pretty floral patterned cushions scattered over it. "This sofa? Where I'll be tonight?"

"I really want to say yes, just to fully creep you out, and tell you that it's the very same sofa. However, sadly, it's Alice's."

"Good to know."

"Although, actually, come to think of it, Alice did ask to keep most of Moira's furniture here when Moira moved out. We were going to put it into storage, but Alice said it was vintage cool. To be honest, I think she just wanted to have something of Moira with her. Which, of course, I totally get." Eve brushed her hand over a dark wood drop-leaf side table that sat under the small front window. "I love this place. I always have."

Eve then stared absently out towards a small conservatory off the sitting room. Soft afternoon light spilled through its glazing into the croft. Roxanne stood silently for a moment taking everything in, for there was simply no denying just how beautiful the space was.

A simple fire grate and hearth was surrounded by candles and a neat wood stack. A hint of lavender from drying bunches in pots here and there delicately scented the air. Half tucked away and nestled by the sofa, a bunch of local pamphlets rested on top of a light blue cardboard box. Everything was tidy but not to the point of feeling bare. It had a lovely atmosphere, cosy and peaceful. It was easy to imagine cuddling up on the sofa and simply not wanting to leave.

Roxanne kicked her boots off and flopped onto the sofa. She patted the bedding pile that had been placed at one end. "Oh, comfy."

"You'll be all right on it for one night, won't you? It opens out to become a bed. We can't really make it up now because there'll be no room left. Alice will help you if you need it. The bathroom is up the stairs to the right. Alice's bedroom is on the left. Try not to mix them up. The kitchen's just through there. If you need to make a speedy exit, you can get to the garden either through the kitchen or sunroom."

"Eve. Stop. Sit. I feel like I've just boarded a plane. If I can't find something, I'll ask. Although maybe I won't."

Eve joined Roxanne on the sofa. "Can I ask—on a scale of one to ten, how scared of her are you?"

"Who?"

"Really? The person you don't want to ask anything of. Alice."

"What? Come on, this is me. Nothing scares me."

"Uh-huh. Oh my God, what's that?" Eve pointed in horror at Roxanne's stocking feet.

Roxanne leaped off the sofa. "What is it? Is it on me?" Eve bent double in pained laughter. Roxanne sat back down and slapped her full in the face with a cushion.

"Ow. Bugger off."

Roxanne lay back in the sofa and rested her hand against her aching chest. "Eleven out of ten."

Eve threw the cushion back at Roxanne. "Knew it."

Roxanne held the cushion against her stomach. "She's made me feel as welcome as a fart in a space suit."

Eve laughed. "She just needs a little warming up, maybe."

"Warming up? The ice caps will likely melt quicker. And what was that about me not knowing you? Cheeky sod."

"She was sticking up for Moira."

"I wasn't attacking Moira."

"It did sort of sound like you were trying to compete with her."

"Well, I'm not. I promise. Although, speaking of sticking up for someone, you didn't exactly stick up for me."

"What do you mean?"

"You could have just said, Roxanne knows me really well. Not implied that you knew me *too* well. Like it was a terrible thing."

"Like I said at the time, I didn't mean it like that. I think the world of you, Rox. I love that we know each other so well. I really value that, in fact."

"Me too."

"And for what it's worth, I totally get that Alice can be a bit... intimidating at first. But really the more I've got to know her over these last few years, the more I've come to see that she's really kind, loyal as the day is long, and fun company."

"Fun? I'm sorry. I thought we were talking about Alice Campbell."

"We are. Okay, so, granted, she may not suffer fools that well, which is tricky for you." Eve chuckled at her own comment. Roxanne raised her top lip in a snarl and growled, which caused Eve to chuckle more. "And now and then her feistiness might get the better of her, but she's really worked on controlling it."

"That last bit's not helping."

"What I'm trying to say is I really like her. She means a lot to me, and it's not just because she's Moira's stepdaughter. Honestly, you'll love her when you get to know her. I just know you will."

"If you say so. And I suppose, in a certain way, she's quite hot."

Eve tugged affectionately at the sleeve of Roxanne's jacket. "Stop right there, Roxanne Barns."

Roxanne laughed. "What?"

"Don't even think it. I'm actually quite serious. She might be in her twenties, but Alice hasn't much experience."

Roxanne sat up straight. "Wait. *You* stop right there, Eve Eddison. Why on earth do you think—"

Eve held her arms up in a what-the-chuff gesture. "Because *you* just said she was hot."

"Come on, I wasn't being serious. Okay, granted, she's sort of pretty."

"Sort of pretty? Who are you trying to kid? We both know she's exactly your type. Feminine with sass.*"

"Two things. There is such a thing as too much sass. And secondly, I've honestly never seen anyone so uncomfortable as Alice that night at The Brewer's. If she is gay, then I'll eat this cushion."

Eve shook her head. "To this day, I still can't believe you thought it was okay to take her there. Without any warning for her and given everything that was going on at the time."

"Hold on, don't blame me for the drama that night."

"I'm not blaming you. And I know you were helping—"

"Thank you."

"But you've got to admit, it was kind of insensitive, all the same. And, actually…"

"What?"

"Well…it's just…I hope that cushion's tasty."

"Why? Do you know something? No way, is Alice gay? Wow. Come to think of it, she was staring at me a lot when I was eating my lunch."

Eve eyebrows rose. "Was she?"

"But then, who can blame her."

Eve laughed. "And that's kind of what worries me."

"What can I say—I am in no way to blame for my irresistibility." Eve smiled broadly and shook her head. "You're such a plonker."

"Yup. Alice Campbell, eh, one of us. Who'd have thought it?"

"It's not quite that simple." Eve tucked her legs up under her and turned her body fully towards Roxanne. "We both know my gaydar's not great, right?"

"You don't say."

"It's just, she had this friend. Like a *best* friend. Milly. She was lovely. They were inseparable. And then out of the blue, middle of last year, we never saw her again. And Alice hasn't mentioned her name since. It had break-up written all over it."

"What does Moira say?"

"I think she makes a point of not commenting on Alice's personal life. And I didn't think it was my place to speculate. At the end of the day, if Alice is gay and she doesn't want to talk about it yet, it's her right—"

They both turned with a start at the sudden noise of the door opening and Alice's shoes brushing against the mat. "That's the bunting properly sorted. We've locked up and all that. I can't believe it's nearly three." Alice hung her jacket on the hook by the door. "Are you two all right? You look a bit startled."

Eve stood up quickly. "Who? Us? We're fine."

"Right, okay. Thanks for waiting." Alice gave an excited clap. "Pressie time. Close your eyes. I meant Eve."

Eve laughed. "Only you, Rox." The moment Eve closed her eyes, Roxanne tickled her.

"Keep them closed." Alice disappeared into the sunroom and returned a few moments later carefully holding something yellow and fluffy with both hands.

"Right, Evie. Hold out your hands."

Eve squealed at the sound of a shrill chirp. "Oh wow. She's beautiful." She gently took the chick from Alice and cuddled it against her chest.

"She has a couple of friends waiting for you in a box in the sunroom. I know how much you've come to love Moira's chickens, and I wanted to give you something unique. And, if I'm honest, I love the thought of you coming over to chat to them."

"That's so sweet, Alice." Eve glanced at Roxanne. "Moira's chickens had to stay here with Alice when she moved in with me. Whenever I visit Newland, I always come over and have a cuddle. It's crazy to think how terrified of them I was at first. One of the older ones died a few months ago, and it broke my heart."

"Uh-huh." Roxanne couldn't decide whether what Eve was confessing was tragic or *tragic*.

"I'm so pleased you're pleased," Alice said, beaming. "I thought we could keep them initially in the sunroom while they grow a bit. I've set everything up for you in a brooder. There's a heat lamp, water, and feed and all that. You'll need to keep the netting in place to keep them safe."

"Will do. Thank you so much. I can't believe this. Can you see, Rox? Isn't she just so cute? Do you want to stroke her?"

Roxanne rolled down her bottom lip. "Erm, maybe later." Like *later* later, like *never*.

Eve's eyes had grown so wide that you could see the chick reflected in them. "Has she got a name yet?"

Alice joined Eve in fussing over the chick. "She's yours to name."

"Well, I think she looks a lot like—"

"Dinner." It had to be said, surely.

Eve and Alice looked at Roxanne at the same time. It wasn't a good look. Alice, in particular, was definitely channelling *arsehole* while Eve, it seemed, was going more for *I can't believe you just said that*.

"Ignore her, Alice."

Alice said, "I already am."

Roxanne laughed. On her own. Was this what Eve was trying to get at by asking her not to take the piss? And when Eve had said that others might not understand, had she meant Alice all along? Eve must feel so torn between them. And she wasn't helping her one bit, was she.

"I'm sorry," Roxanne said, lightly touching Eve's elbow. "I really am. I didn't mean to be so flippant. The chicks are great."

Eve gave a small smile. "Apology accepted. Thanks."

Roxanne then risked a glance at Alice. "It's a really thoughtful gift."

Alice briefly looked up from the chick and gave a quick nod.

"I was going to say Elvis." Eve frowned. "I know it's a boy's name…"

Alice said, "I love it. Do you want to meet the others?"

"Absolutely. I can't believe you've done this for me."

"Happy birthday, Evie." Alice affectionately rubbed Eve's upper arm. "I would hug you, but I think we'd squash Elvis." They both chuckled. And utterly engrossed on names for the other two chicks, they wandered off into the sunroom.

Roxanne flopped back onto the sofa and gave a sigh. How was she supposed to compete with a flock of chickens and a ruby necklace? She reached into the back pocket of her jeans and pulled out a bent white envelope and smoothed it flat. The black ink of Eve's name had smudged. It now read *Ere*. Great.

A bubbly Eve and Alice reentered the sitting room. They were clearly high on all things fluffy.

"Right, we have Elvis, Frankie, and Bing." Eve took a deep excited breath. "I can't wait to tell Moira."

"Oh." A look of worry swept over Alice's face. "I confess I checked first with her whether she thought you'd like them. I hope you don't mind."

"I get that. And she didn't let on." Eve reached for her bag by the sofa. "I've got to go. Thanks again, Alice." Eve gave Alice a quick hug. "See you tonight."

"Bye!" Alice turned and made for the sunroom and the garden beyond.

Roxanne clambered from the sofa. "I'll walk you to the door."

"Okay." Before opening the door to leave, Eve paused with her hand on the door handle and looked down at the mat. "Well, I'll see you later, then."

Roxanne rested her hand on Eve's shoulder. "I get it now. I'll behave, I promise. Look, I got you a card." Roxanne held the card momentarily in the air before handing it to Eve with a flourish.

"Oh, thanks." Eve opened the envelope and smiled. Her expression softened to an affectionate glow.

"A two boob sign-off, as normal."

"I can see."

"I have something else for you." Roxanne dug around in the front pocket of her jeans and pulled out a rainbow-coloured woven thread bracelet.

Eve's eyes sparkled with tears. "That's so cool. It matches the one I gave you when I left Leicester."

Roxanne pulled back her sleeve, revealing a faded and slightly worse-for-wear bracelet. "I never take it off."

Eve laughed. "Feel free to wash it, Rox."

"Here, stick your wrist out." Roxanne carefully wrapped the bracelet around Eve's wrist. "Happy birthday, Eddison."

"I love it." Eve hugged Roxanne tight. Roxanne could feel Eve's tears damp at her neck.

Eve eventually let go and sniffed. She wiped at her eyes with her sleeve. "I really have to go."

"See you on the dance floor."

Eve grinned and nodded. "Sure." And with that, Eve left.

Roxanne turned back to the sitting room. Alice was standing in the middle of the space looking at her. There was definitely a hint of something in her expression. Could it be surprise, or could she even be…impressed?

That was it. Her charms had worked. She was the conjurer of good times. Oh yes. "So, it's just you and me, babe."

Alice folded her arms, and her demeanour visibly stiffened. Her expression sharpened to razor edges from soft surprise, and she became unreadable. Any emotional border that had been briefly opened was now closed, and guards likely patrolled its perimeters. The country of Alice was once again an island with sharks in its seas and cannons aimed at those who dared to trespass.

Roxanne swallowed. Maybe she shouldn't have called her *babe*.

"I'm having a shower." Alice's voice was tight as a drum.

"Okay. Great idea. Relax a bit before the party."

"I am relaxed."

"Oh. It's just you seem a little…" Could she say uptight? No, maybe not. "I'll make the bed up."

Alice gave a concerned glance at the sofa. "Do you know how to do it?"

Rude. "Er, yes."

"Fine." Alice headed up the stairs and closed her bedroom door behind her.

Roxanne pulled off her jacket and dropped it onto the floor.

Should she shower too? She sniffed the collar of her T-shirt. The scent she breathed in was a muddle of everything she'd left behind and was the comfort of the familiar in this unfamiliar place. More often than not, her clothes would smell of hospitals and pubs. And now and then, they'd smell of laundry or the perfume of the girl from the night before.

Her attention was soon drawn from drifting thoughts of how many nights-before there'd been to the stairs, at the sound of humming. That was the last thing Roxanne expected. Who knew Alice had music in her? And it wasn't even angry humming, for it was tuneful and melodic. It was lovely. Wait. The humming had become singing. Wow. Alice could really sing.

Roxanne perched on the edge of the sofa and listened. Each note was smooth and melodic. Her singing seemed as natural as breathing and felt as soothing as the softest down to listen to. Roxanne didn't recognize the song. It was a blend of folk mixed with indie mixed with mermaid on a rock seducing sailors and wrecking the strongest of seaworthy ships. It was intoxicating and haunting, and you wanted to hum it with no reason why.

Imagine having such talent. Why hadn't Eve mentioned that Alice could sing?

The singing drifted to a stop, and the bedroom door opened. This was followed by the bathroom door closing and the sound of the shower beginning to flow.

She couldn't have Alice come down to find the bed not made. It was a matter of pride. Roxanne stood and stared at the sofa, which comprised a jumble of cushions in a wooden frame. How on earth did it work?

She would start by moving the sofa out and away from the wall. As she manoeuvred the sofa towards her, she disturbed the box at its side. The lid slid off, spilling the pamphlets onto the rug and revealing its contents. She gathered the pamphlets into a pile on the hearth. As she lifted the lid to replace it on the box, a photograph nestled amongst the contents caught her eye.

"No way. Is that…?" She cast a nervous glance to the stairs. Alice had begun to hum again against the backdrop of the shower.

Roxanne carefully lifted the photo free to take a closer look. The photo showed Moira standing with a small group of people surrounded by instruments. With their long hair and hippie clothes they looked in every way like a band you would see at Glastonbury. Moira looked so young and geeky and good-looking. She was the only one with short hair. Heartbreaker.

They were all wearing black T-shirts with a white letter across the chest. Standing together the T-shirts spelled out *B-S-E-L-L*. BSELL? Roxanne's gaze slid back into the box. She spotted a couple of T-shirts. Oh, hold on, were these the actual T-shirts? How cool was that. She carefully lifted a T-shirt from the box. The late afternoon light from the sunroom had become shadowed by rain clouds, and only just dimly lit up the letter *B* on the front of the T-shirt. She gently replaced the shirt next to a program of a music festival. At the top right hand corner of the cover of the program, and written inside a star shaped frame, the name *The Bells* stood out. Of course, she remembered now. Wow.

The sound of a hair dryer from upstairs made her jump. She stared one last time at the photo. An absolute stunner stood next to Moira with her arm around her. It had to be the infamous lead singer of The Bells, Iris Campbell. It was crazy to think she was Alice's mum, not to mention Moira's first love. Wasn't that how Eve described her? She'd seen Eve's cheeks blanch every time Iris's name came up. There was only one thing worse than sharing your love with another, and that was for the other to be immortalized, perfect and powerful, by death. Eve had always done her best to keep any toxic thoughts of Iris at bay. It impressed Roxanne enormously.

Roxanne rested the photo back into the box and firmly replaced the lid before sliding the box back into place. She then spent the next ten minutes pressing and pulling in frustration at every obvious knob, screw, and spring that might transform the sofa into a bed.

"Come on you wee—"

"What are you doing?" Alice bounced down the last few steps.

Speaking from half under the sofa, exasperation got the better of Roxanne, and she snapped, "What am I doing? I'm making the chuffing bed up. What does it look like I'm doing?"

"Removing the armrest."

Roxanne scrambled to her feet. She glanced at Alice. "Am I?" And then she gave a double take. Alice? Wow.

"What?" Alice blinked at her blankly. Her soft blond fringe teased at her newly mascaraed eyelashes, and free-flowing tousled hair tumbled against her shoulders and down her back.

"Nothing." Roxanne swallowed at her dry throat, for it seemed a smouldering Alice had evaporated all the moisture in the air. There was no question—as kinky party dressing-up attire went, Alice's outfit was breathtaking.

Alice gave a sharp tug at the waist to the scalloped edge of her fitted jacket. A double line of shiny silver buttons drew the eye from a scooped neckline to the bodice, which hugged against every dip and curve. A traditional kilt, its hem brushing against Alice's legs, matched her jacket perfectly. Knee-high tartan socks lent a fetishy finish to the outfit. Roxanne felt her cheeks warm at the glimpse of soft rose-pink knees that could be seen in the gap between where Alice's skirt ended and her socks began.

She looked hot. Smoking hot. And more than that, she looked familiar. It might have been the dark eye makeup or the tousled hair, but one thing was for sure—she was the spitting image of her mum.

"What exactly are you staring at?" Alice looked down at herself and brushed her skirt flat against her legs.

What would Eve not want her to say right now? "I was just thinking that you look…ready."

"Ready? Thank the Lord, one of us does. Move over." Alice lifted the seat of the sofa, which effortlessly slipped forward to form a bed.

"I was about to do that bit."

"Sure you were. And I was about to knit the clouds into a rain hat. Speaking of which, my phone says it's due to pour down. I have no intention of being late. So if you want a lift, be in the car for six twenty-five. Just so you know—I won't wait."

No surprise there. "Any chance of a snack and a pre-party tipple?" Alarmingly, Roxanne hadn't yet spotted any booze.

"Tea and toast can be found in the kitchen. Obviously, you'll need to use the toaster and the kettle. Please tell me you know how to do that."

"Yeah, very funny. I was hoping for something a little bit stronger."

"Two teabags?" And with that Alice turned away.

Roxanne stood in the small kitchen waiting for the kettle to boil and for her bread to toast. Raindrops began to fall on the window, misting her view of the garden and the wildness beyond.

"Have you been going through my belongings?" Alice appeared in the doorway with unmistakable distress creasing her face.

Roxanne placed her hand on her chest. "Don't creep up on me like that. And no. Why do you ask?" Alice was holding the pile of pamphlets. Uh-oh. "They fell off when I moved the box. That's all."

"You've touched my box?"

Roxanne failed to suppress a snigger.

Alice gave a heavy sigh. "Just leave my things alone. Okay?"

Roxanne held her hands in the air in a don't-shoot gesture. "Sure. Absolutely."

Alice didn't exactly look reassured. "You need to see to your toast. It's burning." From over her shoulder as she walked away, she added, "And grow up while you're at it."

What the...? *Take a breath. Let it go. Think of Eve.*

Roxanne shouted into the sitting room. "I like my toast crispy." With a quieter voice she couldn't help but add, "And I'd like my host to take the stick out of her arse."

Alice reappeared once more.

Help me.

"And *I'd* like my kitchen not burned to the ground. And my guest not to *be* an arse. Guess we can't have everything. And I'm not kidding—if you're not ready, I won't wait for you."

"Message received, several times, loud and clear."

"Good."

Would Alice repeat this conversation to Eve? Of course she would. What she wouldn't give for a drink right now. She shoved a teabag in a mug. What she wouldn't give to be anywhere else right now.

CHAPTER FIVE

Alice watched the intermittent sweep of the wiper blades spread the raindrops to the edges of the windscreen. The radio was tuned to the local station. Now and then a song she knew would come on, and she'd sing a little bit of the chorus. She'd just begun to join in with the melody of a favourite tune when a blast of cold wet air rushed in with the opening of the passenger door.

Roxanne stood on the driveway blinking away raindrops and looking up at her in evident disbelief.

"You waited for me?" Roxanne clambered into the passenger seat. "I couldn't believe it when I came out of the shower and looked at my phone, and it said quarter to seven. And when you weren't there, I honestly thought I'd be walking. Thanks so much." Roxanne seemed unusually flustered, and her smile, rather than teasing, conveyed gratitude and apology. The shoulders of her blue shirt were speckled with black dots of wet, and her flushed cheeks sparkled with sprinkles of rain.

It was frankly annoying that it was difficult to stay cross with her. Alice started the engine. "Buckle up."

"I'll text Eve to say I've made us late."

"I've already let her know."

Roxanne's expression fell, and she looked away to the passenger window. "Right."

How was it she now felt sorry for her? "Eve was fine when I messaged her. Don't worry."

Alice turned the vehicle in the direction of the village hall, and they headed off along the drive that led from the croft onto the road through Newland. The road was only wide enough for one car, and every so often Alice would pull into a passing place to allow an approaching vehicle to pass by.

"I feel a bit nervous, to be honest." Roxanne pulled her seat belt away from her and wafted her shirt. She was either hot or trying to dry the material, but either way she flooded the car with the sweet smell of soap and laundry. "I tend to have a wee dram to take away the nerves before a night out."

Roxanne was nervous? "You don't strike me as someone who finds social stuff hard."

"What can I say—you've got to fake it to make it. 'Cause I reckon everyone gets anxious. Some hide it better than others, that's all. And I think, if anything, I'm nervous for Eve. I want her to have a fab night."

"Me too." They shared an unexpected and distracting smile. "Oops, nearly missed the entrance."

"Wow, there's already quite a few cars here. I'm impressed. I didn't realize Eve knew so many people, and not one of them fashionably late."

Alice laughed. "What can I say, we're a keen lot." She parked as close to the door as she could get. She then turned off the engine, and they sat for a brief moment watching people dashing to the hall from their cars. It was oddly enthralling to watch each partygoer awkwardly jump over or sidestep the puddles.

Roxanne rubbed at the condensation that kept fogging her window. "Oh, cool, there's Eve and Moira. They're just inside the doorway."

A crowd had gathered around Eve, and people were handing her gifts and hugging her. And Eve in turn would introduce them to Moira, who would shake their hands or hug them, depending presumably on whether she'd met them before.

"Do you know these people?" Roxanne sounded decidedly nervous.

"Most of them, yes. Particularly the Newland locals and our centre volunteers. There'll be a real mixture of folk here tonight, so I certainly won't know everyone. There's a chance I'll have met one or two of her work colleagues from the uni library, and a couple of the local LGBT Forum gang she volunteers with. I don't think I'll recognize anyone from the uni's QueerNess group—"

"You've met the Forum members?" Roxanne couldn't have sounded more surprised.

Why was Roxanne so taken aback? More to the point, what had

she presumed about her or heard, even? Oh my God, did she think she was boring? "Yes. You say that like you think I don't leave the croft."

"No, I didn't mean that. I just presumed you and Eve mixed in different...social circles, that's all."

"Okay, well, like I said, I've met a couple of the local group members. I've been to the pub with them when I've been out with Eve. I've also helped her with a series of youth initiatives for the Forum, based here at the centre—confidence building, that sort of thing."

"You have? And you enjoyed meeting them?"

What was that supposed to mean? Did she really think of her as that unfriendly? "Yes, why wouldn't I?"

"No reason."

"I'm not antisocial."

"No, I didn't mean to imply..."

Alice pulled down her visor mirror, focusing her attention away from Roxanne's confusing questions and her scrutinous gaze. She forced herself to concentrate instead on fixing her make-up. "My mascara smudges so easily."

"You look great."

Alice's cheeks stung at the unexpected compliment. She scrambled to brace and protect herself from a follow-up teasing quip that would, no doubt, make her feel exposed and furious. But no. That seemed to be it.

"Thanks." Alice closed the visor. She risked a glance at Roxanne. "So do you, by the way. Blue suits you." Without waiting to hear Roxanne's reply, she added, "Let's go."

"What? Ycp. Yes, let's do this." Roxanne opened the door and jumped out. She then closed the door behind her with a newly struck demeanour of determination.

Whether Roxanne was faking it or not, she definitely seemed to be less nervous. No doubt the prospect of hooking up with a Forum member had just dawned on her, dispelling all nerves. A stab of hurt at the thought surprised and pressed at Alice's heart. She took a deep and steadying breath and repeated in her head, *Roxanne who?*

❖

"Hey, you guys!" Eve waved excitedly at them as they approached, and an onlooker could have been forgiven for thinking it had been four years not four hours since Eve had last seen them.

"After you." Roxanne gestured for Alice to enter first. She couldn't help herself but quip, "Loving your bunting, by the way."

A smile broke from Alice's lips whether she wanted it to or not. "Thank you and thank you. I think."

Eve hugged them each in turn.

As Eve released Alice, she asked, "Everything okay now?"

Alice nodded. "Yes, all sorted."

What was all sorted? What had Alice said? Roxanne's heart squeezed tight in her chest. "I'm so sorry for making us late."

Eve gave a puzzled smile. "There's honestly no need to apologize. A flat tyre's hardly your fault."

A flat tyre? Roxanne glanced at Alice, who was looking out into the rapidly filling room. It was difficult to tell from her concentrated expression what she was thinking. Why had Alice covered for her? Or was she just protecting Eve from the truth that her best mate couldn't even manage to be on time for her big birthday? Yes, that was more likely.

"Rox." Eve's voice startled Roxanne back to the room. "Can I introduce you to Dafne."

"Hallo!" Dafne beamed at her with eyes that shone with a hawklike focus and directness. She had wild flame-red hair set off by a green polo-neck jumper complemented by tartan trousers that hugged her compact frame. Dafne held her arms out wide towards her. "I'm coming in a for a wee bosie, ready or not." She grabbed Roxanne with considerable and unexpected vigour and pressed against her in a tight embrace.

Eve patted Dafne affectionately on the back. "Dafne and I are on the ever-growing local Pride festival committee. And she's responsible for my fab birthday badge." Eve proudly pointed to the large round disc on her chest with the number thirty emblazed in large numbers.

Roxanne gave a muffled, "Great." Had Eve said rugby team, it would have been no surprise, for Dafne's hug was more like a tackle from which it seemed there was little chance of escape.

Roxanne took a large gasp of breath as Dafne let go.

"I've heard so much about you," Dafne said with alarming enthusiasm.

Roxanne readjusted her shirt. "All bad, I hope."

"Ooh, aye." Dafne's decidedly dirty laugh was infectious and full of naughty fun.

"Evie, I'm going to have a last practice with the girls." Alice turned away and began to head off in the direction of a group of women congregating by the stage.

"Sure thing," Eve said. "Thanks so much for organizing tonight's dancing. I can't wait to watch you all."

From over her shoulder Alice shouted, "No worries."

Roxanne called out after her, "Wait. Are you dancing?"

If Alice heard her question, she didn't let on. Instead, she didn't slow her step and carried on walking away.

Eve giggled. "Seriously, you didn't realize Alice was dancing?"

Roxanne stared after Alice. "How was I to know?"

Dafne said, "She's got her outfit on."

Roxanne glanced back to Dafne. "I just thought she was wearing a party outfit."

"Oh, aye, like fancy dress." Dafne gave a knowing nod. "Eve mentioned that you were a nurse. It's a crying shame that you didn't turn up ready for work."

"Yeah, Daf"—Roxanne placed a consoling hand on Dafne's shoulder—"I hate to break it to you, but it's less naughty nurse and more scrubs and Crocs."

Dafne's eyes shone even brighter. "Scrubs, eh?"

Tricky.

Moira had been keeping watch for partygoers arriving. "There's more guests heading our way."

"Oh, it's Enid from work, and that must be her hubby. I'm so pleased they could make it." Eve waved to Enid who was valiantly negotiating the car park puddles. "Okay, you pair, we're on the table where Angus and Elizabeth are sitting. Can you see, Rox? They're just to the right-hand side of the drinks table next to the stage. You're welcome to join us, Dafne. I'll leave you guys to it. I had a feeling that you two would get on."

Roxanne gave Eve a wide-eyed look that she hoped would say, *I can't believe you've set me up.* "Uh-huh."

Dafne rubbed her hands together. "Shall we get a drink, then?"

What was Eve playing at? Keep her distracted so she would cause less trouble? Was that the plan? Fun as Dafne seemed—and who knew, maybe in a different setting on a different day they could have explored Dafne's dressing-up fantasies—tonight a casual hook-up with a stranger was the furthest thing from her thoughts. She had the most peculiar sensation that she had all she wanted right there already. But then she was here for Eve—maybe that was it. Wasn't it? Her gaze drifted in the direction of the stage, and she felt a pinch of disappointment when Alice was nowhere to be seen.

Roxanne placed her hand on Dafne's shoulder. "Tell you what. You go ahead. I'm just going to pop to the loo."

Dafne's face fell. "Okay."

It wouldn't be the first time that Roxanne had found an escape behind a toilet door, or out a toilet window for that matter. It *was* the first time, however, that she found the toilets crammed with Highland dancers.

"Oops, sorry." Roxanne side-stepped two dancers with their arms up in the air while another one stood at the sink adjusting her hair and make-up in the mirror. "I'll come back later."

Alice came out of one of the cubicles and blushed at the sight of Roxanne.

"Hi, again. I'm just…I'll just go to the loo, then." Roxanne nipped into the toilet next door to the one Alice had vacated. She pulled the toilet lid down and sat heavily on it. The dancers chatted away about timings and counting ins, and had Hetty remembered to give their CD to Joe in charge of the music for the night, and why couldn't Lily's Tom make the effort to come? Alice's voice was conspicuously absent. She'd obviously left. And then everything went quiet.

Roxanne opened the cubicle door.

"Hey, lassie."

"Oh, hey, Daf."

"I thought the Loch Ness monster had climbed up the pipes and got ya—you've been that long."

"Have I?"

"I might as well pay a visit while I'm here."

"I would. See you out there." Roxanne left the loo with such haste that Nessie could well have been chasing her. She made her way to their table. "Evening, all."

"Roxanne. How lovely." Elizabeth smiled and pulled out the chair next to her.

"Thank you so much. Before I join you, who wants another drink?"

"We're fine, young lady." Angus lifted his half-pint beer glass, three-quarters full of beer, in a toasting gesture. Another full pint sat beside him.

Dafne returned to Roxanne's side.

"I'm just heading to the drinks table, Daf—"

"There's no need. I've got you a pint of Jane's Jungle Juice to get the party started." Dafne pointed to the glass next to Angus.

"Lovely. Bottoms up." Roxanne promptly lifted the glass and downed it pretty much in one. She rested her hand on her stomach. "Ooh, I wasn't expecting cider. Sharp and fizzy. Good choice. Thanks, Daf. I'll just get another. You're fine, right?"

Dafne's mouth had fallen open, and words now seemed to fail her. She blinked at her own full pint.

"Great stuff. See you in a mo." Roxanne gave Dafne a thumbs-up before heading off in search of a refill.

There was no one at the drinks table. It was self-service. In other words, it was nirvana. She could have a glass of wine, but then the cider was good, wasn't it? The keg of Jane's Jungle Juice sat in between two other kegs. The first keg was labelled The Highland Heavy and the other Highland Heather Ale. Both were frankly tempting. No, she would stick to cider and be responsible and not mix her drinks. It was a mere half a pint later when her fingers and toes began to feel strangely numb. Should she worry that everything in the room seemed to have a double? However, her nervousness seemed to have slipped away. And, as it happened, so had Dafne and her twin who had left their table to join another group of people.

Roxanne stood up straight at the surreal sight of *several* Alices approaching through the mist of alcohol and the muddle of bodies.

Roxanne tidied the collar of her shirt. "Hey, roomie."

Alice looked behind her. "Hey, one night only."

Roxanne laughed. "Has anyone told you you're funny?"

"Has anyone told you you're not?" Alice gave a small smile. She briefly reached across her to grab a bottle of water. She twisted the cap open with a snap and drank down a couple of mouthfuls. Roxanne watched as the moisture gathered on Alice's lips.

Alice wiped at her mouth with the edge of her forefinger. "It's called water. You might want to have some because if you vomit in my car, you're walking home." Alice reached for another bottle and made a point of placing it on the table right next to Roxanne.

"Thank you. Gotcha. Although I'll have you know I'm never sick…" A rolling fizzing sensation in her stomach prompted her to add, "Almost never. Oh, here's Eve. Hey—"

"Oh my God, Rox. How many have you had? You can't even look at me straight."

Roxanne pulled down her bottom lip and shrugged. "Not much."

"If it helps," Alice said, "nearly two pints. That includes the one Dafne gave her."

Wait. Had Alice been keeping tabs on her? Or could she have been... No, no way, was Alice checking her out? Either way, Roxanne definitely felt flattered rather than offended. "You've been watching me?"

Alice's cheeks flushed.

"Thank God you were." Eve peeled Roxanne's fingers free from the glass she was gripping. She took a hesitant sniff of the dregs at the bottom. "That's Jane's Jungle Juice. I'd recognize it anywhere."

Roxanne's stomach gurgled. "It's surprisingly fizzy."

"That's because it's still fermenting. It's lethal. We're not talking Carling, Rox. Two pints would down a herd of elephants. Do you think you can make it back to the table?"

"Of course." The numbness that had started in her toes had now reached her thighs. "In theory."

"I'll help." Alice joined Eve in placing an arm around Roxanne's waist.

They managed to make a discreet exit for their table. Roxanne half sat, half slumped into her seat. Eve pulled up a chair next to her, and Elizabeth diplomatically slipped a packet of crisps in front of her.

"I can't eat the whole pack," Elizabeth said.

"Thank you." Roxanne lifted her finger in the air. "And I can't eat a whole box."

Everyone at the table laughed. Roxanne wasn't quite sure why.

"Oh, Alice, the girls are in place." Eve gestured to the stage and to the dancers getting themselves into position. "Good luck."

Alice brushed at her skirt. "Right. I just need to change into my ghillies." Alice changed into ballet-style soft flats complete with laces criss-crossed through from her foot to her ankle. "Now for a final stretch." Alice stood and arched her back before placing her hands in fists on her hips. With a straight back she carefully bent forward. And then with her legs together and her heels pressed against each other, she proceeded to point her toes out at an angle. As she bent, the scoop of her fitted jacket revealed the white trim of a blouse and the flushed pink skin of her shoulder blades and neck.

"You look great." Roxanne smiled with the half of her mouth that worked. "Really great."

Alice shook her head. "What, both of us?" And with that she headed for the dance floor.

The excited chatter of the hall was replaced by the startling and remarkably sobering wail of a bagpipe.

Roxanne placed her hand on her heart. "Bloody hell. No wonder that put fear in the enemy."

Alice glanced back to their table. Oh no, had she offended Alice? But then, there was no way Alice could have heard her observation, could she? Thankfully, she seemed to be looking towards Eve. Eve was waving at her with an expression full of good wishes.

Angus laughed. "Aye. It's an imposing noise."

Thank God for Angus. Eve was right—he had a real twinkle. He was ace.

Alice took her place at the front left of two lines of two. The group all bowed and then began to dance in perfect unison. They leaped into the air with a ballet dancer's grace, poise, and strength. Sometimes they held one arm aloft, at times two, as they struck a half-crescent shape above their heads with each leap. And each time, they kept their thumbs pressed against their middle fingers to lend the move an elegant flourish. It was simply masterful.

Their dance was a breathless display of sharp angles, lines, and precision, as elbows mirrored knees in forming triangular shapes to their side. Their pointed feet pressed from heel to toe to calf with the dexterity and balance of a gymnast. To say it was impressive was an understatement. To discover that it was sexy was a revelation.

Roxanne undid her top button. "Is it me, or has someone put the heating on?"

Elizabeth leaned in and explained, "You're feeling the energy of the dance."

"Right." Roxanne was feeling something, that was for sure, but she'd never heard it described as energy before.

Roxanne tried in vain to take in the whole group as one moving ensemble, but despite her best efforts her attention returned like a homing device back to Alice. All she could see was Alice.

Alice's skirt wafted and swept about her legs, revealing a glimpse of inner thigh. The tight-fitting bodice of her jacket pressed against the swell of her breasts as they moved up and down with the rhythm of the dance.

Eve placed her hand momentarily over Roxanne's. "You okay, Rox? You've gone clammy and quite pale."

"Uh-huh."

Eve laughed. "Oh, I see. They're good, aren't they. Try not to go blind."

Roxanne chuckled only to stop short when the dancers twirled, whipping up their skirts in a whirl of tartan fabric. Her mouth went dry at a flash of underwear.

Eve slid a glass of water in front of her. "Drink before you pass out."

The dancers froze on the spot and finished with a low bow. The hall erupted in stamping and cheering, outdoing the last gasp of the bagpipe.

Roxanne jumped to her feet, clapping. She slipped her fingers into her mouth and blew a long and loud wolf whistle. Whether it was the effects of Jane's Jungle Juice or the woozy self-conscious sensation of everyone turning to look at her, either way, Roxanne sank heavily back into her seat. She reached for her water and drank down several large mouthfuls.

Alice returned to their table, flushed and glowing.

Roxanne's thoughts drifted to a place they probably shouldn't. No, they definitely shouldn't. They went there anyway. If only she could be the one who made Alice's face look so flushed and glowing. Imagine if…

Elizabeth's exclamation of, "Oh, Alice, wonderful, just wonderful," brought Roxanne soberly back from her illicit daydreams.

The love from everyone at the table for Alice couldn't have been more obvious.

Eve stood and gave Alice a hug. "That was absolutely amazing, and such a treat to kick off the evening. Thank you so much."

Moira, who had been standing and clapping just to the side of them, smiled broadly with evident pride. "Very well done, as always."

Angus's eyes shone with delight, as he said, "Aye, just bonny, young Alice. Just bonny."

Alice went over to Angus and hugged him. "Thank you."

"Yes, that was, erm…" Roxanne glanced at Eve who was busy talking to Moira. "Great. You were great."

Alice looked up at her and smiled. "Thanks. And thanks for the whistle."

Roxanne returned her smile. "My pleasure."

Alice made her way over and sat for a moment in the chair next to Roxanne that Eve had vacated. She leaned down and began to deftly unlace her ghillies. "Keep drinking that water. It'll help."

Roxanne quipped, "Sadly, I'm pretty sure I'm beyond help."

Alice laughed. "Aren't we all."

Moira turned from chatting with Eve to announce, "We think this might be a good time for the buffet."

Was there ever a bad time for a buffet? Roxanne gingerly stood and tested her land legs. "All good now. Lead the way, birthday girl."

Eve shook her head. "How 'bout you stay where you are for now? I'll fill a plate for you."

"You don't have to, mate."

"I kind of do. You still look quite pale."

Embarrassment flooded Roxanne's heart. She'd made a fool of herself, hadn't she, by getting drunk. And no doubt she'd embarrassed Eve. She rubbed at her aching head. She was such a loser. Wasn't that what everyone was thinking? She stole a furtive glance to Alice, who was now helping Elizabeth stand to her feet.

Moira had joined them. "Okay, old lady?"

"Don't look so worried," Elizabeth said. "I'm never better. Just sat a little too long. You go ahead. I shall follow. After all, the birthday girl should have first choice of her buffet."

"Why don't we all go together?" Eve held out her arm for Elizabeth.

Elizabeth gave Eve's arm a squeeze. "That would be delightful."

"And how about I grab a few things from the buffet for you, Angus?" Alice's expression held such affection that it must have felt impossible for Angus to say no to her. "Save you the bother of waiting around at the buffet table. I promise to pinch a few extras." She tapped the side of her nose.

Angus matched the action. "And I won't tell a soul." He turned to Roxanne. "I've never been one to wait around. Too much to do."

"Absolutely. I can see that. A man on the go."

Angus laughed. "Aye."

Alice seemed to hesitate. Her uncertain gaze flitted from Angus to Roxanne.

"You *can* leave us, for we promise to behave. Isn't that so, fella?"

"Aye." Angus's eyes sparkled. "At least we'll try. Go on now, or you'll miss your place."

Alice left for the buffet table. She glanced just once more at them before engrossing her attention upon the task in hand.

With Alice's arrival, Moira tapped a glass with a spoon and

welcomed everyone to come and help themselves to food. An excited chatter erupted along with the scraping of chairs against the wooden floor.

Angus and Roxanne sat watching the party guests forming an obedient queue for the buffet. Roxanne nudged her chair closer to Angus. "I was saying to Alice earlier that it's impressive how many people Eve has come to know."

Angus looked at her. It almost seemed that he'd forgotten she was there next to him.

"Yes." His expression became full of thought. "She is a much-loved addition to this community and to our family. And she makes Moira very happy, and that's such an important thing for us."

"Yep, defo. Eve certainly seems to be completely settled here. And in love, for sure. Although I'm not an expert on that topic." She wasn't quite sure why she'd confessed that. Damn the booze for loosening her tongue and poor old Angus having to listen.

He rooted around his jacket checking each pocket before giving up. "Here's the thing, young lady. Love is less about expertise and more about chemistry and the magic of attraction."

"Okay."

"You can teach someone how to open their hearts to love and maybe suggest how to give love its best chance, but no one can make you an expert." Angus gave a wistful smile in the direction of Elizabeth spooning salad onto her plate. "I learn something new about her every day, and I fall in love a little bit more with each discovery."

Angus's insight and eloquence surprised her. But then, what might be happening to him had nothing to do with intelligence, though it was sadly often the case that the brighter the individual, the more capable and likely they were to try to manage their symptoms and delay help. What was happening to him was just cruel.

Roxanne took a sip of water. "You certainly have something very special. How long have you been married?"

"Nearly fifty-five years." Elizabeth arrived at the table and rested her plate carefully in front of her.

"Wow. That's amazing." Roxanne moved her chair back to where it had been to allow Elizabeth to take her seat next to, literally, the love of her life.

"And I still don't get a word in."

Elizabeth shook her head. "Oh, Angus…"

"Here, trouble." Alice handed Angus his buffet tea. "I went for pretty much two of everything. There's filled rolls, pastries, and salad, so you can just choose what you fancy."

Angus frowned. "I'm not sure I can manage all that. What about the waste?"

"Well…" Alice seemed to struggle with the answer.

"No probs." Roxanne quickly intervened. "I'm here. Anything you don't want, shove it my way. I guarantee zero waste. Although I can't say for certain there'll be zero emissions."

Angus laughed. "Right you are."

Alice gave a broad smile. "There you go. We have our very own recycling solution. Just eat what you can."

Eve and Moira arrived back to the table, and Roxanne sucked her cheeks in to mimic starvation. "About time, Eddison."

"Honestly, you're terrible." Eve's amused expression lent a reassuring warmth to her comment.

"Just kidding, thanks, mate." Roxanne shoved a whole sausage roll in her mouth. Speaking through a flurry of pastry flakes she gasped, "Oh my God, these are just…dirty good."

"Alice made them." Elizabeth couldn't have looked prouder. "She has a real skill with pastry."

"That's because you taught me." Alice and Elizabeth shared a smile that spoke of years of love of the kind that is formed by trust and care. "If I'm any good, it's down to you."

"Surely," Elizabeth said, "it's as much your willingness to learn."

Eve raised her beer glass. "Well, I'm so grateful to the pair of you for this delicious food, and judging by the contented hush around the room, I'm not the only one. So cheers!"

Everyone round the table replied in unison. "Cheers!"

Fifteen minutes later, Roxanne's thoughts were already straying to pudding. She was clearly not the only one, as partygoers had begun to circle the buffet table like vultures. Damn them. Who knew buffet tension was a thing? Hold on, if she offered to clear the table, that would surely prompt the subject of afters. Mercifully, a quick assessment of the progress of her fellow diners showed that they were just a couple of forkfuls behind her.

"So, shall I take the plates." Roxanne hoped her tone of *This isn't a question* would seal the deal.

"Oh yes," Eve said. "Who's for pud? We have amazing trifle, and there'll be to die for birthday cake, of course, later."

Angus scooped up his last bite of sandwich. *Good man.* It sadly turned out that he didn't need Roxanne's help. She supposed that eventually she might forgive him.

Roxanne stood up quickly and began to gather the empty plates. "Oops, oh, all good. Land legs working. Stomach settling." She stuck both thumbs up. "In fact, I can totally carry six bowls. Leave it to me." Before she had time to see their, no doubt, concerned expressions, Roxanne left for the buffet table. "Coming through, mind your backs, emergency mission on behalf of the birthday girl. Wow, now that's a cake."

Eve's birthday cake was displayed pride of place on a cake stand in the middle of the buffet table. It was simply beautiful. Soft cream icing covered the top, and the words *Happy Birthday Eve* were hand-piped in pink. Delicate iced flowers were dotted here and there like stars. If love was cake-shaped, then this would be it.

Roxanne looked back at their table and at everyone chatting and smiling. They were clearly delighting in the evening and in each other's company. Eve was nestled into Moira, who in turn couldn't take her eyes off her. Eve was loved and treasured here. In that instant, and without wishing it, maudlin thoughts darkened Roxanne's heart. Why would Eve need her love any more?

Roxanne turned away. There was nothing worse than a party to make you feel alone.

"I'm not here to check on you." Alice arrived at Roxanne's side. "I just wanted to add some candles to Eve's cake. The cake is so pretty that Elizabeth and I couldn't bring ourselves to spoil it with candles first off. You okay?"

Roxanne sniffed. "Yep. Sorry about getting tiddly earlier."

"To be honest, we should have warned you about Jane's Jungle Juice. It's an easy mistake to make. No harm done. Although the no-puking-in-the-car rule stands."

"Fair enough."

Alice slid the cake carefully towards her and began to delicately puncture the icing with white candles complete with their silver petal-shaped holders.

Roxanne hung her head. "Eve seemed really disappointed in me."

Alice glanced at her and blinked several times. It obviously wasn't a comment she was expecting. "I'm sure she was just more concerned about you, that's all." Alice then hesitated. "We all were."

You were?

Alice's cheeks seemed to colour, and she quickly looked away before sliding the cake carefully back in place. She folded her arms and gave a small nod. "There. All done." As she turned back in the direction of their table, she added, "Don't worry. Eve cares about you very much."

"That's nice of you to say."

Alice shrugged. "It's just true." And with that she walked away.

Roxanne watched Alice take her place between Moira and Angus. Out of the blue and so unexpected, Alice's reassurance meant the world. Eve looked over to Roxanne and waved. Roxanne gave a thumbs-up in reply. Eve looked so happy. Did Eve know how much Roxanne cared about her too? Of course she did. Didn't she? Roxanne fiddled with the bracelet on her wrist. Maybe words were needed as much as gestures.

Roxanne impressed everyone with her bowl-carrying skills, and pudding was devoured in a chorus of compliments. Just before the room returned to its own party devices, Moira stood and tapped at the edge of her glass, calling everyone to attention once more.

"Those who know me will know I'm not one for many words." A murmur of affectionate recognition hummed in the room. "But I, we"— Eve's face shone with emotion as she looked up at Moira—"could not let you go home without thanking you from the bottom of our hearts for joining us tonight to help us celebrate Eve's birthday."

"Happy birthday, Eve!" Enid called out from the table of Eve's work colleagues, who all began to wave at her.

Eve waved back at them. "Thank you!"

"Many happy returns from us too, bonny lass!" Dafne raised her pint glass in the air.

Eve raised hers back. "Thank you for coming!"

The room exploded into a spontaneous round of "For She's a Jolly Good Fellow." The outpouring of affection flooded the hall with more love than Loch Ness had water.

Moira sat back in her seat and held Eve's hand tightly.

Eventually, following another cheer, the room began to settle again. *Fuck it.* Roxanne took a deep breath and stood to her feet.

"And I just want to add…" Strangers' faces blinked back at her. It had seemed a good idea to say a few words. But she now had the sensation of walking into a pub, and all the locals turn and stare at you.

"Go on, young lady." Angus was smiling at her.

"So I'm Roxanne, Eve's best friend, from home, from Leicester that is. I have known Eve longer, a long time, well, for what seems all my life, our life." Eve bit her lip and nodded. "I won't lie—I am very jealous that you all get to have Eve here with you every day." The reserved silence in response was deafening. "But there is a Scandinavian saying that the road to a friend's house is never long. Well, I know that's a lie because it's chuffing miles away." Angus laughed. "But I *would* agree that the distance between two best friends' hearts is no distance at all." She stared ahead, for looking at Eve was impossible. "And I won't lie—that doesn't stop me missing my best mate. But seeing her here so cherished, it could not be clearer that she is in the right place and with the right people and, what's more, being loved by the right person." The room thrummed with approval. "And as her best mate—have I mentioned that?" A chuckle bubbled in the room. "It couldn't make me happier. To Eve. Happy birthday, Eddison!"

Everyone stood to their feet. "Happy birthday, Eddison!"

On cue, and as if it was planned, the lights dimmed, and Alice carried the birthday cake with its candles flickering to their table. As the chorus of "Happy Birthday" began, Alice rested the cake in front of Eve. "Make a wish."

Eve closed her eyes.

Alice looked up and smiled at Roxanne. Roxanne's cheeks tingled hot in response. Alice's mascara had slightly smudged, and her expression was as soft as the flickering candlelight. She held Roxanne's gaze. Alice couldn't have looked more beautiful. And the situation couldn't have felt more dangerous. *Fuck.* This was not good. Not good at all. For Roxanne had seen that look before, and it wasn't one she'd ever been able to resist.

Eve opened her eyes and blew out the candles. "Right, okay, so let's cut the cake. Here goes nothing. You all right, Rox? You look a bit…"

"Me? Absolutely. Unless, of course, all the slices will be that small."

Eve laughed. "I should have known your expression of panic was food related. We've got a second cake in the kitchen. So there's no need for stress."

"Awesome. Even so, how about I finish dividing up this one? Don't look so worried. I've got this."

Eve gave an unconvinced sounding, "Okay."

"And I'll help distribute the slices." Alice picked up the first filled plates and seemed to make a hasty exit.

"Someone's in a hurry." Eve gave a quizzical look in Alice's direction.

"Will we be clearing the hall tonight?" Angus looked about him. He seemed overwhelmed by what he saw.

Elizabeth shook her head. "In the morning, sweetheart."

"Don't we have a school group, our young infants, first thing Monday morning?"

Moira nodded. "Monday morning, yes, but we have tomorrow. Sunday."

"Will that be enough time? There's a lot to do."

"And we've lots of help." Eve placed a plate of cake before him. "And let's not forget—Rox only has to look at bunting and it falls down."

Roxanne paused from cake cutting. "Yeah, let's not forget *that*."

Everyone laughed, and the tension of the moment eased.

Elton John's "Your Song" played into the room. Eve immediately turned to Moira. "It's my favourite song."

"I know." Moira held out her hand to Eve. "Shall we?"

"You requested this for me?"

Moira nodded towards a teenager standing by a small table at the side of the stage. A CD player and amplifier were laid out before him. He was engrossed in fiddling with the volume button and staring up to the speakers mounted either side of the stage.

"This is your evening," Moira said. "I want it to be perfect."

Eve kissed Moira. "It is."

Roxanne watched as Eve and Moira found a spot in the centre of the room and began to slowly dance. Soon the space filled with people dancing. Arms were looped around waists and hands clasped in hands. It wasn't just a disco. No, it was so much more. It was a community.

"Well, Angus McAlister, this is where we take our leave. I fear my disco dancing days are over."

"Surely not." Roxanne set her cake knife aside.

"That's very kind of you to say, Roxanne. But I suspect my slow dance would be very slow." Elizabeth softly rested her hand on Angus's knee. "Time for our bed." She began to fuss and tidy at their table as Angus looked about the room with an expression of concern. It was upsetting to see.

"I'll sort the table, no probs." Roxanne offered her arm for Elizabeth to take to steady herself to stand. "And thanks for your company tonight, fella," Roxanne added. "Maybe you could show me your moves another time?"

Angus looked at Roxanne as if her question seemed odd to him. "Aye."

Alice approached through the crowds. "You pair ready for the off?" She lifted her bag and jacket from the back of her chair.

Wait. Alice was leaving? "You're coming back, though?" Roxanne hadn't meant for her question to sound so panicked. More to the point, why on earth did it seem to matter so much?

Alice laughed. "Don't worry—I won't see you walk home. I'm just dropping these two scamps off. I won't be long."

Roxanne exhaled with relief. "Oh right. I just wondered if you were dancing at all."

"She's a fine dancer indeed." Angus pulled his cap straight, so that it lined up with his forehead.

"And you're biased," Alice said, blushing. "Let's go."

So was that a yes, she would be dancing? "I'll be right here and definitely not eating the last slice of cake number two."

Alice laughed again. "Good to know."

Roxanne watched as Eve and Moira paused from dancing to say goodnight to Elizabeth and Angus. Alice had made her way to the door and was waiting patiently for them. Roxanne hadn't meant to catch her eye. Would Alice think she was staring at her? Who was she kidding? She *was* staring at her. Alice looked down. Great.

Roxanne turned away and stared forlornly instead at the cake left in her charge. She divided the remaining unclaimed slice of cake into two and devoured the wafer-thin slice in one bite. She stuck a candle in the last half. No one would know. Genius. When she looked up again, Angus, Elizabeth, and Alice had left.

Why on earth did Alice's leaving feel like such a wrench? Moreover, when did dreading her suddenly become missing her? It was ridiculous. Alice was a complete stranger, for goodness' sake. She was just a bit lonely, right? But then wasn't this what she feared before she came here—her life exposed for its emptiness when compared with Eve's?

ABBA's "Dancing Queen" tempted the few reticent partygoers onto the floor. Eve waved over at Roxanne for her to join them. *Come on, Barns, get a grip.* She took a deep breath. *Let's do this.* And now only one question remained: Were the Highlands ready for her disco moves? She cast an eye to the door. Was Alice?

"How long do you think she'll be?" Roxanne shouted her question to Eve who was trying valiantly to keep up with the beat with each new track that played. Eve's hands were resting on Moira's hips, and her eyes were focused never far from Moira's admiring gaze. She was engrossed in laughter with Moira with every misstep she made. It looked for all the world that, as far as they were concerned, there was no one else in the room but them.

"Eve!"

"Sorry, Rox. You okay?"

"Yep. Just wondering how long Alice will be."

"Why? Do you want to go back to the croft? Moira could drop you off."

"No, I'm fine. Forget it. As you were. I'm going to sit this one out."

"Okay." Eve returned her attention to Moira and to missing the beat.

Roxanne returned to their table. Some greedy sod had finished the cake. She ran her finger gingerly along the edge of the knife, scooping the last of the icing free. Thank God for sugar.

The music to the Bee Gees' "Stayin' Alive" came on. How she loved this song. It was impossible not to dance to it. Impossible. Wait—was that Alice? Wow.

Through the throng of moving bodies, Alice came into view. She was dancing with Eve and Moira, laughing, and having fun with the music. She effortlessly struck the classic disco pose the song demanded by thrusting her arm in the air and then sharply returning it to her hip. Sod John Travolta—Alice was an exploding inferno of hotness.

For gone was Alice's dancing outfit, and in its place she wore tight black jeans and a black scooped-neck T-shirt. Her blond hair flowed freely against her back as she swung her hips in perfect time to the beat. She could dance. She could *really* dance.

Alice then closed her eyes and tipped her head back. It was as if the music was the sun, and she was bathing in it, revelling in the pulse of its energy and heat.

If Roxanne had a choice of whether or not to dance with Alice, it really didn't seem so. Because before she quite knew it, she was next to Alice on the dance floor, matching her movement with hers. As if drugged, they danced together, breathlessly close but not touching. Roxanne had never felt so entranced by another's body or by another's gaze. Alice Campbell kept surprising Roxanne at every turn.

"You've changed," Roxanne said, leaning into Alice's ear.

Alice blushed deeply. "What?"

"Oh no, I didn't mean…I meant your clothes. You've changed your clothes."

Alice's face relaxed into laughter. "Oh yes. At Angus and Elizabeth's."

"You look…" There were so many things she knew she shouldn't say.

Alice smiled. "Thanks."

"And you can dance. You're really good."

Alice's eyes sparkled as she replied, "You're really terrible."

Roxanne laughed. "Years of practice."

The music finished, and the crowd settled to a satisfied sigh.

"Oh my God, I'm knackered." Eve bent double. "I need a breather. See you both in a mo." Arm in arm, Eve and Moira slipped away in the direction of their table.

Roxanne saluted Eve. "Bye, birthday girl."

"I'll join you," Alice said, turning to follow Eve.

Roxanne reached for her hand. "Please don't."

Alice looked back at her with an expression that seemed both uncertain and intrigued.

Roxanne tipped her head to her side and gestured back towards the centre of the floor. A wail of bagpipe struck up, causing the partygoers to cheer.

"Now we're talking!" Roxanne squeezed Alice's hand. "Teach me? I want to whirl around the dance floor, Highland style."

"You're mad."

"I know."

Alice moved close to Roxanne. "You need to straighten your back." She pressed her palm against Roxanne's lower spine. The warmth of Alice's hand against her shirt sent shivers through her body that fizzed and lingered. "And then raise your arms in the air." Alice lightly guided Roxanne's arms to stretch up above her head. Alice's fingers brushed against Roxanne's shirtsleeves. "Perfect. Now for your feet, you need to bring your ankles together." As she looked down to Roxanne's shoes, Alice's head briefly rested against Roxanne's chest. Could Alice feel the thump of Roxanne's racing heart? "That's great." She looked up at Roxanne and smiled. "And now you're supposed to leap up and down, keeping your core tight. Imagine the floor is hot under your feet." It wasn't just the floor that was hot right then. Roxanne's whole body was ablaze with desire and consumed with the need to touch Alice and to kiss her, to…

"You can put your arms down now." Alice reached up and eased Roxanne's arms back to her sides. "So that's the Highland Fling. Sort of."

When had the music stopped? "Uh-huh."

A voice out of the blue made them both jump. "Well, I'm off, then. I'd say it was nice to meet you, Roxanne, but then you'd have had to have spent some time with me."

Alice and Roxanne turned at the same time to find Dafne pulling on her coat.

"Oh, hey, Daf." Roxanne felt strangely out of breath. "Maybe next time."

"No. I don't think so." Dafne was looking at Alice. "Eve should have really said that you pair were a thing."

"What? No," Alice said, blushing.

Was the thought of being with her that awful? Roxanne swallowed several times, then added, "We're roommates. For the night."

"Is that what they call it nowadays. Most roommates can take their eyes off each other for more than ten seconds."

It seemed that neither of them knew what to say.

Roxanne risked an anxious glance to Eve, who was finishing her wine and chatting to a couple of party guests.

"Well, anyway, say goodnight to Eve for me." And with that Dafne turned and left.

Sobering strip lighting was flicked on to buzz and glare. Eve and Moira became surrounded by partygoers, hugging them and wishing Eve happy birthday one last time.

"Let's clear up," Alice said. She took a deep breath as if to gather herself before she turned towards the abandoned tables.

"Sure." Roxanne looked down. How she hated to see her walk away.

As the guests took their leave, Roxanne helped Alice to clear the tables of debris and then to gather the leftover food from the buffet table and put it in the fridge in the kitchen. An order of sorts was restored in no time.

"Right, home calls," Moira said. "We'll finish the rest in the morning. You two okay?"

Roxanne nodded in unison with Alice.

Alice gestured to the hall door. "You go ahead. We'll lock up."

Moira nodded. "Great, thanks. See you in the morning."

"Thank you both so much for tonight," Eve gave them each a quick hug. "It's been a fab evening."

"Happy birthday, Evie," Alice said, choking up a little.

"Yep, cheers." Roxanne gave a thumbs-up. "Tonight totally rocked. See you tomoz."

And then with a soft splash of Land Rover tyres through the car park's puddles and the sweep of headlights lighting the hall windows, Moira and Eve were gone, and Roxanne was alone with Alice.

"Right." Alice cast a final glance around the room. "I'll just grab my bag, and we'll go."

"Wanna dance?"

"What?" Alice double blinked. "Now? You and me?"

"Yes. Why not?"

Alice's eyebrows rose. "It's nearly midnight."

"And…? It's Saturday night."

A smile played in the background of Alice's bemused expression. "And it's a ridiculous idea."

"They're the best ones. Come on, no one's watching." Roxanne headed for the CD player.

Alice looked at the door. "What if someone comes in?"

Roxanne shrugged. "So they come in. We're not doing anything wrong. Oh, *Hymns from the Highlands* appears to be the only CD left. We can work with it. Come on, Campbell." Roxanne reached out for Alice's hand.

Alice looked at Roxanne's hand. She shook her head. "It's not that I don't want to. It's just…"

Roxanne dropped her hand to her side. "It's just what? You can't exactly say you don't know how to dance."

"Really, I can't."

"Why not? Is it because you don't know me? Or…what? You don't trust me? Is that it?"

Alice looked down. "Let's go back to the croft."

That was one way of saying, *Yes, I don't know you, and I don't trust you.* But then she *was* a stranger to Alice. It was Eve who actually knew Alice, wasn't it? And it followed that it was Eve Alice trusted and not her, surely. What was she thinking? It was a ridiculous idea. What was worse, she was too sober now to blame it on the booze.

"You're right." Roxanne shook her head. "It's a mad idea, sorry. It's this high altitude and thin air, must have gone to my head."

Alice smiled. "I'm surprised you've not had a nosebleed."

"Me too. Let's go."

Alice didn't seem as pleased as she might have done, given it was her decision to leave. "Sure. After you, one night only."

Roxanne laughed. *One night only.* Eve was right—Alice was fun. Fun and oh-so much more.

They locked up the hall and drove back to the croft in silence. Arriving inside, they paused together for a moment in the sitting room.

Alice asked, "Do you need a hot drink or..."

Roxanne winked. "Yeah, I'll have the or."

Alice folded her arms. "Goodnight, then."

"Night."

Alice made her way upstairs.

Roxanne pulled off her clothes and collapsed into bed. She lay there, staring up at the ceiling. Everything about the night had been as predicted. Eve surrounded by friends, colleagues, and loved ones. Speeches, dancing, eating, and laughing. And yet nothing about the night felt quite as expected. Although maybe it wasn't the party. Maybe it was the company. Roxanne looked across to the stairs. For Alice Campbell was not what she'd imagined. No, not at all. The spiky young woman of her memory was in fact funny and talented, kind and tender, and hot as hell. And who could blame Alice for not trusting her? As Eve had rightly said, whether intentionally or not, Roxanne had been insensitive to Alice when they first met. And for some reason she'd expected Alice to dance with her alone tonight. But then when they were dancing together it was...magical. Surely Alice felt it too?

Roxanne turned over, burying herself under the duvet and trying to block out incessant thoughts of Alice's body moving to the music. No. Alice was right not to trust her. Particularly when she wasn't sure she trusted herself.

Chapter Six

Good morning, my beauties. There we go, here's some fresh water. And let's freshen up your bedding, shall we?" A rustle from the duvet across the room called Alice's attention away from Eve's chicks and to a sound asleep Roxanne.

Alice checked her watch. It was ten o'clock. She'd thought Roxanne would have woken at the sound of the shower, or at the kettle boiling, or at least when the porridge pinged in the microwave. Nope. And how the bright morning light streaming into the sitting room made no difference was beyond her. They really should be at the hall already. And they didn't want to be late for lunch with Angus and Elizabeth. What's more, she was sure Roxanne wouldn't want to let Eve down. She should wake her, shouldn't she?

Alice moved to the sofa and to the tangle of duvet wrapped around Roxanne.

"Roxanne?" She gave a gentle shove to her shoulder. She wanted to wake her, rather than startle her.

She stepped back as Roxanne stirred and turned over.

Alice hadn't meant to stare at the bare leg that became uncovered, let alone to allow her gaze to travel from the soft arch of Roxanne's foot up to the curve of her calf and along to the smoothness of her thigh. Wait, what was she doing? She glanced to the garden through the sunroom as if the grasses blowing and the clouds moving across the sky were looking in and watching her and wondering what had captured her so intensely and why.

She cleared her throat and raised her voice. "It's ten. We're due at the hall. Roxanne?"

Roxanne's reply was to begin to softly snore.

Fine. She would go without her. Everyone, including Eve, would understand that it had been a big night for everyone. No one would mind. Alice looked down at the crumple of shirt and jeans at her feet. The image of Roxanne standing in the rain looking up at her came flooding back. She'd had such a soft expression of surprise and gratitude that she hadn't been left behind. How her endearing wonky smile had teased across her handsome face. She was so funny and such a fool. How she'd made Angus laugh. She was good with him.

It had struck Alice how kind and not patronizing Roxanne was. But then, there was such kindness in those eyes…Wait, what was she doing? This wasn't getting the hall sorted. Alice lifted Roxanne's clothes from the floor and placed them on the edge of the bed. She brushed lightly at the shirt collar with her fingertips. How she wanted to breathe the fabric in. How she wanted a good shake, more like. *Enough.*

She moved to turn away, only to pause one last time to look back at Roxanne's face. It was so tender and lost in sleep. How good it had felt last night when Roxanne looked at her. Too good, maybe. And then they'd danced together, hadn't they? How easy and natural it had seemed to move her body with hers. It was almost like they'd always danced together each Saturday night for years. Roxanne had looked at her so intensely as they danced. No one had ever looked at her like that, and with such passion and with such connection. How could two strangers connect like that? Was that what they meant by chemistry? Was that what Dafne saw?

A tinge of fear coloured her thoughts. She didn't know Roxanne. And when they were alone, why on earth had Roxanne asked her to dance? Had Roxanne felt their chemistry too? And then when she'd rejected Roxanne's offer, Roxanne had looked so hurt. But what would have happened if she'd said yes? Where would that chemistry have led?

A thrill of excitement rippled through her chest. She'd kept herself awake last night thinking about the what-if. Somehow everything about being alone with Roxanne felt illicit and thrilling. But with excitement there was always fear at the edges and trepidation of the unknown. There was nothing safe about Roxanne. No wonder she hadn't known what to say when Roxanne implied she didn't trust her. But at the end of the day, what did it matter? Roxanne could be as dangerous and exciting as she liked because the whirl she created around her would soon settle again when she left. And the moment Roxanne arrived, she was already leaving. What use were these thoughts? *You're hurting yourself. Stop.*

Alice turned from Roxanne, and with a renewed determination she headed off for the hall. As she opened the front door to leave, a draught of cold air swept in. She quickly closed the door softly behind her, not waiting to see if the rush of breeze had woken Roxanne.

❖

When she returned an hour later carrying a bag of leftover party food, she found that the bed was restored to a sofa and the shower was running. The smell of burned toast and tea mingled with soap. Roxanne really filled a space with her presence. There was no doubt about that. There was no question, as well, despite all her confusion and reservations, that it felt good to come back to the croft with her there. She unpacked the leftovers into the fridge. Roxanne would be excited to hear of party food needing to be eaten. She chuckled softly to herself at the thought. A wave of unmistakable happiness washed over her, easing her heart and untangling the knots of her worries.

She opened the sunroom door to let in the sweet air. Last night's rain had brightened the flowers to bud and refreshed the greenery to shine. There was simply nowhere else she wanted to be.

She glanced back into the empty sitting room. There was clearly time for her to potter in the garden. She would open the henhouse to let Moira's chickens run free for an hour or so.

"We have a bonny home, don't we, girls? Heh?" The chickens gathered around Alice, and she fussed over them in turn.

A press of tiredness upon her encouraged her to take a moment to sit on the sunroom step. But then it had been a late night. And what a night it was. She closed her eyes. She was back on the dance floor with the music flowing through her. She could feel it in her now. All the different songs and beats and catchy choruses spilled out from her heart, and she began to hum. And then it became simply impossible not to just sing. How free she felt when she opened her heart and sang.

"I thought it was the radio." As if from nowhere, Roxanne arrived at Alice's side. "You have just the most beautiful voice. I mean, professional. But then I guess it's in the genes, what with your mum being a singer—"

Alice stood up and turned so sharply that the action severed Roxanne's compliment, to fall broken in pieces on the floor.

Roxanne looked taken aback and utterly confused. "Sorry, I didn't mean to startle you."

"No, it's okay. I was just..." Embarrassment muddled Alice's thoughts. She'd always been able to hide her singing. For it had always been such a private thing. And so few people mentioned her mum, that hearing Roxanne speak of her could not have left her feeling more exposed. There was Roxanne again, making her feel so undone. It all felt too much. And if that wasn't enough, Roxanne standing there in the sunroom with just a bath mat covering the front of her wasn't exactly helping with Alice's composure.

"Why are you practically naked?"

Roxanne raised one palm in the air. "In my defence, I hung my towel on the radiator in the bathroom last night, and then when I came out of the shower, it was gone."

"Oh. I put it in the wash. Sorry. I'll get you another. Just don't turn round."

"What, like this?" Roxanne flashed her bottom at Alice.

"No." As protests went Alice knew her *no* lacked conviction. It took all her strength and self-control not to let a smile force itself from her lips. Where would encouraging her lead?

A knock at the croft door surprised them both. It felt to Alice like a particularly intimate moment had been disrupted. And if Roxanne's cheeks flushing scarlet meant anything, then she was likely feeling the same.

"I better…" Roxanne nodded to the stairs. Her awkward fidgeting suggested that she didn't quite know how to position the bath mat to facilitate leaving.

"Stay where you are for a sec. I'll go first and see who's at the door, and you can then make your exit."

"Good plan."

Try as she might, Alice couldn't quite stop herself from picturing that glimpse of soft pink cheek, perfectly round and biteable…

Alice opened the croft door. "Eve."

"Alice. Hi." Eve laughed. "Everything all right? You look a bit surprised to see me. I did mention earlier that I might call round."

"Yes, yes, you did." Please God, let Roxanne have made her exit upstairs. Alice hugged the door against her, closing the gap between the inside of the croft and the driveway.

Eve frowned slightly. "Of course, if now's not a good time—"

"It's perfect." Where was the creak of the stairs?

"So can I come in?"

"Uh-huh." Alice stepped aside and held her breath.

Eve headed inside and into the sitting room. "Is Rox about?"

Alice closed the door behind her. *Phew.*

"Rox? Erm. Yes, bathroom. Tea?"

"Sure. Thanks."

Alice made for the kitchen, only to find Roxanne hiding behind the door. Oh no. She asked in a strained whisper, "I thought you were going upstairs."

"I panicked."

Roxanne had wrapped a tea towel around her chest and secured either end of the towel by wedging them under her armpits. Like the mat, there was only so much material available to protect her modesty. In turn, she held the bath mat about her hips. It had something of an extremely short mini-skirt about it.

Eve shouted through from the sitting room, "So, was Rox feeling better when you got home?"

Alice poked her head around the kitchen door. "Yes. Her migraine seemed much better."

"That's good." Eve then clapped excitedly. "Can I give the chicks a cuddle?"

"Help yourself." Alice turned back to Roxanne. "Okay, Eve's gone into the sunroom. Now might be your only chance to make a run for it."

"You covered for me again? Thanks." Roxanne's expression spoke of surprise and gratitude, and there was something else in her eyes that Alice couldn't quite discern.

"You're welcome. But never mind that—what are you waiting for?"

"I'm just building up to it."

"It'll be too late—"

"What will be too late?" Eve had arrived at the kitchen door, cuddling a chick.

"Erm…if I don't sow my tomatoes this week. Here's your tea."

"Thanks." Eve gestured towards the windowsill and the little paper pots of seeds sprouting young shoots. "Aren't they them? Oh dear God." Eve's head jutted back. "Roxanne Barns, I can see you reflected in the window. Why are you hiding?"

Roxanne side-stepped into clear view. "Hey, Evie Eds. How's tricks?"

Eve's mouth fell open as she stared up and down at Roxanne. Even the chick in her arms seemed to chirp with alarm at the sight of her.

"I know what you're thinking—as outfits go, not quite right for lunch."

Eve shook her head. "Not exactly what I was thinking. Actually, you know, I'm not even going to ask."

Alice said, "I think that's best," before she gave a pained cry and collapsed into laughter.

Roxanne quipped, "On that mixed review, I'll just settle on my usual go-to favourites. Won't be a mo."

Alice wiped at her eyes. "Shall we go in the sitting room? I'll bring your tea." Alice led the way, followed by Eve who settled the chick back into its bed before tucking herself up on the sofa next to her.

Eve took her tea from Alice and held it in her lap. "I'm so sorry about Rox, by the way. I promise, she means well—"

"Don't be. I know. She's fun. I really like her." Eve raised her eyebrows in such a manner that Alice instantly feared that she'd given too much away. And by the concentrated way Eve was now looking at her, she very well might have done.

"Yes," Eve said with a newly serious tone. "Rox is fun. And she's very popular. And she definitely likes to have a good time."

"Aye." What was Eve trying to say?

"She tends not to take many things seriously, if you know what I mean. Girl about town. Not that that's a bad thing. Like you say, it's fun. She's fun." Eve took a sip of her tea.

"Yes, she's a daft wee fool, of course." Alice plucked a stray sock that was wedged between the seat pads and that Roxanne had discarded from the night before. She held it in her hand and stared at it. Why did Eve feel the need to make the point to her that Roxanne didn't take things seriously? And by *things*, she was clearly implying relationships. Eve was warning her about Roxanne. But then, why did Eve imagine that there was even a possibility that she would need such advice? Had she guessed something about her? Or was she over-worrying, and they were more general observations?

"And don't feel you have to tidy up after her."

"What?"

Eve gestured to the sock in Alice's hand.

"Oh." Alice laughed. "Don't worry, I don't."

"I'll have you pair know that I shall be all packed and ready," Roxanne said, bouncing down the stairs, "with everything left in perfect order. So no need to stress, Evie Pops." Roxanne settled herself in the single armchair opposite the fire. She had changed into her jeans and

T-shirt. She looked lovely in her uniquely Roxanne kind of way. "So much so," Roxanne continued, "that Alice will not know I've stayed."

Eve responded, "Something tells me, Rox, that's hard to believe." They all laughed.

Roxanne caught Alice's eye, and her warm smile seemed to reach inside Alice to places that had longed to be smiled upon. Alice looked down. Wasn't this the kind of smile that risked her heart? Roxanne was going home, and what's more, she wasn't sure she trusted her, in any case. But then the feel of that smile...

"As I've got you both together, I have a favour to ask." Eve's voice refocused Alice's attention.

"Sure," Alice said with a nod. "Fire away."

"I'm thinking of asking Elizabeth and Angus if I could borrow the Fiesta for a practice this afternoon. Moira's said she'll take me around town. I woke in the night, fretting about roundabouts."

Alice gave Eve's hand a quick squeeze. "Honestly, you've got nothing to worry about. You're a natural. So how can I help?"

"Any chance you could babysit Roxanne? Just for this afternoon, and only if you don't mind."

Babysit Roxanne? Alice's cheeks tingled. "Erm..."

Eve held up her hand as Roxanne opened her mouth to speak. "And before you say anything, it was just a turn of phrase."

Roxanne frowned. It was kind of odd to see her not smiling. A hint of offence tinged her words. "I don't need *babysitting,* mate."

"I know, but it's just I feel bad that I might not be about this afternoon."

"Dude, stop stressing. I live alone. I go to pubs on my own all the time. I'll hang out in The Gunsmith this afternoon. No worries. Really, I don't mind."

"That's even more reason you should mind. I don't want you to be alone this holiday."

Eve's comment seemed to catch Roxanne off guard as Roxanne's cheeks flushed. Could it be that Roxanne, for all her bravado, was lonely?

Alice threw the rescued sock at Roxanne, and it landed in her lap. "I don't mind. I can show you Newland if you want. We could take a walk."

A smile brightened Roxanne's face. "Okay. Can I see it through the window of a car, or is the walk thingy essential?"

Alice shook her head. "The walk thingy?"

"Obviously, it's not a technical term as such."

"I really would appreciate that, Alice," Eve said. "I seem to be asking so many favours of you."

"And I don't mind at all. And I meant it—don't worry about tomorrow."

Eve gave Alice a hug. "Thank you. Okay, I'm having one last cuddle with the chicks, then popping to the loo, and then we better head off for our lunch with Elizabeth and Angus."

"Awesome, I'm so hungry that I could eat my shoes." Roxanne stood and began to hunt around for the sock that matched the one in her lap. She eventually found it further under the sofa. She sat back in her chair and pulled her socks on, then twisted her feet into her shoes, and bent with a groan to tie her laces.

Why was it so hard not to watch Roxanne? There was nothing interesting about her putting her shoes on. When did she become so pathetic? Alice quickly slipped on her jumper and checked her hair in the mirror by the door. She was about to tie her hair back into a ponytail, but then she stopped. She glanced at Roxanne, and without dwelling on why, she simply ruffled her fringe. All she knew was that she wanted to look and feel as free as she did last night. She pulled on a lightweight burgundy puffer jacket and scooped her loose hair to lie flat at her back.

"You look great." Roxanne was nodding. "Really great. I thought I best wear a jumper too for our walk and all that." She pulled at the front of a thick cream-coloured wool jumper.

"Thanks. I love your jumper." And she did. Roxanne looked so cute. Roxanne's footwear, however, caught Alice's eye. "Are they the only shoes you've brought with you?"

Roxanne gave a confused look at her Converse and then at Alice. "These? Yep. Why?"

"Just helps me to plan our walk."

"Don't worry, they're totally all-terrain."

Alice laughed.

Roxanne moved to join Alice. "Seriously, though, Campbell, I just want to say thanks for having me stay last night. I know having a stranger in your home must be hard."

"To be honest, you're my first proper guest."

"Really? I should warn you, for you've peaked early. All other guests"—Roxanne shook her head—"downhill from here."

They shared a warm, amused smile.

"That's better." Eve arrived back into the sitting room from upstairs. "Shall we go?"

Alice gestured towards the door. "After you pair."

Eve and Roxanne made their way towards Alice's Land Rover. Alice watched as Roxanne swung her arm around Eve's shoulders and squeezed her tight. They reminded her of Batman and Robin, Batman all confidence and charisma, and Robin the quiet one with the good sense. They were a gang of two. A sting of loneliness smarted in her heart. Would she always be a gang of one?

The McAlisters' cottage was as charming as its owners. Eve had always spoken of it as chocolate-box pretty, and she was not wrong. Climbing roses, bright green with spring buds poised to open and bloom, trailed along the garden walls. Branches of wisteria twisted and entangled themselves around a willow arch at the entrance to the path that led to the door. The cottage's bright white render glowed under the protection of a sloping grey slate roof, where bee and bird boxes nestled just out of sight in the shade of the eaves.

A curl of smoke billowed from its large chimney, evoking images of roaring fires, steaming bowls of food, and deep-set comfy chairs.

The door opened, and Elizabeth stood at the doorway with an apron on. She finished drying her hands on a tea towel before tucking it under the knot at her waist.

"Hello again, you pair, and welcome, Roxanne. I do hope your headache has improved. There's simply nothing worse."

"Much better, thank you. You have a lovely home."

"Yes. It is our special place. Please, come in." Elizabeth held out her hand to Roxanne, who held it tenderly in hers as they made their way inside. The gesture made Roxanne feel genuinely wanted and in every way their guest, rather than the stranger she was. It was touching beyond words.

Elizabeth led them through the entrance into a tiled-floor dining room. The small space was all but filled with a large oval table which was laid for lunch. A dark wood sideboard pretty much stretched the length of the back wall and was laden with photos. Off to the left was a small kitchen, and leading off from the other side, a fire was lit in the snug of a sitting room. Angus was standing beside it, staring into the flames. It looked like he might be putting more wood on but was waiting for the perfect moment. It didn't look like he noticed their arrival.

"Who's for a glass of sherry? Moira's just nipped out to get some. She won't be a moment." Without waiting for an answer, Elizabeth disappeared into the kitchen. She called out, "Lunch won't be long now. I'm just waiting on the dumplings to colour."

Dumplings? It was instant love. When Elizabeth reappeared with a tray of sherry glasses, it took all of Roxanne's limited reserve not to hug her. "We're having dumplings?"

Eve rested her hand on Roxanne's shoulder. "I think you've just made Rox's day."

"Well, I'm pleased." The fire in the sitting room could not compete with the warmth in Elizabeth's eyes. "After last night's celebrations, I'm afraid a full roast felt a little ambitious, so I hope you'll find my stew an adequate replacement."

"Here, let me." Alice stepped forward, took the tray from Elizabeth, and rested it on the dining table. "Your table looks wonderful." Alice leaned forward and smelt the nodding heads of the springtime daffodils displayed in an ornate glass vase.

Elizabeth slid a chair from under the table and sat for a moment. "I know I promised not to go overboard, and I promise I haven't, but there is nothing more unwelcoming than a bare table."

"Or empty sherry glasses." Angus chuckled his way into the dining room and nodded to the tray of sparkling cut glasses waiting to be filled. "I'm sure we have some sherry somewhere." He began to open cupboards, the contents of which each time almost seemed like a surprise. As he leaned into the sideboard cupboard, the family photos resting on top caught Roxanne's eye.

One photo in particular stood out. It was a snap of Eve and Moira sitting on a garden bench. The bright render and roses in the background placed the setting of the shot in the garden outside. Their hands were entwined and resting in Moira's lap. Their happiness radiated out of the photo and into the room. It seemed impossible to look at it and not smile.

"Angus, sweetheart, Moira has gone to fetch us some more sherry, do you remember—"

"Of course I remember, I'm not a fool, woman." His sharp reply silenced the room.

Alice moved to Elizabeth and rested her hand protectively on her shoulder. Elizabeth stared fixedly at Angus with an expression that spoke of hurt and betrayal.

His face quickly reshaped from red anger to ashen remorse at the sight, no doubt, of his wounded wife. "I just thought I'd double-check." He closed the cupboard softly and began to search in his pockets for something, only to give up moments later. It was the same action that Roxanne remembered from the party the night before.

"Here's Moira now." Eve couldn't have sounded more relieved.

The door opened and the wash of the spring breeze cooled the tense atmosphere.

"Sorry, folks." Moira wriggled hurriedly out of her coat and hung it up on the rack. "There was a queue." She stopped short as she looked at everyone. "Everything okay?"

"Yep." Eve kissed Moira. "All good."

"Right, shall I do the honours with the sherry?" Roxanne pulled off her jumper and threw it over the back of a chair.

Moira handed her the bottle. "Not for me, thanks."

"Or me," Eve said. "I'm not sure it will improve my driving."

"Sure thing. Everyone else?"

"Just a small one for Angus and me," Elizabeth said. "Thank you, Roxanne."

"Okey-dokey." Roxanne looked at Alice who shrugged and nodded.

Roxanne promptly unscrewed the top. What she wouldn't give to take a swig from the bottle. *Pour it quick, Barns. Pour it quick.* "Okay, everyone." They all moved to the table and lifted a glass. Moira filled hers and Eve's with water from a jug on the table.

Roxanne raised her sherry glass in the air. "Cheers, everyone."

A resounding "Cheers!" filled the room.

Roxanne downed her sherry in one. The afterburn was a surprise and caused her to cough. "That's one fiery friend."

Alice chuckled. "You're meant to sip it."

Roxanne whispered under her breath, "Sipping is for pussies."

Alice coughed to cover a laugh.

Eve widened her eyes at Roxanne before turning her attention to Elizabeth. "Would you like me to check on the dumplings?"

"Oh gosh, Eve, well remembered. Everyone, lunch is served. Find a place, and help yourself to bread and butter. Angus, perhaps you could help me with the plates."

Lunch was as delicious as Roxanne had hoped. And a dessert of steamed treacle pudding and custard left her in a near coma of pleasure. Her eyelids sank heavily, and a yawn pressed from her throat. What would finish her meal perfectly would be a snooze in front of that fire...

"You look like you need some fresh air, young lady." Angus gestured to the window. "I think we might even have a little afternoon sun."

"Huh?"

"Oh, actually, talking of that, I wanted to ask you something." Eve looked at Moira and then to Elizabeth and Angus. "Please say no if it doesn't suit."

"Of course, Eve," Elizabeth said. "Whatever we can do to help." Angus nodded in agreement.

"Could I possibly borrow your Fiesta this afternoon?"

"It would help Eve to have another practice in town before her test tomorrow." Moira placed her hand over Eve's. "We obviously have the plan in place to borrow it first thing and that still stands."

"Of course, that would be fine—wouldn't it, Angus?"

"Aye. I don't see why not. But you won't be wanting to come back and forth this evening, will you? Why don't you just borrow it now and bring it back tomorrow?"

"We don't mind." Moira shook her head. "It's not right to leave you without your car overnight."

Elizabeth frowned. "But won't you be leaving your Land Rover here, in any case?"

"Yes, I suppose."

"Well, there you are."

"Would you be okay with that, Angus?" Moira looked anything but convinced. She added gently, "It has been a while since you've driven it."

His cheeks flushed. "You seem to forget it was me who taught you to drive one in the first place."

"I haven't forgotten that, old man. I'll never forget it." Moira's tender reply seemed to soften the bristle of his reaction.

"Aye." He seemed sheepish. "So off you go. Catch the afternoon while she's still young enough."

"So, what, this afternoon's walk with Alice is off then?" Since when did she feel sad about not walking? But then she knew in her heart it had nothing to do with the walk. It was Alice she had been looking forward to being with. "And I'll need to collect my stuff from Alice's place."

"Oh right. I see what you mean," Eve said. "I'm really sorry to mess you both about like this."

Elizabeth nodded enthusiastically at Roxanne and Alice. "So you pair have a walk planned? How wonderful. What an excellent way to spend this afternoon. Perhaps up to the tor would be lovely. The view from the top is just such a joy. Even now it takes my breath. I only wish I could walk it more often." She gave a heavy sigh. "Old bones."

Moira shifted on the spot.

"Don't look so worried, brave girl. I'm not done yet."

"That's good to hear," Roxanne said. "It would be a real tragedy if that was the last dumpling of yours I'd eaten—" Roxanne stopped herself short. *Okay, that sounded less selfish in my head.*

Thankfully, there followed a general chuckle around the table.

"Yes, up to the tor was what I'd had in mind." Alice's eyes seemed to mist over, and her voice wavered a little, prompting her to clear her throat. "Another time maybe."

Was Alice disappointed they were not walking too? Or was it Elizabeth's comment about ageing that now shaded Alice's face in sadness?

"Why?" Elizabeth looked at Moira. "I can't imagine it will be much fun for Roxanne on her own this afternoon."

Roxanne raised her hands. "It's fine, really. If it fits for me to come with you now—"

Eve rubbed her brow. "And come to think of it, you'll be on your own for tomorrow morning too."

"Like I said, no probs."

"Why don't you stay with us until after Eve's test?" Elizabeth looked from Roxanne to Moira. "You'll be back at around lunchtime, anyway. That's right, isn't it, Moira?"

"Yes, I wanted to exchange the Fiesta for the Land Rover and do a few hours at the centre."

"Well then, bring Eve with you after her test, so that she can be with Roxanne, and then you can all head home together when you leave later in the afternoon."

Roxanne shook her head. "Thank you so much for the kind offer, but really, I couldn't let you and Angus put yourselves out—"

"You can stay with me another night. If you want?" Alice's cheeks coloured a little with her invitation.

Roxanne's face heated a little in return. "You wouldn't mind?"

"I wouldn't go that far."

Roxanne laughed. "Okay, if you're sure."

"That's really good of you, Alice," Eve said. "I think this officially gives you hero status. You've helped me out so much."

"It's no probs. Come to think of it, it would be great to have another pair of hands with the infants in the morning."

What? Could she say she was thinking of more of a lie in? No, probably not.

"That's settled, then." Moira pushed her chair back. "Eve and I will see you all at lunchtime tomorrow."

"And you know where the Fiesta's keys are." Angus stood and placed his hand on Eve's shoulder. "All the best for tomorrow. And if the instructor's hair's blowing, you'll be going too fast."

Everyone laughed and then gathered by the door and took turns hugging Eve and wishing her every success.

Roxanne waited her turn before holding Eve in a tight squeeze. "Good luck, Eddison."

"Thanks. So you've got everything you need to stay tonight?"

"Yep."

"And you're okay with the plans?"

"Positive. What's that face for? Do you need a poo?"

Eve pulled Roxanne aside from the group and lowered her voice to ask, "I don't know how to say this without seeming like I'm constantly having a go at you, and I don't want you to think I am, but you'll behave, won't you?"

Roxanne laughed. "I'll try. I can't promise—"

"You need to. You need to promise me you won't flirt with Alice."

"What?" Where did that come from, and more to the point, where was it going. "I have *zero* idea what you mean." What had Eve seen that had evidently freaked her out so much? Or were they back to the fact that Roxanne happened to mention in passing that she thought Alice was hot? "Zero idea."

"Okay. If you say so."

"I do."

Eve lowered her voice even further. "It's just, I worry that you're being too entertaining. And that Alice might…"

"Might what?"

"Look, I don't want her to get hurt, Rox."

"How would Alice get hurt? We're just having fun." She hadn't meant to say that so loud. Maybe no one else heard? Alice's newly pink cheeks suggested otherwise. Tricky. With a hushed voice, Roxanne added, "And who says it might not be Alice who hurts me?"

Eve double blinked and then gave a small laugh. "What makes you say that? Why would Alice hurt you?" Eve glanced to Moira who was pulling on her coat. "I've got to go. Promise me?"

"Sure. I promise, no *entertaining* Alice. See you tomoz."

"Love ya, Rox."

"Yep, love you too. Good luck."

Why wouldn't Alice be the one who hurt her? It couldn't be that Eve thought she wasn't capable of developing feelings for someone enough to get hurt. Could it? Or was it that the notion of her and Alice was ridiculous, and that Alice was out of Roxanne's league? Or was it simply, as it sounded, that Eve didn't trust her. When your best mate didn't trust you, what did that mean?

Elizabeth and Angus and Alice and Roxanne stood at the door and waved them off.

"Right, you." Alice couldn't quite look Roxanne in the eye. "Jumper on. Let's go."

"Do we need some Kendal mint cake? Alice?"

"I'm not even going to answer that." And with that Alice slung a small rucksack over her shoulder and headed out the door.

"I think we're off now. Thank you for lunch."

Elizabeth laughed and gave Roxanne a hug. "Our pleasure."

"Now enjoy our wonderful Newland, young lady, and all it has to offer." Angus's playful smile lit up his eyes to twinkle in the afternoon light.

"I will." As she stepped into the spring sunshine and saw Alice slip on her sunglasses and ruffle her hair into place, Roxanne was pretty sure she'd never meant anything more. Yes, she was just going to enjoy everything Newland had to offer, regardless of what Eve Eddison might have to say about it.

CHAPTER SEVEN

Alice walked a couple of paces ahead of Roxanne, leading the way up the hill path past the black peatbogs, blowing grasses, and curling ferns. Now and then, Alice would point out a particular flower or vista or the history behind a mossy earthwork, but other than that they mostly walked in step, in silence. Roxanne seemed to be conserving her breath and energy for the climb, for she was unusually quiet and simply listened on the occasions that Alice spoke.

In the interludes of silence, Alice kept wondering about what had prompted Roxanne's outburst. What had Eve said? Why was Eve warning them off each other? Was she really that worried that Roxanne might hurt her? And what would happen if she told Moira about her concerns? Anyway, there was nothing for anyone to worry about because Roxanne couldn't have been clearer that they were just having fun. Nothing more.

"Please tell me this is the mountaintop rather than a pile of stones marking the spot where climbers didn't make it." Roxanne bent double, her hands pressing on her hips and her eyes closed tight in an expression of pain.

Alice laughed. "How do I break it to you that we think of it as more of a hill than a mountain, as such. Therefore, we're kind of more walkers than climbers." She held out her hand for her gasping rosy-cheeked companion. "Come on up."

"A *hill?*" Roxanne took Alice's hand and heaved herself the last few paces. "Well, you can just bugger off because I can see snow on the *hills* across the way."

Alice gazed out into the distance and to the horizon of mountain peaks beyond. "Actually, those *are* mountains."

"Well, enough said, as I'm pretty sure we're much higher."

Roxanne gripped one hand on the large rock in front of her and held Alice's hand tightly in the other.

"And I'm pretty sure I can't feel my fingers," Alice said.

"Frostbite?"

"More the grip of death."

"Huh?"

Alice chuckled and nodded to Roxanne's hand clasped in hers.

Roxanne promptly released Alice's hand. "Oh, sorry. I was just making sure you weren't going to fall."

"Oh, I see. That's very gallant of you."

"What can I say, that's me. I might sit down." Roxanne half sat and half slipped her way to sit with her back resting against the largest of the rocks that made up the tor.

"Good idea. Have some water." Alice reached into the mesh side pocket of her rucksack, pulled out a sports bottle, and handed it to Roxanne.

"Oh, great—cheers." She gulped down half the bottle in one go.

"And here. I didn't bring Kendal mint cake, but I brought a Mars bar if that's of any interest."

Roxanne wiped her mouth on her cuff. "Hell yeah. Are we sharing?"

"All yours. Try at least to chew it." Alice brushed at a makeshift stone seat and sat next to her.

The Mars bar hardly touched the sides. Roxanne then blew out her cheeks and fussed with her hair. "I'm boiling." She began to strip off layers of clothing, beginning with her jumper. "No, that hasn't helped. I might take this off as well." She undid the buttons on her shirt, pulling it down and tangling herself in the cuffs. She soon gave up trying to free herself. And instead, Roxanne sat, breathless, in her newly revealed creased white T-shirt. Alice tried and failed not to stare at the delicate sweep of the exposed lily-white skin of her arms.

"That looks sore." Alice gestured with a nod to Roxanne's forearm. "How did you do that?"

"What?"

"This." Alice brushed her hand lightly over an angry red burn mark. They both stared for a moment, watching Alice's fingers caressing Roxanne's skin.

Roxanne shifted slightly, prompting Alice to remove her hand. "Oh, that. I burned it, taking out pizzas from the oven and by not paying enough attention. Serves me right."

Roxanne then closed her eyes and rested her head back with her chin lifted to the sky.

"You okay?" Alice couldn't help but notice that Roxanne's chest was still heaving up and down. She could even smell the soap she recognized as hers evaporating from Roxanne's hot skin.

"I'm fine. Just hot."

"Yes, I can see." There was no denying that Roxanne smouldered in a don't-give-a-fuck kind of way. She gazed at Roxanne's lips, parted with her panting breath. How many mouths had pressed urgently, desperately against them? How many women had wanted her so badly it hurt? And when had she become one of them? There, the simple truth was out in her head, and the untamed thought ran rampant. Maybe it took being a few hundred feet up to dare to release it. It was crazy. Hadn't she always craved order and neatness? Now all she seemed to crave was disorder, disarming openness, and the feel of Roxanne's skin against hers. Where were the mistrusting doubts that had always kept her feelings in check?

Her gaze fell to Roxanne's pink cheeks before slipping down to her neck and then to her chest. She lost her breath at the sight of the soft peaks of Roxanne's nipples revealed beneath the cotton that clung against her beautiful breasts.

"You need to stop checking me out—it's making me horny." Roxanne opened her eyes and smiled knowingly at Alice.

"No, I wasn't. *No.* What a ridiculous thing to say." Alice's cheek burned. She quickly looked away, reached for her water bottle, and drank down several mouthfuls. "And stop looking at me like that."

"Like what?"

"Like you know me. Because you don't. Okay?" Alice stood up and stared out and away from Roxanne's gaze.

"Okay."

"And may I suggest you put your clothes back on before you get cold."

Roxanne sat up straight. "Now that you mention it, I am feeling a bit nippy."

Alice glanced over her shoulder at Roxanne and quickly looked away again as Roxanne re-buttoned her shirt and pulled on her jumper. "Sorry if I offended you or—"

"I'm not offended, just…Look, let's change the subject." Alice pointed into the distance underlining her wish that far away was where she wanted their discussion to go. "So, as the crow flies, if you carried on that way to the left you'd get to the Affric mountains, and then that way behind us to the north you'd reach Ben Wyvis. Oh, look, there's a wee roe deer. It looks like she might be pregnant. She's wandered a little way from the woods. Mid-afternoon, I would have expected her to want a bit more cover, but then, she looks well."

"Where?" Roxanne stood with a groan.

"There, can you see, fluffy white behind, by that small stream?" Alice risked another look at Roxanne taking her chance while she was utterly engrossed. Why had she made it so obvious by staring at her just then? What possessed her to give so much away? Oh my God, what if it was her staring that Eve had seen before that prompted Roxanne's outburst? She needed to get a grip. What could she do? She would properly change the subject. Yes. And fast.

Alice returned to her seat amongst the rocks. "Do you know this takes me straight back to the first time I met Eve and her family."

Roxanne slid down next to her. "Really?"

"Yep. They'd randomly turned up at the centre. It was right at the beginning of their holiday." Alice shook her head at the memory. "They'd just done this very walk."

"Actually, now that you mention it, I can remember Eve saying how knackered she was after it."

"They all looked utterly exhausted and a bit in shock, to be honest. Eve's dad was so proud and triumphant to have conquered a mountain." Alice looked at the ground. It was stony like the rubble remains of her guilt. "Until I told them it was a hill."

"Blimey," Roxanne said. "Steal his thunder, why don't you."

Alice looked up at Roxanne and nodded. "Eve was so polite and sweet. Looking back, I can see how lovely she was." Alice reached for her water and finished it off.

A smile drifted over Roxanne's face. "I can even remember the first time Eve mentioned Moira. She got in a right fluster over her. It was clear she fancied the pants off her from the get-go. It's mad, isn't it, to think how far they've come?"

"Yep. Can I be honest and say I didn't think Eve would cope here?"

Roxanne turned sideways on to face Alice. "You can, and neither did I. Still, she proved us both wrong and hung in there and has really made a go of things."

Alice hung her head. "In spite of me."

"Yep." Roxanne kicked Alice's shoe with hers, prompting Alice to look up. "And in spite of me too. Look, the last thing I wanted was for Eve to stick it out. I just wanted her to forget about Moira and to see it as a lucky escape when they nearly didn't get together. But Eve just couldn't let Moira go even though Moira just seemed to be hurting her."

A sickening sense of shame rose in Alice's heart. "You should know…" Alice forced back tears that pressed in her throat. What she was about to say would surely make Roxanne hate her, and who could blame her? But not saying it and not being honest with Roxanne just didn't feel right.

"You don't have to, Alice."

"I do. I hurt Eve too." There, she'd told her. "Moira didn't mean to, but I did. I was awful to her."

"I'm sure it wasn't as simple as that."

Alice shook her head. "It was. There was this time I found Eve crying in the middle of the hens. She was sobbing her heart out and throwing food at them to keep them away."

Roxanne shifted in her seat. "Really?"

Alice nodded. "It was years ago now, and early on when she was trying to make things work with Moira."

"Okay. Go on."

"I don't think it was about the hens."

"Yeah, I'd guessed that."

"I can remember that day as if it was yesterday. As Eve stood there with tears rolling down her cheeks"—Alice took a deep breath—"I told her to fuck off. I said that she'd ruined our lives and that Moira would soon realize that she wasn't right for her. I was a total cow."

Roxanne's pink cheeks drained of their colour. "You don't say."

"Not that this is any excuse, but I was freaked out by her."

"Freaked out?"

"Maybe even a bit frightened."

"Frightened? Are we talking about the same Eve?"

"I mean of how she was turning our world upside down. Moira was in this emotional turmoil. I'd never seen her like that before. My dad had left. I was petrified that I would lose Moira too. Looking back, I didn't deal with it very well. And before you say anything, I know that's an understatement."

Roxanne's eyes widened and she nodded.

"I know you're probably thinking *What a bitch*."

"Something like that."

Oh God, no. She took another, even deeper breath. "And it wasn't the only time I told her to fuck off."

Roxanne stood and folded her arms. She stared out towards where the deer had been. "I think I've heard enough, to be honest."

"I need to tell you. Please. I have this weird feeling that if I don't tell you, I'm somehow lying to you, and I'm letting you think that I'm someone better than I am. It feels dishonest. I want to be honest with you."

Roxanne turned back to face her. "Why?"

"I don't know. It feels like it matters."

"Look, Alice, newsflash, all human beings are flawed, and most of us don't feel the need to tell people about the less flattering stuff."

"Well, I do. I feel I owe you—"

"You don't owe me anything. I'm thinking you might owe Eve an apology, though, even after all these years."

"Believe me, I have apologized to her and to Moira many times. I promise. Not only that, but I've worked on my temper and on getting a grip on myself. In fact…I've had counselling."

"Good for you. I hope it's helped."

"Massively. We sifted through all the noise to get to the nub of the sound. They wanted me to hear what was wrong. To use their language." Alice fiddled with her bootlaces. "Turns out the anger issues stemmed from insecurity and unresolved grief."

Roxanne nodded. "Your mum? Eve has mentioned her."

Alice swallowed several times as buried emotions rose free in her throat. "She died when I was seven." Alice shrugged. "So there, you know it all now." She couldn't decide if she felt better for confessing all. And she had no sense as to whether it meant anything to Roxanne or if she'd just completely embarrassed herself. Roxanne was just staring at her. God only knew what she was thinking.

Roxanne eventually said, "Grief is a tricky one, for sure. I'm sorry you've gone through that. How was Moira about you having counselling?"

"Moira? Fine. She seemed pleased and even possibly relieved, I think. She came to a few sessions with me, in fact. We certainly talk more now, for sure, particularly since Eve moved up here. Moira's just so happy and far more open than she's ever been."

"Yeah, Eve's good to be around, but don't tell her I said that."

Alice laughed. And then she fell silent as her guilt returned to steal her joy.

"I'm amazed you haven't walked away after hearing this. You must hate me for how I behaved."

"Hate you? Okay. While we seem to be in confession mode, the truth is I did hate you, you and Moira."

Alice's chest ached at Roxanne's confession. But she had asked her, and what else did she think Roxanne would say? She stared at the ground. "I get that."

"And the truth is, I didn't want to come here at all. Brace yourself— you were frankly the last person I wanted to see again."

Alice's breath caught at the wounding comment. Then to her surprise, Roxanne bent forward and lifted Alice's chin from her chest where it rested.

"But by all accounts, you both seem to be making Eve very happy. And being here with you is not that shit after all. Go figure."

"Thanks. I think."

"Try to let it all go now, though. Life's too short. Oh, Alice, the deer's back."

Alice stood, and they watched together as the deer grazed, and the afternoon grew old. "Can I say one last thing?"

Roxanne smiled. "Can I stop you?"

"Nope. It's just...I'm sorry if I was rude to you, back then in Leicester. That's what I need to say. I know you were trying to help me that night we met. I should have been grateful, but I was so caught up in, well, blinding panic and fear. Thanks for being the one who had the guts to tell me the truth."

"Moira would have got there in the end. And Eve still hasn't forgiven me for taking you to The Brewer's, by the way. I can see her point now, given everything. It was thoughtless of me. I'm sorry, for it was clear how uncomfortable you were there."

She nodded. "It was just, I'd never been to anywhere so... liberated."

"No?"

Alice felt her cheeks tingle. "No. Not then."

"It's my second home, so..." Roxanne shrugged.

"It's who you are. I remember you saying that to me. I like who you are, Rox."

"I like who you are too, Alice Campbell."

Alice's heart thrilled in her chest at Roxanne's words. "Thanks. I bet you and Eve must have had some wild times in The Brewer's."

"Well, maybe me more than Eve."

"Why doesn't that surprise me. Did you mean what you said in your speech, that you're jealous of us that we have Eve now?"

"Defo."

"You must miss her very much."

"Ah, you know…I'm starving. Shall we go?"

"Sure."

"I'll race you."

"If you fall, I'm not carrying you."

"Good to know! I'm winning already."

Roxanne ran ahead, screaming and swearing most of the way down. How she stayed upright was frankly a miracle.

By the time they made it to the bottom, each gasping for breath, Alice couldn't help but notice that she felt lighter.

"I'm glad you're here." The words escaped Alice before she realized they were out. Not that she regretted saying them.

Roxanne's expression opened wide into a broad smile. And were her red cheeks suddenly glowing even redder?

"Me too, roomie. Me too."

❖

Roxanne lay crashed out on the sofa. A full mug of tea grew cold on the floor at her side because moving to lift it to her mouth hurt. Their walk had occupied the whole afternoon and into the early evening. It had left Roxanne punch-drunk on Highland air and unsettled with curiosity.

She couldn't help but be surprised at Alice's need and openness to talk. What had prompted it? Alice certainly didn't owe her anything. And why did it matter so much to Alice that she was honest with her? Most other people were at great pains to hide their flaws, but not Alice, it seemed. But then, Alice wasn't most people. She'd honestly not met anyone quite like her. She was so many things all at once. She was open and warm, yet at times reserved to the point of frosty. And she was vulnerable with shadows of self-accusation, yet confident and capable in equal measure. Alice Campbell was such a complicated mix that it kept Roxanne on her toes. And that was just how she liked it, for it was utterly captivating.

She lay there completely contented and listened to Alice humming in the bath. Occasionally Alice would forget herself and sing a few lines. It was so peaceful that sleep overwhelmed Roxanne without her noticing, and only the distant approach of clucking hens signalled the reemerging reality of the world outside.

"Was I snoring?" Roxanne rubbed at her eyes as she sleepily disentangled herself from the cushions and comfort of the sofa and made her way to lean against the frame of the open sunroom door that led to the garden and to Alice feeding the chickens.

Alice was dressed in jeans and a navy jumper with a scoop neck that set off the soft pink of her skin. She smiled. "Let's say more of a snuffle."

"Why do I think you're being kind."

"No, I'd say."

Roxanne laughed.

"I've fetched your bedding back out of the laundry bin. It's just on the stairs."

"Right, okay. Thanks again for putting up with me for another night. And to show my appreciation, I was thinking of treating us to a takeaway." Roxanne pulled out her phone with a triumphant flourish and scrolled though her Deliveroo app. "Perfect. Inverness. Okay, so what do you fancy, there's pizza, oh—Mexican, or maybe KFC? Why are you looking at me like that?"

"I have an awful feeling I'm going to break your heart."

What? An unmistakable crush of panic gripped at Roxanne's chest. What was she so afraid of? Surely to fear heartbreak meant you were invested in someone or something enough to care, and enough for something to break? "You've lost me."

"Deliveroo is, well, Deliverdon't."

"No way, really?"

"Yep, we're too far out from the city."

"I've lost all hope."

Alice shook her head. "Then maybe I can restore it with the news that I do have a fridge full of leftovers from the party."

"You have? I have no words."

Alice laughed. "That's surely a first. Can you carry on feeding the chickens for me? I'll be right back with supper."

The chickens seemed to stop pecking at their feed and looked up at Roxanne. It was frankly unnerving. Maybe she could excuse herself by checking on Elvis and his crew?

"What's up, tennis balls?" They were undeniable cute. Roxanne gently lifted one into her arms and cuddled it. "Don't tell anyone about this, right. Keep that beak zipped."

"Too late."

"Damn you, Campbell." Roxanne gently placed the chick back with its siblings.

"Here, eat. Not that I need to say that."

A hungry silence fell upon them both as they sat on the sunroom step and devoured their supper. The food tasted even better than the night before.

Alice set her empty plate aside. "Can I ask you a question?"

Roxanne gave a distracted nod as she licked her fingers. "Only if it begins with *What would you like for pudding?*"

"Not exactly, although I do have ice cream. It's just, I'm curious. Why didn't you want to come here? You said it earlier."

"Did I?"

Alice nodded.

"Well, I guess I get homesick. An hour spent away from The Brewer's, and I develop a tic." Roxanne emphasized the point by twitching her shoulder.

"So it's not because you're in love with Eve, then? And that seeing her with Moira would hurt too much?"

Roxanne gasped. "What? In love with *Eve*? Romantic love? You're kidding, right?"

Alice shrugged.

"Oh my God, that's gross. I *do* love her, though, but not in *that* way. She means everything to me. Eve and the Eddisons, well, they're in every way my logical family."

"Logical family?"

"It's the idea that some people create their own *logical* family. It's often made up of close friends. They provide each other with the love and support that for, whatever reason, their own *bio*logical family can't or won't."

Alice gave a slow nod. "Logical family. I love that."

"You see, Eve isn't just my friend—she's my best friend in the whole world. There isn't anything I wouldn't do for her."

"Then I'm confused. Why didn't you want to come here, and why haven't you come before? You said you were jealous of us all for having Eve, so are you also jealous of Moira and Eve, and of what they have?"

"Nope. I'm not jealous of them. Why so many questions?"

Alice shrugged. "I'm just curious."

"Trust me. I'm really not that interesting."

"I disagree."

Roxanne laughed. "Seriously, there's no great depths here. We're talking paddling pool, not Loch Ness."

Alice giggled. She then tilted her head slightly. "Maybe you were worried seeing them would make you feel lonely?"

What was this? "Lonely? No. I know loads of people. I could just pick up my phone, and I would have a date in seconds."

"I don't doubt it. I've seen the postcards."

"How do you mean?"

"The ones you send Eve. I was round at theirs when your last one arrived. Eve said you tended to travel when a love affair ended. And that you travelled a lot. I thought that sounded sad."

Why had Eve felt the need to say that? "Eve said that?"

"Yes, but not in a gossipy way. She worries about you."

"There's no need for her to worry about me. I'm totally fine." Roxanne stood up. "So, ice cream?"

"So if you're not pining for Eve, and you're not lonely, then—"

"Oh my God, Alice, you're like a dog with a bone."

"I'm just trying to understand."

"Why? Why do you need to understand? Why do you even care?"

Alice's cheeks glowed red. "I don't. Obviously. We're strangers. I'll get our pudding."

She returned with two bowls of vanilla ice cream. She handed a bowl to Roxanne, and they both took their places once more on the sunroom step.

"Thanks." Roxanne bumped at Alice's shoulder with hers. "Sorry for snapping. I'm not good with questions."

"I'm sorry too. I didn't mean to pry."

"The truth, for what it's worth, is that I feel like I'm being judged in comparison with Eve, and not in a good way." Roxanne scooped the ice cream into her mouth, emptying the bowl in a matter of seconds.

"Judged by who?"

Roxanne set her bowl aside. "Everyone. I know everyone is judging me for living the way I do. For not finding my life partner and settling down. I like my life because I'm in complete control of what happens to me. Okay?" The thought of being judged kindled anger to rise and warm her cheeks. "And I know Eve thinks I lead people on and break people's hearts."

Roxanne noticed Alice's cheeks flushing as she stared at her ice cream dissolving at its edges. Had her comment struck a chord with Alice? Was Eve right?

Roxanne cleared her throat. "I always make it clear right from the start that I don't do relationships, and I'm not the girl of their dreams."

Alice glanced up at her. "Have you never wanted to settle down with someone, commit?"

"No."

"Right." Alice bit at her lip. "I suppose you get to leave them before they leave you. And before they can hurt you. I can see that attraction."

"Exactly. Your ice cream's melting, by the way. And I don't see it as leaving someone when there's no relationship to leave."

Alice scooped up several mouthfuls of her ice cream. She then held her spoon briefly in her mouth before tossing it lightly into the bowl with a clink. "I suppose that's one way of looking at it."

"Thank you. At last, a fellow believer."

"I don't believe what you believe. I want to commit to someone. I'm just not very good at it."

Was she talking about the Milly girl? Could she ask her? Should she? Or would Eve be mad with her for crossing the line and for going too far with Alice, yet again?

Alice rested her hand lightly on Roxanne's arm. "No one's judging you, you know. I remember my therapist saying that sometimes we project onto others what we fear or believe ourselves."

"Are you sending me a bill for *this* therapy session?"

"Definitely. And I should warn you, I'm expensive."

"Of course you are."

Alice reached out for Roxanne's bowl. "There's no shame in being lonely either, you know. Not that you are, obviously."

"Obviously. So are you?"

"What?"

"Lonely. I mean, it must be hard for you to see Moira and Eve together. And you must miss Moira now that she's based in the city."

"Sometimes. And now and then, for sure, I find it hard not to have someone who's there for me. Who"—Alice swallowed—"loves me."

Surely this was the moment to ask Alice if Milly was her girlfriend, the one who left her before she had the chance to leave? It must be so painful, damaging even, to feel the need to be so private. And why did Alice feel she couldn't say anything, particularly given now that Moira had Eve? They—actually, the whole of Newland, if Eve's party was anything to go by—would never judge her. Surely Alice knew that?

"Alice, if there's anything you maybe haven't been able to talk to someone about before, then you can always talk to me."

Alice gripped the stacked bowls against her. "Like what?"

Alice's phone rang startling them both.

"It's Elizabeth. Hi. Everything okay?...You can't find him?" She covered the phone and whispered, "Angus is missing."

"Missing?"

Alice's cheeks blanched as she nodded.

Roxanne urged, "Ask how long for."

"How long has he been gone?...A couple of hours."

"We'll go over."

"We're coming over. No, honestly, it's no trouble. Don't worry, we'll find him."

Alice ended the call and stared at her phone. "It's not like him to just wander off."

"So this is new?"

Alice's face creased with concern. "Yes."

"We'll find him, don't worry."

"It's almost dark out."

Roxanne pulled on her shoes and jumper and headed for the door. "Well, lucky for you, I eat my carrots."

Alice gave a distracted laugh. "Right, I'm pretty sure we have all we need in the Land Rover."

"Great." Roxanne held the door open for Alice. "Let's go."

As Roxanne settled herself into the passenger seat, Alice turned to look at her. "Thanks for coming with me."

There was such feeling behind Alice's words that Roxanne's cheeks grew warm in response. She quickly rallied to say, "No place I'd rather be."

Chapter Eight

A lice gripped the steering wheel with all her might. It was difficult not to imagine the worst. Had Angus thought to take a walk and fallen? Was he out there in the cold, all alone, and in pain? Had he got himself lost? Was Newland—his home, his companion—slowly becoming a stranger to him?

"I don't know how much you know about Angus's recent struggles with his memory and confusion." Alice glanced at Roxanne who was scanning the landscape. "You see, we're all losing him, slowly, heartbreakingly, right in front of us. And he's too proud to admit that he's ill. Moira has tried everything to get him to the GP, but he refuses."

"Yeah, she mentioned that."

"They've even rowed about it, which is really out of character for him. It upset Moira terribly. And she's worried sick about Elizabeth, who's bearing the brunt. I've tried to help, but…"

"You are helping. It's clear all of you are."

"It never feels enough."

"It's sadly not an illness that knows the meaning of enough."

"And now tonight, I can't help thinking the worst."

"We don't know for sure what's happened. There could still be a less alarming scenario at work."

"I can't think of one. He would never dream of not telling Elizabeth where he was going. I've honestly never heard such fear in her voice."

"I don't suppose she mentioned whether he took Moira's Land Rover?"

"No. She just said he'd gone missing. I do hope he's not crashed somewhere if he has taken it."

"How's his driving normally?"

"We've noticed that he tends to stick to the local area he knows well. Within this routine he seems to be quite safe. Moira and I have both been keeping a discreet eye on his driving. When I've been with him, his judgement and decision-making seemed fine. I'm pleased, though, that he has been self-limiting. Actually, now that I think about it, I don't think he's been driving at night for many months now."

"Okay. It sounds like it's unlikely he's driven far, then. So I think the local area is where we should—Hold on."

"What?"

Roxanne strained to look behind her. "I'm pretty sure there's a light on in the hall."

Alice slammed on the brakes and reversed back along the road. She then swung into the hall car park, throwing them around in their seats and splashing in every pothole.

Alice wrenched on the handbrake. "I can't see the Land Rover. Can you grab the torch? It's in the side of your door."

"Got it."

They clambered out, and Alice ran to the entrance only to find the door locked. She tried to see in through the partly curtained window that stretched the length of the doorway. "Maybe someone just left the light on by mistake."

"Is there another entrance?"

"Yes, at the side, but it hasn't been used in a while. It'll be muddy, so take care." Alice followed Roxanne to the side door, which again, they found locked.

No. Alice pushed at the handle. She resorted to banging a couple of times on the door with her palm. "He's obviously not here. Let's go to Elizabeth."

"Okay." Roxanne turned with a jolt, ending up pretty much in Alice's arms.

The sensation of Roxanne's warm body pressing against her was the last thing Alice was expecting. "Did you stumble?"

"I've just walked into a spider's web. Oh my God, there's the spider. It's *huge*." Roxanne brushed frantically at the web that clung to her.

"Before you say it, I doubt it's eaten Angus."

"You say that like it's not a distinct possibility."

In spite of everything, Alice couldn't help but laugh. "Here, let me help you. Stop shining the light in its eyes—you're blinding the poor thing with your torch. Turn it off."

"Why would I turn it off? I've not got a death wish."

"The only thing that will kill you is me, you eejit. Turn. It. Off."

"No way."

"Give it." Alice wrestled the torch free of Roxanne's grip.

"Aye, our friends with eight legs can see without a torch, young lady. Such a commotion indeed."

"Angus?" Alice spun round, blinding Angus with the torchlight. He protected his face with his hands. Alice ran to him and hugged him.

"What's all this, young Alice?"

"We thought something—" Alice stopped herself. The last thing Angus needed was an overreaction to worry or stress him. She needed to be calm. She took a deep breath. "Nothing. Erm, I just need to make a call. One sec." Alice pulled her phone from her pocket and stepped away a few paces to ring Elizabeth. At the same time, she kept Angus in her peripheral vision.

"You okay, handsome?" Roxanne rested her hand on Angus's shoulder. How Alice loved the way Roxanne engaged with him.

"Yes, for goodness' sake, why wouldn't I be?"

"Fair enough. So you're just having some me time?"

"Me time? I have no idea what you mean. I was preparing the hall for the infants tomorrow. It seems everyone's forgotten about that."

Why would he say that? Alice stared at her phone, ringing out unanswered. And where was Elizabeth?

Roxanne glanced up at Alice with a worried expression. "Oh right, of course. And you've finished now, I'm guessing, as it's quite late."

"Finished? I've only just begun."

"Alice?" Elizabeth finally answered the phone, sounding breathless and understandably flustered.

"Hi," Alice said, pressing her phone to her ear. "We've found him."

"Oh, Alice, that's such a relief. Is he okay?"

"Yes, he seems…fine." She had wanted to say physically fine, but with Angus in earshot, that would surely be insensitive.

Angus's face screwed to a frown. "Of course I'm fine. Now, if you'll excuse me."

Alice mouthed *Go with him* to Roxanne, who gave a thumbs-up in reply and followed Angus back round the side to the front door.

"Are you bringing him home now?" Elizabeth asked.

"We'll bring him home right away. Perhaps put the kettle on."

"Yes, I'll do that."

"See you in a minute. Try not to worry any more."

"Yes. Thank you so much."

"No worries. Bye." Alice couldn't decide who worried her more, Angus or Elizabeth. It was just so heartbreaking. But this was not about her. If she was to help them, she needed to be strong and objective. She needed to be more like Roxanne.

Alice caught up with Roxanne inside the hall. Roxanne was crouched and brushing nothing into a dustpan while Angus swept at a clean floor.

Alice stared around the immaculate room. "Please say you have a plan."

"Absolutely."

"You don't, do you?"

"No. I'm just going with the flow." Roxanne made her way to Angus. "I don't know about you, but I think we're about done. Good job. Go us." She raised her hand in a high-five gesture, which Angus ignored. Instead, he narrowed his eyes to stare at the tip of his brush. "I can't see any more dust."

"That's because this hall is cleaner than a nun's joke book."

Angus laughed. "Aye. Cleaner than a hungry man's plate."

"Ooh, good one. Cleaner than—"

Alice gave Roxanne a look. *Really?*

"Right, yes, let's go. There's a girl waiting at home for her man." Roxanne held out her hand for Angus's brush, as if giving it to her was the natural thing for him to do.

"Aye." With a discernible numbness in his demeanour, Angus gave Roxanne his brush. He then looked about him as if he was trying to decide upon something, but that the decision was just out of reach.

Roxanne rested their brushes against a bench and then tenderly said. "After you, fella."

"No, young lady, after you."

"Well, thank you very much. Don't mind if I do."

Angus followed Roxanne out the door without protest or even looking back.

Relief brought tears to Alice's eyes, which she quickly blinked away. She had braced herself for a row. But no, instead there was a joke which allowed for a shift of focus. As no-plans went, it was a great plan and masterfully carried out, that was for sure.

Alice turned off the hall light and locked the door behind her. A warm feeling glowed inside her at the sight of Roxanne sitting in the front middle seat of the Land Rover chatting away to Angus.

Alice climbed in. "There we go, that's the hall all locked up for the night."

"Great stuff," Roxanne said, adding, "Easy on the bumps when we set off, Campbell."

Alice laughed. "Okay." She willed herself to concentrate on the journey ahead rather than on the feel of Roxanne's thigh against hers. "So, home then to Elizabeth, Angus." Alice turned on the engine and reached for the gear stick.

"She is my beginning and my end." Angus looked dreamily ahead into the darkness as he spoke.

Alice bit her lip. She would *not* let Angus's comment upset her. No. This was not the time for tears but for strength. Wasn't that what she'd told herself? Please God, let her be strong. To her surprise, the warmth of Roxanne's hand rested over hers.

"Good job, roomie," Roxanne whispered. "Good job."

In what felt like the most natural thing to do, Alice reached over and hugged Roxanne tightly, burying her face momentarily into her neck.

"Lucky we're in no hurry." Angus chuckled to himself.

Alice let go and lingered a while in the comfort of Roxanne's affectionate gaze. "Okay, we really are going now." And with that they swung out onto the road.

Roxanne leaned towards Angus. "Cleaner than the conscience of an innocent man."

Angus turned to Roxanne, utterly bemused. If ever proof was needed, it couldn't have been clearer in that very moment that for Angus the memory of the recent past was lost as easily as one's breath. And that memory for him was less a preserved thought and more a dream lost on waking.

Roxanne gave Alice an apologetic look.

"Don't worry. I have no idea either, Angus," Alice said. "There's a possibility it was an attempt at humour."

Roxanne wiggled her eyebrows. "What can I say—I'm here all week, folks."

How Alice wished it would be true.

❖

"Angus." Elizabeth hugged him tight.

"What is all this for, Betty? I was gone just a wee while. Wasn't I?"

Elizabeth seemed unable to let him go. "Don't leave me again like that. Without telling me where you are going."

"I'm sorry to have worried you, my love. I just took a turn up the hill."

"The hill? But I thought—"

"You thought what, my love?"

"Nothing."

It was heart-wrenching to see. No wonder Alice turned away as she said, "I'll make us all a hot drink."

Elizabeth released her hold of Angus and held his hand tightly as she led him to the sitting room and to his armchair, pushed a little nearer to the fire.

"Won't you join us, Roxanne?" Elizabeth opened a folding side table flat before settling into a chair next to Angus. "I can't thank you and Alice enough."

Roxanne pulled off her jumper and slung it over a small formal sofa for two. The sofa had a firm back and was upholstered in a floral-patterned fabric. It wasn't uncomfortable as such, but it wasn't exactly a seat to lounge in. It took Roxanne a moment or two to decide how best to sit in it. She opted in the end for an upright stance and crossed legs. "No problem at all," she said. "Really. And what's not to love about toasting your cockles by a roaring fire in wonderful company."

Elizabeth smiled. "Aye. Indeed."

Alice came into the sitting room, carrying a tray laden with steaming mugs of tea, a stack of white side plates, and a fruit cake. She carefully placed the tray on the side table. "Here we go."

"Thank you. Wonderful. Cake all round?" Elizabeth's hand shook slightly as she cut the first slice.

Alice took her seat next to Roxanne. She crossed her legs in the opposite direction.

Roxanne gestured to the knife. "Why don't I do that?"

"No, you are our guest."

"You do know," Alice said, "that you're denying Roxanne the chance to cut herself a large slice."

Roxanne chuckled. "Did you teach Alice mind reading as well as pastry making?"

Elizabeth shook her head and laughed. "Well, in that case." She turned the cake towards Roxanne.

"Okey-dokey," Roxanne said. "So, shall I divide it into four? Angus, what do you reckon?"

Angus had left them, it seemed, in that moment for the mesmerising flicker of the fire in the hearth. Roxanne gently leaned across and slipped her fingers to rest softly at the pulse at his wrist. Over the years she has mastered the art of disguising a pulse read as a warm touch. Helpfully it took him a few moments to stir. His pulse was a little fast, but then, given everything, it wasn't that surprising.

"Angus, sweetheart."

Angus turned to Elizabeth and then looked at Roxanne's hand on his wrist. Roxanne gave a soft pat, and in response he placed his other hand over hers.

"Hey, fella."

"Hello, young lady."

"How does a slice of this cake and a cup of tea sound to you?"

"A fine idea."

"And then I think we'll retire." Elizabeth glanced at Alice who nodded.

"Party pooper," Angus said, mischief mixing with the flicker of the fire in his eyes.

Elizabeth looked genuinely cross. "Angus McAlister, what a thing to say."

Roxanne laughed. "You're lucky I've got the knife."

"You are my party, Betty."

"You can keep that sweet talk for someone who's amused." She pinched at her forehead. "What a night."

Alice nudged the plate of cake towards Elizabeth. "Try a little bit of cake yourself before bed."

"I'm fine. Please don't worry about me."

"But I can't help it. I love you, both of you, so much."

"Oh, Alice, and we love you." Elizabeth reached out to find Alice's arms wrapping around her.

Angus adjusted his cap several times and began to rummage in his pockets. Was he looking for the words that seemed to evade him?

They ate and drank, accompanied by the ebb and flow of gentle conversation deliberately chosen to help ease the upset of the night. Alice and Roxanne spoke of the weather and their walk that afternoon up to the tor. How excited they had been to have a magical glimpse of the pregnant roe deer. How the afternoon had become evening without them really noticing. Elizabeth and Angus listened as best they could but with eyelids growing ever heavier with tiredness.

Roxanne gave a deliberate yawn. "Well, I'm beat."

Elizabeth set her teacup aside and steadied herself to her feet. "Yes. Bed for everyone. Goodnight, both."

They all stood at once.

"I shall stay with you." Alice glanced from Elizabeth to Angus.

"Really, Alice, that's not necessary." Elizabeth looked to Angus. "We'll be fine now. Go home with Roxanne."

"Indeed. Not required, young Alice." Angus's face wrinkled with confusion as he shook his head. Was this evening just another memory lost for him? How frightening to have so much stolen from you, day in, day out.

"Why don't you lead the way, sweetheart." Elizabeth reached for Angus's hand. "I'll be right behind you."

"Aye."

"Sleep tight." Alice gave Angus a hug.

"I will indeed." He looked behind him to his chair. He seemed to be checking for something.

"Night, fella," Roxanne said with a tone as gentle as the moment deserved.

He looked up and blinked into her eyes. "Yes. Goodnight."

They watched as he made his way out of the sitting room and headed through to the dining room and to the hallway beyond.

Speaking softly, Alice said to Elizabeth, "It doesn't feel right leaving you. And I'm not sure that Moira would forgive me if I left you this evening."

Elizabeth sat once again in her seat. "I understand that, but I promise we'll be fine. Any problems, I shall ring. And as for Moira… why do we need to tell her? It would only worry her."

Alice looked at Roxanne. "I don't know…"

Roxanne shrugged. "It might worry Moira more if she feels you're keeping things from her even if for very understandable reasons. But the decision, of course, is yours."

Elizabeth nodded. "I'll have a think. Now, go. Please."

Roxanne lightly rested her hand on Alice's arm. "Come on, roomie. We have been told."

"Okay." Alice's feet didn't move.

What could she do to help her? Turning to Elizabeth, Roxanne asked, "Would it be of use, maybe, if you had my number as well as Alice's? I'd like to help if I can."

"Yes." Elizabeth nodded. "Good idea. Thank you, Roxanne. Let me get some paper."

Alice smiled at Roxanne. "Thanks."

"Sure."

Elizabeth returned with a floral-patterned paper notelet and handed it to her. "Here we are." She stood over Roxanne as she wrote out her mobile number.

"There you go."

"Wonderful. I shall put it by the phone." Elizabeth made for the dining room and the sideboard where their phone sat in the corner, all but hidden by the photos.

Alice dug in her back pocket and pulled out her mobile. "Maybe I should have your number too?" Alice's cheeks flushed. "For emergencies."

"Okay. Let me have your phone and I'll stick it in."

Alice tapped with her thumbs at her screen before handing over her phone. "I've created a new contact entry for you. I'll then send you a text, so that you have mine too."

Roxanne laughed at Alice's entry of *Wee Eejit*. She added her number and handed her phone back to Alice.

Alice smiled. "Done, I've sent you a text."

Roxanne checked her phone for the message which read, *Thanks x*

The latch on the front door opening drew their attention from their phones to the task of leaving. As hints went, not so subtle. Roxanne glanced across to Elizabeth, who stood holding the door open and smiling. "I think that's our signal to go."

They made their way to her, and Alice gave Elizabeth a final quick squeeze. "Night."

Elizabeth tenderly rested her palm against Alice's cheek. "No more worrying."

Alice nodded, and with that she brought herself to leave.

They were home in no time. And before they'd even stepped much beyond the front door of the croft, Alice suggested, "How about a drink? I'm fairly certain I've some cooking brandy in the back of the kitchen cupboard."

"You don't drink, normally?" Roxanne turned on a side lamp and collapsed onto the sofa.

Alice shouted through from the kitchen. "Me, teetotal?" Alice laughed. "God, no. I don't drink and drive, so that may have given you the impression that I'm a nun."

Roxanne laughed. "A nun? I love it."

Alice emerged from the kitchen carrying the brandy bottle in one hand and two glasses in the other. "To be honest, I finished my last bottle of white the night before you arrived. I meant to get some more. And I suppose I thought we had the party and that you were just with me one night. Sorry."

"And I should have brought some with me. But it was all I could do to carry, or should that be drag, my bloody rucksack. And I didn't realize until the last minute that I'd be staying with you."

"We're even then." Alice sat next to Roxanne and poured her a generous measure of brandy. "Here. Cheers." Alice rested the bottle on the floor, tucked her legs up underneath her, and snuggled into the sofa with her body turned towards Roxanne.

"Thanks. Cheers." Roxanne took a sip and the afterburn stung at her lips. "Oh, that's got a kick. Fab."

Alice swirled the amber liquor to lick and coat the side of her glass as if she was conjuring it to reveal every answer to every question she might wish to ask.

"I think you were right about not keeping things from Moira," she said. "I'm sort of noticing that, when it matters, you always seem to know what to say."

"Me? Nah. Remember, it's easier for me—it always is for the person not directly involved. And I'm sure it also hasn't escaped your notice that I have the knack of saying the wrong thing. More often than not, I never know what to say."

"No?"

"Nope." In that moment, with Alice looking at her with such affection, Roxanne was certain that nothing coherent would escape her lips.

"I totally get why Elizabeth's hesitant about telling Moira. I would be, in her place. I can't bear upsetting and worrying her either." Alice took a sip of her drink. "And seeing Moira hurting, well, it's awful." Alice's eyes misted over, and she chewed on her bottom lip in an attempt, no doubt, to stem her tears. What upsetting memory had triggered such sadness?

"It's such a difficult situation for you all to be in. On the one hand, it's clear that you are trying not to overreact, and yet on the other, you can't ignore things either. It's hard."

Alice looked up at her and nodded. "Yes. You must see this a lot in your job."

"Yep, unfortunately." Roxanne finished her drink. "In A&E we often have to deal with some of the more challenging moments of the disease. Like when a crisis has happened or when the illness has taken its final toll."

"I imagine it's heartbreaking."

"And rewarding because I'm there for people when they need me. Look, I meant what I said about wanting to help. And even when I go home, I'll be just a phone call away." Home couldn't have felt further away. Time had seemed to slow in these last few days. How she hoped that the next few would linger just the same.

Alice smiled at her. "That means a lot. Thank you."

"And I know it's easier said than done, but don't worry too much about Moira, for she'll be all right. After all, she's got you and, of course, Eve as well now."

"Yes, I guess you're right." Alice drank down the remainder of her drink in one. She laughed as it stole her breath. "Another?" Without waiting for Roxanne's reply, Alice refilled their glasses and resettled herself. She rested her elbow on the back of the sofa and tilted her head to rest against her palm. She was looking at Roxanne with curiosity clearly bubbling under the surface of her expression.

"What?"

Alice laughed. "Nothing. I was just wondering..."

"Here we go."

Alice nudged at Roxanne's knee with her foot. "If Eve is your logical family, then does that make your own family—"

"Illogical? Yep. My so-called family are, quite frankly, arseholes, and that's being kind." Roxanne took a slug of her brandy.

"I'm sorry to hear that."

Roxanne shrugged. "My mum and dad got divorced when I was a kid. At first, I thought thank God, no more rowing. But then they both remarried and had sprogs with their new partners, and they literally forgot to give a fuck about me. They moved on without looking back. Useless, selfish shits, the pair of them."

"Wow. That's terrible."

"My father's new wife, in particular, hated me. She looked at me with such suspicion." Roxanne stared into her drink. "I was a child, for God's sake. If you can't trust your parents to love you...?" She shook her head. "If it wasn't for Eve and her family looking out for me, then who knows what would have happened. I honestly never really knew for sure when the bell went after school whether anyone would be there to pick me up."

"Oh, Roxanne..."

"Eve used to wait with me when they were late to collect me. This one time when it happened, Eve's dad confronted my dad and said, *Look, we couldn't help but notice that your daughter is waiting for you more than she should have to.* I really thought my dad would punch him. And then Henry asked, did he want me to go home with them, and they would drop me off home after tea. My father, of course, bit his arm off. Lazy shit, he was thrilled to be rid of me."

"Good for Henry."

"The Eddisons pretty much fed me for all my teenage years. And as soon as I could, I'd go travelling during the holidays to avoid being stuck with my family. Still, it gave me a love for travel. Wherever I went, I'd always send the Eddisons a postcard. And, as you know, I still send them to Eve."

Alice nodded. "If it wasn't for Moira taking my dad and me in when my mum died, then, like you, God knows." Alice shifted a little in her seat. "Although, you thought your parents' rowing was bad. You ought to try silence."

"Moira and your dad?"

Alice hugged her brandy glass to her chest. "Looking back, I have no idea why they married and why they stayed married as long as they did. I think they told themselves it was for me, but I just don't think they knew what to do. So that just leaves you with the status quo, doesn't it?"

"I guess."

Alice held Roxanne's gaze. "However lonely that might be."

"Yes." They were sitting so close now that Alice's knee brushed against her leg. It felt good. Too good. But they'd just been talking. Surely that was okay?

Alice looked puzzled. "You okay? You've gone a bit..."

"Yup. I'm fine. Just pooped. You must be too." Roxanne scrambled to her feet. "I best get this bed made up while I still can."

"Oh right. I'll give you a hand." Alice inched herself off the sofa and pulled the bed out flat.

Roxanne unfolded her bottom sheet and flapped it into place, then bent to tuck it into the sides.

"Here." Alice tossed over Roxanne's pillow, which hit her on the head. She giggled. "Sorry."

Was that accidental? Or could Alice be playing with her? Teasing? Either way, it was war.

Roxanne picked up the pillow and gripped it like a bat.

Alice placed her hands on her hips. "Really?" She lunged for a cushion and with effortless grace walloped Roxanne on her shoulder.

"What the...! If Eve asks, you started it." Roxanne swung her pillow into Alice's middle only to receive a follow-up blow to her face. "Right, you asked for it." Roxanne grabbed the duvet and slung it over Alice's head and wrestled her onto the bed.

Alice gave a muffled squeal as she struggled. Roxanne's only option was to straddle Alice's hips using her weight as ballast. When the wriggling and squealing stopped, she gingerly peeled down the duvet to reveal a pink-cheeked opponent blinking up at her.

"I suppose you think you've won?" Despite Roxanne's advantage, Alice managed to free an arm before she finally gave up with a groan. "Okay, you win. I give up."

"You surrender, eh?"

"More a tactical retreat."

Roxanne chuckled. "Fair enough." She shifted her weight a little as Alice lay warm underneath her. Their play-fighting had left Alice's breath raggedy as she stared up at Roxanne. Alice's expression seemed to have changed from warrior to something tamed or rather softer. Her lips were parted as if poised for something...or someone.

Alice reached up and lifted a stray feather free from Roxanne's collar. "You look so serious."

"Me? Serious? Never."

Nothing had ever felt more serious. For wasn't *everything* resting perilously in that moment upon her ability not to kiss Alice and not to bury her lips into her neck. Hearts, friendships, and relationships could all be at risk for just one kiss. It was madness. What on earth would Eve say? She needed to get off her. Right now.

Roxanne climbed away from Alice who, in turn, untangled herself from the duvet. The hot energy of their tussle lingered in the room as they proceeded to make the bed in silence.

"I'll leave you to it, then." Alice looked towards the stairs.

"Uh-huh. Night."

Alice nodded. She seemed to hesitate just for a second before turning and making her way upstairs.

Roxanne pulled off her clothes, turned off the side lamp, and climbed into bed. This wasn't good, was it. How close had she come to kissing Alice. Without question she was playing with fire as she no doubt risked hurting Alice. Because where would a kiss lead in the longer term? She'd never hung around long enough before to find out. But who was to say that her future had to be determined by her past? No one, not Eve, not anyone. A sense of defiance swelled in her chest. What happened if she wanted a different future, and with someone who made her feel excited and curious about where a kiss might lead? And what would happen if that someone was Alice?

She stared up at the ceiling. What was Alice thinking? Maybe Alice wasn't thinking anything. That was more likely. Sure, it seemed that Alice was amused by her, even now and then admiring of her, maybe. And they did seem to have more in common than she could have imagined just a few days ago. But that certainly didn't mean that she meant anything to Alice.

Oh my God, why did that thought hurt? Did she want Alice to have feelings for her? Was this what having feelings for someone was like? What would she know about that? Love was always something someone else had.

Her head hurt. She was just tired—after all, it had been a long day. She just needed to sleep. Everything would feel different in the morning.

CHAPTER NINE

"Thank you, everyone. Settle down now." Alice held her arms out with her palms pressed flat, and she slowly moved them up and down, softening and stilling the excited chatter. Roxanne's impression of the Monarch of the Glen's mating call had triggered an eruption of laughter and excitement amongst the class of young children, so much so they were literally rolling around the hall floor in delight.

How everything about the space felt so different from last night. Where there had been shade, and worry, and sadness, there was now light and laughter and fun. It was fair to say the teaching assistant was a hit.

"Thank you, Roxanne." Roxanne sat back on the stage next to Alice and dangled her feet off its edge. Roxanne looked up and beamed her a smile. Alice quickly steadied herself. They were not up a hill or in the croft—this was her place of work. She was the professional responsible for delivering a worthwhile learning experience. So why on earth was she feeling like an excited teenager full of raging hormones, having met someone affecting and special? She must concentrate.

She returned her pen to the pad on the flip chart and pointed several times to the next bullet point on her list. "Okay, we have red deer in our woods. What other creatures might you find?"

Roxanne raised her hand in an urgent manner, causing the children to erupt again in laughter. Alice ignored her.

A young girl with tight braids gingerly raised her hand. "Yes, Aileen," Alice said, "do you have a suggestion for us?"

"A squirrel, Miss Campbell."

"Yes, that's right, the *red* squirrel. The red squirrel is native to the Highlands. It is endangered in the rest of the United Kingdom because of the dominance of the non-native American grey squirrel. So we must be vigilant and care and protect them, mustn't we?"

A united and very sweet "Aye" floated up to the stage from the obedient faces staring up at them.

A lad with tufty hair and one collar turned up beneath his school jumper shouted out, "Golden eagle."

"Yes, now, what a special bird. And what do eagles like to eat?"

Aileen raised her hand again and called out, "Fish."

"That's right. One of their favourite treats is salmon. And they like to nest in the cover of our hillsides and swoop down to feed from the loch. It is the perfect home for them. Now"—Alice flipped over her paper—"tell me, can you think of *another* animal who has made Newland its home?"

Roxanne raised her hand again. The class pointed to Roxanne. Annoyingly, this made it difficult for Alice to ignore her.

"Yes, Roxanne." Alice hoped her fixed stare would help manage Roxanne's answer. It was wishful thinking.

"Tyrannosaurus Rex." Roxanne proceeded to raise her hands in a small-claws gesture and began to roar. The class screamed with pleasure and began to repeat Roxanne's impression. It was *Jurassic Park* on speed.

It took a further five minutes for the prehistoric excitement to settle and for Alice to then bring the lesson to a close.

With the teaching complete, the children filed out. It was incredibly sweet to see them high-fiving Roxanne on the way and skipping over the few remaining puddles in the car park. Their teachers, without exception, made a fuss over Roxanne and her unique teaching methods. Although it was clear from their bemused expressions that they'd never seen the non-native, rather dominant *Roxanne* species before.

"I was thinking pine marten." Alice shook her head as she finished clearing away the teachers' chairs. "Grab the chart for me."

After a few seconds of head scratching, Roxanne lifted the flip chart free of its frame. She then passed it down from the stage to Alice, who tucked it on a shelf in the store cupboard. Roxanne joined her at the cupboard door and handed her the frame to put away. "Oh right, I see. But you have to agree, a ferrety friend is less enthralling than a dinosaur. And are you absolutely certain they are not in Newland?"

Alice softly closed the cupboard and made for the exit. Over her shoulder she added, "I think we would have seen one by now."

"You say that, but has anyone actually seen Nessie, yet totally a thing."

Alice reached the entrance door and held it open for Roxanne. "Well, one thing's for sure, those little ones will not forget this class for a while. Thanks for helping."

Roxanne smiled. "I think we both know I was more a distraction than a help. But it was fun. And you're a great teacher, by the way."

"Thanks." Alice rested her shoulder against the door. "I love teaching, and I've always wanted to be a teacher, right from the start. I'd watch Moira leading a lesson, and I'd see the attendees gain in confidence and happiness with each day. It was totally inspiring. I even went to the same college, the Scottish Agricultural College, or Scotland's Rural College as it's now known, as Moira and my mum."

"Really? That's cool."

"Yep. I focused on environmental sustainability and added modules on business, land management, and forestry. I wanted to be able to help care for Newland. I know that must sound—"

"It sounds great. I love your passion for your home."

"That means a lot." And it did, and until Roxanne had said it, she'd had no idea how much. "I then completed a postgrad teaching qualification, and well, I haven't looked back. I want to inspire and help people as Moira and my colleagues do every day."

"Well, FYI, you certainly inspired the youngsters today. It couldn't have been clearer how much those rug rats adore you."

Alice's cheeks tingled at Roxanne's compliment. "I adore them too. They take everything in with such wonder." Wonder was something Roxanne had provided in spades, that was for sure. And it wasn't just the kids whose morning had been brightened by her or who felt sad when time ran out.

Alice cleared her throat. "Right, let's open the centre." Alice locked the hall, and Roxanne walked by her side to the waiting Land Rover. It felt as natural as if they had always worked together, as if Roxanne's place was right by her side rather than hundreds of miles away.

An oddly heavy silence accompanied the beginning of their short journey. As they turned off from the road to the track that led to the centre, Alice broke the sombre quiet and asked, "So, what about you?"

"What about me?"

"Why nursing?"

Roxanne blew out her cheeks. "I didn't really know what I wanted to do when I left school. I knew I preferred science to art. Then I had a fling with a hot girl I met in the pub who was doing nursing, and that was it really."

"Oh, so she inspired you?"

"Kind of. It was more the thought of hanging out with hot nurses and doctors like her and the mention of subsidized accommodation."

Alice laughed. "You're not joking, are you."

"Nope."

"Do you take anything seriously?"

"As little as possible."

"Right, I see." Roxanne was so difficult to work out. Last night she was focused and even serious at times, but today she was playing the fool and wanting Alice to believe that she cared about nothing. Why? Was she scared to admit she cared?

As they drew up at the centre, Roxanne nodded in the direction of the two composting toilet huts located just to the side of the car park. "Eve has warned me about the loo situation." Roxanne opened her door and climbed out.

Alice laughed as she jumped down from her seat and swung her driver's door shut. "I won't ask what else she has warned you about." She stopped herself when she realized what she had said. She hadn't meant to make reference to what Eve might have warned about Roxanne not hurting her. Thankfully, if Roxanne heard, she made no comment.

Instead, Roxanne was looking about her. "Yep, just as Eve described. Eco chalet in the Alps. Lead the way, Fräulein Campbell." She began to hum "The Lonely Goatherd" from *The Sound of Music*.

They reached the entrance, and Alice unlocked the door. She flipped the notice over to read *Welcome*. "So, welcome." She smiled at Roxanne and gestured for her to enter.

Roxanne gave a small bow finished with a warm smile in return. "Why, thank you." As she stepped inside, she asked, "So is it just schoolchildren you teach here?"

Alice began to pull up the window blinds. "We teach a whole variety of people. The school-aged children we help are often struggling in the mainstream system and need a bit of support and direction. Oh, poor thing." Alice lifted a pot plant from the windowsill and held it briefly under the painting sink's tap. She brushed her fingers softly over its leaves and returned it to the sill. "And, actually, a lot of our time these days is spent facilitating learning for adults. We give lessons in healthy eating and greener lifestyles as well as traditional bush skills."

"Bush skills?" Roxanne pinched her lips tightly together as she clearly tried and failed to suppress a snigger. "Sorry, I'm listening."

"But the work I'm most proud of"—Alice handed Roxanne a leaflet—"are our mental-health and well-being partnerships."

Roxanne nodded. She seemed impressed by what she was reading. "Branching Out?"

"Yeah, it's a partnership programme funded and supported by the Forestry Commission and by mental health teams in the region. It enables green space on referral for those adults who would benefit from positive structured time here with us. It's been really successful."

Roxanne handed back the leaflet. "Nature as part of a healing plan sounds so much better than turning to drugs as the only answer."

Alice rested against the counter. "Yep, definitely. Being outside in nature helps me every day, and I swear it keeps me well. And talking therapy, as you know, helped me loads, but even so, it's certainly exposing to open up to someone." Alice folded her arms at the thought.

Roxanne nodded with an expression that seemed so soft with compassion and understanding. It had been okay telling Roxanne about her struggles, hadn't it. She was so easy to talk to and a natural listener who didn't seem to judge.

"Even though you say you kind of fell into nursing, I bet you're great at your job."

Roxanne laughed. "Me? You'd have to ask my patients or my colleagues, maybe. I'm part of a team, in truth."

"Same here. I like to think working in partnership we may have helped save some people's lives. I feel proud about that. We all do."

"So you should. I for one couldn't be more impressed. Eve said how cool this place was, and…" Roxanne briefly looked down. When she looked up again, she was blushing. "How cool *you* were, in fact. She couldn't have been more right."

"Really? Eve said that about me?"

"Yep."

Alice's heart surged in her chest. *Cool* was the last thing she thought of herself. And for Roxanne to think so too…"I'm glad you think I'm cool."

"I do." Roxanne looked at her with such a focused and serious intensity. "Very much."

Was it her imagination, or was Roxanne trying to say she liked her?

They both jumped as the centre's door swung open, and Elizabeth walked in carrying a cloth bag with some children's books sticking out from it. She stopped for a moment and looked at them both in turn.

"You two look guilty."

Alice stepped forward to Elizabeth and took the bag gently from her, placing it next to the bookshelf. "Us? Not at all."

Elizabeth gestured to the books in the bag. "For the youngsters."

"Thank you." Alice gave a shake of her head. "I could have collected them from you."

"No need. To be honest, I was pleased to come here and have a break from the cottage."

Alice looked outside to the car park. "Did Angus drop you off? I didn't hear the Land Rover."

"Yes, but I asked to walk the last fifty yards. After last night I was so desperate for some air, and I thought a change of scene would do me good. So here I am. He's calling in, as he does, on the neighbouring farm." Elizabeth looked at Roxanne. "Do you know, he will stand there, Roxanne, nattering with Hugh and his wife, ankle-deep in slurry, no doubt, and oblivious to the time or the cold."

Alice slipped her arm around Elizabeth's waist. "They'll look after him, don't worry."

Roxanne's eyebrows rose. "So your neighbours know about Angus's condition?"

"Not directly." Elizabeth shook her head. "He's sensitive to anything I might say to friends, or anyone, really. It's ludicrous because after any real time spent in his company, you would know that something wasn't quite right. He drops the thread of conversation so easily and then repeats himself, and this all adds to his confusion and defensiveness. It's exhausting."

Elizabeth made her way over to a craft table, which was part covered with water pots and paint brushes. She pulled out a wooden chair from under the table and sat heavily down.

Alice bent down next to her. "Would you like a cup of tea?"

"No, I'm fine. But thank you anyway. You see, Roxanne, if people know about Angus's difficulties, it's simply by spending time with him. Look at me. I came here for a break from him, and all I've done is talk about him."

Alice lightly rubbed Elizabeth's arm. "We don't mind."

"You should."

Alice winced at the unusual exasperation in Elizabeth's tone.

Roxanne rested her hand lightly on Alice's back. "Well, I fancy a brew. How about I make you and me one?"

"Great, thanks. The kitchen's just tucked behind the bookshelf. There's some biscuits knocking about somewhere."

"I'm on it."

Alice returned her attention to Elizabeth, who looked so washed-out and tired. She couldn't bring herself to ask if she had spoken to Moira about last night. "So…"

"Don't worry, I can see you're fidgeting to ask. I've done the deed and updated Moira."

Alice gave a sigh of relief and pulled up a seat next to Elizabeth. "Oh right. Good." She wouldn't push the subject by asking how Moira took the news.

"She'd not long left Eve at the test centre when I spoke to her." Elizabeth absently lifted a fallen brush back into the pot. "Which was good. I would have hated to have upset Eve with such news ahead of her test."

Roxanne brought over two steaming mugs of tea and a packet of shortbread. "Here we go." She drew up a chair and made short work of opening the biscuits.

"Thanks, Rox. I hope Eve wasn't too nervous." Alice blew over her tea. "I tried to tell her that she was a fab driver."

"Now," Elizabeth said, "if I remember correctly, Moira said Eve was a little quiet, but otherwise fine."

"That makes sense." Roxanne took a sip of her tea. "Eve tends to close down when she's frightened. I could always tell when she had a dental appointment."

Alice and Elizabeth laughed.

Elizabeth pointed at Roxanne. "You'll be pleased, no doubt, to have Eve back with you, so you can continue your holidays."

Roxanne silently shrugged and nodded in response.

"And I'm sorry again to you both that your evening was so disrupted."

Alice shook her head. "Oh gosh, no. We're just pleased everything's okay."

Roxanne bit into a biscuit. "Yep. And honestly, no worries at all. These things happen."

Elizabeth briefly patted Roxanne's hand. "That's very generous of you. All the same, it's not quite what you imagined for your time here, I bet."

"To be honest, I had no expectations for my holidays, and so far, if I'd had any hopes, they have been exceeded." Roxanne beamed a smile at Alice.

To Alice's mortification Elizabeth noticed. *Act nonchalant.* How she managed to control her newly beating heart, she really didn't know.

"Well, that's good to hear." Elizabeth gave a loaded sigh and checked her watch.

Alice glanced outside. "Are you expecting Angus to collect you?"

Elizabeth's eyes brimmed with tears in response. "I think those days of expecting something are gone now." She reached for a handkerchief from her handbag. She pressed it to her nose. "Just one moment. How silly and weak of me."

It was all Alice could do to stop from crying too. She wrapped her arm around Elizabeth's shoulders. "I'm so sorry. I didn't mean to upset you."

"I'll be okay, Alice. Please don't worry."

Roxanne said, "I've been thinking."

Alice looked up. "You have?"

Roxanne fiddled with her mug. "I'm not sure if it would work."

Elizabeth glanced at Roxanne with eyes rimmed in red. "We'd try anything."

"I could maybe have a chat with Angus for you and see if I can persuade him to go to his GP. You never know, I might be able to win him over with my irresistible bedside manner."

Alice's heart surged with the possibility of help. "That would be amazing."

"It is a long shot, I'm afraid. And to get the best result might be a bit too complicated."

Elizabeth urged, "How do you mean?"

"You see, it would ideally require you to see if you can get a GP appointment for Angus tomorrow, given that I'm going home on Wednesday—"

"Goodness, your stay has gone so quickly. Hasn't it, Alice?"

Alice bit her lip and nodded.

Roxanne cleared her throat. "And then I would match the timing of my chat to the appointment."

"Hold on," Alice said, "don't you have a boat trip with Eve on Loch Ness tomorrow?"

"Crap. I'd forgotten about that. It's booked for the morning, but if I miss it, it doesn't matter. This comes first. *You* come first."

To hear someone say *You come first*, and for Roxanne to be the person saying it, meant everything. "Thank you."

Elizabeth shook her head. "I hate the thought of spoiling your holiday. I promise to try my hardest for an afternoon slot. If I can get one, perhaps come for lunch after your boat trip and speak to him then. I could make some pasties."

"Okay, that could work. If I manage to persuade him, from what I have seen, we have to assume that we'll have a relatively small window of time to get him in that moment to the doctor."

Elizabeth nodded. "I understand. Do you really think it could work?"

Roxanne frowned a little. "I think the key, if there is one, is for Angus to want—in that moment at least—to seek help. His doctor will also need to see it come from him."

Elizabeth glanced at Alice. "Right."

Alice nodded emphatically. "We so much want it to come from him and for it to be his wish to seek help."

Elizabeth rested her finger momentarily over her lips. "I'm wondering if I should ask for the appointment to be a home visit?"

"Why," Roxanne said. "Is your GP practice not local to here then?"

"It's just a few miles away in the next village of Drumnadrochit."

"Okay, good. My only hesitancy with his GP calling round seemingly out of the blue is whether Angus will be suspicious of that. It's so important not to lose his trust. He might just half believe that you were able to get a cancellation."

"Are you saying that what I would need to do is to pretend to ring them after he's agreed and appear to get him in by good luck?"

Roxanne nodded. "Like I said, it's complicated and a bit of a long shot. The closer the plan is to what you would normally do, the better. Although it would be good if Moira or Alice could go with you. I'm guessing this probably doesn't happen usually?"

Elizabeth shook her head. "Half the problem is he's really proud. He always drives us to appointments, and it's normally just the two of us."

Roxanne tapped her forefinger at the side of her mug. "Okay. Then it's best you go alone. The bottom line is the more he feels he is in control, the less resistance you might get."

Alice turned to Elizabeth. "So, what do you think? Rox deals with people like Angus a lot."

"I'm keen, but what do you think Moira would say?"

"I think she would think we have no choice but to try something. So I say let's give it a go. But, of course, it's up to you."

Elizabeth nodded. "I agree. When you have nothing, something seems everything."

Relief swept in, swelling Alice's heart with gratitude. Alice covered Roxanne's hand with hers. "This means so much to us."

Roxanne blushed. "I'll give it my best shot."

Elizabeth tucked her handkerchief back in her bag. "Yes, thank you. It's really kind of you."

"Like I said, no worries, happy to help. I need to warn you both, though"—Alice's hand slipped from Roxanne's—"that even if it goes okay, it will be just a small step on the road to triggering the support you all need, but at least it's a start. Establishing a diagnosis for Angus will be the important next stage."

Elizabeth resolutely pushed her chair away from the table and stood. "I shall try our doctor's using the centre's phone, right now. There's no time like the present, particularly given that Angus is out of earshot. They've been our practice for so long I know their number by heart." She went over to the reception desk and perched herself on its edge. She dialled the surgery's number with the concentration of someone who didn't want to miss a digit. When she eventually got through, she repeated Roxanne's plan to the receptionist.

"You okay, Alice?"

Roxanne's voice startled Alice from her focus on Elizabeth. "Yes." How she wanted to add, *Now that you're here.*

"Oh, it's my phone." Roxanne rummaged for her mobile in the pocket of her jeans. "It's Eve."

Alice reached for Roxanne's arm.

Roxanne pressed the speaker button. "Hey, Eddison."

Eve gave an excited squeal. "I've passed!"

"Congratulations, mate!"

"Oh my God, Evie." Alice bent forward towards the phone. "Well done!"

"Thank you! I couldn't have done it without you. We're just leaving the test centre now and heading your way. Moira's picked up sandwiches for us all. Our plan for the afternoon is for Moira to drop me off at the croft to have lunch there with Rox, and then she'll drop food off with Elizabeth and Angus. And then after that, she'll team up with you, Alice, for lunch at the centre. How does that sound with you two?"

Alice leaned in again. "Yes, that's fine, Evie."

"Sure thing, mate. I'll meet you at the croft."

"Fab! See you soon. Bye."

Elizabeth returned to her seat at the table. "I'm so pleased Eve has passed her test. How wonderful."

"Yes, I'm so pleased for her." Alice's excitement faded, as she asked, "But even more importantly, how did you get on?"

"Well, the receptionist says she'll talk to the doctor, but I got the feeling they would support our efforts. She has suggested I ring first thing for one of their emergency same-day appointments."

"Just like us nurses"—Roxanne gave a knowing slow nod—"the receptionists are the key to everything."

"That's great." Alice's excitement began to fade even further at the realization that as soon as Eve returned, her time with Roxanne would come to an end. The sound of an engine drew her attention from her aching heart to the window. "Oh, Elizabeth, would you believe it's Angus."

"Really? I'm not sure whether to be pleased or confused or cross or all three."

Alice stared out at Angus jumping from the Land Rover with the spring and verve of a sprightly young man. He paused to refix his tie and straighten his cap. It looked for all the world like he was picking up Elizabeth for their first date.

Alice turned back to Elizabeth. "Maybe it's his own way of telling you those days of counting on him are not over yet."

"And that you'll always be his girl." Roxanne gave Elizabeth a soft nudge on her shoulder. "Whatever happens."

A hopeless romantic on the quiet, eh, Roxanne Barns?

Angus swung the door open, lifted his cap, and gave a sweeping bow. "Your carriage awaits, my lady."

"I'm amazed you are not covered in slurry. Was Hugh not in?"

"Hugh? Why would I have gone to Hugh's?"

"I thought…never mind. Thank you both."

Alice gave Elizabeth a tight hug. "Get some rest when you get home."

Elizabeth cupped Alice's cheeks. "Don't fuss. Would you like us to drop you back at the croft, Roxanne?"

"Oh yes. Thanks."

Elizabeth glanced from Roxanne to Alice. "We'll be waiting in the car park. Give you two a chance to say your goodbyes."

And with that, they were left alone.

Alice swallowed down a pressing urge to cry. She dug in her gilet pocket. "So, here's the croft keys." A tear embarrassed her by falling. She quickly swept it away.

Roxanne took the keys and shoved her hands deeply into the pockets of her jeans. "I'll miss you too, Campbell. Please tell me that's what you were thinking."

Alice laughed and nodded.

"Don't forget, even if we don't get to see each other again today, I'll see you tomorrow, all being well, for my chat with Angus. Whatever happens, I'll make sure I say goodbye properly. I promise."

The Land Rover's engine rumbled into life.

"I'd like that—thank you. But I'm just being daft." Alice folded her arms. "Now go on before Angus forgets he's waiting for you."

"Right." Roxanne quickly made for the door. At the threshold she looked back and waved. "Bye."

Alice raised her hand. "Bye."

It looked like Roxanne wanted to say something more. But instead, she turned away and left, leaving the door to swing closed behind her.

Alice returned to her seat at the craft table and rested her face in her hands as tears overwhelmed her. Why, oh why did Angus have to be poorly? Why did Elizabeth have to grow old? And why was *she* stupid enough to be falling for a person who didn't do relationships, let alone love?

Chapter Ten

Roxanne closed the croft door behind her, then pulled off her hoodie and slung it over the coat hooks. It was crazy how much this place felt like home.

She stood for a moment taking in the croft, for she wanted to commit every detail to the memory it would soon be. Here was the sitting room with its sofa, whose every lump and bump she knew by heart. A smile pressed at her lips at the memory of Alice's horrified face at the sight of her attempting to unscrew the sofa's armrest. What a fool Alice must have thought she was.

Was she a fool? Had she been foolish to say to Alice just then that she'd miss her too? But then she would miss her, and where was the harm in admitting it? She'd stood watching Alice cry while pinching at her own leg through her jeans pocket to stop herself from welling up too. There was only so much you could hide.

The soft chirp of the chicks drew her attention to the sunroom. She opened the sunroom door and bent to check on Eve's birthday pressies.

"Hey, fluffballs." She stroked their soft down. "Shall I give you a top up of water?" She went to the kitchen, filled their water feeder, and returned it back in place. "A quick cuddle? So, which one are you? I'm guessing you're Elvis or maybe Bing." She held the chick gently against her chest and carefully opened the door to the garden.

She sat on the step with the chick in her lap, just where she'd sat chatting with Alice yesterday. It was crazy how easily conversation always flowed with her. They'd shared such personal feelings and trusted in each other to listen without judgement. Maybe that explained how Alice managed to get her to talk so openly about difficult private subjects that she'd never spoken to anyone about before, not even Eve.

There was no shame in being lonely, wasn't that what Alice had said? But once you admitted to being lonely, what then?

"Rox?" The comforting familiarity of Eve's voice calling to her from the sitting room lightened the heaviness of the moment.

"Hi, I'm in the sunroom." Roxanne gently placed the chick back in its box. "I swear they're twice as big already. If they carry on maturing at this rate, they'll have graduated from school by the time I leave."

Eve laughed as she carefully rested a carrier bag against the sofa and shrugged off her coat. "And be moody, demanding their own personal space, and pining over the rooster next door."

"Who you won't approve of."

"Exactly."

They shared a warm, amused smile.

"Congratulations, you clever bugger." Roxanne held out her arms, and Eve in turn hugged her tightly.

Speaking into Roxanne's shoulder, Eve said, "I'm so chuffed, Rox. I don't know why it took me so long to learn to drive because I won't lie—I feel a bit proud of myself."

"So you should be. Have you told your mum and dad? Oh, and I meant to ask, how's Esther doing?"

Eve released her tight hold, but her smile, unsurprisingly, remained in place. "She's much better thankfully. There's even talk of discharging her. Mum kept me on the phone all the way here. She wanted every party detail and has already lined up places she wants me to drive her to when I visit next."

Roxanne laughed. "I'm pleased Esther's on the mend. So, you're getting a Lamborghini?"

"Hah, nope, something cheap and reliable. My mum sends her love to you, by the way."

"Right back at her."

"*And* I've brought some celebratory booze for us. And some sandwiches." Eve made for the carrier bag. It did not escape Roxanne's notice that it clinked when Eve lifted it. Eve dug around in the bag and pulled out a couple of packs of sandwiches. She tossed them to Roxanne, who caught them awkwardly. "There's a couple of bottles of fizz for Alice that need to go in the fridge. And a cheeky Bud or two for my cheeky bud."

"I see what you did there. Nice. I'll stick them in the fridge. Don't eat my sandwiches." Roxanne disappeared into the kitchen.

Speaking through from the sunroom, Eve said, "Moira told me about last night."

Roxanne opened two beers with a sharp fizz. "Yeah, poor sods." She joined Eve sitting on the step from the sunroom into the garden. "Here you go. Cheers."

"Thanks, cheers. And thanks so much for helping and for being there for them all."

Roxanne gulped down several glugs of her beer. "Oh my, that's good. No worries. Thankfully, we found Angus quite quickly in the end."

"Was he okay?"

Roxanne drank down more beer and nodded. "Yep. He was a bit cold and confused, and like I said, it was good we found him quickly and that Elizabeth had the sense to raise the alarm. Otherwise, he was generally all right, given everything."

"Was Alice all right? It must have been a shock to receive that call."

"I think so. I get the impression she's as worried about Elizabeth as she is about Angus."

"I get that. Moira is too. She's worried sick about her. With your medical hat on, and being serious for a moment, has she got reason to be?"

"Let's just say, I'd keep an eye on her. There was no question that she had a proper shock last night. She was shaking quite a lot, and it's clear to see she's frail."

Eve's bottom lip wobbled.

Roxanne gave her a comforting rub on the back. "I agreed with Elizabeth and Alice this morning that I'm going to try to speak to Angus, in the hope that I might be able to persuade him to see his GP."

"You have? Oh my God, Moira's going's to be so relieved when she hears."

"There's no guarantees."

"Even so." Eve hugged Roxanne. "Thank you. And we fully intend to keep a close eye on Elizabeth. In fact, Moira mentioned on the way over moving back here."

"Really?"

"Nothing's been agreed. But I'm certainly relieved to have got my license so I can get to the uni library for work."

"Yes, of course. Does Alice know?"

"Not yet. Like I said, it's very early days. And I don't think Moira wants to say anything yet until plans are a bit firmer in her mind. If it happens, it will likely be at the end of the year at the earliest when the holiday bookings slow down for Foxglove."

"So you'll move into Foxglove?"

Eve shrugged. "I guess."

"Cool." Roxanne ripped her sandwich pack open and crammed a large bite into her mouth. She then chased it down with her beer. She stretched out her legs. "I'm still aching from my walk yesterday."

Eve giggled. "I bet. It's beautiful here, but with that comes hills."

"How do you feel about moving here? It's certainly different from the city."

"Good, actually. Don't get me wrong, I've loved living in town. But there is something magical about Newland. It's always felt like home to me."

Roxanne nodded. "Yeah, I get that."

Eve's face spread wide with evident surprise. "Really? That's fab to hear. Does this mean you're going to come again?" Eve nudged Roxanne's shoulder and added, "In another three and a half years?"

"I was thinking more for your fortieth."

Eve laughed out loud and shook her head. "You're terrible."

"Yep, always. Seriously, though, being here"—Roxanne gazed around the garden and glanced behind her back into the croft—"I understand why you love it."

Eve took a sip from her beer. "I've so many memories of Moira here. So much so I wonder if maybe the affection we have for somewhere is sometimes less about the place and more about the person who lives there." Eve looked at Roxanne. "Do you know what I mean?"

Roxanne gave a nonchalant, "Sure." She couldn't have understood more.

"So for me, home is Moira."

"Makes sense."

And for her? Did it follow, then, that she was homeless? For there was no one person in Leicester who made Leicester *home* for her. And Newland was Eve's home, not hers. She took a couple more bites of her sandwich, only to push it aside. The thought of a homeless heart sounded like the saddest thing in the world and made her feel sick.

Eve looked at Roxanne's half-eaten lunch. "You okay, Rox?"

"Uh-huh."

"I mean, really okay? I know we had a quick chat Friday, but we haven't had a chance until now for a proper catch-up."

"Me? Never better. Ducking and diving. You know."

Eve nodded. "And work's okay?"

Roxanne shrugged. "Yep, busy as usual."

"And everyone at The Brewer's, are they all good? Any pink paint casualties?"

"Numerous."

Eve laughed. "And any new hottie on the scene who's caught your eye?"

Roxanne's chest squeezed against her lungs. "How...how do you mean?" She slugged down the last of her beer.

"Don't look so worried—it was just a casual question." Eve poked teasingly at Roxanne's leg. "After all, there's normally someone you're—"

"*Entertaining?*"

"Oh my God, you're not cross with me about our Alice chat earlier. Are you? I didn't mean to offend you. And I really wasn't getting at you when I mentioned the Alice flirting thing."

"It made me feel like you don't trust me."

"*No.* I trust you implicitly. You know that."

Roxanne shrugged. "I thought I did."

"I'm so sorry. That's not what I intended. I just feel a bit protective of Alice. That's all."

"Why? She's an *adult*, Evie. If anyone can take care of herself, it's Alice."

"Maybe."

"And, in any case, you're talking as if Alice needs protecting because she's developed feelings for me. Why would you think that?" Roxanne held her breath. What would Eve say?

"Funnily enough, it was something you said about her not taking her eyes off you Saturday lunchtime."

"Oh, come on."

"I then kept noticing that she literally can't seem to take her eyes off you. Not to mention, she often visibly blushes when you speak to her."

"That doesn't mean anything."

"Her eyes light up when you enter a room."

Roxanne thought her chest might burst. *Do they?*

"I can't believe you haven't noticed."

Roxanne said, "Nope." She *had* noticed but had questioned every reaction in Alice because she couldn't quite believe it could be that she was feeling the same as her. "Really, I doubt you've got anything to worry about. I'm sure Alice knows the score, and she certainly knows I'm going home Wednesday."

"Alice knows the score? Are you saying she knows you don't do serious?"

"Yes. But that doesn't mean I *can't* do serious."

"I never said you couldn't."

"You laughed when I said it could be Alice who hurts me."

"I didn't mean…Look, you have to agree, you have tended in the past to, well, not settle on anyone in a particular."

"But that doesn't mean I'm fixed by my past. What if I want to do things differently? What if I want to try to change?"

Eve placed a tender hand on Roxanne's arm. "Then that's your right."

"Exactly."

"It's just…" Eve removed her hand.

"Just what?"

"Okay, I'm just going to say it. It's going to sound worse than I mean."

"Yeah, then don't say it."

Eve scrunched her eyes shut and blurted, "I'm not super keen on you practicing changing on Alice." She opened one eye. "I'm sorry."

"What makes you think I'd be *practicing* on her? And, be honest now, is this because you think I'm not good enough for her?"

Eve shook her head vehemently. "*No.* She'd be lucky to have you. Anyone would. But relationships are hard. They don't always work out, do they? And long distance relationships are even harder. I knew I had to move here if Moira and I were to have a chance. You see, my worry is, what happens if it ends badly? Alice isn't just anyone. She isn't some girl you met at The Brewer's—"

"*No*, I know she's not." Hold on, was this on Eve's mind when she made that postcard comment to Alice? Was she giving Alice the heads-up? Warning her off, even then?

"Rox, if Alice ends up getting hurt, it is inevitable that Moira and I will get mixed up in the fallout. Moira will defend Alice and I—"

"Will defend me. Right?"

"It's not as simple as that."

"Hold on, I always defend you. I always have. When Moira was messing with your head, who stepped in and stuck up for you? Tell me that?"

"It's not the same thing."

"Isn't it? I'm meant to be your best friend in the whole wide world, and you don't seem to care that if Alice gets hurt, then I'd be hurting too."

"That's not fair. Of course I'd care. I'd be heartbroken for you. But they're my family—"

"And I'm not?" Roxanne stared at her beer. Had she been shot at point-blank range, it would have hurt less. She could swear that her heart was bleeding out inside her chest.

"I didn't say that. Look at me. Rox."

Looking at Eve was the last thing she wanted to do. She begrudgingly looked up.

"I love two people in the world more than anything. One is my partner, and one is my best friend. There is *nothing* I wouldn't do for either of them. But Alice is Moira's stepdaughter, and understandably and rightly I feel responsible for her. The simple truth is I am Moira's. She's my *one*. What hurts or worries Moira hurts and worries me. She's my everything."

"But wait a minute, you're assuming Moira would get involved. Didn't you say she makes a point of not commenting on Alice's personal life?"

"She may not comment, but it doesn't mean she doesn't care."

What could Roxanne say to that? Of course Moira would defend Alice, and Eve would support Moira. Who would be there for her?

Roxanne cleared her throat. "Anyway, this is a pointless conversation because there is nothing between Alice and me. Nothing. She thinks I'm a wee eejit, in fact."

"Okay." Eve took a deep breath. "Then please finish your sandwich—you're worrying me."

Roxanne shoved the remaining bite of her sandwich in whole. "Happy?"

"I am if you are."

"Like I said, I'm never better. Let's have more beer." Roxanne stood and made for the kitchen. She could tell Eve was still looking at her. She'd been right earlier, then, hadn't she, when she'd sensed that kissing Alice would be a perilous thing to do. And that if something happened between her and Alice, then she risked so much, including losing Eve. That it was Alice *or* Eve. One thing was certain—she had an awful feeling that her heart was sure to break either way.

Chapter Eleven

Roxanne sat on the edge of the bath, flicking wet from her fingers into the foam. The bath she had drawn soon after Eve left had taken an age to fill. But, at last, it was ready. She scrambled out of her clothes and climbed in. She slid down under the water until it lapped at her ears and tickled at her chin. The taste of salty tears mingled with the bathwater, and for the first time in years, she began to cry.

Roxanne's emotionally charged conversation with Eve about Alice seemed to have shaken them both. They had done their best to rally by drinking more beer and chatting about everyday stuff. Eve described her work at the library, and how she had found the new responsibilities that had come with her promotion at first daunting, but she was now finding her feet. Her colleagues were just lovely, and maybe Roxanne could meet them when she was next up. And Roxanne chatted about the redecoration debacle at The Brewer's and the changes Eve would notice to the city in general when she next visited. But somehow, despite their best efforts, an atmosphere hung heavy about them. It was like something had broken or had been lost. It was simply awful.

Eve had arrived at the croft from her test so full of excitement, and just an hour or so later, she had excused herself early to return to Moira wearing an expression that looked like she might cry.

Was Eve crying just like her now? Roxanne sank even deeper into the bath. Tears always embarrassed her. From a young age she'd determined that tears got you nowhere, and she'd resolved to be emotionally resilient and self-sufficient. But hearing Eve say, *They're my family*, and even though she had quickly said that she hadn't meant that Roxanne wasn't, it had nonetheless managed to puncture the walls of Roxanne's resilience and left her wounded and overwhelmed.

Her time in the bath passed with her trying not to think—or for that matter *feel*—and soon her hands were crinkled and her water lukewarm. When she eventually rallied to get out of the bath and dry herself and then dress to return to the sitting room, she couldn't have been more relieved to hear Alice's humming floating through from the kitchen.

Roxanne folded her arms and leaned on the kitchen door frame. "Hey. I was just taking a bath. I didn't hear you come in. You're back early."

Alice's fingers were caked in dough and a smudge of flour dust marked her right cheek. Her face was a picture of concentration as she held a rolling pin over a pie dish.

"Hey. Just one moment—tricky bit." Alice unfurled a square of pastry from the pin to rest over the pie contents. She pinched the edges of the pastry and then made a slit for the tip of a pie funnel to poke through. She puffed out a ball of breath which caused her fringe to ruffle. "I'm always pleased to get that bit done." Alice brushed her hands free of dough and glanced up at Roxanne and smiled. "Given all of the excitement last night, Moira suggested I head home early."

"That's sounds fair enough."

Alice brushed a wash of egg over the pastry top. "I don't feel too tired after last night, do you?" Alice looked up again at Roxanne, and this time she seemed to study her more closely. "Actually, don't take this the wrong way, but you don't look so great. You okay?"

Roxanne gestured to the pastry heaven in progress. "Who wouldn't feel unwell at the sight of a homemade..."

"Roasted sweet potato and feta."

"...pie literally being made in front of you that you can't eat because you won't be here for tea."

"Ah, I see." Alice smiled. "In that case, you'll be relieved to hear that I have news on that front."

"Please tell me that news involves me eating that pie."

"Yep. Eve and Moira are staying with Angus and Elizabeth tonight."

Roxanne stood up straight. "Really?"

"Yep. When Moira arrived at the centre, she asked me if I would mind having you for another night as she was worried by how she'd found Elizabeth when she dropped off their lunch."

"Has Elizabeth's condition deteriorated since this morning?"

"I don't think so. Moira just said she looked tired. I tried to reassure her that Elizabeth had not long been with us at the centre and was all right. It didn't seem to help."

"It's understandable that she's worried. Do you know if Elizabeth had a chance to update Moira with our plan? I mentioned it to Eve, and she was pleased."

Alice shook her head. "Elizabeth couldn't say anything because Angus was there. So I updated her. She was really grateful, as we all are. You're our hero."

Alice's comment should have made Roxanne's heart surge with pride, but instead it hurt. She certainly didn't feel like anyone's hero.

Alice threw a piece of pastry at Roxanne. "It's a compliment."

"Huh? I know." Roxanne mimed pulling open her shirt front. "Under this shirt—massive *S*."

"For Superwoman?"

"Superhungry. How long does that pie take?"

Alice laughed. "Well, if I put the oven on now, like so, once it goes in, half an hour maybe."

"I'm counting the minutes. Thanks for having me with you again. And for the pie."

"Mainly for the pie, right?"

"I didn't like to say."

Alice chuckled. "And we have Eve to thank for"—Alice reached into the fridge and pulled out the Prosecco—"refreshments. She was so sweet and kept saying thank you to me. I told her I wasn't the one who passed the test."

"Did she say anything about me staying with you again?"

"Eve? No. Actually, she was really quite subdued. And particularly when she first arrived at the centre, Moira was surprised to see her. I think she thought you two would be celebrating all afternoon. So did I, to be honest."

"We did, good times, we had beers and sandwiches." The last thing she wanted was to rehash what happened. And she couldn't imagine Alice would be delighted to hear that she was the topic of conversation.

Alice gave a sceptical, "Oh, good. Here, open this, Superhungry." Alice pushed the bottle into Roxanne's chest. "I'll grab some glasses. Oh, and speaking of Eve, that reminds me…" Alice reached up to the top shelf of her cupboard, stretching to the back to reach the wine flutes.

Roxanne gripped the bottle, cold against her. Before she realized she was staring, she was staring. She stood transfixed by the sight of Alice's firm and shapely behind with the slight suggestion of an underwear line hinting at her body beneath.

"She told me to tell you sorry about The Gunsmith and that she would call for you for your Loch Ness trip tomorrow around half past nine. Fingers crossed, eh, that she comes with news that Elizabeth has been successful in getting an appointment for the afternoon."

The sobering mention of Angus's appointment brought Roxanne back from soft denim and warm skin to the coldness of the bottle, wet in her arms. As for The Gunsmith, she hadn't given it a thought. "Okay. Roger that."

Alice closed the cupboard and rested two flutes on the counter. "Right, let me get this pie in the oven." She opened the oven door and dug her hands into oven gloves. She then slipped the pie onto the middle oven shelf before closing the door again with a push of her hip. "So, we have thirty minutes before pie lift-off." Without missing a beat, she deftly dropped the oven gloves over Roxanne's head. The glove's pads rested like dog ears at the sides of her face.

Roxanne curled her lip and growled.

Alice pulled the pads together, cradling them under Roxanne's chin. "Very scary. And unless you're deliberately heating that wine up, how about opening it and pouring us some." She tugged off the oven gloves and slapped Roxanne on the shoulder with them before dropping them on the counter next to the oven. "See you in the sitting room. I'll put on some music."

Roxanne released the bottle and rested it next to the glasses. A smile broke at her lips. There was no doubt she'd met her match in Alice. And she simply loved it.

She popped the wine deliberately, sending the cork into the sitting room, then filled the glasses to the brim. She took a massive glug from one and refilled it before joining Alice on the sofa.

"So, cheers!" Roxanne passed Alice her wine and raised her glass in the air.

"Cheers! And well done, Eve."

"Yep." Tears surprised and forced their way, unwanted, to sting her eyes. "Sorry, it's a bit fizzy."

"You can tell me to mind my own business—"

"Mind your own business."

"But it doesn't take a genius to work out that something might have happened between you and Eve. I'm pretty sure I was also let off early by Moira so she could ask Eve in private if everything was okay."

"It's fine. We're fine." Roxanne took a large mouthful of wine. "The music's nice. The singer's got a great voice." The soft and yet strong tone of the woman's voice blended in a haunting harmony with the bellowed breaths of an accordion. There was something visceral and earthy about it. It felt like it was of this place, for it was wild and on the edge.

Alice sat quietly with her glass pressed into her lap listening to the music. Roxanne hoped Alice would take the hint that came with a change of subject not to pursue the upset with Eve.

Alice tucked her legs under her. "It's my mum. The singer, that is."

"Your mum? Wow."

"She recorded it with The Bells a couple of years before I was born."

Could she say her mum's voice wasn't as good as Alice's? No, maybe not. Alice obviously wanted to talk about her mum. Once again Alice was trusting her, and Roxanne wasn't about to blow it by saying something foolish. She didn't want to be the usual fool. For the first time she wanted to be more than herself. Better. Worthy of someone like Alice.

"She was still with Moira then." A shadow of sadness passed over Alice's face. "I used to think that if I hadn't been born, they'd still be together." Alice shrugged.

"Please tell me you don't still think that. Because, frankly, if they were meant to be together or, rather, *wanted* to be together, my guess is nothing would have stopped them. That's how it works. I'm older than you, so I know these things." She didn't, but her hunch sounded right.

Alice smiled. "You're Eve's age, right?"

Roxanne nodded. "Brink of retirement."

Alice laughed. "I don't think that any more, by the way. Moira set me straight."

"Good for Moira. And for what it's worth, guessing what might have happened in life or what could have been tends to hurt us. And dwelling on the past, let's just say I'm not a fan." Roxanne pushed away crowding thoughts of how her past had led to such a lonely place. "And let's not forget you wouldn't be here. And that would be"—she wanted to say *unthinkable*, but if she said that, she might as well say she loved her—"boring."

Alice frowned a little. "Boring? It's good to know I'm entertaining."

"Very."

"Talking of entertaining, I've got the cassette tape and tour brochure that go with this single. Would you like to see them?"

"Sure. And I'll refill our glasses." Roxanne went to the fridge, and when she returned to the sitting room she found Alice bent by the side of the sofa, pulling forward the box the contents of which Roxanne had already had a sneak preview of.

Resting on her knees, Alice lifted the lid, along with the pamphlets stacked on top of it, away from the box to rest on the floor.

"When my dad moved out, he gave me a beat-up box of my mum's things that he'd kept from the days of The Bells. I was going to store it as my dad had done, but then Moira encouraged me not to put it away and to keep it out. She said that my mum would want me to have her things around me."

"Wise words."

"So I treated myself to this prettier box, so I can keep her things at hand. Ah, here's the tour brochure." Alice tenderly stroked the brochure's cover, which displayed the image of her mum and bandmates, standing together and smiling. An image of the Highlands had been Photoshopped behind them as a backdrop. It spoke of Scotland, and of tradition, and of Alice's world, so foreign to Roxanne. Alice held up the brochure to show her.

It felt like Alice was showing her some of the most precious things she could show her. "Cool. It's amazing you have all this."

"I know. I treasure them." Alice then gently replaced the brochure next to the group snap, which included Moira. "Oh, cassette tape."

"Retro. I remember Eve's dad winding the shiny black ribbon back into place on one of his cassettes and trying not to lose his temper or swear in front of us when it tangled beyond help."

Alice smiled broadly. "I know what you mean. Thankfully, my dad has most songs converted into digital format, so I don't have to risk playing it."

"Smart."

"Yeah."

"You must miss him."

Alice nodded and stared at the brochure cover again. "That's him." Alice pointed at the bandmate at Iris's side. He had his arms folded, and another band member had his arm around him. "And that's Hamish draped over him. Dad said he drank a bit too much but was one of the best folk guitarists out there."

"Well, they both look very groovy. Loving their hair."

"Dad's hair's really short now and receding at the front. You wouldn't recognize him."

"Do you see him regularly?"

"No. He lives with his new girlfriend on the borders. He works away a lot as well. He's a consultant for the—now let me get this right—the Agriculture and Rural Delivery Directorate, or something like that. We FaceTime now and then. But it's not the same."

"So he's not a musician any more?"

"Not professionally, no."

"You weren't tempted to go with him when he left here? See the world, maybe?"

Alice shook her head. "I was in the middle of my college course. And in any case, as you know, I love it here. And I couldn't leave Moira or Angus and Elizabeth." Alice took a sip of her wine. Her attention strayed to the group snap with Moira with her arm around Iris. "Even though for those first few months after he left I was upset with Moira, it never crossed my mind to leave. I love her."

"And it couldn't be more obvious how much she loves you. Her face bursts with pride when she looks at you, Alice."

"I know. Moira and Angus and Elizabeth are all so protective of me, and particularly Moira. I can tell, even when she's trying to act nonchalant. I can feel her concern now and then, you know."

"Right." That's what Eve had said too, wasn't it.

"Moira and I went through this box together over a couple of months or so after I was given it. She didn't want to, but she did it for me. We took it steady, selecting just a couple of items at a time. Moira would get upset at certain things that seemed to prompt a particular memory." Alice stared intensely at Roxanne for a moment. It was like she was trying to gauge something. Was she asking herself if she could really trust her? After all, what Alice was sharing with her wasn't just about Alice. It was about everything and everyone who was important to her.

Alice then gently eased a black T-shirt from the box. "This one belonged to Moira. My mum gave it to her. She told me one evening that for many years she slept with it under her pillow, and that she would wear it at night particularly when she was missing her. I think… when she gave it to me she was letting my mum go a little." Alice's voice broke.

"Oh, Alice." Roxanne crouched down by her side and put an arm around her shoulders.

"I know now that she was opening her heart to Eve." Alice stared at the T-shirt. "She was moving on. It was a good thing."

"Maybe being open to love needs you to be brave and let go of stuff. Not that I know."

"Me neither."

They shared a smile that felt so much more than a smile, for it felt like understanding and intimate connection. It felt…dangerous.

Roxanne let her hand fall from Alice's shoulder, and she rearranged herself to rest on the floor with her back against the sofa.

Alice returned her focus to the memorabilia as she lifted a purple-covered notebook free. "My mum wrote songs and drafted them in these notebooks. There's one in this one called 'Highlander.' It's about Moira. It's quite intense. I won't read it to you."

"Fair enough." This would be the moment, wouldn't it, when she'd say something daft to ease the embarrassment. Not tonight. She wanted to be Alice's hero, not her fool. *Just let her speak.*

"I write songs."

"Okay."

"I'm working on one at the moment. I've called it 'To My Future Love.' I know it's a sentimental title." She glanced up at Roxanne and gave a curious smile. She was expecting a smart remark from her, wasn't she? "I wrote it at the end of this same book as my mum's song for Moira." Alice turned to a page marked by a gold-embossed green bookmark. "I could read you a few lines."

"Or sing it to me, maybe?"

Alice blushed. "No, I don't sing for people."

"But it's just you and me, if you don't count Elvis and co."

Alice shook her head. "I can't, sorry. It's not that I don't want to. I do. I'd love to sing for people but…"

"You don't have to explain."

"I'm not sure I know how to explain. You see…" Alice paused to close the notebook and to return the memorabilia back in its place, as if to protect her treasured memories once more. "When my mum died, the music stopped. Life stopped. The last time I sang for people was at her funeral, and the minute I opened my mouth to sing, everyone started crying. Moira started crying. My dad just wept and wept with his head in his hands. In that moment I vowed never to sing again for anyone. I was seven, and to this day I've not broken that vow." Alice hung her head. "I've never told anyone any of this before…"

"No?"

"No. Just you." Alice looked at Roxanne as so many girls had looked at her before with soft dreamy eyes that spoke of admiration and longing. But Alice wasn't any other girl, was she? Eve couldn't have made that clearer. She was Moira Burns's Alice. Eve's Alice.

The timer rang out from the kitchen.

"I'll get the pie." Roxanne scrambled to her feet. Her heart raced in her chest. She wanted to run away, and she didn't want to run in equal measure. She was so confused. She wanted to leave and to stay, and she wanted to go home and yet make her home right here. *What's wrong with you? Get a grip.*

"Thanks." Alice's knuckles had turned white from clutching her glass. Did she feel like she was losing her grip too?

"Won't be a mo." Roxanne busied herself fetching the pie from the oven. She returned in a blink, holding two forks, two napkins, and the pie dish half wrapped in the oven gloves.

Alice shook her head and smiled. "I do own plates."

"Yeah, but let's face it, not a dishwasher."

Roxanne led the way by plunging her fork into the steaming pastry and blowing the mouthful all the way to her lips. "Ow. It's hot."

Alice shook her head. "Eejit."

The sweet yet savoury, sticky yet smooth, crisp yet soft, delicious beyond words pie made Roxanne want to weep once more. It wasn't food. It was ecstasy. "Oh my God, Alice."

Alice laughed and matched Roxanne's emotional smile with her own. "That good, eh?"

"I'm honestly not just saying this, but I don't think I've tasted anything more—"

Alice stole the words from her lips with the press of her mouth against Roxanne's. If the pie was ecstasy, then the feel of Alice's mouth tenderly kissing hers was quite simply heaven.

Roxanne let her fork fall to her lap and kissed Alice in turn. She placed her palms lightly against Alice's hot cheeks. Their kisses brought their mouths ever closer into each other with every surge deeper and with each brief release for a moment's breath. This was it. No more running away. Her homeless heart was home.

It was all kinds of agony when Alice eased herself away. "We're literally covered in pie."

"What?"

Alice smiled with such warmth that it felt like it would be impossible to ever be cold again. She brushed lightly at Roxanne's shirt, and her fingers caressed at her collar and the skin at her neck.

"You've gone all serious on me." With that, Alice stood and held out her hand to Roxanne. "Come upstairs?"

"Yes." Her phone beeped in her pocket as she steadied herself to her feet. "I'm sure it's nothing. Let's go."

"If that was your phone, I better check mine."

Roxanne held onto Alice's sleeve. "Leave it."

"Just one sec."

Roxanne reluctantly let go, and Alice went to her gilet hanging on the hook by the door.

Oh for God's sake. "I'll check mine." Roxanne roughly pulled her phone free from her pocket. It was a message from Eve. *Hey. Sorry about earlier. I hate the thought that I upset you. I know you'd never hurt Alice. Talk more tomorrow? X*

Alice tossed her phone onto the sofa. "No messages for me. Is that Eve?"

Roxanne nodded. Tears burned in her eyes. She held her hand over her face. Alice moved to her and wrapped her arms around her.

"What is it?" Alice said. "What did Eve want? Is there something wrong?"

"I can't, Alice." Roxanne guided Alice free of her body and held her softly by her arms.

"You can't what? I don't understand."

"You're everything I want—"

"And I want you too—"

"And everything I can't have."

Alice's cheeks blanched and she swallowed several times. "Why not?"

"I risk losing Eve for sure. She seems certain I will hurt you, and I won't risk hurting you."

"Is that what her text said? You don't know that."

"I *do*. Because I always do. I hurt people."

"You're just afraid."

She was. She'd never felt so frightened. "I'll clear up if you want to go upstairs. We should call it a night."

"I don't want to."

"Please, Alice. For your own sake."

"But…" Alice's words seemed to fail her. She looked utterly lost and confused as evident hurt muddled with the tears in her eyes as she turned and made her way upstairs.

Heartbreak ripped through Roxanne at the sound of Alice's bedroom door closing. How could she do such a stupid thing and return her kiss? Why had she ignored Eve's plea and casually played with Alice's feelings?

Eve would find out eventually, wouldn't she? And then that would be that. How could life change so slowly you didn't notice it, and yet so quickly that it brutally and shockingly stole the beat from your heart.

❖

If Alice had managed to get any sleep, it didn't feel like it. Why did she think it was okay to kiss Roxanne? What madness had possessed her? She was such a fool. A fool who'd ruined everything. And if that wasn't enough, she had the nerve to call Roxanne afraid when it must have taken so much courage and so much willpower not to follow her upstairs. She could tell by how Roxanne kissed her just how much she wanted her, for her lips had pressed against hers with so much passion and with so much need. God, how much she needed her too. How much she wanted her right now.

The sound of a phone alarm ringing drew her ear to the sitting room. She held her breath as Roxanne groaned. The alarm stopped. Had Roxanne managed to get any sleep? Should she make her a tea?

She pulled on her clothes and ruffled her hair roughly into place. She made her way downstairs. The bedding on the sofa was tangled but empty. The kettle began to boil in the kitchen.

"Hey."

Roxanne turned round. She was standing at the kitchen counter dressed in just her T-shirt and underwear. She had the kind of body that made you want to hold her and feel her close. Roxanne stirred the tea in two mugs that rested in front of her. "Hey. I figured you'd need a brew too."

"Yes, thanks."

They said in unison. "I'm sorry."

Roxanne gave a tired smile. "Wanna join me in bed as we come to?"

That was the last thing she wanted. How could she sit under the covers with Roxanne and not touch her or kiss her? She wanted to slip her hands underneath Roxanne's T-shirt and caress her breasts before sliding her underwear over her hips. She didn't want to drink tea with her like best friends.

"You know I do." Perhaps that came out a little too earnestly.

"I know."

"But I'm not sure I trust myself to be in bed with you."

"I get that." Roxanne led the way and climbed under her covers. She patted at the bottom of the bed. Alice settled herself to sit cross-legged in the dip left by Roxanne's palm. Roxanne blew nonchalantly over her tea. "So, you're gay then, Campbell?"

Roxanne's direct question caught her breath. After last night, she couldn't really tell her that it was private. "Yes."

"So that Milly girl was your girlfriend?"

Milly? What? "I thought maybe we were going to talk about us." Or was there no us? Roxanne looked down. If she was looking for the answer it was right there in Roxanne's silence. She cleared her throat. The last thing either of them needed was her tears. "Yes, Milly was my girlfriend. How do you know about her? Has Eve said something?"

"Not much. Just that you had a best friend who then suddenly wasn't around. It made Eve wonder."

"Just Eve? Does Moira know?" Fear pressed into Alice's stomach. What would Moira think?

"Does it matter if she does?"

"I was so awful to her when she came out to me. I couldn't have made her feel worse about Eve. I made her cry, Rox." Alice's throat thickened. She swallowed and swallowed again to free her words. "I hate myself for how I treated her. I was so unkind that to expect her to understand about me, given my terrible behaviour, is asking too much. I don't deserve for her to be okay with it."

"She *will* be okay with it, though. And you said that you've apologized to her and to Eve many times. And surely Moira more than anyone will understand. And there is another way of looking at it."

"How can there be? How can I look her in the eye ever again?"

"Newsflash, let's assume she's guessed already, so then you've been looking her in the eye for ages. She'll have likely been waiting for you to say something to her. She's not going to bring it up because *you* haven't. And let's face it, this is Moira. And, like I said, there is a different way to see things. Because my take on it, for what it's worth, is given how closeted Moira was with you, how she can expect you to feel open about your sexuality is beyond me. Alice, she kept from you how much she loved your mum. That's not a small thing."

"I hadn't thought of it like that."

Roxanne gave a deep sigh. "It's messed up, isn't it, how we inherit the traits of our parents, or at least how much their behaviour and their choices influence us? You need to keep in mind that Moira's sensitivities are Moira's, so don't let them shape who you are. Being too private and risking a relationship because of it, that's just how Moira behaved with Eve. Except, as we know, Eve wasn't that easy to dump." They shared a smile. Roxanne leaned forward and placed her hand lightly on Alice's knee. "From what I've seen here, everyone without exception has welcomed Eve. They couldn't be happier for Moira. It seems to me that you're in a good place to be you."

Roxanne, her wee eejit, was so wise, wasn't she? Her comforting words were soothing Alice's confused heart. "I can see that," Alice said. "And there've been times I thought I might say something. And particularly with my therapist, I came so close to speaking about it. But I've kept my feelings to myself for so long that I honestly don't know how to share them."

"You couldn't talk to Milly?"

Alice shook her head. "Milly and I, well, we just sort of happened. She wanted us to talk about it. Looking back, I just closed down on her. It's ridiculous isn't it. I'm ridiculous."

"No. You're human. We're all ridiculous, Alice."

Alice laughed. "I love your take on things. I meant what I said last night about you being the first person I've properly shared stuff with." Alice's heart caught and ached. "And look what's happened. I've ruined everything." Alice stood up. "I'm going to make you late for Eve. It's half-past eight already."

Roxanne reached for Alice's wrist. "What happened, actually, was the most awesome kiss I've ever had. Believe me when I tell you I've had a few. I wouldn't have missed that kiss for the world."

You wouldn't? "Really? Me too. I lay awake all night willing you to come to me."

"I lay awake all night trying not to. It was fucking agony."

Alice nodded. "I hurt all over."

"I'm sorry, really I am." Roxanne climbed out of bed and gathered her clothes in her arms.

"What are we going to do?"

"You'll go to work. I'll go on the boat trip with Eve, and then we'll team up at lunchtime to help Elizabeth and Angus."

"As if nothing has happened?"

Roxanne looked down. "It's not what I want."

"So you know what you want?"

"Yes. And I can't have it." And with that, and without another word, Roxanne made for the bathroom.

By the time Eve arrived, bang on half-past nine, Roxanne was dressed in her hoodie and jeans. The sofa was once more a sofa, and Roxanne and Alice were, for appearances' sake at least, once more roommates.

"You okay, Alice?" Eve was standing in the centre of the sitting room, poised to leave. Unnervingly, this didn't seem to stop her from looking quizzically at Alice.

What? How? "I'm fine. A little hungover maybe." Alice rubbed at her head. "Thanks for the wine."

"My pleasure." Eve zipped her jacket up. "I wasn't sure what to wear today. With being out on the water and everything." Eve was dressed in a grey V-neck jumper and blue walking trousers. She wore a lightweight black rain jacket on top, and a pair of binoculars dangled from her neck.

"You look great. Perfect, in fact." Alice pulled on her coat. "And were Elizabeth and Angus okay this morning?"

"Yes, given everything, they seemed fine. A little quiet but no more than that."

It had been a relief that Eve and Moira had stayed the night with them. Alice never really thought of herself as on-call, but then she never gave caring for them a thought. They were so much part of her life, and that's how she liked it. Alice then asked, "And did Elizabeth manage to get an appointment for this afternoon?"

"Yes, she did. Three thirty. We agreed that Moira and I would give you some space for the chat. So I'll drop you off, Rox, with the McAlisters after our boat trip."

A sleepy Roxanne said, "Sure thing."

Alice added, "And I'll head over to them when you arrive back at the centre, then."

"Cool, sounds like a plan." Eve looked at Roxanne. "Are you hungover too, bugalugs?"

"Me? Nope. In fact, ahoy me hearties, all ready for the open waters."

Eve laughed. "You do look a bit pale, though. Some fresh air might do you good, for I've seen you look brighter after a hectic night shift." Eve sounded apologetic as she added, "You would say if you weren't okay, wouldn't you. I noticed that you didn't reply to my text."

"Oh. Right. Sorry about the text. I thought I had replied." Roxanne pulled up the hood of her top. "Anyway, let's go, Eddison. I've a date with a dinosaur."

Alice watched Eve hesitate as she stared for a moment at Roxanne. What was Eve thinking?

Alice gestured to the door. "Come on, I'll walk you both out."

She hoped Roxanne would turn to say goodbye, but instead she carried on out the door with her gaze resolutely fixed to the ground. Either Roxanne didn't care or cared too much, but either way it hurt.

Eve shouted after Roxanne from the doorstep, "It's the Fiesta, and it's open." Roxanne climbed into the passenger seat. She had something of the sulking teenager about her. Eve turned back to Alice. "It's really kind of Angus to lend me his car again. I'll return it to them when I drop Rox off at lunchtime." Eve then stared back at the Fiesta with a decidedly anxious expression. "It's my first solo trip. I'm a bit nervous."

"You'll be fine. In any case, you've got Rox with you."

"Yes, that's why I'm a bit nervous."

They both laughed.

"Thanks again for having her for another night. I know it was asking a lot of you, and I'm really grateful."

"No worries at all."

"Well, at least you've got your place back now. If it's okay with you, we'll collect her rucksack later this afternoon just before we head back to the city. I promise I'll take her home with me tonight."

Alice folded her arms in the hope that it would ease the crushing ache in her chest. "Great. That's a relief."

Eve laughed. "I bet." She squeezed Alice's arm. "This afternoon will be all right, I promise. For all her bluff and bluster, Roxanne will look after them."

"I know."

"Good. Bye then. See you later."

Alice watched Eve join Roxanne. Roxanne appeared to be staring at her phone. Eve started the engine and reversed with the concentrated care of a new driver.

Alice pulled her door closed. She paused to take one last look at the Fiesta being gingerly manoeuvred by Eve so that it faced the road out of Newland. *Please look up Roxanne. Please look up.*

As if she had willed it, Roxanne looked across at her. At the same time, Alice's phone bleeped. Roxanne raised her hand, and Alice's heart surged. She waved back. And then with a slow crunch of tyres on gravel, Eve eased them on their way.

Alice checked her phone. A text from Wee Eejit. Alice opened Roxanne's message, and it took all of her might not to cry when she read, *Best pie ever. Thank you, roomie x*

Alice couldn't help but wonder what Eve had said in her text last night that changed everything in an instant. In a matter of seconds, Roxanne went from wanting to spend the night with her to being freaked out by the thought that she might hurt her. And why did she think she would lose Eve? Unless that's what Eve had said to her? It just didn't seem like Eve at all. Surely Eve would want Roxanne to find someone as she had done. And why couldn't that someone be her?

Alice gripped her hand into a tight fist. Why was it so hard for everyone to get that, above all, all she wanted was love and not protection. Just love.

Alice stared down at her phone. Roxanne's love.

Chapter Twelve

Eve leaned her elbows against the boat's railings. "I'm regretting lending you those binoculars, for I've barely been able to squeeze two words out of you since we left the quayside." She tugged at Roxanne's hood. "Rox?"

"Hmm?" Roxanne lowered the binoculars to just under her chin. If Nessie was here she would find it. And, frankly, if Nessie spotting meant not talking, then that suited her just fine. And with the prospect of this afternoon with Angus, some quiet time beforehand seemed a good idea. And, in any case, surely Eve had said all she wanted to say yesterday afternoon.

Eve chuckled. "You've got red rims round your eyes. Don't press them so tightly against your face. It's not going to improve your chances of seeing Nessie."

"It's really quite choppy out on the water, isn't it? Twice I thought aha, hump, but it was just a bobbing seagull." Roxanne replaced the binoculars to her eyes.

"Yeah, the water's a bit more treacherous than it looks. The wind funnels and whips up the water, which makes it difficult for boats. It looks idyllic with its trees and farmland sweeping down to its shores, but in truth it's quite wild and untamed. Which pretty much sums up the Highlands. Are you listening at all?"

"Wild and untamed…"

"Oh wait, what's that at the far shore?"

"Where?"

Eve slipped a toy Nessie in front of the binoculars' lenses and made a bobbing motion.

"You've left the tag on." A smile broke free from Roxanne's lips as she let the binoculars swing at her chest.

Eve smiled back. "You can keep it. Holiday memento."

"Oh, thanks." Roxanne made a roar. It took her straight back to yesterday's lesson and to the kids laughing and to Alice. *Alice.*

Eve cleared her throat. "I just want to say I'm sorry if I upset you yesterday. I really didn't mean to."

Roxanne shrugged. "Don't worry about it." She then quickly returned the binoculars to her face.

"But I do worry. I worry about you."

She was probably just tired, but Roxanne had an awful feeling that if Eve kept asking if she was okay or saying that she was worried about her, it would all come out. How lonely Roxanne felt at times. How much she was missing Eve. And, moreover, how much Alice really meant to her. She had to keep it in, didn't she?

The boat's recorded guided tour burst into action with a piercing squeal, and a monotone nasal voice informed passengers that they were approaching Urquhart Castle, should they wish to disembark.

"Do we get off here?" Roxanne asked, as the stone ruins of a medieval tower perched on the edge of the loch came into view. "Maybe they have a visitor restaurant."

"Well, I wasn't sure what we'd be up for, so I just bought the boat ride. But we can get off if you like and change our ticket. It is interesting."

"I guess we could get an ice cream."

"The history is interesting, not the cafe." Eve pulled at Roxanne's sleeve, forcing her to drop the binoculars. "It's clear you're not really in the mood. So there's not much point, is there?"

Roxanne shrugged. "Another time."

Eve nodded. "Fair enough. So I was thinking maybe we could head over to The Gunsmith tonight. Make up for not going out last night?"

"Okay. Maybe Alice could come too?" Her words were out before she could take them back.

Eve raised her eyebrows. "Alice?"

The boat jolted into place at the castle's jetty, and people pushed past them to disembark.

"Or not, obviously."

"It's fine. There's no problem if you want Alice to come."

"I didn't say I *want* her to come. Just that she could come."

Eve frowned. "Okay. Tell you what, why don't I get us an on-board coffee?"

"Great idea. Thanks."

"Oh, and just to be clear, I won't believe you if you say you've seen Nessie while I'm gone."

Roxanne laughed. "Damn."

Eve turned and headed downstairs to the bar on the deck below.

It felt so good to laugh with Eve and be silly with her and to just be *them* once more.

The boat pushed off from the jetty with a diesel engulfed shudder to make its return journey back to the quayside where they began.

Eve re-emerged from below deck, carrying two coffees and two KitKats. "Here."

Roxanne pulled down her hood. "Thanks."

Eve broke her KitKat in two. "Your hair's all flat."

Roxanne pinched at her hair, which flopped rather than spiked at her touch.

"Usually, when your hair's droopy, you're either ill or sad."

Roxanne gave a two-finger gesture with her KitKat fingers in reply.

Eve giggled, and then her face straightened to a serious expression. "I spoke to Moira last night."

Roxanne sipped gingerly at her hot coffee. "Okay." Where was this going?

"When I left you, I just felt awful. I knew I'd hurt you with our conversation about Alice."

"Eve, really…"

"I know, but please just let me say this. Obviously, Moira could tell I was upset about something. And I don't like keeping things from her. So I told her."

"You told her?"

Eve shook her head. "Just that I had asked you to take care with Alice. And before you say anything, I know nothing's happened between you, and I told Moira that."

"I kissed her."

Eve double blinked. "You kissed her?"

"It was just a kiss. Nothing more. And, actually, Alice kissed me, and I kissed her back. It was awesome. She's awesome. I really like her, Eve. More than I've liked anyone before."

Eve rested her coffee and KitKat next to her. "I just need a minute to…"

Roxanne rested her hand on Eve's back. "You're my best friend,

Evie." Eve looked at Roxanne and nodded. "You're the one I always tell stuff to. And you're the one I want to tell *this* to. What's happening with Alice, I think it might be a big deal for me. And I want to share it with you. I miss you and I miss us."

Eve hugged Roxanne tight. "I miss us too."

Speaking into Eve's neck, Roxanne said, "By wanting Alice I don't want to lose you."

Eve released Roxanne. "I don't understand. Why would you lose me?"

"Because you said if I chose Alice, then you would choose Moira and—"

"Wait. No. I was just trying to explain my worries about the potential hurt that might happen if things went wrong. That's all, I promise."

"So are you saying you'd be okay if Alice and I—"

Eve stuck her fingers in her ears. "I don't need the details."

They both gave a small giggle.

Eve looked Roxanne in the eyes. "Can I ask you something, though?"

"Sure."

"Why Alice? What makes her different to all the others?"

Could she say *everything*? "Well, she's kind and compassionate and smart, with bags of common sense. And she's funny and sharp-witted and feisty—I can't bloody well get away with anything."

Eve laughed. "True. You've certainly met your match."

"But most of all, maybe, she looks at me like no one else has ever done. As if she sees through the bullshit and…"

"Sees you?"

"Yes. And she still really seems to want me nonetheless. Go figure. And I know it's really, really, early days—"

Eve gave Roxanne's shoulder an affectionate nudge. "Four days. But then, to be fair, I knew pretty much straight away with Moira that this was something new and special."

"And I took the piss out of you and made you doubt your feelings. Sorry, I feel a right ignorant twit now."

Eve smiled. "Maybe just a twit."

Roxanne laughed and shook her head. "I just didn't think you could feel so strongly for someone so quickly." Roxanne pointed to her stomach. "Something in my gut tells me that it's not just because we're both lonely."

"You're lonely? You know, I feared you were. Why didn't you say something to me?"

"You had your new life."

Eve reached for Roxanne's hand and held it tight. "It doesn't mean my old life doesn't matter any more. That you don't matter any more."

Tears pushed and bullied in Roxanne's throat. Eve's eyes misted over at the same time.

"To be honest," Roxanne said, swallowing several times, "I didn't know what to think or do. So I just carried on as I was and pretended not to care about anything much or anyone in particular. For some time now, I've wanted to change. But until Alice, I'd never met anyone who's made that feel like a possibility. She makes me want to be better than I am, so that I stand the slimmest chance of being hers."

"I think it's quite a good chance. I don't get the impression she goes around kissing everyone."

They smiled together with such warmth, just as they had always done.

"No, me neither. She can be incredibly private. On that note, what did Moira say when you told her about our conversation?"

"Given that it was Alice we were talking about, she was remarkably matter-of-fact. She simply said for me to stop worrying so much, and for me to feel reassured that whatever happened it wouldn't affect us. She also said that Alice must make her own choices."

"That's very cool."

Eve's face went all melty. "She is. I think it was her way of saying I was overreacting and that I shouldn't feel insecure about her and me. And she's right. Now I feel like a twit. Sorry again that I hurt you."

"Two twits together, eh?"

"Defo."

The jetty came into sight, and the engine changed from a soft pumping to a disgruntled rumble.

"Okay. That's us." Eve stood and looked about her. "Give me your cup, and I'll find a bin."

Roxanne watched the hills of Newland loom up above them as they reached the quayside. She wanted to run to Alice to tell her that she wanted her and for them to start their future right now. But first there was Angus who needed her to be strong and to concentrate. And having said no to Alice, would she get a second chance to say yes? Would Alice's own fears make her change her mind? What would she do if Alice changed her mind?

They disembarked and were soon back in the car with Eve carefully going through the process of starting the engine.

"Eve. Wait a sec. Can I ask a favour?"

"Sure. Don't worry, I will take it steady up the hill."

"No, it's not that. I'm not sure how Alice will feel about me telling you."

"I won't say a word."

"So you won't tell Moira? It's just, I think it should come from Alice."

"Okay. I understand. And thanks again for helping with Angus this afternoon."

Roxanne took a deep breath. "I'll try my best."

"And thanks for telling me about Alice. For trusting me when I had let you down by making you think I didn't trust you."

"You never let me down, mate."

"Not even when I left? I know I hurt you by leaving." Cars started to circle the car park for a space ahead of the next trip.

Roxanne shrugged. "You found your one, and she just happened to be miles away."

"Yep. I need you to know that it hurt me too to leave you. Finding your one can—"

"Hurt?"

"Yes. You'll take care, won't you, of both yourself and Alice?"

Roxanne nodded. "I promise."

"Right, we need to go. Or we'll be late. Brace yourself for the hill."

It wasn't the hill Roxanne was bracing herself for. It was seeing the heartbreak of Angus and Elizabeth. For if ever there was proof that finding your one hurt, then it was them. For wasn't he her sweetheart, and her his beginning and his end.

Chapter Thirteen

When Alice arrived at the McAlisters' her heart was beating faster than a bird's. Her emotions were all over the place. On the one hand, she was excited to see Roxanne again and had willed the morning to end quickly. But on the other hand, she was fearful for what the afternoon would bring. For wasn't this the last time she might see Roxanne, and what would happen if they couldn't persuade Angus? But then she must trust Roxanne. She'd surprised her before.

She found Angus in the garden, pulling up the last of the winter's carrots.

"Hi, Angus, I hope you've saved me a pastie."

He looked up and beamed a smile at her. "Hello, young Alice. You'll have to ask the chef about that. I'm in the middle of showing Roxanne what a purple carrot looks like. Apparently, she thinks I have made it up."

Alice laughed. "Good for you. I'll see you inside."

Elizabeth stood up and then immediately relaxed when she saw it was Alice.

"Good timing. He's just finished his lunch. Although why he suddenly feels the urge to garden is beyond me. We've been terribly rude and eaten too. I've been fretting about time. Please have yours, though."

Alice rested her hand on her stomach. "On second thoughts, I couldn't eat a thing. As to Angus's gardening urge, I have it on good authority that there's a score to settle about carrots." Alice tilted her head at Roxanne.

"What?" Roxanne stood at Elizabeth's side, brushing flakes of pastry free from her jumper. "I just happened to say that carrots are orange and that he didn't honestly expect me to believe they were all the colours of the rainbow." Roxanne shrugged. "And then next thing we knew, he was pulling on his wellies."

The door burst open, and Angus strode up to them in a triumphant fashion. He waved a bunch of carrots, complete with their green tasselled fronds, in the air. "Hah." He rested them, soil and all, on the kitchen table and fanned them out to display their multicoloured shades of orange, purple, red, white, and golden. "So, what do you say to that?"

Roxanne puffed out her cheeks. "Are you sure you haven't had your felt-tip pens out, fella?"

It was impossible not to laugh. Was this part of a plan? Had Roxanne intended to relax the room and ease the mood? Or was she just being herself, for there was surely no one quite so warm and charismatic.

Alice's cheeks tingled when Roxanne glanced up at her and smiled.

Alice smiled back at her as she said, "I'm not sure who is encouraging who when it comes to you pair."

Angus's expression was full of impish delight. "Aye. And a bunch of carrots just like these helped me to woo my girl."

Roxanne's eyebrows rose. "Really?"

Elizabeth wafted away his comment with a wave of her hands. "Oh, Angus, please, I'm sure Alice and Roxanne don't want to hear such stories."

"I don't mind. Shall we? I think this calls for a comfy seat." Roxanne gestured to the sitting room and to the two armchairs by the fire. "I'm always keen to glean some top wooing tips from a pro."

Angus looked at Elizabeth as if to say *I told you so.*

"Tell you what"—Alice rested her hand on Angus's shoulder— "why don't we leave these two Casanovas to share stories. Did you mention you wanted my help to change the sheets in the spare room?" Alice nodded until the spark of understanding lit in Elizabeth's eyes.

"*Yes.* Thank you."

"Come on then." Alice ushered Elizabeth towards the hallway. They found a spot just out of sight but still within earshot. They sat perched on a wooden settle bench and all but held their breath as they listened. At what point would, or rather could, Roxanne find the moment to mention the GP?

"That's much comfier." Roxanne's confident and playful tone

drifting to them from the sitting room was reassuring in itself. If anyone could convince Angus it was her.

"So, I'm all ears," Roxanne said. There was a brief silence. "You were about to tell me about how those magnificent veggies won Elizabeth over."

Elizabeth looked at Alice. She whispered, "It's not going to work, is it? If he can't remember that?"

Alice shrugged.

"Ah, yes. Well, here's a story for you. We'd been friends for a little while, and I suspected she knew I liked her, but she'd been playing hard to get, you see."

"The temptress."

Angus laughed. "Exactly. But I was more than man enough to step up to the challenge."

"I don't doubt it."

"I needed an edge. Something the other boys didn't have."

"I like it."

"They kept sending her bunches of flowers, roses, you know."

"I do. That old trick."

"So one day, I got up early, beating the sun to its breeches, and I went to my vegetable patch. I pulled up the most magnificent bunch of carrots of every colour you have ever seen, and I tied them together in a red ribbon. I got on my bike, and I pedalled over the fields until I reached her family home. I was more than aware that her father owned a gun, mind."

"A gun? You took your life in your hands to win her love?"

"I did indeed. I threw a couple of well-aimed stones at her window. She opened it quick as, but I was quicker and managed to hide out of sight, leaving my bunch of carrots to glow underneath her window."

"No note?"

"No. I did this for two weeks until I'd dug up every carrot. And with empty hands and a full heart I returned to her window. I threw my stones as usual, but this time I knelt down on one knee and pressed my palm against my chest. She opened her window and said, *Angus McAlister, please, I beg of you, no more carrots*."

"So she knew it was you all along."

"Aye. I said, then will you accept the harvest sown from the seeds of our friendship, for I offer you this bounty of my love? Will you marry me, Elizabeth Fraser?"

Elizabeth lifted her apron to her eyes and dabbed softly. She'd been mouthing some of his words along with him. "He knelt in nettles, the daft fool."

Alice smiled and then placed her finger softly to her lips.

"And on our anniversary each year, I give her a bunch of carrots. She's just as cross to receive them now as then."

Roxanne laughed. "I think that honestly might be the most romantic story I've ever heard."

"She's my beginning and my end."

"And you are hers, fella. It is plain to see how much you love each other."

"There's nothing I wouldn't do for her."

"Then I know I can speak of something important with you, for it is something I have promised I would ask. And, what's more, I know you'd want me to ask it. Because it's for your girl, and only you can help with it."

"Of course, what is it?"

"I must be honest here and tell you that in order to help, you will likely need to be as brave as that day when you got on one knee. Even braver, maybe."

Alice reached out and held Elizabeth's hand.

"Please just tell me how I can help her."

"Well, Elizabeth has noticed that you've been finding things hard that at one time perhaps would have been no problem at all. You see, she's worried about you, Angus, to the point that it's taking its toll on her. And with my nurse's hat on, I'm worried about you both. We all are. I think it might be wise for you to go to the doctor and have a bit of a check-up."

"I'm not sure I understand, young lady. What *things*?"

Alice winced at the beginnings of the defensive tone in his voice that they had come to know so well.

"For some people, the world around them might in small ways begin to not feel quite right or as familiar as they'd like it to be, and that can make them feel stressed and anxious. Perhaps the detail of things might be a little harder to grasp and hold than before, and that often makes planning or completing tasks feel overwhelming or confusing even."

Roxanne paused at that point. Alice noted that Angus hadn't stopped her as he had stopped them so many times before when they'd tried to raise their concerns with him. But then they hadn't spoken so dispassionately and so calmly and clearly, had they. Was he recognizing what Roxanne was explaining? Was he properly listening to her?

With a gentle and kind tone, Roxanne then continued, "They might find that the threads of their thoughts and of their conversations are lost a bit too easily, or are hard to recall, and this can make them feel isolated or pressured. Life becomes exhausting simply by their effort to pretend everything's okay for themselves and for their loved ones."

"I get tired a little more easily now, but I don't know about these *things* you're talking of."

"You don't have to know or be sure. You just have to be brave for your girl. She needs you to trust in her and in your doctor and in how much you are loved and to let this give you the reassurance to get yourself checked out. That's all."

What did the following further silence mean? Was Angus okay? She could feel Elizabeth's hand gripping tighter in hers. But then Rox was there by his side, and this comforted Alice in a way she'd never felt before. There was no question the world was a better, less scary, and less lonely place with Roxanne in it.

Roxanne gently broke the silence and said, "I know what we've spoken of is hard to take in."

"And you say she's very worried. And you're worried about her?"

"Yes, and so are Moira and Alice. They're worried about both of you."

"What do I do?"

"Let Elizabeth see if she can get an appointment with your doctor. You never know, we might be able to get one this afternoon."

"This afternoon?"

"Absolutely. I suspect you're not a man to wait around. After all, would you have delayed another day to have asked your girl to marry you?"

"No, not at all. I'm not a man for dilly-dallying."

"Thought not. We'll get the ball rolling ASAP." Roxanne's chair scraped lightly against the sitting room tiles.

"Do we go in?" Elizabeth sat even further on the edge of her seat.

"And you're staying with Alice at the croft tonight?" Angus asked.

Alice's breath caught in her throat. She lightly rested her hand on Elizabeth's arm to signal for her to wait.

"Oh, erm, I'll need to check with her first, but yes, I can do if you'd like me to."

"Good. If we get an appointment, it might be useful if you are close by. I'm not asking for me, you understand. I think it would help Elizabeth."

"Yes, of course."

Elizabeth strained her neck to look into the sitting room. "Shall we join them?"

"Yep." Alice helped Elizabeth to her feet. She watched as Elizabeth brushed her apron flat against her legs and straightened her beads at her neck before holding her chin high and making her way into the sitting room.

Elizabeth took a deep, shaky breath. "Well, thanks so much for your help, Alice, with the sheets…"

Angus quickly stood and went to Elizabeth and held her hands to his heart. "My love, Roxanne has told me how worried you've been. I had no idea. Why didn't you say something sooner?"

"We just need to get you checked." Elizabeth's voice caught. "No more than that."

"And you'll stop worrying?"

"Yes. I thought I might try the doctor."

"Yes. Do. I'll drive us. Tell them we can make this afternoon." He pulled her into him almost as if she was falling and he had quickly caught her. "Forgive me that I didn't know."

Elizabeth hugged Angus close. "Oh, Angus, there's nothing to forgive."

Alice swallowed down the urge to cry. She whispered, "Thank you," to Roxanne who gave a simple nod in reply. Alice then gathered herself to suggest, "I'll make some tea, shall I?"

"I'll give you a hand." Roxanne followed Alice into the kitchen.

Alice checked her watch. "They'll make it in good time. If he can just hold on to this moment, it might just work. And yes to you staying with me, by the way. I'd love that."

Roxanne's cheeks flushed pink. "Me too." Roxanne then looked away and picked up the carrots. "Would you be wooed by a bunch of these?"

Alice laughed. "Would you?"

"I think you know I'm more of a pie girl."

They turned at the sound of Elizabeth pretending to speak to the GP practice. "A cancellation? That's great. We'll come now."

"Fingers crossed, eh." Alice bit at her lip and watched Elizabeth rest the phone back on its receiver and take a moment to find her breath.

"They'll be okay, Campbell." Roxanne reached out and curled her warm fingers around Alice's hand and gave a light squeeze. She quickly let go as Elizabeth bustled in.

"I'm sorry, Alice. We've no time for tea. I don't know how long it will take."

"No problem and no rush," Alice said. "We'll be right here, waiting for you and with the kettle on, for when you get back."

"Really, there's no need for you to wait here for us. I have no idea how long we'll be. Please. You've got your work at the centre, and I'm sure Roxanne would like to spend what remains of her last afternoon with Eve. I promise to ring when I get back to let you know how we've got on."

Alice nodded. "Okay, if you're sure?"

"I am."

"And Alice is right," Roxanne said. "This is your time to ask for help. Don't let yourself feel pressured or rushed."

Elizabeth held them both against her. "Thank you both so much."

Roxanne whispered, "Go now."

"Yes. I must strike while the iron is hot."

"Exactly. If needs be, you could try small gentle reminders on the way if you feel he might be forgetting. He's going for you, so keep with that theme."

"Okay."

"And remember"—Alice held Elizabeth's hands in hers—"we're on standby to come to you if you need us."

Elizabeth's expression firmed to become one of steely determination.

Angus stood at the door, waiting for her. There was no question, he'd never looked braver. He took Elizabeth's hand, and with that they were gone.

Alice turned to Roxanne. "Thank you so much."

Roxanne smiled and nodded. "So far, so good."

Roxanne certainly looked brighter and happier than this morning. She'd looked so sad and tired when she'd left for the boat. And Alice had felt so responsible for the kiss that had thrown them both.

"You seem a bit happier," Alice said. "I was thinking about you all morning and hoping that you were okay. Did you have a good trip?"

"Yes." Roxanne rested against the counter. "It turned out to be fab, actually. Eve and I had a really good catch-up. Crazily, I don't think we've chatted properly since she left Leicester to be with Moira."

"It must be hard with the distance." Was that what they would have to contend with if there was ever a *they*? Eve and Roxanne were so close, so if that could happen to them…

"It hasn't helped." Roxanne frowned. "But I can't blame it on that. I think I was being too proud. I wanted to give the impression that I was all self-sufficient and not bothered that she'd left. I kind of pushed her away, I guess."

They were standing so close together as they chatted that their bodies all but touched.

"I'm pleased that you've sorted things between you."

"We have."

The way Roxanne was looking at her wasn't the expression of someone backing away. No. For if she wasn't mistaken, behind Roxanne's gaze was a desire for something more. Had something changed from this morning's resolve?

Alice took a deep breath. She could be brave too. "Later for our supper, I thought, if you wanted, I could make more pie."

Roxanne's eyes shone. She stood up straight and reached out again for Alice's hand. "I'd like that. A lot."

Alice's heart surged in her chest. Roxanne was looking at her like she was everything to her. There was a time that such a look would have made her feel exposed, but now it was exactly how she wanted Roxanne to see her.

Roxanne's response bolstered Alice to say, "You see, I've all that we need. That you need."

Roxanne's cheeks flushed from pink to scarlet. "You sound pretty certain of that."

"That's because I am." And she was. She didn't want to think about what she was doing or might do, for she just wanted to live in the moment, unprotected and free. She wanted to be everything for Roxanne.

Without moving an inch, Roxanne said, "We should update Eve and Moira to let them know so far, so good."

"Oh right, yes." Alice shook her head. "You might need to let go of my hand." In that instant she was back on the hill and at the beginning of it all.

Roxanne smiled. She was clearly there too, as she said, "I was just making sure you weren't going to fall."

Alice smoothed her palm against Roxanne's hot cheek. "I think it's too late."

❖

"Hey both, only us." Alice brushed her shoes against the coir matting, and Roxanne held the door for a visiting family to make their way out. She then closed the centre's door behind them.

Moira looked up from the paperwork she was completing at the reception desk, and Eve turned off the tap where she'd been washing out paintbrushes.

"How did it go?" Moira's words were thick with concern.

"Amazingly, just as planned." Alice glanced at Roxanne and smiled. Alice's face glowed with relief.

Eve beamed at Moira. "That's wonderful news."

Moira moved to Eve, who held her close. "I take it they're with Angus's doctor now."

"Yes," Roxanne said, lifting herself up to sit on the edge of the reception desk. "They set off about fifteen minutes or so ago."

"We offered to wait for them at the cottage," Alice said. "But Elizabeth insisted we get on with our day. She's promised to ring us with an update when they get back."

Moira shook her head and looked across at Roxanne. "I honestly can't quite believe you got him to go."

Roxanne shrugged. "It might have been that he was just ready."

"But we've tried so many times."

"Why don't we take a seat." Eve spoke to Moira with such tenderness as if trying to soften the moment. "How about here." Eve led Moira by the hand to the craft table where they pulled out chairs and sat together. She then held Moira's hand in her lap.

Moira's face creased with a frown. She looked so tired. "You'd think the doctors would have stepped in like that and saved us all this heartache."

Eve said gently, "We know it's not as simple as that."

"I know, so they've told us. But really, why isn't it?"

Roxanne felt lost for words. What could she say? It was a process, and whilst it protected Angus's rights, it put a dreadful strain upon his loved ones.

Alice moved to lean against the reception desk next to Roxanne. "In hindsight," Alice offered, "it maybe took someone like Rox to provide an independent take on things. She isn't Angus's doctor, and she isn't his family. She's just Roxanne—someone he likes and who he knows we all like." Alice's admiration flowed with her words into the room.

Roxanne glanced at Eve. Her best mate seemed completely lost in worry for Moira.

Moira gave another shake of her head. "I just can't imagine what you said that changed his mind."

Roxanne nodded. "I get that. But you know, it wasn't so much that I changed his mind, for he was just as surprised as all those times you've tried to talk to him. I guess I just tried to help him to see, in that moment at least, what he needed to."

"She was just really clever in reaching him," Alice added. "She got him chatting about Elizabeth and how much he loved her and how he would do anything for her."

"It opened the door for me to talk to him about how worried Elizabeth was about him," Roxanne continued. "This took the focus off Angus himself and made it about Elizabeth, and I think that made him less defensive."

Eve asked, "He didn't resist the suggestion to go to the doctor?"

Alice shook her head. "Oh no, he began to bristle like he always does for sure, but Rox calmly persisted and explained what a theoretical someone—not him—might be feeling if they were poorly. He just listened quietly. I think deep down he recognized what she was describing."

Moira looked at Alice as if the pieces of their chat with Angus were falling into place for her. "Right."

"She even appealed to his pride in not dithering by suggesting that she would be sure he would want an appointment that very afternoon. So smart, so intuitive."

"So Rox came up trumps," Eve said. She was looking at Roxanne with an amused and impressed smile. "And I think that calls for several well-earned pints on us at The Gunsmith tonight. You'll come too, Alice. Right?"

Eve's invitation meant the world to Roxanne. It said *I am your best mate. I care. And I'll do what I can for you.*

"Oh, erm…I don't think we can make tonight." Alice looked at Roxanne. Eve looked decidedly confused.

The word *we* fluttered in Roxanne's heart. She slid down from the reception counter. "Yes, sorry, mate, but I think we'll have to raincheck The Gunsmith. Angus has asked if I can be around in Newland tonight. He assumed I was staying with Alice at the croft."

Moira looked taken aback. "Angus asked?"

"I know," Alice said. "I nearly fell off my seat. And what's more, it sounded like he was asking for himself, even though he said it was for Elizabeth. It's like Rox makes him feel safe."

"And we don't?" Hurt bubbled in Moira's voice. "I can't bear the thought that I've let him down."

Alice went over to Moira and crouched beside her. "Of course we make him feel safe, but maybe in a different way."

Roxanne shook her head. "And in no way have you let him down." It took no imagining how confused and helpless Moira must feel. Roxanne caught Eve's eye and Eve smiled her thanks.

Moira nodded. "Yes. Of course, I'm sorry. I'm very grateful to you, Roxanne. I'm just trying to take everything in."

"I get that." Roxanne shrugged. "No worries. And so, obviously, I said yes, that I would stay in the croft if it was okay with Alice."

Alice said emphatically, "And I really don't mind."

Eve gave Alice an affectionate smile. "Thanks, Alice."

Moira pushed her chair back and stood. "Yes, it certainly helps. We'd talked about staying tonight ourselves, but Eve's been called in for an early meeting. And I wasn't sure whether Elizabeth and Angus might need a bit of space, just the two of them, to digest everything."

Eve looked apologetically at Roxanne. "Enid rang, and the meeting I'm chairing, which was scheduled for next week, has been brought forward to nine o'clock tomorrow morning. Bless her, she tried to rearrange it for me with no luck. Will you be okay if Moira collects you and takes you to the station?"

"Sure."

"I can always drop Rox off at the station," Alice said. "If that helps?"

Moira shook her head. "We can't ask that of you, Alice. You've helped so much already."

"I don't mind. Oh no—wait. I'm teaching."

Roxanne stepped forward and touched Alice lightly on her back. "It's all right. I'll go with Moira."

Moira looked at her watch. "I hope they're doing okay."

"Dr. McBride's really kind," Alice said. "I understand they'll have to wait for a diagnosis, but my hope is the doctor will have some practical measures to put in place for them, as quickly as they are able."

Moira nodded. "And we can always come up with some sort of rota of our own, as well. I mean, take Sunday night as an example. It's not fair that you are always on call because you're closest."

"It's fine—"

"It's too much, Alice. And it'll only get more difficult. So we'll need a plan."

"Do you have something in mind?"

"Let's see what today's appointment brings."

"Okay."

Moira made her way back to the chair behind the reception desk. "I'll try to finish these forms. You're welcome to take Roxanne back to the croft, Alice. Catch your breath a bit. I'll finish up here."

"Okay, if you're sure. Thanks." Alice turned to Roxanne. "You'll no doubt want to say goodbye to Eve first." Roxanne nodded. "How about I finish cleaning the last of these brushes then. And I'll see you outside." Alice rolled up her sleeves and tipped a paintbrush pot into the sink.

"That's kind of you, Alice," Eve said. "Thank you."

"Come on, Eddison. Let's get some air." Roxanne followed Eve outside. They found a log bench and sat together. It felt in every way both an ending and a beginning all at once.

Eve nudged Roxanne's shoulder. "Sorry we didn't make it to the pub."

"I know. Total chain yank. I honestly never thought I'd say this, but I'll live."

They laughed.

"And I can't believe I won't be there at the station to see you off tomorrow. I am officially a terrible friend."

Roxanne nudged her back. "Yep. The worst. You could have tea with Alice and me before you go home tonight. Alice is making pie." *Did that sound convincing?*

"I have a feeling it might be pie for two. But thanks anyway."

"We could make it stretch."

"We both know you're just saying that, Rox."

Tricky. "No."

They giggled.

"And why shouldn't you?" Eve turned to face Roxanne. "Listen to me. Pie for two that doesn't include me is okay with me. You're allowed to want to be with her. You've a right to change your life and look forward. Okay?"

Roxanne hugged Eve. "I'll miss you."

"Then come back a bit sooner than my fortieth."

Roxanne laughed. "I hope to."

"Well, if that's the case, then don't leave a mess in the morning for Alice to clean up. Moira will come for you in good time for your train. Travel safe tomorrow, and text me when you get home."

"Will do." Roxanne stood. "Goodbye then, Evie Eds."

"Goodbye, Roxanne Barns."

The centre's door opened, and Alice held her phone in the air. She called over to them, "That was Elizabeth. The doctor managed to get Angus to agree to some tests. Fingers crossed this means we've got the ball rolling."

Moira arrived at Alice's side. Eve rushed over to Moira, and Moira wrapped them both in her arms.

After a few moments, Alice gently broke free and came forward to Roxanne.

"Good job, roomie."

"Good job, us. Shall we head back? I'm hoping you're hungry."

"You can't imagine."

The way Alice blushed so deeply in reply suggested that she might just be able to.

Chapter Fourteen

S o what do I do with these?" Roxanne held the sweet potatoes in the air.

Alice glanced at Roxanne. "Just so you know, I find that question vaguely horrifying."

Roxanne laughed. "I do *know* what to do with them. After all, doesn't everyone know that a sweet potato is just a well-behaved spud."

Alice chuckled and shook her head. God help her. "You're such a—"

"A lovable wee eejit?"

Lovable? As Roxanne stood close to her with her shirt crumpled from wearing her hoodie all day and with her smiling eyes and lazy grin, she was certainly lovable, not to mention kissable. "Aye. Something like that."

"I was asking if there was any particular special pie way you wanted them prepared."

"Nope. Peel and chop them. Tell you what, why don't I do that, and you grab the baking tray, stick the oven on high, and I'll pass you the cut-up pieces to go on the tray. You'll need to season and oil them for us."

"How about, while we work, I open the other fizz Eve brought. Chef's treat."

"Perfect."

Roxanne fetched the bottle from the fridge and opened it with a pop. She grabbed two mugs from the draining board and filled them half full. "What? Drink up."

Alice raised her mug. "Fair enough. A mug it is, then. Cheers." If Alice didn't know better, she would say Roxanne was nervous.

"Up your bum." Roxanne downed hers in one.

"Better?"

"Yep."

Alice put the bottle back in the fridge. "Good. Now concentrate. Oven, tray, veg prep. Unless you plan to eat tomorrow."

"When you put it like that…" Roxanne put on the oven and began to season and oil the potatoes in earnest.

"I can sense you eyeing up my mug."

Roxanne laughed. "Actually, I wasn't. I was checking my phone, which I just happened to have left by your mug, for any missed calls from Elizabeth."

Alice was sceptical. "Okay. None, I hope?"

"Nope."

"How do you think he'll be tonight?"

"I honestly don't know. Emotions have a habit of lingering beyond the detail, so he'll likely *feel* the day rather than recall the details of it. I think they'll be fine, though. And I agree with Moira that a quiet night just for the two of them is likely what they'll need."

"I guess. It's hard not to worry about them."

"I know it is. And that's why Moira's idea of setting up a rota is a good one too. Establish some time off for you."

"I don't need time off from them."

"Of course, but"—Roxanne softened her tone—"things might get harder. Time out will help you care for them."

"I see what you mean. I suppose so."

"In any case, when they move back, it will be easier for both of you for sure."

"What?"

Roxanne's face emptied of colour.

"Nothing."

"It's hardly nothing. You said they were moving back here?"

"Did I?"

"Rox."

"Okay, Eve mentioned in passing that they were in the very early stages of talking about moving back to Newland, that's all."

Why had Moira not mentioned this before?

"I shouldn't have said anything, Alice. Please forget I said it."

"It's not for you to feel bad about telling me. It should have come from Moira before now." Disappointment and hurt smarted in her heart. After everything they'd been through together, you'd think Moira would be more open with her. Or had nothing changed, and was she being left in the dark yet again for her own sake?

"I don't think anything's happening immediately. Eve sort of thought it wouldn't be until the end of the year at the earliest. Alice?"

"You heard her too. All Moira mentioned today is that we need a plan. I even specifically asked her if she had something in mind, and all she said was let's wait to see what happens today. She didn't even hint that they'd even thought about coming back."

"Like I said, it's very early stages. They've likely not even started planning—"

"What happens if they want to move back in here?" An awful sense of panic swept in. This wasn't just a building—it was her home.

"They've got Foxglove."

"But it's let out for holiday makers."

"Hence the end of the year."

"I can't believe I'm the last to know. Neither of them said anything to me."

"I doubt it's been mentioned yet to Elizabeth and Angus."

"But you'd think, as it directly affects me, they'd care enough about me to say something." Alice gripped the knife and chopped roughly at the last of the potatoes.

"Take it easy with that knife. You should see the number of chopped fingers I have to bandage—"

Alice poked the knife in the air. "It's like my feelings—no, *I*—don't matter."

"Yeah, waving it about is not much better. And you know that's not true."

"Do I?" Alice dumped the last of the chopped potatoes onto the tray before opening the fridge door and refilling their mugs.

Roxanne slipped the tray in the oven. Alice grabbed the timer from the windowsill and screwed it to the time required.

Roxanne smirked. "Just wondering whose neck you were thinking of then."

Alice took a large mouthful of wine. "Well, if they're not thinking about me, then I'm certainly not going to worry about what they might be thinking—about me or about us."

"Actually, on that note, I spoke to—"

"I want to get drunk, and"—Alice reached for Roxanne's hand and took a deep breath—"I want to get laid. And as you seem very interested in my *pie*, can I interest you in any of those options? Please say yes."

Roxanne's cheeks flushed pink. "What? Right here, right now?"

Alice pulled off her jumper, revealing her bra and her intentions.

"Yes. Both. I'm totally up for both." Roxanne pulled Alice into her and kissed her with so much need that Alice wondered if her legs might buckle. It was a relief to feel the press and gentle squeeze of Roxanne's hand against her bottom, holding and steadying her ever closer against her.

Alice slipped her hands under Roxanne's shirt to reach up to her breasts and began to fondle them. How badly she had wanted to touch her that day on the hill. How achingly badly. She could feel Roxanne's breath catch under her hands as she brushed her thumb lightly over her hardening nipples. She then broke her lips free from Roxanne's to breathlessly exclaim, "I love your boobs."

Roxanne whimpered. "I swear I'm going to come if you keep touching me like that."

"What, like this?" Alice massaged harder and pinched softly at Roxanne's nipples.

Roxanne clamped her lips together.

Alice leaned in to Roxanne's neck, and as she kissed the hot skin, she pressed her lips ever more tightly, sucking until Roxanne moaned. "Am I hurting you?"

"You're killing me." Roxanne smoothed her hands over Alice's back and unhooked her bra. She placed her warm lips to Alice's shoulder, teasing her with featherlike kisses.

The intense thrill of the sensation of Roxanne's mouth on her skin flooded down her body to between her legs. She tugged at the button of her jeans and unzipped her fly. Roxanne clearly didn't need telling what Alice needed her to do as Roxanne's hand slipped between Alice's legs and underneath her underwear.

Alice pressed her body into Roxanne's palm and bit down on her lip at the feel of Roxanne's fingers inside her. Her legs would surely give way as the desperate need for sweet release consumed her strength and stole her every last breath. She wrapped her arms around Roxanne's shoulders and buried her face into her neck. "I need to lie down."

Roxanne eased Alice onto the kitchen floor.

"I wasn't really thinking the kitchen—oh my God."

The rush of arousal at the press of Roxanne's body upon her

chased reason away as soft chest pillowed against soft chest, and hip
slid beside hip, and thigh writhed against thigh.

Roxanne slipped her fingers beneath Alice's underwear once
more, this time pressing deeper and faster inside her. Alice, in turn,
squeezed at Roxanne's bottom, relishing the soft and giving sensation
of her body. She felt so good to touch, just so...

Alice arched her hips to meet the intense rhythm as the surging
waves of sweet pressure broke against her and threatened to break her
into millions of pieces and to spin her out into the hills and beyond on
the drifts of endless air. For she was utterly undone, unfixed, as the
last unrelenting urge to climax broke all restraint and set her free in a
shuddery gasp of release.

Roxanne's warm body partially collapsing into her brought Alice
back to the grounding reality of the hard floor and the feel of their
bones bruising against it and the softness of their breath evaporating
away.

She held Roxanne tight against her, taking her weight and enjoying
the sensation of her hot, spent body. She then rested her hand against
Roxanne's chest. "Your heart is like a bird's. It's beating so fast. It must
feel like it might explode."

Roxanne nodded, and with ragged breath she said, "That was
just..."

Alice laughed. "Just?"

"Wow." Roxanne rolled away and lay on the floor with her arms
out wide as if she'd been shot.

Alice snuggled up next to her and rested her cheek against
Roxanne's heaving chest. "How was that for you? Was it good?"

Roxanne's answer was to undo the button of her jeans and unzip
her fly. She reached gently for Alice's hand and guided it down between
her jeans and underwear.

Alice's body reignited instantly at the feel of the warmth and
wetness against her fingers. "You're really..."

"I think there's your answer."

"Did you completely come? Even though we didn't, I didn't..."
Alice moved her fingers over the swollen lips beneath the soft cotton
of Roxanne's underwear, brushing and rubbing them and encouraging
a wash of new wetness against the material.

Roxanne's breath became unsteady again, and she swallowed
several times. "I was all but there when you took your top off."

Alice laughed. "So if I did this…" Alice tucked her fingers into Roxanne's underwear, seeking out the source of the wetness and the essence of her need. She pushed her fingers inside Roxanne, easing them in and out in a rhythm which teased of the pleasure to come.

Roxanne closed her eyes. "I can't decide whether you're fucking me or torturing me."

"Really?" Alice repositioned herself and climbed on top of Roxanne, straddling her hips. She slipped her fingers back inside her and found her rhythm once more. Roxanne was staring up at her with pupils wider than a hawk's at sunset.

With her free hand, she pushed up Roxanne's shirt and with it her T-shirt to reveal her bra. She leaned over her and teased at her nipple with her mouth.

Roxanne wriggled underneath her.

She reached under the base of the bra's cup and lifted it over Roxanne's breast and began to suck at her nipple. She began softly and then more firmly matching the pace of her sucking with the rhythm of her fingers inside her.

Roxanne closed her eyes tightly and gripped at Alice's thighs. If this was a rollercoaster ride, then everything about Roxanne's demeanour suggested the climb to the big dip was nearing the top.

"I…" Roxanne opened her eyes and stared up at her, stark and unblinking. She lifted her torso slightly from the floor, and Alice felt Roxanne's body stiffen under her and then the warm release of wetness against her palm.

Alice leaned over and kissed her, and Roxanne wrapped her arms around her, pulling her close in a tight embrace.

They lay there with their hot bodies cooling on the tiles until the timer rang.

"I don't think I can concentrate to make pie. I could ping a rice sachet, and we could throw in some feta and the potatoes. What do you think? Rox?"

"I can't quite believe I'm saying this, but I couldn't eat a thing."

"Shagging ruins your appetite?"

"It normally increases it." She reached for Alice's hand. "You fill me up, Alice Campbell, in a way that other girls have not."

Alice's heart raced. That was the very last thing she thought she'd hear Roxanne say. "I don't want to worry you, but that sounded decidedly romantic."

Roxanne laughed, and then her expression became serious. "It frightens the shit out of me."

"Me too." And it did. After all, there was nothing scarier than actually finding what you have been longing for. "Let's try at least to have something to eat and some booze, of course." Alice released herself and unsteadily got to her feet. She pulled on her jumper and ruffled her hair into place. "Right, food." She reached for the oven gloves and slipped the tray from the oven and assembled their makeshift tea.

Roxanne, in every way clearly dazed, eventually gathered herself to pour them both more wine. She discarded the empty bottle on the floor by the bin and gathered together forks and napkins. She then gestured to the garden. "I think I need some air. Meet you on the sunroom step."

"Sure. Oh, and Rox?"

Roxanne looked back at her with an expression softened and hazy with lovemaking.

"You don't have to be afraid, you know. I won't hurt you."

Roxanne nodded. "I know. See you out there, Campbell."

Alice waited for the reassurance to be returned. But nothing. She wouldn't read too much into it. Roxanne had just said she wasn't like other girls. And she definitely meant it. Didn't she?

Alice shrugged off all invasive doubts and joined Roxanne. "Eat what you can."

"Thanks." Roxanne took a couple of mouthfuls and then paused and seemed to tease at her food with her fork.

"You don't like it?"

"I won't hurt you either." She looked at Alice with an expression that carried with it a blend of sincerity and vulnerability that she had not seen before.

You won't? It was all Alice could do not to cry. She called upon all of her calm to reply breezily, "Cool." She then quickly leaned across and kissed Roxanne's cheek, only for Roxanne to turn and for their lips to meet.

"Oops." Alice laughed. They kissed again, all but oblivious to their food growing cold and the strength of the day's sunlight beginning to fade.

Just kissing was so hard because with each kiss Alice always wanted more. She wanted to feel Roxanne against her and to touch her, and to make her whimper again.

Alice drew herself away. "I have to stop before I can't."

Roxanne smiled. "I love that you want me so much."

"A bit too much if your poor neck's anything to go by. I've given you a right bruise." Alice brushed lightly at the deep pink mark she'd made.

"You're an animal, Alice Campbell. A wild one at that." Roxanne held her hands in the air and shaped them into claws and made a roar noise, which made Alice squeal with delight. This seemed to encourage Roxanne even more as she nuzzled her mouth into Alice's neck, returning the hickey Alice had given her.

It hurt like hell and felt like heaven. Was that what loving Roxanne would be like?

She playfully pushed Roxanne away and scrambled to her feet. "Let's go to my bedroom." Alice began to gather the supper things together, not helped by Roxanne biting at her behind. "You are nothing but trouble. Nothing. But. Trouble. Bring the mugs." With her arms full, Alice turned for the kitchen, then called over her shoulder, "I know you're staring at my arse."

Roxanne laughed. "Goddammit, you know too much."

If only that was true. She scraped the uneaten food into the bin and dropped the bowls into the sink. Roxanne came into view through the kitchen window. She had taken a few steps into the garden and was looking out at the loch and the mountains. If only Alice knew what Roxanne was thinking right then and there. But much more than that, if only she knew how to ask to see her again and maybe even for her not to leave. But this was Roxanne, wasn't it? And if Alice knew anything at all, having a girlfriend wasn't Roxanne's plan, and leaving was what she did best.

❖

"Morning, Campbell."

Alice opened her eyes to see Roxanne placing two mugs of tea on the bedside table. She was wrapped in a towel that seemed to reveal more than it covered. Still, a hand towel was slightly better than a bath mat.

"Hi." Alice asked through a stretch. "What time is it?"

"Just gone half eight. Would you like me to burn a piece of toast for you?"

Alice laughed. "Lightly charred with marmalade. Perfect." She held out her hand, and Roxanne took it, discarding the towel and sliding back under the covers.

Alice snuggled up to Roxanne. "I'll have to go to work soon. I should have got up earlier. Have you been up long?"

"Nope. Just long enough to make a brew and to try to work up the enthusiasm for showering, getting dressed, and packing. I'm not quite there yet."

"Can I say I'll miss you?"

"You can. I'll miss me too."

Alice groaned. "Seriously, it's gone so quickly. One minute you arrived, really annoyingly."

"Lovely, thank you."

"And now you're leaving, really annoyingly."

Roxanne smiled. "I'm generally annoying then."

"Yep."

This would be a good time for Roxanne to reassure her, promise to keep in touch, but instead her attention was caught by the oil painting on the wall opposite, depicting the loch and the mountains in the distance.

"Moira's father painted it."

"Really? Wow. It's good."

"It used to hang on the wall downstairs above the fireplace. When Moira moved out, I assumed she'd take it with her, but she thought it might look out of place hung in somewhere modern. So I suggested she could leave it in the croft along with a few other pieces of furniture. She seemed surprised that I'd want it here. But I love that painting. I used to stare at it as a child so hard that sometimes I'd swear the ripples on the loch actually rippled."

"I get that. Eve's parents had polystyrene tiles on the ceiling in their living room that I used to stare at until they shrank and travelled towards me in a trippy way." Roxanne shook her head. "I must have seemed a really weird kid."

"Me too."

Roxanne reached for their tea. "Well then, here's to all the weirdos in the world."

Alice sat up in the bed. "Yes, cheers."

"Amazingly, despite my weirdness, they kept having me round. Looking back, they were very accepting of difference. When I accidentally outed Eve—"

"You outed Eve?"

"In my defence, I happened to mention it to Eve's sister who totally blabbed."

"Oh my God, Rox. That's terrible. I would hate that. What did Eve say?"

"It was fine. She was fine. She was a little freaked out at first, but then when she got her head around it, she was okay. That's kind of how she is with news that's…new."

"Isn't all news new?" Why did Roxanne look all of sudden so uncomfortable? "You all right?"

"Absolutely. Yep. No probs at all. Whatever happens, I just want you to know that I honestly felt things with you that I've never felt with anyone else."

Whatever happens? "What things? Sex things?" Alice tucked the bedding under her arms, protecting her heart from view.

"Hands down the best orgasms I've had."

"I see. Great."

"Alice. Look at me. The *things* I felt were emotional, not just physical. For the first time in whenever, I thought there could be more. I wanted more."

You did? "So are you saying you'd like to see me again?"

"Alice! Anyone? Hello!"

"Shit. Rox, it's Moira."

"What?"

"Moira." Alice scrambled out of bed and frantically pulled on her clothes. "It's not even nine. For heaven's sake, what time's your train?"

"It's not for ages. Does she usually just walk in?"

"No. Never. She always rings. Where's my phone?"

"I'm pretty sure I last saw it in the kitchen with mine."

"Oh my God. No wonder we didn't hear if she rang. What if something's happened to Elizabeth and Angus? We were meant to be on duty."

"Don't stress. I'm sure they're fine."

"Don't stress? You're *naked*. Get dressed. Quickly."

"All my clothes are downstairs. Tell you what, I'll jump in the shower. You go and entertain her. Go! Before the intruder comes upstairs."

"Hi, Moira, just coming." Alice ran downstairs, only slowing her pace for the final steps. "I didn't hear you knock."

"I did. Several times. And tried your phone. Both your phones. I was on my way to Elizabeth and Angus for breakfast. As I passed the croft, I thought I'd stop by and ask you if I could cut some flowers from the garden to take for them. When you didn't reply, I was going to leave you to it, but then I thought maybe I should check in case there's a problem. I had the sense you get when something's up. I hope you don't mind that I let myself in."

"No. And everything's fine here. As you can see." Alice looked past Moira to the sight of their clothes strewn around the sitting room. Her own bra and jeans were slung over the banister. "Erm, laundry day."

A smile played on Moira's lips as she said, "Aye." Moira's gaze had fallen on the sofa, which would have looked less incriminating if it had looked less like a sofa and more like a bed.

The shower began to run in the bathroom. "Rox is just taking a shower. Can I make you a tea?" Alice made for the kitchen and for her phone. Please let there be no calls from Elizabeth. She gave a sigh at the sight of no missed calls.

Moira followed Alice into the kitchen. "No thanks, like I said, I've made plans to have breakfast at the cottage before I take Roxanne to the station. No problems I'm guessing with Angus and Elizabeth?"

"No. No calls." Alice tucked her phone into her pocket and leaned against the sinkful of dirty dishes.

Moira's foot knocked against their wine bottle, which rolled along the floor to Alice's bare feet. Maybe Moira hadn't noticed it.

Moira gestured to Alice's feet. "Eve was hoping that you two would enjoy the wine."

"She was?" Alice picked up the bottle and rested it on the counter. "It was great— really kind of her."

"Good. Right then, I'll leave you to it. If it's okay with you, I'll go and take the cuttings from the garden. But I'll go out the side way—I won't come back through the house and disturb you again."

"That's fine, and you haven't disturbed us."

Moira smiled at her. "Even so. Can you tell Roxanne I'll call for her in about three-quarters of an hour?"

"Sure."

"Great. Have a good morning, and I'll see you back at the centre in a bit."

"Yep. Bye."

Moira left for the garden. Alice watched her bending amongst the flower beds and choosing just the selection that they both knew would bring Elizabeth such joy. Before long, she had gathered a small bouquet of bluebells, heather, and cuckooflowers. With her task complete, Moira looked up at her and they exchanged a wave goodbye.

Roxanne bounced downstairs. She gingerly poked her head into the kitchen. She was wearing Alice's dressing gown. "Moira okay?"

"Yes. She'd just called to pick some flowers for Elizabeth. She's having breakfast with them and then she'll call for you."

"Right. I better be ready." Roxanne went into the sitting room. Alice stood and leaned against the kitchen door and watched her as she rummaged in her rucksack and retrieved her underwear and clothes. She slipped off the dressing gown, revealing her beautiful naked body. It took all her might for Alice not to move to her and hold her and kiss her. She wanted her so much. Just as she had wanted her so much last night, and all night, for that matter.

Had it shown on her face this morning? Moira couldn't have somehow sensed this, could she? Although she'd hardly had to sense anything—their underwear being all over the place was a huge hint.

Roxanne pulled on her T-shirt. Her hickey shone out against the white material. Oh no. Alice rushed to the mirror by the door. Her own hickey was just visible beneath her hair.

"Do you think Moira could have seen this?" Alice swept her hair back to reveal her neck.

Roxanne looked at Alice and shrugged. "Maybe."

"What if she guessed about us? It didn't look like you'd slept on the sofa—"

"Alice. Take a breath. It doesn't matter."

"How can you say that? You're saying you're not bothered if Eve finds out?"

"She knows. I tried to tell you last night. Well, not about us sleeping together, obviously. But that we kissed. I told her on the boat trip. I told her that I liked you and that I was serious about you."

"You told her we kissed?" Alice sat down in the armchair. "What did she say?"

"Well, granted she needed a moment to digest everything, but then when I explained how awesome I think you are, she came round to the idea."

"So this means Moira will know, won't she." Oh God. "I can't believe you outed me to Moira. Just like you did to Eve—"

"What? *No.*" Roxanne moved to her and bent down at her side. She placed her hand on her knee. "I haven't. We haven't, I promise. I asked Eve not to tell Moira. I knew you would want it to come from you."

"You did? And Eve said she wouldn't?"

Roxanne nodded.

Alice gave a heavy sigh. "Okay, that's good."

"And just to reassure you even more, Eve and Moira did have a hypothetical discussion about me and you."

"What?"

"It was when Eve wasn't so keen on the idea. You know when she arrived upset at the centre, and Moira sent you home early."

"But you just said Moira didn't know about me."

"She doesn't. Like I said, it was a hypothetical chat. And Eve didn't give me the impression Moira was remotely fazed by it. Apparently, Moira just said you should make your own choices."

Alice stood up. She didn't know what to say or to think. But she knew what to feel because she'd felt it many times before. They were once her constant companions. Fear and anger.

"It's okay, Alice."

"It's not okay."

"But I thought you'd got it that Moira will be the last person to judge you for wanting to be with a woman. She's just waiting for you to tell her when you're ready to. When you've met someone special."

Alice could hear what Roxanne was saying, but at the same time all she could hear were the words *Go to hell* that she herself had screamed at Moira when Moira had tried to explain about Eve. How on earth could she even begin to explain about Roxanne. "I'm not ready."

"Sorry? I thought—"

"I can't do this."

"What do you mean?"

She couldn't look at Roxanne. She knew her words would surely wound her, and that her heart would no doubt be breaking. And she didn't know what to do about it. She just didn't know what to do. All she knew was that she was late for work. "I ought to get to work."

Roxanne reached out for her arm. "But what about us? To answer your question from before, yes, it does mean I want to see you again. Please, Alice, you're being irrational."

"Irrational?" Alice clenched her hands into fists and stared ahead to the door. "Well, you're well rid then. Just how you like it."

"That's not fair."

Alice glanced at Roxanne. All the colour and all the joy from this morning had drained from her face. It was beyond awful to see. "But isn't that what you said? You don't do relationships. You're not the girl of any girl's dreams."

"Yes, but I didn't mean it. Well, I did mean it. But that was before us. But as you clearly don't think I'm that someone special, then I guess maybe I was right all along. Maybe relationships aren't for me." Roxanne stuffed her remaining clothes and belongings back into her rucksack.

Alice quickly turned away at the sight of Roxanne's tears. She went to the door, pushed her feet into a pair of trainers, and grabbed her keys and her jacket. She paused. What on earth was she doing? What on earth had she *done*? She turned back to look at Roxanne. Roxanne was sitting on the edge of the sofa with her head in her hands.

She took a deep and painful breath. "I think the world of you. And you deserve someone better and braver than me." And with that she opened the door and stepped out of the croft. She closed the door, and before she could take another step her legs gave way beneath her, and she sobbed her broken heart out. Anger and fear had won just like they always did and always would. Wouldn't they?

CHAPTER FIFTEEN

"We're here." Moira pulled into Station Square and found a spot to park. She jumped out of the Land Rover, lifted Roxanne's rucksack from the boot, and slipped it onto her shoulder. Roxanne climbed out and numbly followed her into the station.

Moira had collected her from the croft just as she had promised Eve. And Roxanne had willed herself not to cry just as she had promised herself. Roxanne had taken care to leave the croft tidy. She had said her farewells to Elvis and the crew. She then left with Moira without looking back, for she had no need to collect memories with a last look. Weren't memories for those who would have occasion to recall them?

They drove the winding ten miles that led from Newland to Inverness pretty much in silence, listening to the radio. Not that Roxanne heard a word the DJ said, nor could she have recalled a song to hum on the journey home, nor for that matter, would she have commented on the passing scenery, as it turned from lush green hills to the brick, concrete, steel, and wood facades of the city. For everything was a blur, an unreal blur.

"Still not wearing his trousers, I'm afraid." Moira smiled and shook her head in the direction of the statue of the Highlander.

Roxanne managed a small hollow laugh. She couldn't muster or stomach a witty quip in reply, for nothing seemed funny any more.

The soldier stood fixed, proud as he was five days ago, and as if nothing had changed when literally everything had. When she'd first stared up at the statue, her carefree heart was free to roam at will, untethered by romantic entanglements. But now it ached, for it had been ripped and torn from the fragile new connections it had made to a girl in a croft. And not just any girl. This was Alice. Wasn't that what Eve had said? Moira's Alice.

Roxanne swallowed. She caught a glimpse of them reflected in the station windows. Did she look as awful as she felt? If she did, then surely Moira would ask if everything was all right. And what could she say?

Roxanne followed Moira past The Ness and Thistle and into the station concourse. Moira then rested the rucksack on the floor at her feet and glanced up at the departures board. "Your train's running a bit late. Shall we grab a coffee?" Moira gave a nod in the direction of Costa Coffee.

"Oh, erm…" Wouldn't Moira just want to get back to work? Or had Eve told her to wait until she was on the train? "Honestly, you don't have to wait with me. I'll be fine." Waiting with Moira would mean talking. But if Moira left, wouldn't she just be left waiting with her own thoughts? That was the last thing she wanted.

Moira gave a warm smile. "I know you'll be fine. We don't have to—"

"No. Coffee sounds great. Thanks."

"Okay, you find a seat," Moira said. "I'll get the coffees. Are you okay with the rucksack?"

"Definitely. I've got it from here. No problem." Moira moved the rucksack towards Roxanne, who took it from her and immediately let the floor take the weight once more. What had possessed her to pack so much? What had possessed her to come in the first place?

She dragged it to an empty table and sat fiddling with a sachet of sugar.

Moira soon arrived with a tray loaded with two coffees, a Coke, a couple of packets of biscuits, two packets of sandwiches, a bag of crisps, and a slice of Dundee cake.

Blimey, was she planning a long chat? There had been no opportunity for Moira to speak to Alice, had there? None of what happened was her fault, as such. And Moira would understand. Wouldn't she? Roxanne said, "Thank you."

Moira nodded. "Sure. I know there'll be a buffet car on the train, but I can hear Eve asking me whether you had food for the journey."

"Oh wow, thanks. Can I give you some money for all this?"

Moira waved away the suggestion. "Actually, I should have asked for a bag for you."

"No need. I'll just fill my pockets. They probably won't make it off the platform."

Moira laughed. "Aye." She reached for her coffee and took a careful sip. "I just want to say again that I'm incredibly grateful to you for your help with Angus."

Roxanne cleared her throat and forced down the urge to cry. Moira's warmth and gratitude weren't helping one bit. *Stop being so kind to me.* This was Moira Burns. Wasn't her thing to be a woman of few words?

Roxanne shrugged. "It's totally shit and unfair what's happening to you all. I was honestly pleased to help."

"Well, thanks to you we have a clearer way forward now, which is so valuable in helping to manage the stress of it all."

"Defo." Roxanne peeled the lid free from her coffee and blew over it. "Eve mentioned that you were thinking of moving back to Newland at the end of the year to be closer to them."

"Did she?"

"Just in passing. She said it was early days in the planning."

Moira nodded. "Things always take longer to sort out than you think. So you have to get a plan before you *have* to. If you know what I mean."

"Sure."

"To be honest, I feel bad asking Eve to leave. She loves it in the city and then there's her work commitments."

"If it helps at all, she said how much she loved Newland, and that it had always felt like home to her. Actually, no, that's not quite true. She said *you* were her home."

Moira's cheeks flushed, and she swallowed several times before she seemed able to reply. "That's helpful to know, thank you."

"Yeah, erm, I may have been slightly less helpful by also mentioning your move to Alice." Roxanne's voice broke a little at the mention of Alice. *Keep it in.*

"Right." Moira was looking at her in such a way that suggested she was about to ask if everything was okay.

Roxanne gripped her coffee cup. "I know I may have inadvertently taken away your chance to tell Alice yourself. I'm sorry."

"What did she say?"

"Well…she was…surprised." Roxanne took a sip of her coffee. She stared fixedly at the table rather than Moira's face.

"And I'm guessing not in a good way."

"She was a bit hurt, to be honest, not to have been included in the planning. I think she felt a bit left out. And she's also worried about losing the croft." Roxanne glanced up at Moira.

Moira was frowning into her coffee, and her eyes were darting about as if chasing the meaning of what Roxanne was saying in the swirl of milk. "But we haven't begun the details of the planning, so there's nothing for her to be left out of. And as for the croft, I thought she understood that I consider the croft to be hers. I really can't believe she thought I would see her homeless." Moira nodded. "I'll have a chat with her. Thanks for telling me."

"It was the least I could do. Sorry again for blabbing."

"Anything else you feel I should know? After all, you seem to have a magic touch in getting Alice to open up."

Moira didn't need to know about her magic touch or, for that matter, how much Alice had enjoyed it. The sudden pain at the memory made her heart ache. That was a conversation for Alice to have with Moira. After what had happened, it would be a conversation that would now be all but impossible to avoid. For surely Alice couldn't hide her pain after this morning, let alone how much these last few days together had meant. Could she?

She'd tried her best to help Alice feel able to be open about her sexuality, but none of it seemed to do any good. And Alice could think the world of her, but at the end of the day they were both alone again. How could nothing good come out of something so magical? But there *was* something. Should she say? Why not. She simply had nothing to lose.

"She wants to sing."

Moira sat up a little straighter. "How do you mean? Professionally?"

"I don't know. But I do know how much she adores her work at the centre, that's for certain. And she spoke with such pride at having always wanted to be a teacher. It's just, she writes these songs. I think she's worried that if she sang in front of people, and in particular in front of you and her dad, that it would upset you both and remind you of her mum."

Moira looked down at her coffee again.

"I mention it because I don't think she will ever tell you herself. And not telling you is hurting her." Roxanne's words caught in her throat. "Anyhow, I thought you should know and that you'd want to know."

Moira shook her head. "I really had no idea."

Roxanne looked away to the concourse. Had she said too much?

The departure board showed that her train was due in ten minutes. "My train's due in."

"You better get to your platform." Moira pushed her chair away from the table and stood.

"If I hugged you goodbye, would that be weird?"

"Yes." They both laughed. Moira held out her hand, which Roxanne shook firmly. "Travel safe. And come back soon. Yes?"

"Will do."

Moira turned to leave for the exit.

"Moira? Will you tell Alice...Will you tell her that I think the world of her too?"

Moira's eyebrows rose for a fleeting moment before her face formed the kindest of smiles. "Yes, of course. Goodbye, Roxanne."

"Cheers, and thanks for the lift."

It felt in every way that she'd just said to Moira *I love your stepdaughter. I love Alice.* She felt a rush of unmistakable relief. It was short-lived as the memory of her last conversation with Alice pierced her heart with sharp arrows of sadness.

Roxanne shoved the food and drink in her pockets and made her way out of the coffee shop and to the ticket barrier. She looked back towards Inverness one last time to see Moira's Land Rover drive away. Moira had listened calmly and without judgement, and she had made her feel cared for, and that couldn't have meant more to Roxanne. Eve had always said how special Moira was, and maybe it had taken Roxanne until now to completely see it.

Just gone eight o'clock in the evening, Roxanne arrived into Leicester, half dazed with crushing fatigue.

She'd tried to sleep on the way, but every time she drifted off, she would wake and remember with agony her last heartbreaking moments with Alice. So she'd drunk cans of Coke and numerous strong coffees and struck up conversations with fellow travellers in an effort to stay awake. She was now so tired that she was beyond tired as she half carried, half dragged her rucksack to The Brewer's.

"You look like shit." The barman poured Roxanne a pint of Carling.

"Thanks. Nice to see you too."

"Rox!"

"Hey, Bel."

Belinda hugged Roxanne and then drew away, sniffing at her jumper. "You smell."

"I've been on the train for nine and a half hours—"

"No, it's not just the sour train stink, it's more like—Oh my God, is that a hickey?" Belinda pulled at Roxanne's shoulder for a closer look.

Roxanne shrugged and drank her beer in large thirsty gulps.

"Spill. I want to hear all the sordid details."

"I can barely stand, let alone speak. And there's literally nothing to spill, not a drop."

Belinda tilted her head and waited.

"Okay. I met a girl, hung out with the girl, shagged the girl, and got dumped by the girl." Roxanne shrugged. "And my heart hurts so much I can't breathe."

Belinda double blinked. "Your heart?"

"Yep. And now I just want to go home and sleep and ideally never wake up."

"Then maybe you should have added, *I fell for the girl and got hurt by the girl.* Just a thought." Belinda hung her head and walked away.

Roxanne pulled her phone from the pocket of her jeans. There were no messages. She quickly texted Eve. *Home safe x.* What would Eve think when she found out? A text from Eve came straight back *Fab. See you soon x*

"Another?" The barman gestured to Roxanne's empty glass.

"No, I'm heading off, thanks anyway."

"Get some sleep."

"I will." She knew she wouldn't. She dragged her rucksack with her onto the street outside and leaned with it against the wall. How had things gone wrong so quickly? Had Alice really meant for it to end this way, or even for it to end at all? They had felt so good. One minute they were in bed together, cherishing the intimacy they had found in each other, and the next they were strangers doubting every choice they were making. But they had been so certain. *Alice* had been so certain. *Fuck this.* She dug again for her phone and scrolled down for Alice's number. She took a deep breath and pressed dial. It rang out and rang out until her call went to voicemail.

"*Hi, you have reached Alice Campbell's phone. If your call is in relation to the Newland Trust Education Centre, then please call the centre directly. For all other matters, please leave a message. Thank you.*"

"Hi, Alice, it's me. Just wanted to let you know I…I'm home safe and I…" Would she pick up? No of course not, she probably wouldn't even hear this message for hours. "Okay then. Bye."

Everything about the call felt futile. What did she think she was doing anyway? Who was she fooling? Alice was right. Roxanne had told her emphatically that she didn't do relationships. What made her think she could do this one? But then Alice was different in every way from anyone before. And didn't everyone she cared about leave in the end? Maybe it was good that it ended before it began. Damage limitation and all that.

Except how come everything felt damaged already, and there was certainly no limit to her sadness and pain.

CHAPTER SIXTEEN

A lice was never one to lie in. She was more often than not up with the lark, at just a suggestion of light through her bedroom curtains. And this past week she was out of the croft and up into the hills before the sun had risen fully in the sky.

At first light she'd drive to the centre and leave her Land Rover parked, ready for the start of work a few hours later. And then she'd walk up through the woodlands and out to where the grasses and heathers of the moors began.

Those first few hours breathing in the sweet woodland air and listening for the sounds of morning bird calls and the soft rustle of waking animals quite simply carried her through the day. It kept the hurt that sparked her anger at the edges of things. It made the heartache almost bearable.

This morning was no exception, for she had made for the woodland and sat leaning against the same tree at the edge of the woods where she had mended the fence with Moira and Angus. How crazy to think that was just over three weeks ago now. It was where it had all begun, with Moira asking her if she would have Roxanne for the night of the party. She remembered how nervous she had been at the mention of Roxanne's name.

She felt so stupid. "You fool!" Her cry startled the birds in the trees. They burst into flight, turning and swooping in the air before resettling again.

Why had she let her guard down so easily and let Roxanne in? Was her resistance to Roxanne's charms that pointless? Why had it felt so inevitable that they would give in to their desire for each other?

Alice raised her fingers to brush at her lips. How she'd wanted

Roxanne so much that just the thought of her touch was ecstasy in itself...

She dropped her hand to feel the ground and to grip the solid earth. She buried her fingers into the soil, cold and damp at her touch. How carelessly had she thrown caution to the wind and sailed with Roxanne to the sun. And now, charred, they had fallen to the earth with their feelings and their hearts burned to ash. She hugged her knees to her aching chest, then sat with her forehead resting on them and her eyes closed. The solemn call of the willow warbler sang out from the woodland, its notes lifting and falling.

"Alice?"

Alice jumped at the sound of Moira's voice.

"Sorry. I didn't mean to startle you."

"What time is it? It can't be time to open the centre, can it?"

"No, it's still early. Barely eight. Eve had an early meeting, so I thought I might as well get a head start on the day myself. And when I arrived and saw your Land Rover and that you weren't in the centre, I was a bit worried. I tried to think where you might be. Lucky first guess. And the walk up here's always nice, so I thought I'd head this way."

"There was no need. I'm absolutely fine. Just getting some morning air. Shall we go?" Alice gathered herself to stand only to see Moira gesture for her to stay seated.

"Why don't we sit for a while?"

"Oh, okay." Alice shuffled a little bit over to allow Moira to rest her back against the tree.

Moira settled herself by Alice's side. She glanced at the line of fence that separated the woodland from the crofter's land. "Our fence held, then?"

"Yes. For how long, though, who knows. Wee vandals."

Moira laughed. "Aye. It seems much longer somehow than just a few weeks ago."

Alice nodded. "Yes, I was just thinking about when we were last here. We were all so excited about Eve's upcoming birthday."

"Yes, indeed. It was a great night."

"So, how is Eve? All this last week, I've kept meaning to ring to say hi. But then I know she's back at work now and trying to catch up, no doubt, so I didn't want to disturb her." In part that was true. But in the main Alice wasn't ready to speak to or to see Eve. Eve had texted her the day after Roxanne had left to ask if she was okay. Alice had wondered whether it was just Eve checking in with her like she usually did, or whether there was something more behind it. Surely Roxanne had updated her. Eve would likely know everything. She'd replied, saying she was great. Eve had sent a kiss by return. But it didn't feel like the end of their chat, more a pause in it. Roxanne had said that Eve wouldn't tell Moira about their kiss. Did that mean that Eve would keep what happened from Moira too? Alice gripped at the soil.

"She's okay." Moira gave a shrug. "She's missing Roxanne. I think she's found it hard, having enjoyed her being here and then for her to leave." Moira looked at Alice.

"Uh-huh. I imagine they've spoken a lot since Roxanne's left then."

"Yes. Several times. I'm not sure Roxanne's doing that great, actually."

Alice's heart choked in her throat. "No?"

Moira shook her head. "But Eve seems to be sorting it."

"Right. That's good."

"Aye. Looking back, Roxanne didn't look so well when I took her to the station. I didn't want to pry."

What could Alice say? *I did that to her. I hurt us both. And now I don't know what to do?*

"We had quite an interesting chat, nonetheless, while we waited for her train."

Alice's mouth felt like it was full of dust. "You did?"

Moira nodded. "She helped me, actually. She drew my attention to a couple of things that she thought I needed to know about."

Oh God. "I'm not sure I understand."

"She mentioned that you felt hurt when you heard that Eve and I were thinking of moving back to Newland. That you'd not been included in the planning."

Why? Why would Roxanne care any more? Alice had spent the last week stewing over the thought that nothing had or would change for her. Love was out of her reach, and she would always be alone and on the outside of everything. "Oh, right. Well, I do feel hurt, to be honest. It feels like I was the last to know. Again."

"You haven't been left out, I promise. And that's because we haven't actually made any plans yet. And other than Roxanne, no one else knows."

"But you've decided?"

"I don't think we have any choice. Like I said, I'm not leaving you to be at the sharp end of things with Angus and Elizabeth on your own. And Alice, Roxanne also mentioned that you were worried about losing the croft if we moved back. That will *never* happen. The croft is your home now. In fact, to make my intentions clear, I've decided to ask my solicitor to transfer the deeds into your name."

"You'd do that for me?"

"I'd do anything for you. I hope you know that."

Alice hugged Moira. She whispered, "I do. I don't know what to say. Thank you doesn't seem quite enough."

"It's absolutely enough."

Alice held Moira's hand tight in hers as they sat in silence, taking in the moment. Now was the opportunity, wasn't it, to be truly honest and open with Moira. And if not now, when? Roxanne and Eve had clearly not said anything to Moira about what had happened. They had kept her privacy and given her the opportunity to tell Moira for herself. They had done right by her, and Alice couldn't have valued that more. It was now her turn to do the right thing and have the courage to be honest. Moira deserved that from her. Moreover, Roxanne deserved that from her. But where could she begin?

Alice took a deep breath and turned to face Moira. "So did Roxanne get home okay?" It had been a week since Roxanne had left. Moira had just said that Eve had spoken to Roxanne several times since. It was a ridiculous question. And one she'd known the answer to, as well. But when you didn't know where to begin, sometimes the question you knew the answer to was the place to start.

Moira frowned and sat up a little straighter. "Yes. She didn't let you know?"

"She did. She left a message on my phone when she got back to Leicester." That night, Alice had sat up with her phone tucked in her lap, trying, and failing, to concentrate on a book. She'd told herself having her phone close was in case Elizabeth needed her. But she knew in her heart she was hoping for a text or a call from Roxanne. She had convinced herself that this was so unlikely that when her phone rang with the caller ID *Wee Eejit* she couldn't believe it, and it rang off before she could gather herself to answer. And then she didn't know what to say if she was to ring back. And the longer she left it, the harder it got.

"And you've not returned her call?"

Alice shook her head.

"Right. I think it might help you to know that one of the last things

Roxanne said to me was would I tell you that she thought the world of you too." She looked at Alice. "I've been waiting for the right moment to mention it. It seemed so personal."

"She said that?"

"Look, tell me to mind my own business—"

"Don't mind you own business. Please."

"Did something happen between you and Roxanne? It's not just Roxanne who looked like she'd lost everything—so do you."

"I messed up." Alice bit at her lip. *Don't cry.* "I pretty much told Roxanne I didn't want to see her again. And the thing is, I do. I really do. I want to be her..." Alice swallowed. The miles of fresh air around them suddenly didn't feel like enough for her to breathe. "Girlfriend." There, it was done.

"Oh, Alice."

"Are you cross with me?"

"Why on earth would I be cross? I take it Roxanne asked you out."

"Not as such. We slept together. And then she was trying to tell me that she wanted to see me again, but then you arrived, and I panicked and ruined everything. I was so frightened of what you would think of me if you found out."

"Why? I promise you that who you choose to be with or to love makes no difference to me or to my love for you."

"But I treated you so badly when you came out to me."

"And I treated *you* badly by keeping too much from you. Anyone would have been as hurt and cross as you. I'm thankful every day that I still have you in my life."

"You'll always have me in your life." Alice bit at her lip again, but this time it didn't help as tears stung in her eyes and drizzled down her cheeks.

"Come here." Moira held Alice tight in her arms. "For what's it's worth, I very much like Roxanne."

"I think the world of her. She *means* the world to me."

Moira released her hold and smiled. "Well then, maybe return that call."

"I want to..."

"But?"

"I don't know whether I can trust her. Eve thought, at first at least, that Roxanne would hurt me. And even Roxanne confessed she didn't take anything seriously. I *am* serious about her, and so where does that leave me?"

"Oh, okay. I remember chatting to Eve about her worries about Roxanne. Eve's very protective of her—and of you."

"I know."

"And it's got to be pretty scary for Roxanne too. I get the impression you would be her first proper girlfriend."

"Yes. She said that she was frightened by her feelings. She also said she wouldn't hurt me."

"There you go. And I will offer you one more thought, and I know it's not quite the same thing, but if you're trying to seek some certainty, there is one person who does completely trust Roxanne, and that is Angus."

"So you're saying I should trust her?"

"I'm saying you should at least ring her back or even…"

"Even what?"

"I'm not saying you should do this, or that I'm recommending you do this, but when Eve and I were apart, both hurting and confused, Eve did the bravest thing for us. She just got on a train and came to me. No phone call to ask if she should come. She literally just turned up in my garden. I even remember what she said when I asked her why she'd come all that way. She replied, *How could I not?*"

"But Rox's so far away too. And I would need to take time off work—"

"Take it, then. Have a few days. You're certainly owed them. I'll look after things here, and we've plenty of volunteers I can call on to help me at the centre if I need them."

"What if she doesn't want me there?"

"Then at least you'll know where you stand, saving yourself wasted weeks of pining and wondering."

"I don't know."

"Maybe it's not about knowing. Eve said something else. It was one of the wisest things I'd ever heard. She suggested that the head was too clever to be honest. She had simply trusted in her heart."

"I risk getting mine broken."

"So did Eve. So did I. Don't make the same mistake I kept making and protect your heart too much." Moira took a deep breath. "Right. I really have said all I have to say. Come on, let's head back while we're still a bit ahead of our day."

"Yes."

They stood and brushed at their clothes.

The willow warbler began his song again. They paused for a moment to listen and to stare up at him where he sat high in the trees.

Alice shielded her eyes from the strengthening morning sun. "It has such feeling, his call, doesn't it?"

"Aye. His heart always sounds so full."

"He's not the only one. Thank you for always being here for me. For being my mum."

Moira's cheeks flushed. "I love you, Alice."

"I love you too."

Alice wrapped her arm around Moira's as they made their way back down to the centre and to their morning's work. The warbler followed them for a little while longer as if determined to finish singing for them with all his heart and might.

Chapter Seventeen

"Knock, knock, it's just me." Alice closed the McAlisters' door softly behind her.

"Oh, Alice, how lovely to see you." Elizabeth greeted her with a tired smile. She reached out for Alice's hands and held them in hers. "I do look forward to our Friday evenings. I was only saying to Angus this morning at breakfast what a treat it is."

"I look forward to it too. Although"—Alice nodded towards the table and the plate of meringues that greeted her—"I thought we said I was making my shortbread, and that there was no need for you to go to the trouble of baking this week."

"Oh yes, but I had eggs that I wanted to use up, and so I thought meringues, and I might use the yolks for a crème caramel tomorrow."

"I see." Alice placed her tin of shortbread on the table. "Really, I'd rather you did less thinking and more resting."

"And I'd rather you did less worrying and more, I don't know, whatever young people do these days."

"When you find out, let me know."

Elizabeth chuckled. "I'm hoping whatever it is it doesn't involve a Friday."

"Never. Shall I warm some milk?"

"Perfect." Elizabeth tilted her head in the direction of the sitting room. "Angus, it's Alice."

Angus wandered into the dining room with his cheeks rosy from the fire. "Well, that's good, otherwise we would have a stranger in the house eating my meringues. And that wouldn't do at all." He quickly snaffled a meringue from the plate and popped it into his mouth, leaving a trail of sugary crumbs down his waistcoat.

"Oh, Angus, really. Why couldn't you at least have waited until we were seated. There are no words, Alice, are there?"

Alice turned from her milk pan at the Aga to see Elizabeth brushing at Angus's front. He couldn't have looked more mischievous or less repentant. What's more, he looked happy and like someone who had unloaded a worry, for his eyes seemed brightened as much with relief as happiness. It was just so good to see.

Alice laughed and turned back to her pan. "Brush that naughty fairy off his shoulder while you're there. Okay, the milk is ready. Three hot chocolates coming up." Alice carefully poured steaming milk into three mugs and spooned in hot chocolate powder before giving each a quick stir.

"Oh, wonderful. Gosh, these shortbreads are delicious." Elizabeth examined the buttery biscuit finger in an admiring way. She took another careful bite, cupping her hand under her chin to catch the crumbs.

Alice rested their drinks on the table and took her place next to Elizabeth. "My pleasure."

"In fact, it's rather a shame Roxanne isn't here to enjoy them. Just imagine her delight." Elizabeth dabbed at her lips with a napkin. "You'll have to post her some."

A rush of pain flooded Alice's heart at the mention of Roxanne.

Angus raised his nibbled biscuit in the air. "Good idea. Just not my allocation."

Alice shook her head. "I don't think so. They sell shortbreads in every supermarket."

"Ah"—Angus shook his head—"but not your shortbreads, young Alice, with your special touch."

She had no clue whether Roxanne was interested any more in her special touch or not. She just had no clue. Moira had said she should at least ring her and find out. But each time in the last day or so she thought she might ring, she bottled it. What happened if Roxanne didn't want her? She didn't think she could bear to hear Roxanne turn her down. And so long as she didn't know, there was always hope.

"Do you know, she rang me last night to check if we were okay. What a thoughtful thing to do."

What? "Roxanne rang you?"

"Yes. She had been thinking about us and hoped we were all okay. I said we were doing just fine." Elizabeth reached for Angus's hand, and he rested their entwined hands on his leg. "I told her not to be a stranger and that she was welcome here anytime."

"What did she say to that?"

"Oh, let me think. Yes, she thanked me. She was a bit quiet—for Roxanne, that is. But then she was on her way home from work so she would have been very tired, no doubt. Such a responsible job. I hope she found her break with us of some benefit at least."

More likely she regretted ever coming, particularly given that she didn't want to come in the first place. Wasn't that what she'd said? "Maybe."

"Angus McAlister. Is that your third biscuit? Perhaps it might have been polite to ask Alice if she minded you finishing them off."

"It's okay. I've more made at home."

"Ah, but here's the thing…" Angus released his hand from Elizabeth's and patted at his breast pocket. "Have you seen my pipe?"

Alice glanced at Elizabeth who seemed as surprised as she was by the reference to something so long forgotten.

Elizabeth lifted her chin as if she was willing herself to be strong. "It will be where you last left it."

"Yes, of course." He frowned and then shook his head. "Where was I?"

Alice said softly, "Something to do with biscuits?"

"Ah yes. I didn't *ask* if I could have another biscuit because I didn't want to be told no. It is as simple as that. If you do not want the answer to your question to be *no*, then don't ask it."

"But then you would never have asked Elizabeth to marry you."

"But then I was certain of her reply."

"Oh, Angus." Elizabeth stood unsteadily from the table. "You always have had a way with words." She walked to the Aga and lifted the pan to the sink for washing. "Before you say anything, Alice, we are both leaving it to soak."

"Fair enough." As Alice stood to gather herself to return home she leaned towards Angus and whispered, "You can have my biscuit anytime."

"Thank you. Although it was not *your* reply I feared."

"I heard that, Angus McAlister." Elizabeth moved to Alice and gave her a hug. "Goodnight. Have a lovely weekend. And please do something for yourself this weekend. I'm sure we keep you from your own time too much."

"Nonsense. Night, both."

"Goodnight, young Alice." Angus slipped Elizabeth's biscuit from her plate into his pocket and pressed his finger against his lips.

She couldn't help but smile in reply, even though some things were best not to see. And perhaps not to ask? Maybe Angus was right. You should just do the thing you want to do. No questions. No permission. No hesitation.

As Alice drove home, there was one thing she wanted to do above all. She wanted to see Roxanne. And she didn't want to ask anyone whether or not she could, or should, not even Roxanne herself. She would be as brave as Eve had been and risk her heart, rather than protect it as Moira had once done and risk losing the most precious thing of all, a chance at love.

Chapter Eighteen

A lice glanced down at her phone and at the Google Map with its pin stabbing at her destination across the street from where she stood. This was it.

It was impossible to miss the rainbow flag billowing proudly from a pole beneath the second-floor window of a building that might once have been handsome. It spoke of distinctive Regency elegance with its flat rendered off-white facade punctuated with long rectangular inset windows. Sadly, like a movie star in retirement, the power of its charisma had faded over the years. But judging by the star-shaped lights around its name, The Brewer's Arms' sparkle had not dimmed at all.

A small group of Saturday-night revellers excitedly approached and pushed their way through the scuffed brass and dark wood entrance. A tall woman with a blond wig cut into a bob came out and stood on the threshold. She was dressed in a fur coat and thigh-high boots with heels that would no doubt leave an imprint on the pavement where she stood. She lit a cigarette, taking care to protect her lipstick from smudging. She was a figure of contradictions—something about her seemed both fragile and shy, yet glamourous and extroverted at the same time. She was mesmerizing. The woman looked across at Alice. Alice quickly turned away. The last thing she wanted was to attract attention to herself. She pretended to be looking at her phone as if she was busy or entirely unbothered by where she was. *Unbothered* was the last way to describe how she felt. *Unprepared* in every sense was nearer the mark.

It's not like she hadn't formulated a plan, because she had. By the time she'd arrived home from her Friday night with the McAlisters, she'd decided she was going to Roxanne the very next day. She'd texted Moira, letting her know what she'd decided to do and to ask her for Roxanne's address. Moira had simply replied with a thumbs-up and the information she needed.

She'd then booked her train ticket and left Inverness the next morning at eight forty-five. She didn't allow herself to worry or to think or to doubt. She just followed her fired-up heart the three hundred and fifty-seven miles to Leicester.

Simple. At least, it would have been if Roxanne had been home. Still, she had a plan B and that was to try her at the hospital. Except the hospital was horrendously busy. But then, what had she expected? A health spa? So disturbing Roxanne at work, if she was at work, didn't seem right.

Plan C it was. God help her.

She had no memory of the outside of The Brewer's Arms at all. She could just remember standing on the pavement, trying to keep her world from collapsing about her. And, of course, there was Roxanne at her side walking her back to the hotel. Roxanne had been her unlikely hero, and yet she had responded by telling her to go to hell. Alice gripped the strap of her knapsack as fear and regret crept up like silent muggers intent on stealing her resolve.

What was she doing here? Wait, she was thinking. No, she wouldn't *think*. Instead, she risked another look. The woman had gone, and in her place was a younger woman in jeans and a sheepskin jacket. She couldn't have been much out of her teens and was trying to get her cello through the door. It was painful to watch.

It would be easier to go in with someone, wouldn't it? Alice crossed over the road and mustered all her bravery. "Do you need a hand?"

The young woman blushed as she looked up at Alice. "Yes, that would be great. If you can hold the door, then I could maybe hug her to my chest and walk her through."

"Okay." Alice dutifully held the door, and the young woman and her cello squeezed by.

"Oh, crap, there's an inside door."

"No worries." Alice leaned over the woman and her instrument and pushed at the inner door.

The girl inched her cello inside. "It's lucky you're tall and strong, and really beautiful." The young girl looked down and shook her head. "I can't believe I just said that. Sorry."

If ever Alice needed a compliment, it was then and from such a sweet girl at that. "Don't be. And thanks. I'm Alice, by the way."

"I'm Ruby. Pleased to meet you."

"Are you playing here tonight?"

"That's the plan. I've never been here before. It's an open mic night." Ruby pulled out a folded leaflet and held it up to Alice. "From eight. I'm meant to book in at the bar." Ruby blinked into the crowded pub becoming ever more crowded with every person who pushed past them. "It's very pink in here, isn't it?"

"Aye." Even with pink paint covering what seemed like every surface, Alice could still remember the inside of The Brewer's as if it was yesterday. There was the booth under the window and then the long bar where people leaned to look and be looked at. And in the corner, as before, was the snooker table with its sharp crack as ball met ball. And how could she forget the groups of people huddled together, laughing and so intimidating with their tribal power. She should have been at home here with these likeminded people. But she felt in every way a stranger, far from home and out of place.

"Well, I'm off to book in." Ruby clutched her cello case against her.

"I'll come with you. I'm looking for someone who the barman will probably know. I'll lead the way for you."

"You're a lifesaver."

Alice gently encouraged people to move aside, and Ruby and her cello followed as they made their way to the bar.

Alice raised her hand, catching the barman's eye.

"What can I get you ladies?" He looked down at the leaflet in Ruby's hand. "Oh, you're here for the open mic. Excellent." The barman lifted a clipboard from under the bar.

Ruby leaned forward. "Yes, I'm Ruby."

The barman dragged a pencil down the list. He squinted. "Ruby. Queen's 'Bohemian Rhapsody' reworked for cello?"

"Yes."

"Well, that'll be a first." The barman pointed through the crowds to a small stage, where a man stood, adjusting a microphone stand. He wore a painted-on T-shirt with a rainbow logo that stretched from nipple to nipple. "Andy's just setting up now. Let him know what you'll need in terms of a chair or whatever. Your performance should be no more than ten minutes, and there'll be a short break after each act."

Ruby turned towards the stage. "Wish me luck."

"Good luck," Alice said, mustering an encouraging smile through her own nerves. "Have a good one."

"Thanks. Bye, and I hope you find the person you're looking for."

"Thank you." So did she.

The barman looked with expectation at Alice.

"Oh no," she said, shaking her head. "I'm not on the list."

"No probs. How about we fit you in then after Ruby and before Dave the builder's Tina Turner. I'd take that slot as Dave's always hard to follow."

"No, it's okay—"

The microphone squealed, piercing the air and causing a united wince and groan.

The barman unclenched his face. "I'm sorry, I missed that."

"I said no. But thank you anyway."

"Suit yourself. Can I get you a drink?"

"Erm, well actually, I was wondering if you knew if Roxanne Barns would be in this evening?"

"Rox?" The barman looked at his watch. "Yeah, she should be in later. Oh, hi, Bel. What'll it be?"

A petite woman eased herself onto a bar stool. She had cropped red hair and wore a low-cut blouse and shiny black denim skirt that spoke of danger and desire.

"Four Virgin Marys." She gave Alice a slow coquettish smile that felt more like a lingering kiss than a passing acknowledgment. Alice had the oddest urge of wanting to wipe the woman's red lipstick off her own lips. "Get me, who am I trying to kid? Make them bloody ones. So, you're looking for Roxanne? I couldn't help overhearing. I'm Belinda."

"Aye. Yes." *I remember you. You and your friends laughed at me.* "Sorry, I've changed my mind. I will have a drink. Could I get a glass of Prosecco, please?"

The barman nodded, glancing at Belinda and then back to Alice. "Play nicely, Bel."

"Always. So you're from Scotland then?"

"Yes." Maybe Bel wouldn't remember her?

Belinda narrowed her eyes. "We've met before, haven't we? Alice, isn't it? Eve and Moira's Alice?"

Oh God. "Yes. I'm surprised you remember me."

"Oh, let's just say, meeting you was memorable."

Alice swallowed hard.

The barman slid a tray of drinks towards Belinda.

"Put it on my tab, will you?"

The barman scowled. "I'd rather put it on your card and you settle the tab." Belinda gave him a pained expression, and he relented. "Okay. Just this last round."

"And how is Eve? Well, I hope."

"She's fine. Thank you." Alice glanced behind her to the door. Please let Roxanne be early.

"Good. Say I say hi. So, did Roxanne enjoy her holiday with you?" Alice's cheeks tingled. "You'd have to ask her."

"Oh, I have. Seems she met a girl who she rather fell for. Fancy that. And fancy you turning up here…"

The barman rested Alice's drink in front of her. She took a large gulp before reaching into the pocket of her jeans and pulling out her cash card and waving it over the payment machine the barman offered.

"That's great, and here's your receipt. See, Bel, that's how it's done."

"Really…I'd always wondered." The barman laughed and turned his attention to his many waiting customers. "Don't worry, by the way"—Belinda gestured to the door—"the one thing Roxanne *can* be counted on for is to come here straight after work. Why don't you join us while you wait?" Belinda lifted her tray of drinks and nodded in the direction of a group of women sitting on stools underneath a sign that read *Bitches' Corner*. "Ignore the sign. It should read *The Roxettes*."

"You're a girl band?"

Belinda laughed, causing the drinks to tip a little onto the tray. "We're Rox's exes."

"Oh, I see." Of course they were. "Thanks, but no. I'm just going to wait here for Roxanne."

"Aren't we all, honey. Waiting for her." Belinda curved her way through the crowd to her friends, who all looked up at Alice. Except this time they didn't laugh—they just looked at her with a sort of pity in their expressions, like they knew what was coming.

Alice turned away and drank her wine. The many miles that her excitement had absorbed now collapsed upon her as tiredness pressed and bullied. What made her think she was any different to The Roxettes? Was she about to make a fool of herself? Again. For where on earth was her heart leading her? To humiliation? Well, she wasn't going to give them a show.

She turned and made for the door. She'd go to that hotel she and Moira stayed in last time. Book in and then leave for home first thing. And then it would be over. Forgotten. Done. She stepped out onto the pavement and looked up and down the street. So, which way was it?

Wait, what was it even called? For goodness' sake, why was every decision so hard? She'd go left to start, and she'd recognize it when she saw it. She could track a sick animal over the moor, for God's sake. But then this wasn't home. It was anything but home.

❖

"Hey you guys. Move over." The Roxettes nudged along to make space for Roxanne to pull up a stool next to Belinda.

Belinda tucked her arm around Roxanne's. "Evening, Ms. Barns."

"Hi." Roxanne turned to face the stage. A cellist was settling herself into her seat.

"Goodness, that cello's nearly as big as she is. It's amazing how far such a small girl can spread her thighs. But then, needs must." Belinda gave a seductive half bite of her bottom lip in Roxanne's direction.

"Seriously, do you not think of anything else?"

Belinda looked at her fellow Roxettes, and they all looked back at Roxanne, open-mouthed.

Roxanne stared back at them. "What?"

"I'm sorry, did *you* just accuse *me* of being sex obsessed?"

"Yeah, yeah, whatever." Roxanne focused on the stage. "I hope she's good. This crowd can be fuckers when they want."

The girl began to play a passionate rendition of the Queen classic with concentrated vigour. It was good in an absolutely off-the-wall way. When it got to the distinctive chorus, the crowd sang along, so loudly in fact that the girl could barely be heard. Still, she carried on like a pro.

The barman weaved his way around the room, gathering up people's empty glasses. He arrived at their table flushed and slightly sweaty.

"Oh, Rox," he shouted. "I nearly forgot—there was a woman in here earlier, asking after you—an Alice someone or other. She didn't leave a message or anything. And before you ask, I don't know where she went."

"Alice was here?" All the blood in Roxanne's body rushed to her heart. She glanced urgently around them, even standing on her seat to try to see above the crowds. "I can't see her." She hurriedly checked her phone for a missed message or phone call. Nothing. Maybe it wasn't *her* Alice. "What did she look like? Did she have a Scottish accent, by any chance?"

The barman nodded and adopted a dodgy Scottish lilt to his voice. "Tall, blond, a wee bobby dazzler."

Roxanne reached again for her phone. "I'll give her a call."

Belinda held her arm. "She's gone, Rox. I even invited her to sit with us. She's obviously changed her mind."

"You spoke to her? You let me sit here, and you said nothing?"

"I'm sorry. It's hardly *my* fault she's done a runner. And good for her. She's clearly out of your league."

"Will you just fuck off, Bel. Don't you think I know that?"

Belinda's face turned bright red. "Fine. Sod you."

"Look, wait, I'm sorry. I shouldn't have snapped at you. Forgive me?"

"I don't know. I mean you could maybe settle the tab."

"Uh-huh. And then I'll be forgiven."

"Let's not be too hasty."

Without needing to be asked, the barman who'd been lingering at the table next to them swiftly printed off a receipt and handed it to Roxanne.

"What the chuff? How many Bloody Marys?"

"Not enough. Oh, I think Ruby's reaching her climax. Where are you going?"

Roxanne hung her head. "I honestly don't know."

Belinda gave a sigh. "For pity's sake, if you have to, then just ring her, or you could always try the train station, or maybe she's staying overnight somewhere."

"Yeah, maybe." Roxanne pulled on her jacket to leave. She fumbled in the pocket of her jeans, pulled out some cash, and left it on the receipt. "And I really am sorry. For everything."

Belinda swallowed and blinked. She gave an indignant jut of her chin. "What do they say, *Je ne regrette rien.*" She then turned away and wolf-whistled at Ruby. Her voice broke a little as she shouted, "Go girl!"

Roxanne slipped away and out onto the pavement. How many people just like Belinda had she hurt over the years, just as Eve feared she would do with Alice? No one's heart was safe in her hands. No one's.

She pulled her jacket close about her as she glanced up and down the street, preparing to cross to the other side to make her way back to her flat. Was she hallucinating? Was that Alice?

"Alice!"

Alice looked up and walked at pace towards her. "Rox. Hi." She couldn't have sounded more relieved.

Alice's hair was tousled, and her mascaraed eyes had something smoky and of the city about them. Roxanne knew how soft Alice's hair would feel against her skin, and how their bodies would fit against each other with such perfection if they were to hug. She knew the smell of her and the taste of her. It was almost too painful to look at her and not be able to touch her.

Roxanne shoved her hands in her pockets. "Hi."

Alice fidgeted with her knapsack on her shoulders. "Turns out the hotel was the other way. I got a bit lost."

"It is, yes." What was she doing here? What did she want?

"Look, before you ask why I'm here, I just want to say that *you* are my someone special. I shouldn't have let you think you weren't. I panicked. I'm so sorry. I've told Moira how much you mean to me. You mean *everything* to me. So how could I not have come?"

She told Moira? She was Alice's someone special? But then why hadn't Alice returned her call? And as for how could she not have come... "Er, you could have just not got on the train."

"You didn't want me to come? Oh God."

"Alice—"

"Then why did you ring me?"

"Why didn't *you* return my call?"

"I didn't know what to think or what to say. But I do now."

"There's no point." Roxanne didn't even try to keep the dejection out of her tone.

Alice said, "But your call gave me hope. You told Moira that you thought the world of me. Why would you do that, say that, if there's no point?"

"Because that's what I do. I lead people on, not deliberately, but I do. And then I hurt them. I'm a terrible person. So go home. Really, it's for the best." Roxanne's heart crushed her breath from her lungs. But she had to be cruel to be kind, didn't she? She had to make Alice go. She couldn't hurt her even more than she was already.

Alice pressed her hand against her chest. "No, please, wait."

"I'll take you to the hotel."

"You're just scared."

"What? I don't think so."

"Yes, you are. Because you're not a terrible person. And I know you want me."

"Of course I *want* you. You blow my mind. You're just awesome. When I think of you, I want to cry and come at the same time. Do you know how that messes with a person's head? But this isn't about what I want."

"Why not? That's exactly what it's about. And what's more, I'm pretty certain this isn't about protecting my heart—this is about protecting yours. You won't take a chance on us because you're frightened of getting hurt yourself."

"Really? Like you're an expert on me."

Alice held out her hand and started counting off. "One. You say stupid things when you're nervous. Two. You don't iron your clothes, not because you're lazy, but because you don't want people to take you too seriously. Three. You have spiky hair to look sort of tough when you're soft and kind. Four. You care about things far more than you let on. And five. You twitch when you fall asleep." Alice shrugged. "Shall I go on?"

Blimey.

"And I'm frightened too. Do you know what it took for me to go in there?" Alice pointed at the door of The Brewer's. "But I did it for you."

"I didn't ask you to. I didn't ask for any of this, this pain." Roxanne hugged her jacket ever closer about her. "Go home. Please. *I* can't do this." Roxanne forced herself to turn away. She went back into The Brewer's, the one place she was certain Alice wouldn't follow her.

The barman's eyebrows rose as Roxanne approached, and he wordlessly poured her a pint. She sat at the bar watching the head dissolve in her glass. She was relieved to find the sharpness of the pain dulling to numbness.

"Well, I never." The barman clicked his fingers under Roxanne's face. "Rox."

"Whatever it is, I don't want to know." The microphone squealed. They both winced. "Please tell me it's not Tina Turner."

"It's not Tina Turner. You might want to take a look."

"Hello. I'm Alice Campbell from a small hamlet outside of Inverness. I write songs. And tonight I thought I might sing one for you."

Roxanne spun round in her chair. Nothing was numb any more.

The cellist, now sitting at the bar, clapped like a seal. "Yay, Alice!"

Alice acknowledged the girl and gave her an obviously nervous smile. Then she caught Roxanne's eye.

Roxanne looked down. What on earth?

Alice stumbled a little over her words and then cleared her throat and tried again. "I don't have any music. I just have my voice and my heart."

The pub's patrons continued to chat over her. If Alice's last visit had been difficult, then this one had trauma written all over it, and there was no way Roxanne would let that happen. No way.

"Oh, for fuck's sake." She stood up and went to Alice. "You really want to do this?"

"I don't know, but I do know I want to show you what bravery looks like."

"I'm not a coward."

"I didn't say you were. I said you were frightened. Just listen to the words. I finished the song when you left. I rewrote it for you."

"Can I stop you?"

Alice shook her head.

"You're a wee eejit, Alice Campbell." Roxanne leaned into the microphone and shouted at the top of her voice, "For one night only"—a hush of curiosity fell upon the room as heads turned towards the stage and chairs scraped on the wooden floor—"please give a warm welcome to the songbird of the Highlands, where mountains are hills and the snow never melts, Alice Campbell."

Roxanne led the clapping and left the stage and retook her seat. She couldn't have been more nervous if she was singing herself.

Alice took a deep breath. "This one is called 'To My Future Love.'"

Alice began to sing. She sang with the effortless ease and beauty of someone for whom music flowed in their heart and rested in their soul.

Roxanne didn't have to ask the crowded pub to listen, for they hung on every softly rising and gently falling note. Alice Campbell brought the Highlands to a pub in the Midlands and freed its tamed industrial heart to run wild in the heathland and moors, and to breathe in the heather and the gorse, and to listen to the songbirds sing.

As she listened, it was the chorus that Roxanne knew would stay with her. But more than that, it was the sight of Alice standing on the stage with such a natural presence that Roxanne would remember forever, as if she was born to be there.

This is for my future love.
This is for my bonnie lass.
This is for the dreams we'll share
until our time has passed.

This is for the girl I've met
For my bonnie lass.
This is for your heart, safe with mine
until our time has passed.

The pub remained silent after Alice stopped singing.

And then as if the magic spell dispersed, they burst into clapping and whistling. Alice stood holding the microphone lightly in her hand, taking it in, as if she'd seen the most beautiful view for the first time and it had caught her breath and left her reeling.

Roxanne finished her pint and left. For this moment was Alice's and hers alone.

Stepping out onto the pavement, Roxanne was struck as never before by the starkness of the city with its gaudy harsh lights and sooty grey air, so far away from the clean, green glens and slopes of the Highlands.

Just a few moments later, Alice emerged from The Brewer's and stood in front of her, breathless and flushed. Her eyes pleaded with Roxanne as if she wanted her to say something or to feel something or both.

"You didn't like it?"

"I…"

"That's okay, really." Alice held her palms up to Roxanne. "I'll go to the hotel, then home first thing. I'm sorry that I got it so wrong." Alice turned away and began to walk off.

"Alice. It's this way."

"No. I tried that way."

"To my place. It's this way to my place." Roxanne held out her hand. Alice swiped at tears that rolled down her cheeks.

Roxanne held Alice tightly against her. She whispered, "You're amazing. What you just did for yourself, for us."

"I just want to give us a chance, at least."

"I'm worried I'm not good enough for you."

"Well, my heart disagrees. It wants you. It will surely break without you."

"And mine thinks it might burst it feels so much for you."

"Then why don't we just do it. No thinking. No worrying."

"Okay, roomie. Let's see where this goes."

The street grew busier around them as Saturday night revellers crawled from pub to pub.

"Come on, Campbell, follow me."

Alice adjusted her knapsack. "I'm excited to see your place."

"Okay, about that...so, there's a high chance when you see my place, you might wish you'd gone to the hotel. Let's just say I wasn't expecting you."

Alice laughed. "That bad, eh?"

Roxanne entwined her fingers in Alice's. "Well, some would say *informal*."

"And others?"

"That I've been burgled, and have I rung the police?"

Alice's laughter, tinged with clear relief, lasted pretty much the few streets to Roxanne's building and up the stairs to her tiny flat.

Roxanne pulled off her jacket and dropped it on the floor.

Alice's eyes widened and her mouth fell open. "Okay, you weren't joking."

"It's all clean clothes, I promise. I just—"

"You don't know how wardrobes and drawers work? I'm not sure where to stand."

"Oh well, in that case." Roxanne pushed her bedroom door open. "You could always lie down?"

"Smooth."

"Thank you."

"I really need a shower, and do you have any food? I had something on the train, but that feels like ages ago."

"Food? Yes, I most certainly do. The meal of champions coming up."

"Great. Is this the bathroom?" Alice pointed to the only other door in the flat.

"Yep. Help yourself."

Roxanne tried in vain to concentrate on preparing food as Alice pulled off her gilet and dropped it onto the pile of clothes on the floor by the door. She then lifted her jumper over her head. She let the jumper fall at her feet.

"Here." Roxanne's mouth went dry at the sight of Alice down to her underwear.

Alice looked in the bowl Roxanne gave her.

"Coco Pops. They're fortified with vitamins and everything."

"Oh, very healthy." A smile spread across Alice's face, and her eyes sparkled with something that might have been hunger. "Tell you what." Alice rested the bowl on the floor. "Why don't we save this for now and put it just here by the...plant pot, with soil and no plant."

Roxanne thought she was having a heart attack at the sight of Alice bending. She barely managed to say, "I'm in the process of replacing my dearly departed spider plant."

"I see. How about you put those green fingers on me and we share a shower?"

"Hell yeah." Roxanne got in the bath and turned on the shower full blast. She pulled Alice in with her. They both screamed and gasped at the sensation of the cold water.

"You're fully dressed—you're such a fool." Alice wrestled with Roxanne's wet clothes, peeling her jeans down her thighs.

"And you're so gobsmackingly beautiful. Do you actually know that?"

"I don't really think about stuff like that too much, to be honest. Oh my God, please say this water gets warmer."

Roxanne was certainly thinking about it as Alice's underwear became see-through when the water seeped in, and the delicate fabric clung against every curve and peak. Roxanne kissed Alice's neck, her breast, her nipple, only to lose her breath at the sensation of Alice's hand reaching between her legs.

"I love the feel of your mouth on me. Let's lie down." Alice guided them to lie in the bath with the shower water splashing at their half-naked bodies.

She freed Roxanne of her shirt and then her T-shirt and then her bra. She pressed her wet chest against hers and eased Roxanne's underwear down her thighs, stopping where her jeans had gathered. She slid her palm between Roxanne's legs and pressed her fingers inside her.

"I'm scared." The words were out before Roxanne could stop

them. Alice began to remove her fingers, but Roxanne stopped her by pressing her hand against Alice's.

"I know. Me too. But it doesn't make me want you less or need you less." Alice gently began again, easing her fingers deeper and moving them in and out, in and out.

"I know I've said it before, but I won't hurt you...*oh God.*" Roxanne lifted her hips to receive Alice's fingers.

If Alice heard, she didn't reply as she kissed her way to Roxanne's breasts, sucking and licking and teasing them to peaks of sweet agony.

Roxanne grasped at the edge of the bath. She squeezed her eyes tightly shut. She needed to come more than she'd ever needed anything before, but she just couldn't let go. Everything was changing so quickly...

Alice's chest lifted from hers. Roxanne opened her eyes to find Alice sitting with her bottom resting warm against Roxanne's thighs. Alice had paused for a moment with her fingers remaining in place.

"Will you take my bra off?" Alice's expression was so concentrated, her eyes fixed on her with such intensity, that it seemed like nothing else existed in the world apart from them and this very moment.

Roxanne reached up and unclipped Alice's bra, slipping the material free. She brushed her fingers over Alice's breasts, tracing over her nipples with her fingertips. Her body instantly reignited with need at the feel of Alice's soft skin.

As if she sensed it, Alice began to move her fingers inside her again returning to the steady rhythm as if she'd never stopped. Except this time, Alice reached with her free hand around Roxanne's back and pressed her torso against her. She then held her in a tight embrace as they moved together, hips rocking with hips in a synchrony of soft groans.

Alice pressed her mouth to Roxanne's ear. "I've got you."

Roxanne believed her. Believed her and trusted her and it was frightening, for after all, hadn't believing and trusting always ended in pain?

The shower water flowed over them, rushing, urgent and warm, as the feel of Alice inside her urged Roxanne nearer and nearer to the edge. "I'm...so...frigging scared."

"Maybe it's because you care."

"I don't just *care*. It's much worse...I think I fucking love you." Roxanne cried out, and Alice held her tight as the exquisite compulsion to climax overwhelmed her, wrecking her body against the devastating shores of the hazardous and uncharted territory of love.

Alice eased her fingers free as Roxanne lay back, broken, staring up at Alice as she reached to turn off the shower.

Finding her breath, Roxanne said, "About what I just said."

"It's okay—I won't hold you to it. I guess people say all sorts of things as they're coming." Alice got out of the bath and stepped out of her underwear. She then placed them with her bra on the radiator.

Roxanne untangled her legs from her jeans. "You can hold me to it, if you want."

Alice turned back to face her, and her smile lit up the bathroom. "I just might do that. Now shift it. I need an actual soak, and please say you have tea."

Roxanne clambered out with her legs unsteady and her heart swollen in her chest. She grabbed a towel. "I have tea, and I'll even burn you some toast." Her eyes fell upon Alice's body.

"No."

"What?"

"Stop looking at me like that."

"Like what?"

"Out. Go. Get dried."

Alice pushed Roxanne out of the bathroom and closed the door.

Roxanne quickly dried herself and then stood naked with her arms folded, waiting by the bathroom door. She would give it ten seconds. Max. One, two, three—

Alice burst out. "This is really annoying." Alice furiously rubbed at her hair with a towel. "I need a proper bath and some food, and I need to sleep, but all I want…" Alice shook her head.

"Come on, Campbell." Roxanne held out her hand. "There's a bed and an orgasm with your name on it."

Roxanne led Alice to her bed and nestled them both under the covers.

"I love you, Rox. I know I don't have the excuse of coming."

"Not yet."

Alice screamed as Roxanne made devouring noises as she nuzzled her face into Alice's neck. They made love until the early hours and until their tired bodies eventually let them be.

When the morning arrived, and as she folded the last item of her clothing into her drawer, Roxanne was quite convinced an alien had taken over her mind. She looked at Alice sound asleep, and it took every ounce of her self-control not to slide back in bed and cuddle next to her. But she knew this would wake her, and that would be no less than a crime.

Instead, she crept back out of the bedroom and stared at the immaculate living space she had spent the last hour tidying. She didn't recognize herself or her flat, and it filled her heart with joy.

Her phone buzzed with a message.

Hi Roxanne, no probs to covering Wednesday's shift for you. Mother in law staying, glad of an excuse to be out. Dan.

Awesome. On waking, Roxanne had sent out feelers to see if one of her colleagues could cover the first night of her upcoming night-shift rota. No work for a few days. How she hoped Alice didn't have to rush back.

Roxanne replied, *Ta! Glad to be of help.* She dropped the phone on the breakfast counter and filled a kettle for a brew. The last thing she expected was for her phone to ring.

Oh no, he hadn't changed his mind already. She glanced down at the caller ID. Wait. Eve?

Roxanne had rung Eve first thing the day after she left the Highlands to let her know what had happened. Eve had been as heartbroken for Roxanne as she'd said she would be. She had rung pretty much every other day since to check on her and to reassure her that, even though it might not feel like it, everything would be okay. Eve had kept her going through it all with her constancy and love.

"Hey, Rox. It's me."

"Hey, bud. How's tricks?"

"Not so good, to be honest. The thing is Elizabeth's in hospital. She's had a stroke. Moira's gone to be with her. I'm here with Angus."

What? Roxanne stared at the phone and glanced into her bedroom where Alice slept, oblivious. "Oh no, mate."

"Moira's told me that Alice has gone to be with you, and I'm guessing she's with you now. That's so cool, Rox. I'm rooting for you both."

"Thanks." The last thing Eve needed in that moment was a blow-by-blow love life update. "I want to help. What can I do?"

"Can you let Alice know?" Eve's voice broke.

"Oh, Evie, I'm so sorry."

"It will be okay if you tell her, I know it will. Because everything's okay when you're about." It was clear Eve was struggling to keep everything together. "I can't believe this has happened."

"It'll be okay, I promise. I'll let Alice know, and we'll get straight on a train and come back."

"You'll be able to come too? What about work?"

"Sorted. I won't leave Alice or you. Never." Eve was silent at the other end. "Eve, mate? Try not to cry if you're with Angus."

"He's in the garden. It's almost like he's totally oblivious."

"Maybe try and keep it that way, at least until we get there, or until Moira gets back. And then we'll get a plan. He'll need to see Elizabeth, and she'll need him."

"Will do. I've been given a number to ring for help from his doctor if we need it."

"That's great. I'll text when we leave. And we'll see you tonight. Tell Elizabeth to say yes to everything they offer her."

"She's unconscious, Rox." The sound of Eve's voice breaking was almost unbearable.

"We're coming. Hang in there."

"I'll be fine. I'll get a grip. Sorry."

"You don't have to be sorry. I know how much she means to you. I'll see you soon."

"Okay. Thanks. Bye."

"Bye."

"What's going on?" Alice stood at the bedroom door blinking sleepily at her.

"That was Eve."

"Yes, I figured it was. Is she all right?"

"She's fine...But I'm sorry, she was ringing with some properly crap news. Come and have a seat with me."

Alice sat perched on the edge of the sofa with her knee touching Roxanne's.

"Elizabeth's not so well, I'm afraid. She's been admitted to hospital. But she's being looked after, and Moira's at her side."

Alice covered her mouth. "Oh God. What happened?"

"They think she's suffered a stroke."

"No. Is she going to die?"

"I don't know the details, but I have to be honest—from what Eve briefly said, there's a chance she's really quite poorly. I'm so sorry."

"I shouldn't have left her, Rox. What on earth was I thinking. What if she dies, and I don't get the chance to say goodbye?"

"Look, we'll get the next train. I could even see if there's a flight. We'll be back in no time, I promise."

"We?"

Roxanne squeezed her hand. "I won't leave your side. You can hold me to it."

Alice hugged Roxanne. "Thank you."

"No worries, you know that."

"Elizabeth said she wanted me to go and do the things young people do and have the weekend for myself. I shouldn't have listened. I should have stayed. I could have been there."

"Don't beat yourself up. How were you meant to know? Surely you were just following her wishes."

"I was following my heart."

Roxanne held Alice tight. "I wouldn't wish this for the world, but I'm so pleased you did."

Alice loosened her hold and shook her head. "I've never felt so many things all at once."

"I can imagine. Tell you what, let me make you a brew, and I'll get our travel sorted for us. At least my clothes will be easier to find."

"You've been busy." Alice looked around the tidy-to-the-point-of-empty room.

"Yeah, I have no idea what came over me."

"I'll help you pack," Alice said. "Maybe a few items less this time?"

"I have no idea what you mean."

They shared a soft smile of broken-hearted understanding and love.

Packing to go to the Highlands would be very different this time, for sure.

Chapter Nineteen

Roxanne gazed back along Ness Walk to the city of Inverness spread out before her. "The city looks fab from this vantage point, Eddison."

In the distance the impressive castle stood embattled, and the fading afternoon light caught the red stone of the towers of the cathedral. They'd taken a break and walked the couple of miles through town from Raigmore Hospital where Elizabeth was receiving care.

"Moira and I often take an evening walk along the river at night and find ourselves on this spot enjoying the view."

"And the bounce, no doubt." Roxanne made the pedestrian bridge they were standing on move up and down.

Eve gripped the railing. "Seriously, that's not a good idea. This bridge is already in need of repair without you bouncing us on it."

"Evie, come on."

"I'm not joking—it's at least a hundred and fifty years old, and they close it when there's big events in the city."

"Really?"

"Really."

Roxanne stood stiff. If she thought about it, the impressive ironwork structure with its trusses, latticework towers, and suspension cables could have looked a bit more robust. She gingerly leaned over the railings to see the River Ness foaming and rushing beneath them.

"Point taken. In fact, I'm now shallow breathing to minimize movement."

Eve laughed. "Good plan." Her smile faded, and she stared down at her feet. "I can't believe you're leaving again."

"I've got work. Nights from Thursday. I have to go tomorrow because if the trains are late, then I'm buggered."

"Sure, of course. I'm just pleased I managed to grab you for a bit. It's been so heartbreaking, hasn't it?"

"Yes. Sorry about not having time before now for a chat. Alice needed me, and I wanted to be with her."

Eve squeezed Roxanne's forearm. "Sure, of course. I understand." Roxanne felt her cheeks burn at Eve's not so subtle knowing and delighted smile. "I'm not sure what *any* of us would have done without you these past couple of days."

"You'd have been fine. I'm glad if I made it a bit easier, that's all."

"I don't know. I think we would have been overprotective of Angus. Moira is convinced it was him being there at Elizabeth's side as you had encouraged that made all the difference to her gaining consciousness."

"It's amazing what love can do. What? Why are you looking at me like that?"

Eve smiled. "Nothing."

"I'm really pleased for you all. It's such good news. And the tests they've done so far look really positive. And the physios will help her to gradually gain strength and movement, particularly in her left side. The fact that she can swallow and speak, even if a little slurred, is such a good sign. She'll be whirling round that dance floor before we know it."

"I'll settle for her home with Angus."

"Fair enough, I get that."

"How long do you think they'll keep her in?"

"It will depend on the tests they've still to do. Getting her actually home will be a staged process, likely over several months, and possibly in different care settings, particularly with a rehab focus. You'll need a firmer plan for Angus's care."

Eve nodded. "Moira and I were talking last night. We're going to give notice to the holiday agents looking after Foxglove. The only snag is we will have to honour the bookings in place. It's pretty full over the summer. But just for a few months, we can cope with Moira staying regularly with Angus. I'll join her at weekends and stay in town during the week, so we don't overwhelm him with too many people in his home. And Alice has pushed for Moira's rota idea."

"And I'll come up as often as work allows. I'm not sure I'll be able to commit to a rota, but I'll commit to being there for you all."

"Thank you. That means the world. I can only imagine how much it means to Alice too. You've been amazing with her. Really tender."

"You didn't think I would be?"

"It's just I've never seen you this way before. It's new."

"I've never felt this way before. I have this overwhelming urge to protect her and care for her. I want to show her I'm serious about us and the future."

Eve smiled. "You've made a fab start on that. And I know what you mean about feeling protective. In fact, can I show you something?" Eve moved a few paces further along the bridge.

"Is it worth risking my life for?"

"Here. Come look." Eve bent down and lifted a padlock locked to the railing of the bridge alongside other padlocks. She held it loosely in her palm. Roxanne bent down next to her. "Moira etched our initials, just here, can you see?"

Roxanne nodded as she stared at the fine light metal outline of a heart and an *M* and an *E* either side of it.

"We were having our evening walk as usual this Friday just gone. And we paused here to admire the view. That's when Moira took the padlock from her pocket and said, *Sometimes words don't feel enough to show you how I feel about us.*"

"Don't take this the wrong way, Evie, but isn't this kind of soppy for Moira? I mean, a ruby heart necklace, maybe, but this?"

"I won't lie—even I was a bit surprised. Totally loved-up by it, but surprised. But then she told me a bit more about why she'd wanted to do it. She wanted to find a way of expressing that whatever happened around us that we weren't expecting, like you and Alice, or that might be challenging, like with Elizabeth and Angus, that she wouldn't let it affect us, or affect our love. That our love was safe as if locked away from the mad world." Eve gently let the padlock slip from her palm. She then stood up and leaned against the railing, facing Roxanne. "She hoped it would help me feel safe. And I know it might seem silly, but it really does."

"It's sweet. Good for Moira."

"You're the first to see it."

"What, other than everyone who walks on the bridge?"

"*No*, I mean the first person I've shown. You know, when you said you wanted to share things with me that were a big deal to you—I feel the same. You're the best friend, Rox. The best friend in the whole wide universe world." Eve hugged Roxanne, holding her close. "And I'm really pleased you've found happiness."

"Thanks. She's the most amazing girl."

Eve let go. "And don't forget—so are you. I know you're not meant to tell people what you're thinking when you blow out candles on a cake, but do you know what I wished for at my birthday party?"

"Bigger boobs?"

"That the evening would never end, and you would stay forever."

Roxanne swallowed down the ever-embarrassing urge to cry. "You did?"

"Yep." Eve rubbed at Roxanne's back. "Do you need pizza, maybe?"

Roxanne nodded. "Uh-huh. Four. And can we get off this bridge now?"

They laughed and walked away arm in arm, leaving the view for others to admire and the waters of the River Ness to flow on its journey far away to the sea.

CHAPTER TWENTY

"Oh, come on you…there." Roxanne stood in stocking feet, wobbling on a dining room chair and reaching up to hang a glittery banner that read *Happy Anniversary* over the door of the McAlisters' cottage. "Surely it's straight now?"

Alice tilted her head and placed her hands on her hips. "I don't know. What do you reckon, Eve, maybe to the left?"

"Yes, defo to the left, or maybe to the right?"

Roxanne looked over her shoulder at them and squinted. "Maybe you should both sod off and stop taking the piss."

Alice and Eve collapsed in laughter.

Roxanne jumped down. "It's not funny." She cupped her ear. "No, no one's laughing. Apart from you two wee eejits, of course."

Alice took a deep breath. "Anyway, so we have some news, Evie. I wanted to tell you while it was just us rather than steal the show from Elizabeth and Angus. I'm too excited for words—"

"Oh my God, you're pregnant."

Alice laughed. "No, not yet."

Roxanne's eyes grew saucer wide. "What do you mean *not yet?*"

Eve guffawed. "Your face, Rox. It's a total picture."

With the most serious expression she could muster, Alice turned to Roxanne and said, "You don't want babies?"

"I didn't…I didn't say that. I'm just thinking we've been together just over five months—maybe it's a bit early for that chat."

Alice nodded in earnest. "You're right. And come to think of it, maybe after we're married."

"Uh-huh." It was clear Roxanne wasn't absolutely sure whether Alice was teasing or not. "I refer you to my previous answer. And in any case, if anyone should be tripping the light fantastic down the aisle…" Roxanne bumped Eve's shoulder.

Eve smiled broadly and gave a coy shrug. "Oh, you never know. So, your news?"

"Rox's got a job at Raigmore Hospital."

"Really? That's so cool. Congrats, mate." Eve gave Roxanne a hug. "So does this mean you'll be moving in together?"

"I refer you to my previous answer. They've offered me accommodation. Alice is delighted."

"I'm not delighted. You know I hate not falling asleep with you."

Eve covered her ears. "*T-M-I.*"

Alice continued, "All I said, to be exact, is *That's great—you can keep your mess there.* It's a total win-win."

Eve said, "I'm properly pleased, and so will everyone else be. Oh, speaking of which, they're here, guys. Hi!" Eve waved as Moira's Land Rover pulled up outside. Moira, Elizabeth, and Angus waved and smiled back.

Moira climbed out and went round to the front of the vehicle and opened the passenger door. At the same time, Angus jumped out from the back seat.

Supported by Moira and Angus, Elizabeth in turn eased herself down from the passenger seat.

"Now, take it steady, and please use your stick," Moira said, looking ahead at the ground Elizabeth would walk.

"Aye, there's no rosette for first place to the door." Angus offered his arm, which Elizabeth took with a smile that spoke of love and relief.

Elizabeth paused at the threshold. "What a wonderful banner. Thank you so much."

"Our pleasure. Happy anniversary and welcome home." Alice's voice caught as she gave Elizabeth a tight hug. "We've missed you so much."

"And I've missed you all so much too. I am so pleased to be finally home. So many months of such fussing in hospital—I've never seen the likes. Can I do this, can I do that…"

Roxanne held the door wide. "Those occupational therapists are never happy until you've nailed a handstand."

Elizabeth laughed. "Oh, and the forward roll. It's so lovely to see you, Roxanne."

Roxanne took Elizabeth's hands in hers. "You too."

"And thank you, Roxanne, for all your support. It's meant so much." Elizabeth looked from Roxanne to Alice.

Alice's cheeks tingled. "Yes, she's been my rock, for sure."

"Aye. It's so lovely to see you both so happy." Elizabeth smiled so warmly that it was like Alice's heart had been hugged.

Roxanne was biting hard at her lip, clearly struggling not to let the emotion of the moment overwhelm her. She turned away in the direction of the Land Rover and Moira lifting luggage from the boot.

Alice cleared her throat. "I've made my shortbreads."

"What are we doing standing on the doorstep, then?" Angus guided Elizabeth inside and to a seat at the dining room table.

Roxanne caught Alice's eye. "I'll help Moira with the bags. The light ones, obviously."

Alice laughed. "Obviously." She discreetly pointed in the direction of Angus, who was slipping out into the garden, and whispered. "Can you keep an eye on him too?"

Roxanne nodded. "Sure."

"And I'll pop the kettle on." Eve gave Elizabeth a hug. "Welcome home."

"Thank you."

"Let's get you a tea." Eve made her way into the kitchen.

Elizabeth called after her, "Goodness, you and Moira must be in the middle of unpacking yourselves."

Eve shouted through from the kitchen. "Do you know, thanks to help from Alice and Rox, we've got sorted quite quickly."

"Good. I for one will be unpacked before bed."

"You for one will be taking it easy." Moira placed Elizabeth's bags momentarily on the dining room floor. She wagged her finger. "I'm serious. You're to promise me."

With a contrite tone, Elizabeth replied, "I promise to behave— you're not to worry. And I'm so pleased you're settling so well into Foxglove. Such a beautiful house."

"Aye." Moira beamed a smile to Eve as she rejoined them from the kitchen, carrying a tray with a teapot, milk, and mugs. "We're busy making it our home."

Eve nodded. "We love it." She poured the teas and joined Moira to sit with Elizabeth at the dining table.

They all turned at the sound of Angus banging his boots on the coir mat at the door. A soil smudged bunch of rainbow carrots hung in his hand, green topped with their tasselled fronds.

Roxanne followed behind him and rested a couple of bags on the floor with the other luggage. She moved to Alice and stood at her side and tangled her fingers in hers. She whispered in her ear, "He's had his felt tips out again."

Alice laughed and whispered in reply, "Leave you two alone for just a moment…"

Angus made for Elizabeth, slipped off his cap, and knelt on one knee. He smiled up at his wife. "I love you, my dear, dear, girl, my love. I love you today on our anniversary more than any man could ever love."

Roxanne held Alice's hand ever tighter.

"You are my beginning and my end. Thank you for being my love, my Elizabeth, and for receiving these carrots every year, when I know you would rather have a bunch of roses."

Elizabeth took the soil smudged offering into her lap and rested her palm against his rosy cheek. "No, my sweetheart. What other wife has such a unique gift? And what other wife could ask for more than a life lived with you? I love you, Angus McAlister, with all my heart. Now please get off that cold floor with that knee of yours."

Angus dutifully got to his feet, and Moira stood and gave him her seat. She moved and stood behind Eve and rested her hands lightly on her shoulders.

Alice stepped forward. "I think this calls for a toast. We've brought some champagne, and I've prepared some sandwiches for tea. I know we've just had a well-needed cuppa, but can I tempt anyone?"

Elizabeth and Angus shared a delighted smile. "That would be wonderful," Elizabeth said. "Just perfect."

"Great. They're just in the fridge. I'll bring them out."

Eve jumped to her feet. "I'll grab the flutes from the sideboard."

"And I'll give you a hand in the kitchen." Moira joined Alice. "I wanted to have a quick word."

"Of course."

Roxanne kissed Alice's cheek. "I'll see you in a mo, Campbell."

Alice nodded. How could just a kiss mean so much? "Okay." She gathered herself and went to the kitchen, followed by Moira. "Right, then." She bent into the fridge and brought out covered plates of sandwiches. She passed them out one by one to Moira along with the bottle of champagne. "What did you want to talk to me about?"

"I wanted to give Elizabeth and Angus a special gift."

"Okay. Sounds good. And you want my opinion?"

"If possible, I'd like to commission it from you."

"I'm not sure I understand. I think that's everything." Alice stood and began lifting the foil from the plates.

"Do you remember I mentioned that Roxanne and I had a chance for a good chat when I dropped her off at the station? After her first visit here?"

Alice stopped unwrapping the sandwiches and turned to face Moira. Suspicion joined curiosity. "Yes."

"There was something else Roxanne mentioned to me that I've been thinking about a lot since then."

"Okay."

"She said that you composed songs and might even want to sing them in public. But you didn't feel you could because you were worried about upsetting me because of the connection with your mum."

"She told you that? She hasn't said anything to me."

"She was worried about you because she said not singing was hurting you, and she thought I ought to know. She was right, Alice."

"So what are you saying, that you wouldn't mind if I sang now and then?"

"I wouldn't mind if you sang all the time if that's what's in your heart to do."

"I don't want to be a singer. I just want to be able to sing. I love my teaching, for that's where my heart lies. Here in Newland. But I'd be pleased to write you a song for them."

"That's great. Thank you. I don't suppose you have something you could sing now. I'd love to hear you. We all would."

"Now? I don't know, I mean, there's a song I sang for Rox. It's about love. I could check with her if she'd mind if I sang it."

"Yes. Do. And, Alice, I don't want anything to hurt your heart."

Alice hugged Moira. "I know."

Moira gave a sigh that sounded so full of feeling. She gave a small shake of her head as if to rally herself. "Let's get these goodies out to them." Moira left the kitchen with the bottle of champagne, and Roxanne replaced her at Alice's side.

"Hey, you."

"Hey. So, turns out I've been asked to write a song for Moira to gift to Angus and Elizabeth."

Roxanne blushed deeply. "Oh, so she told you."

"Yep."

"I wasn't gossiping."

"Thank you for caring about me enough to tell her. Even then."

"I'm pretty sure I loved you even then."

"I loved you too. She asked if I had a song I could sing now, as it happens. The only one I know well enough is our song. Would you mind if I sang it for them?"

"Mind? Nope. I'd be pretty damn chuffed. And proud. Proud that you're mine."

"I am. Always."

The sound of champagne popping in the background called their attention to the party getting under way in the dining room.

"Come on then, mine. Your audience awaits." Roxanne led Alice by the hand and announced as they reentered the dining room, "Everyone, will you join me in welcoming Alice to sing for us this afternoon."

A united chatter of approval and excitement buzzed about the room. Roxanne stood beside a beaming Eve and Moira.

Alice stood in front of them and took a deep breath. "I first began to write this song many years ago when I dared to dream for a day like this. So here we go."

Alice Campbell sang for her loved ones with a heart so full of love that a lifetime well-lived would never be enough to run it dry.

This is for my only love.
This is for my bonnie lass.
This is for the dreams we'll share,
For love will time outlast...

About the Author

Anna is an English Literature graduate with a passion for LGBT heritage. She has master's degrees in museum studies and the word and the visual imagination and has written and curated a permanent exhibition of LGBT voices and memorabilia, based at Leicester's LGBT Centre.

Anna's debut novel, *Highland Fling*, was a finalist in the 2018 Golden Crown Literary Society Awards. Her second novel, *Love's Portrait*, was a finalist in the 2019 Rainbow Awards and in the 2019 Foreword INDIES Book of the Year Awards. Her short story "Hooper Street" can be found in the BSB anthology *Girls Next Door*. Her poems have been published with Paradise Press and the University of Leicester's Centre for New Writing. Find her at her website, www.annalarner.com, or on social media. Facebook and Instagram: @anna.larner.writer; Twitter: @annalarnerbooks.

Books Available From Bold Strokes Books

A Fairer Tomorrow by Kathleen Knowles. For Maddie Weeks and Gerry Stern, the Second World War brought them together, but the end of the war might rip them apart. (978-1-63555-874-6)

Changing Majors by Ana Hartnett Reichardt. Beyond a love, beyond a coming-out, Bailey Sullivan discovers what lies beyond the shame and self-doubt imposed on her by traditional Southern ideals. (978-1-63679-081-7)

Highland Whirl by Anna Larner. Opposites attract in the Scottish Highlands, when feisty Alice Campbell falls for city girl about town Roxanne Barns. (978-1-63555-892-0)

Holiday Hearts by Diana Day-Admire and Lyn Cole. Opposites attract during Christmastime chaos in Kansas City. (978-1-63679-128-9)

Humbug by Amanda Radley. With the corporate Christmas party in jeopardy, CEO Rosalind Caldwell hires Christmas Girl Ellie Pearce as her personal assistant. The only problem is, Ellie isn't a PA, has never planned a party, and develops a ridiculous crush on her totally intimidating new boss. (978-1-63555-965-1)

On the Rocks by Georgia Beers. Schoolteacher Vanessa Martini makes no apologies for her dating checklist, and newly single mom Grace Chapman ticks all Vanessa's Do Not Date boxes. Of course, they're never going to fall in love. (978-1-63555-989-7)

Song of Serenity by Brey Willows. Arguing with the Muse of music and justice is complicated, falling in love with her even more so. (978-1-63679-015-2)

The Christmas Proposal by Lisa Moreau. Stranded together in a Christmas village on a snowy mountain, Grace and Bridget face their past and question their dreams for the future. (978-1-63555-648-3)

Wisdom by Jesse J. Thoma. When Sophia and Reggie are chosen for the governor's new community design team and tasked with tackling substance abuse and mental health issues, battle lines are drawn even as sparks fly. (978-1-63555-886-9)

The Infinite Summer by Morgan Lee Miller. While spending the summer with her dad in a small beach town, Remi Brenner falls for Harper Hebert and accidentally finds herself tangled up in an intense restaurant rivalry between her famous stepmom and her first love. (978-1-63555-969-9)

A Convenient Arrangement by Aurora Rey and Jaime Clevenger. Cuffing season has come for lesbians, and for Jess Archer and Cody Dawson, their convenient arrangement becomes anything but. (978-1-63555-818-0)

An Alaskan Wedding by Nance Sparks. The last thing either Andrea or Riley expects is to bump into the one who broke her heart fifteen years ago, but when they meet at the welcome party, their feelings come rushing back. (978-1-63679-053-4)

Beulah Lodge by Cathy Dunnell. It's 1874, and newly betrothed Ruth Mallowes is set on marriage and life as a missionary…until she falls in love with the housemaid at Beulah Lodge. (978-1-63679-007-7)

Gia's Gems by Toni Logan. When Lindsey Speyer discovers that popular travel columnist Gia Williams is a complete fake and threatens to expose her, blackmail has never been so sexy. (978-1-63555-917-0)

Holiday Wishes & Mistletoe Kisses by M. Ullrich. Four holidays, four couples, four chances to make their wishes come true. (978-1-63555-760-2)

Love By Proxy by Dena Blake. Tess has a secret crush on her best friend, Sophie, so the last thing she wants is to help Sophie fall in love with someone else, but how can she stand in the way of her happiness? (978-1-63555-973-6)

Marry Me by Melissa Brayden. Allison Hale attempts to plan the wedding of the century to a man who could save her family's business, if only she wasn't falling for her wedding planner, Megan Kinkaid. (978-1-63555-932-3)

Pathway to Love by Radclyffe. Courtney Valentine is looking for a woman exactly like Ben—smart, sexy, and not in the market for anything serious. All she has to do is convince Ben that sex-without-strings is the perfect pathway to pleasure. (978-1-63679-110-4)

Sweet Surprise by Jenny Frame. Flora and Mac never thought they'd ever see each other again, but when Mac opens up her barber shop right next to Flora's sweet shop, their connection comes roaring back. (978-1-63679-001-5)

The Edge of Yesterday by CJ Birch. Easton Gray is sent from the future to save humanity from technological disaster. When she's forced to target the woman she's falling in love with, can Easton do what's needed to save humanity? (978-1-63679-025-1)

The Scout and the Scoundrel by Barbara Ann Wright. With unexpected danger surrounding them, Zara and Roni are stuck between duty and survival, with little room for exploring their feelings, especially love. (978-1-63555-978-1)

Can't Leave Love by Kimberly Cooper Griffin. Sophia and Pru have no intention of falling in love, but sometimes love happens when and where you least expect it. (978-1-636790041-1)

Free Fall at Angel Creek by Julie Tizard. Detective Dee Rawlings and aircraft accident investigator Dr. River Dawson use conflicting methods to find answers when a plane goes missing, while overcoming surprising threats and discovering an unlikely chance at love. (978-1-63555-884-5)

Love's Compromise by Cass Sellars. For Piper Holthaus and Brook Myers, will professional dreams and past baggage stop two hearts from realizing they are meant for each other? (978-1-63555-942-2)

Not All a Dream by Sophia Kell Hagin. Hester has lost the woman she loved, and the world has descended into relentless dark and cold. But giving up will have to wait when she stumbles upon people who help her survive. (978-1-63679-067-1)

The Secrets of Willowra by Kadyan. A family saga of three women, their homestead called Willowra in the Australian outback, and the secrets that link them all. (978-1-63679-064-0)

Turbulent Waves by Ali Vali. Kai Merlin and Vivien Palmer plan their future together as hostile forces make their own plans to destroy what they have, as well as all those they love. (978-1-63679-011-4)